The Way to London

By Alix Rickloff

The Way to London
Secrets of Nanreath Hall

The Way to London

ALIX RICKLOFF

wm

WILLIAM MORROW

An Imprint of HarperCollins*Publishers*

P.S.™ is a trademark of HarperCollins Publishers.

THE WAY TO LONDON. Copyright © 2017 by Alix Rickloff. All rights reserved. Printed in the United States of America. No part of this book may be used or reproduced in any manner whatsoever without written permission except in the case of brief quotations embodied in critical articles and reviews. For information address HarperCollins Publishers, 195 Broadway, New York, NY 10007.

HarperCollins books may be purchased for educational, business, or sales promotional use. For information please e-mail the Special Markets Department at SPsales@harpercollins.com.

FIRST EDITION

Designed by Diahann Sturge

Library of Congress Cataloging-in-Publication Data has been applied for.

ISBN 978-0-06-243320-6

17 18 19 20 21 LSC 10 9 8 7 6 5 4 3 2 1

For Tom & Matt—my own little sprogs

Chapter 1

Singapore, September 1941

Troop movements. Battles. Sinkings. Bombings. Russia resisting. England persevering. Japan rattling sabers. America dithering.

Boring. All of it completely dulls-ville.

Lucy Stanhope turned the page and her attention to the announcement of a Portuguese woman giving birth to septuplets, an Australian man being sued by a wife he claimed he'd never met, a strike of the Great World amusement park's cabaret girls.

Now, this was news.

Yet still hardly worth more than a quick scan.

She tossed aside the newspaper and waved a languorous hand to signal one of the Singapore Swimming Club's white-jacketed waiters. It was one in the afternoon. Surely, not too early for a cocktail.

"Miss Stanhope?" he said with a little bow.

"A gin rickey. Heavy on the gin. And could you do something

with this umbrella? If I lounge out here much longer, I'll be pink as a lobster."

"Of course." The waiter shifted the wide beach umbrella, casting a shadow over all but her trim ankles. "Will that be all?"

"Can you conjure a breeze? Not one of these pesky little things more water than air, but an honest-to-goodness gust that brings with it a tang of wood smoke and a rattle of leaves?"

"Pardon, miss?" She'd clearly confused the poor chap. He probably assumed she'd started on the gin rickeys with her bacon and eggs this morning.

She didn't know why she'd spoken. Maybe it had been the six-month-old copy of *Woman's Own* just arrived in this morning's post. All those photographs of sweet fresh-faced girls in hand-knitted cardigans and crocheted wraps like sweet old Granny used to make. Well, not Lucy's granny. She doubted either the dear departed Countess of Melcombe or the Main Line society grande dame Mrs. Carlton Stanhope III would be caught dead doing anything so plebeian as crocheting. But other people's grannies. Other people who posed on picturesque stone walls while equally fresh-faced smiling young men in sleeveless sweaters looked on in innocent adoration. Other people who sipped cocoa by roaring fires while playing Parcheesi with Mom, Dad, and little gap-toothed Junior.

One big happy family.

Talk about fictional. Almost as far-fetched as the article she'd just read about Hitler's being eaten by his pet alligator.

"Never mind. Just the drink, thank you."

The waiter made another little bow and scurried his way around the crowd of swimsuit-clad women basking on lounge chairs in the equatorial sun, past the patient Chinese amahs leading their little charges toward the pool like ducklings in a row, and finally through clusters of wrought iron tables where wealthy European tuans and their memsahibs picked at their three-martini lunches and chatted about tonight's dance at the Tanglin Club; the recent arrival of Mr. Duff Cooper and his stylish wife, Lady Diana; and which wives had strayed from their marriage vows with the dashing officers arriving fresh on the island's shores like a sampan's catch of the day.

It would be the same tomorrow and the day after tomorrow. On and on into infinity. She was so tired of it all—the pettiness, the triviality. Surely, this wasn't the best life had to offer.

Lucy turned her gaze to the sea, watching the to-ing and fro-ing of ships in the harbor. Merchant cruisers, great wallowing cargo ships, and passenger liners refitted as troop transports, while the little lighters and trading junks circled like minnows. She fanned herself against the tropical heat and accepted her drink with a smile. The sweet bite of it slid cool and far too easily down her throat.

If she wasn't careful, she'd be pickled as an onion by sunset.

Not that it mattered. This afternoon's jam-packed schedule included shopping for a new pair of shoes to go with the frock she'd bought last week, wandering past the Padang to watch the cricketers practice, then dinner and dancing at Raffles Hotel with Lieutenant Chambers . . . Chandler . . . Chalmers . . . or was he a captain? She couldn't remember and frankly didn't care.

He'd talk to her about England, his wife and or sweetheart back home, Malaya's bloody (insert "heat," "humidity," or "bugs" here), while kneading her knee with one hand and smoothing his pencil-thin mustache with the other. Then they'd drive home to her stepfather's wide verandaed house on Orchard Road, where he'd offer her a chaste kiss good night on the steps to the clashing sound of cicadas and the clinging hothouse scent of frangipani.

It had become a dully familiar ritual in the two years since she'd been forced to give up her dream of a flat in Paris to come to live with her mother and stepfather in British Malaya—thank you very much, Mr. Hitler. Perhaps that's why she'd been waxing nostalgic about board games and long country rambles. It was simply tedium with the status quo. Had to be. She'd never rambled in her life and she'd rather jab herself with a sharp stick than play a game of Parcheesi.

She lit a cigarette and lay back, sipping her drink.

She didn't even have Yoon Hai to divert her from this attack of restlessness. He remained trapped on his father's rubber plantation in Penang playing dutiful son until who knew when. She closed her eyes, imagining their reunion. The way his glossy hair slid like silk between her fingers, the long slender shape of his hands, and the feel of his golden skin against hers. A frisson of delight shivered up her spine to lift the hairs at the back of her neck, and . . .

Wow, golly!

Cold water obliterated her daydream like a dropped bomb. She gasped, her body unconsciously lurching to escape, her gin rickey spilling in a sticky mess across her brand-new swimsuit to ooze down her thighs and between her legs. A half-inflated beach ball rolled under her lounge chair.

"So sorry. Are you all right?" A young man stood over her, water sluicing off his chest and down his legs to puddle at his feet.

"What do you think?" she fumed.

"If I had to make a guess, I'd say you'll live to tan another day."

Talk about someone who looked as if he'd stepped off the pages of a magazine—here was fresh faced with a capital FF. He slapped wet hair off his forehead, cloudless blue eyes barely hiding his amusement at her expense. Had she met him on the dance floor or at the club bar, she might have thought him handsome in a gee-whiz vicar-y sort of way. But as he stood over her dripping pool water, his mouth twitching in silent laughter, she wanted to punch him square in his Roman nose. "I might, but your continued survival is very much in doubt."

He watched her wipe pointlessly at her legs with a towel. "You could just dive in and wash it off."

"What did you say?" she asked through gritted teeth.

"The water's perfect. Just dive in . . ." His words trickled to a halt as he took in her well-coiffed hair, her expertly applied cosmetics, a bathing costume never meant to actually touch water. "Forget it." Then he grinned—the fiend actually grinned—and stuck out his hand. "Corporal Michael McKeegan. And you are?"

"None of your damn business." She looked around, hoping someone would take pity on her and drag this madman away.

"You don't sound like a Brit. You a Yank or an Aussie?"

"A citizen of the world."

The same waiter who'd brought her the drink and moved her umbrella came puffing up, his face a mask of concern. "Miss Stanhope? Can I help?"

He fluttered around her like one of the growing cloud of fruit flies until she shooed him away. "I'm fine. Just . . ." She took a deep breath. "Just clean up this mess and bring me a whiskey neat."

She stood up, flinging off her silk wrapper, feeling Corporal McKeegan's smug gaze turn to a look of approval. She started to walk toward the edge of the pool.

"Miss Stanhope?" he said softly, almost apologetically.

She swung around. "What do you want now?"

He pointed to her chair. "Could you hand me the beach ball? There's a good lass."

She threw it at him as hard as she could.

It turned out the night's menu consisted of two wide-eyed navy ensigns happy to leave behind the perils of the North Sea for the sultry—and safer—Malacca Straits.

Lucy laughed at their jokes, listened to their stories, and flirted unabashedly when she wasn't being swept around the Raffles Hotel dance floor as the orchestra played the latest from Glenn Miller and Tommy Dorsey. Her gown floated like a cloud, candles flickered like millions of tiny glowworms from every table, and she'd drunk just enough to feel deliciously alive and perfectly content.

A feeling she knew couldn't last.

A tinkle of musical laughter underpinned by a masculine chorus signaled her mother's arrival, and an immediate clenching of Lucy's stomach.

Lady Amelia Fortescue retained the youthful exuberance and delicate girlish features that had captured not one, not two, but three wealthy and influential husbands, and continued to tempt men to her side like bees to a honeypot.

She and her entourage took a table in a small alcove shielded by a bank of potted palms, but Lucy continued to hear snatches of sparkling conversation above the clink of glasses and the pop of champagne corks. Waiters hovered like dragonflies, and every eye in the place seemed focused on the dazzling beauty mugging for her admirers like a starlet to the cameras. In a steel-gray silk organza gown by Schiaparelli and drenched in diamonds, Amelia—as she had always insisted Lucy call her—was the epitome of style.

Lucy's façade slipped. Suddenly she felt frumpy and out of step, her outfit too gaudy, her manner too gauche. She dismissed her own small following, now sadly less attractive, and sank into a chair as far away as possible from the newcomers without retreating completely.

She fumbled in her purse for a Sobranie. Damn. Her cigarette case was empty. She sighed and settled for a gin fizz . . . make that two. It was shaping up to be that kind of night. At least her step-father had chosen to amuse himself elsewhere.

"Alone, my dear? You must be losing your touch."

Speak of the devil, or what she imagined the devil must look like—tall, lean, dark, and smiling.

"Hello, Father." Fortescue hated being reminded of their familial relationship. He frowned as he offered her a cigarette from his own gold monogrammed case.

"I thought you were dining with Captain Chambers tonight," he said with a flick of his lighter.

She leaned forward, dragging in a relaxing lungful of smoke. "I did. He had to be back on base at ten. I wasn't ready to leave so I gracefully declined his invitation of a ride home."

"My little girl is flying solo tonight."

"I'm not your little anything, and I have two eager young men vying for my attentions. We came up with a game. I've set each of them a task. Whoever returns first gets the honor of my company the rest of the evening."

"But you're free now, so how about a dance? I've had a hellish day and a turn around the floor with a pretty young thing is just what the doctor ordered." His eyes shone with a challenging gleam.

"None of your usual pretty young things available?"

His gaze narrowed. "Hasn't your mother taught you yet that it's not polite to bite the hand that feeds you?"

"At least not until someone with a better menu comes along. Yes, I've learned the lesson well."

Fortescue's hand upon the small of Lucy's back was overwarm, and his fingers linked with hers squeezed ever so slightly as he guided her steps in a slow graceful waltz. "You're looking particu-larly nice tonight. One of your little creations?"

"Yes, actually." She had purchased the gown from a stall in Change Alley, the design ghastly but the fabric a perfect shade of peacock blue. With the removal of the ugly glass beading and cheap lace, along with a few alterations to the bodice and sleeves, it had turned out rather dashing.

"I'll admit you seem to have a flair for that sort of thing. Can't imagine where you come by it. Amelia can barely dress herself without assistance, much less sew her own damned clothes."

"You'd be surprised how much you pick up in the name of academic discipline."

His smile held nothing of pride or amusement. His eyes remained cold, but for a dark assessing glitter she knew all too well.

"Did you come with Amelia?" she asked in a bid to deflect his unwanted attention.

"No, is she here?"

"You know that she is. It's why you asked me to dance. You're well aware that it annoys her."

"Does it?" He spun her so that she was forced to concentrate on her feet instead of her questions. "Actually, I've been at the office since dawn. Nonstop meetings with chaps from the government. Everyone's up in arms about our lack of preparedness in case of attack."

"Are we unprepared?"

"Don't be absurd. The Japs wouldn't dare attack from the sea. And what army would ever manage to trek through all those miles of jungle? You needn't worry, my dear. You're quite safe."

"I never doubted it for an instant."

He sought to guide her toward a darker corner of the room, but she quickly pivoted, throwing her weight backward as she one-two-three-ed toward the middle of the floor. He had to follow or look as if he were being tugged like a dog on a leash.

Out of the corner of her eye, she caught sight of one of her ensigns standing with a ridiculous umbrella high in his hand as if carrying the king's scepter. At the back of the crowd, the other boy pushed his way through waving a bunch of bananas over his head like a trophy. Then Fortescue spun them away and into the shadows of a terrace door and out of sight. His grip never faltered. His hand ran up her back in a gesture of possession.

"I remember when you first arrived in Singapore, fresh from that expensive Swiss finishing school. Tall and skinny like a giraffe on stilts. And now here you are, a ravishing young woman. Quite a coup for the man who finally wins your hand." He fingered one of her shoulder straps, his gaze taking on a predatory glitter. His breathing grew harsh, the odor of whiskey thick enough to knock her back a step. "I won't say your heart because you haven't got one. If you had, you'd have seen how much I desire you and you'd have taken pity."

"You're drunk."

He pawed the bare skin of her arm, his pinky ring scratching her. "We're not related by anything other than serendipity, you know."

"A fact that has always been of great solace to me." She slid from his grip just as he lowered his head to take her in a sloppy kiss. By now, her stomach fluttered, and her knees trembled. She tried to keep the waver from her voice, angry at letting her stepfather's boorish behavior affect her. "If you'll excuse me."

She stepped into the light of the dance floor, where he could not follow, though she sensed his angry gaze drilling into her back. Sinking into her chair, she sought to slow her breathing and calm the shudders racing up her spine. Fortescue's attentions were growing more tiresome and more frequent. Amelia would be no help. A twenty-one-year-old daughter only served to emphasize her own fading charms. She saw her as a rival who must be thwarted at every turn. Normally, Lucy didn't mind, but tonight she would have given almost anything to be able to curl into her mother's arms and pour out her troubles.

"Miss Stanhope?" The hotel's maître d' hovered respectfully. "A message just arrived for you. The caller said it was most urgent."

"Thank you." She read the short note, the knots immediately loosening, a smile touching her lips. *Just arrived and must see you. Meet me in an hour. The usual spot.* She folded Yoon Hai's note and placed it in her purse. "I'll be leaving. Have my car brought round."

"Of course, Miss Stanhope. And your tab?"

She gathered up her wrap and bag as she rose, her moment of weakness tamped down where it would never show. "Put it on Mr. Fortescue's account."

The Botanic Gardens were quiet this time of night, the visitors having departed with the sun. No one would trouble them with disapproving glances or insults hissed behind clenched teeth as they meandered the paths hand in hand or stole a kiss beneath the trees. She met Yoon Hai here as frequently as subterfuge would allow. For both of them, inventing excuses to slip away alone had grown difficult, and finding a place where they would not be discovered by her family or his, nearly impossible.

She leaned her head on his shoulder as they passed cultivated beds of orchids and low ferns, thick groves of rain trees and palms, a long ornamental lake thick with lotus. The loamy, pungent aroma of earth mingled with a salty sea breeze. The unexpected shriek of a macaw or cockatoo punctuated the steady whirr of cicadas and trumpet beetles. "I didn't expect you back until next week at the earliest."

"My uncle desired my presence at a stockholders' meeting. Times are tense, and the Yoon family must present a solid front if we're to survive any unrest."

"Do you think it will really come to war?"

"It's not a question of will it come, but when. My family back in China has been fighting this enemy for many years. I've been lucky that I've been living here and can pretend for a little longer."

"Fortescue says Singapore is impregnable. That between the British defenses and the terrain to the north, we're safe."

Hai didn't answer right away. She felt his fingers close around hers. "I hope your stepfather is right."

Suddenly afraid, she pulled him off the path into the shade of a palm grove, her arm sliding behind his neck. He smelled musky and sweet and tasted of wine. "I don't want to think about it anymore," she said, cold despite his arms around her. "It's nothing to do with us."

He caressed her rib cage and drew her close until she pressed lengthwise down his body. She felt his excitement and heard the quick hitch of his breathing. Her skin prickled with anticipation as he rained kisses along her collarbone and up her neck. The bark of the tree he backed her into was rough as his kisses grew more demanding, his touch more insistent. "Hai?" she whispered.

"Don't be afraid," he murmured. "I won't ever hurt you."

"I'm afraid I'll hurt you. I don't care what people think. You do."

He laughed, his voice gentle, his caresses turning her limbs to honey. "You care more than you let on."

She ducked her head, unnerved at the way he seemed to see things within her she dared not admit even to herself. She'd gone to great pains to cultivate her aura of cynical indifference. One was able to conceal so much behind a set of bared teeth and a rapier tongue. Perhaps it was time to move on from Hai. Too close meant too comfortable. And too comfortable meant trouble.

Always had. Always would.

Hai laughed again and then left no more time for breath or speaking.

On second thought, maybe she'd keep hold of him a little longer.

Chapter 2

Raffles Place and the bustling streets leading off it were a shattered-mirror reflection of Paris elegance and London efficiency. The fashionable department stores of John Little and Robinsons stood alongside the imposing financial edifices of the Chartered Bank, the Bank of Taiwan, and Hong Kong Bank. Clerks and managers from the big firms like Shell and the Netherland Trading Company scurried like ants from a kicked hill, their minds full of account balances and letters of credit, seeing nothing of the exotic oasis around them. Lush palms swayed in the humid breeze amid riotous colorful beds of canna and bougainvillea. Coolie-driven rickshaws warred for space with electric trams, buses, and long sleek passenger cars while a burly bearded Sikh in turban and uniform directed traffic amid a harsh chorus of a dozen languages.

Once, not so long ago, Lucy might have taken delight in the enchanting chaotic crossroads of disparate empires, but two years of life lived within the narrow-minded confines of what passed for society in Singapore had dulled her pleasure and deadened her curiosity.

"I'll only be a moment, Jim," Lucy said, tilting the brim of her hat to cover her eyes against the glare as her stepfather's Malaysian syce helped her from the car.

She stepped into the cool quiet interior of Renee Ullman's, her eyes taking a moment to adjust after the bright afternoon sun. Immediately, three eager shopgirls descended upon her. She allowed them to shepherd her through half a dozen dress changes until she settled on a tea gown in cream chiffon that, with a few minor touches, might be just the thing for next month's yacht club ball; three new hats; and a dozen pairs of silk stockings. Her packages approved, wrapped, and placed on her stepfather's account, Lucy made her way through to a counter where men's watches lay in long glass cases and a haberdasher's dummy sported a handsome sharkskin dinner jacket. This time of day, there were few shoppers about, and the attendant was at the far end of the floor folding shirts.

She was alone as she perused the choices of Rolexes and Longines, when a young Chinese businessman browsing a spinner rack of leather replacement bands cleared his throat.

"You came," he murmured under his breath. "I wasn't sure if you would."

Lucy didn't look up or acknowledge Yoon Hai in any way. "You're playing with fire. They're growing suspicious."

A young shop clerk watched them from the far end of the counter. A soldier browsed among the guidebooks and cheap tourist souvenirs. And was it her imagination or did the pair of aging matrons by a display of foundation garments look a bit more interested in Yoon Hai than in the girdles on display?

Ignoring her words, Hai edged closer. She could smell his cologne and the fresh scent of his skin. "Listen to me, Lucy. You must leave Singapore. Buy your passage immediately and go home to England, where you'll be safe."

"Have you read the papers? England's a smoldering ruin."

"Singapore will be worse."

"What have you heard?"

"I don't need to hear anything. It's in the very air, the whispers on the street, the eyes watching. It's a matter of time before our peace is shattered. I want you safely out of here before that happens."

"Fortescue will never leave his business behind, and Amelia will never leave Fortescue."

"Then you must leave without them."

"And go where?"

"Your real father lives in America, does he not?"

"As far as I know. I haven't heard from him in years. He has a new family to occupy his time and spend his money on."

"Then your mother's people in England." Throwing caution to the wind, he turned toward her, his expression urgent.

"We don't hear from them except for the obligatory Christmas card. Amelia has a way of burning her bridges." The shop clerk continued to eye them questioningly. The soldier glanced up from his copy of *Willis's Travel Guide*. Lucy recognized the young man from the swimming club. Today, he wore the uniform of the Royal Engineers. In the store's bleak overhead lights, his jungle tan was sallow, dark sooty circles trapped beneath his pale eyes, skin stretched tight over the angled bones of his face. His blond hair had been smoothed down with oil, though the island's eternal humidity had already caused small curls at the nape of his neck and just behind his ears. He stared at her, and she found herself coloring under his gaze.

"Please, Lucy. I can do nothing for you but this one small thing." Hai put a hand on her sleeve.

Lucy stepped subtly from under his touch as the clerk headed in their direction. He cast a sidelong glance at Hai, who wandered away to browse among the ties. "Is there something I can help you with?"

"I'd like to see the gold one there with the grommeted band," Lucy replied.

"Of course."

She pretended to ooh and ahh over the watch while her mind churned with questions. "I'll take it. Put it on Reginald Fortescue's account."

He took the watch and headed toward the register while Lucy meandered toward Yoon Hai, feigning delight in a blue silk tie with yellow dots. "Don't worry about me. I'm like a cat. I always land on my feet," she whispered under her breath.

"Miss Stanhope? Is that you?" A handsome older gentleman with wavy blond hair and a California bronze smiled across a display of the latest in leather footwear. "It *is* you. I'd know that profile anywhere. One part Greta Garbo, two parts Irene Dunne, with a splash of Rita Hayworth and a twist of Carole Landis."

"You make me sound like a cocktail."

"One sip is all it takes to be knocked flat." He placed his hands over his heart in mock surprise as he took a few staggering steps backward.

Though the soldier's attention was seemingly directed at a map of the Cameron Highlands and the pleasures to be found there, Lucy would swear he was listening to every word spoken.

"I'm surprised to see you here, Mr. Oliver. I thought you'd be at lunch with Lady Amelia. I know she mentioned it when I saw her this morning."

Mason Oliver was reputed to be an influential producer from Hollywood. Since his arrival in Singapore, he had become a fixture at the big airy house on Orchard Road, his constant presence at Amelia's side accepted by everyone—Fortescue included. Lucy's stepfather probably found himself relieved at his wife's preoccupation. It meant he could conduct his own affairs with greater ease.

Normally, Lucy took pains to avoid the men Amelia corralled for her amusement. They tended to be arrogant sods with the personality of jungle hyenas—her stepfather being a case in point—but Mr. Oliver, despite his artificiality and outrageous personality, was of a different mold. He made her laugh. He was kind in a generous-uncle sort of way. And not once had he tried to get her alone in a dark corner. The man was either a saint or a poof, and personally, she didn't care which. She liked him. Not something she was able to say about very many people.

He smiled, the corners of his hazel eyes crinkling, his veneered teeth unnaturally white. "I'm just headed to pick her up. I've discovered the dearest little club off Bras Basah Road, very exclusive. Very avant-garde. There are only four tables in the whole place. Lady Amelia will love it."

Lucy doubted it. Amelia liked to create a spectacle. If she couldn't be seen, it wasn't worth the trouble.

"It sounds tip-top. Just her cup of tea. And after, you should take her to the Great World. It's her favorite. She loves the *bangsawan* theater."

"Really?" Oliver clapped his hands together. "I never would have thought it, but sure. It sounds like fun."

Lucy wished she could be a fly on that wall. Amelia despised the rowdy crowds and cheap entertainments to be found among the stalls and stages, but for the chance to be Hollywood's next leading lady, she'd stand on her head singing "Rule, Britannia!" if Mr. Oliver suggested it.

"Who's your gentleman friend?" Mr. Oliver asked. His gaze wandered over Yoon Hai with avid curiosity. "I don't think we've met."

"Yoon Hai is a business associate of Fortescue's. His family runs one of the most successful trading syndicates here in the city," Lucy evaded. Hai held out a hand, which Oliver shook. "No enterprise makes a move here without consulting the Golden Seas Corporation."

"I'm sure with tailoring like that; Savile Row?"

"Tsim Sha Tsui," Hai replied in perfect Etonian English.

Oliver waved a breezy hand as he sighed dramatically. "Stunning."

Lucy wasn't certain whether he referred to Hai or his suit.

"Ah well, I can't hang around. I'm already late. Lady Amelia will fret, and I want everything to be perfect for our farewell luncheon."

"You're leaving Singapore?"

"Duty calls, and I'm needed back at the studio." He handed her his card, a thick white stock embossed in looping black script. "If you're ever in the States, look me up. I'll make you a star. Right up there with Carole Lombard."

Yes, she was sure of it now. The soldier was definitely eavesdropping. The guidebook he read was completely forgotten as he chuckled to himself. How dare he laugh at her? The ridiculous Mr. Oliver, fine, but not at her. And why couldn't she be the next Carole Lombard? She wasn't exactly an ogre in the looks department, and hell, if she'd learned anything from Amelia, it was how to playact.

Anger pricked her, tiny needles of heat burning through her usual cool ambivalence. She pushed them away, refusing to let some no-consequence corporal with a warped sense of humor ruin her afternoon.

She took the card with a smile of thanks and tucked it in her handbag. "I just might do that, Mr. Oliver." She couldn't help a swift glance toward that odious smirking soldier. But he was gone. As was Yoon Hai.

In their place stood the store clerk with the wrapped watch and a knowing expression she wanted to wipe off his greasy face.

G et up." Amelia's voice rocked Lucy into consciousness.

The late-morning sun slanted through latticed shutters and a haze of mosquito netting to burn red against Lucy's eyelids and straight to her brain. She rolled over, hoping to escape the onslaught beneath her pillows, but that only disturbed her still-wobbly stomach. She lay perfectly still while her nausea settled and tried to recall last night's entertainments. There had been dinner followed by drinks at the club and then dancing. She vaguely recalled a taxi and more dancing, much more drinking, and there had been some sort of commotion involving a rickshaw, two rather boisterous RAF officers, a ladies' brassiere, and the imposing statue of Sir Stamford Raffles that stood in pride of place outside Victoria Memorial Hall. "What time is it?" Lucy asked.

"Nearly ten."

"What are you doing up . . . and dressed?"

"I've been up since half eight, thank you very much. That's when I was rousted from my bed by a call from Fortescue and ordered to attend him at his office downtown."

Lucy's wobbly stomach nearly rebelled. She rolled over to face her mother, who stood crisply coiffed and coutured beside the bed. Her rich auburn hair was barely threaded with gray, her delicate features hardly touched by age. Even dragged from her bed, she maintained her glamorous air. For a moment, Lucy thought of that damned copy of *Woman's Own* and wished she had one of those comfortable parents who baked cookies and knitted doilies rather than this cool untouchable queen.

"Fortescue told me what happened. How could you do such a thing?" Amelia's voice emerged in a harsh half whisper. She ran an agitated hand up and down the string of pearls at her throat. "It's too dreadful to contemplate."

Lucy struggled up, her head swimming with more than a hangover. "Whatever he's told you, he's lying. The man's a toad I wouldn't touch with a six-foot stick."

Amelia's bright red lips thinned to a scarlet gash in her pale face. "You'll show your father more respect."

"Stepfather," Lucy shot back.

Amelia's eyes flared as if she'd been pushed to a dangerous edge. "You're not too old to feel my hand, young lady." She pulled a frock from the closet and tossed it on a chair, dislodging one of the ubiquitous *chi-chak*, small lizards that infested the house despite all her efforts to have them eradicated. "Get up and get dressed. Fortescue will be home any minute. He's furious, and I don't blame him." Her voice broke on a sob, something more alarming than all her frozen rage. "What were you bloody thinking? What kind of daughter have I raised?"

Lucy wanted to argue that Amelia had had very little to do with her upbringing aside from financing it. What care she'd received had come from a succession of nannies until, at the age of seven, she was sent away to school. From then on, her wayward parent had exploded into her life once every few years, at which time she would introduce Lucy to her newest father and shower her with gifts and attention before departing in a cloud of Chanel with barely a backward glance.

Her school friends had been envious of her stylish and alluring mother.

If they only knew.

"If it's about that brassiere we tied on old Raffles's head, I can explain. At least, I think I can. It's all a bit muzzy."

"Stop your damned chattering. Be downstairs in fifteen minutes or, so help me, I'll drag you down by your bloody hair."

Not only upright and assembled before lunch, but using post-cocktail-hour vocabulary.

Lucy's hangover swallowed by a new and greater fear, she rose and dressed quickly. With a hasty glance in the mirror to assure her all buttons were fastened, all seams were straight, and her hair and teeth were suitably brushed, she headed downstairs to the high-ceilinged drawing room.

The long open room faced west, keeping it cool even this late in the morning. The louvered windows threw long slatted shadows across the polished wooden floor, and a fan creaked softly overhead, accentuating the awkward silence. Outside, she could hear the gardener, or *kebun*, scything the lawn. His slow even strokes steadied her leaping pulse.

Amelia sat on a couch by a wide stone hearth, purely decorative in nature. Temperatures rarely dipped low enough to warrant any kind of fire, though smudge sticks burned nearly continuously in every room to ward off the bugs.

"Did you have a nice afternoon with Mr. Oliver?" Lucy asked innocently.

Amelia stiffened, her gaze narrowing. "I should have known you had a hand in that."

Before she could enlarge, the houseboy Bin-Bin set a tray down on the table beside her. On it stood a glass of water and a bottle of pills. It was only as Lucy sat down in the chair opposite that she realized the water was gin.

"What's going on? You didn't drag me out of bed over a few hours of bad opera, I assume."

Amelia took two of the pills and swallowed them down. Her color was high, her face haggard in a way Lucy had never seen. "Did you ever stop to think what might happen if you were discovered with that young man? Or was it all just a game? Another of your ridiculous schoolgirl larks, like sneaking out to the pub or getting caught smoking in the loo?"

"I'm assuming we're not talking about a brassiere."

"Forget the damned brassiere." Amelia's voice turned shrill, sending Bin-Bin scurrying for cover. Her tantrums were legendary among the staff.

"You've outdone yourself, Lucy." Fortescue's oozing tenor voice shot her heart into her throat. Lucy swung around to see him seated at his desk. No fortifying drink sat to hand, but he possessed the same strained tension she'd found in Amelia. "You've managed to offend one of the most powerful men in the Straits Settlements. Someone who could run my firm into the ground with one lift of his bloody hand."

She gave a shaky laugh. "You nearly frightened me to death lurking back there."

He rose, coming around to lean against the desk, ankles crossed and arms folded. "Where did you meet him? Was it at the dinner last month?"

"Meet who?"

"Yoon Jianguo's nephew."

Lucy's mouth went dry. Her already-pounding head vibrated like a coiled wire on her neck. Had Oliver mentioned seeing her with Yoon Hai? Or had it been that nosy clerk spreading tales? Either way, she was sunk unless she could bluff her way clear. "I don't know who you're talking about."

Fortescue pushed off his desk to pace slowly toward her, a tiger moving in and out of shadow and light. She couldn't stop the shiver down her back or a darting glance around the room as if she might escape the inevitable. "Let me refresh your memory. His name is Yoon Hai. His uncle and father between them own one of the largest trading agencies with connections and subsidiaries all over the Far East. We had them to dinner when the Golden Seas Corporation and Fortescue, Myers, and Brill were contemplating a stock swap. I told you to make nice with the young one while I conducted business. Coming back to you yet?"

"That's right. I remember now." Lucy tried for a dismissive shrug. "Sorry. Was my idea of nice not exactly what you had in mind?"

Fortescue grabbed her upper arm, his fingers digging into her muscle as he yanked her to her feet. "Don't you dare joke with me. Not now." His face was inches from her own, his pale eyes glittering dangerously. "This morning, Yoon Jianguo made an unscheduled visit to my office to let me know I'd better keep my whore of a stepdaughter away from his precious heir or there would be serious financial repercussions."

"Hai and I were—"

"I don't care if you rogered him ten ways to Sunday, but Yoon Jianguo does. I've been ordered—*ordered*, mind you, as if I was a lowly junior clerk—that you're to leave Singapore immediately. They don't want any complications while they negotiate Yoon Hai's marriage contract."

"Marriage?" she managed to croak through numb lips. "To whom?"

He flung her away to pace before the hearth, hands behind his back. His Brylcreemed sophistication shattered, revealing the bullying thug beneath. "How the hell should I know? Some Chinese bitch with wide hips and a hefty dowry. Did you think it would be you?"

"Of course not. But where am I supposed to go? You can't just toss me out. You're my father."

"Stepfather. And I'll arrange passage for you on one of the troopships heading for England. If you're lucky, you'll be back in old Blighty by Christmas."

"And if I don't want to leave?"

"You don't have a choice. If Yoon Jianguo's firm withdraws its backing of my Borneo project, my company is sunk. You're leaving, and that's it."

"Amelia?" Lucy swung around, hoping her mother would act like one for once and come to the rescue. She despised Singapore, but it was home—of a sort. At least it was the closest thing to a home she'd ever had.

Only the empty glass and the slight tremor in Amelia's voice spoke of any emotion. "I'll cable your aunt in Cornwall. She'll have you."

Lucy was watching her mother drive away in a cloud of Chanel all over again.

She straightened, her chin clamped high, her hands curled into fists at her sides. "Don't bother. I'm twenty-one years old. Old enough to look after myself."

Her stepfather gave a bark of disbelief. "With what? If you think you're going to live off me, you've another think coming. I've had enough of your sponging. What have I ever seen of gratitude?"

Lucy managed a snide smile and a flash of her eyes. "Are you saying if I'd slept with you, you'd have been happy to set me up with a little flat in London? I guess it's too late to take you up on your offer."

Amelia's slap rocked Lucy back on her heels. "Shut your mouth." Her hand trembled, bracelets jangling. "You have one week. Then you're on a boat to England. Let your aunt deal with you. I'm done. I should never have brought you out here. You've been nothing but trouble."

Lucy's face burned and tears pricked her eyes, but the rest of her felt empty and slightly sick. "I'm exactly what you made me, Mother dear."

As the car took the curve by the football ground on Kampong Bahru Road, Lucy caught her first glimpse of the P&O liner *Strathleven* straining at its moorings in Keppel Harbor. Its funnels had been repainted a steel gray and the gleaming brass and polished wood fittings shone dull and scuffed after two years of troopship duty. Lorries loaded khaki-clad British reinforcements for the trip into the city or to the military base at Changi while Tamil porters with handcarts and canvas-covered removal vans mingled with money changers and government officials. Passengers stepped from yellow-topped taxis, touring cars, or in some cases rattling rickshaws driven by Chinese coolies in their woven bamboo hats.

Fortescue's Rolls nosed its way through the crowds, uncaring of those it shoved aside as it approached the wharf. Lucy clutched her handbag as she eyed the activity from behind dark glasses, half-hoping to spot Yoon Hai come to see her off.

A stupid hope.

She'd tried a dozen times in the past week to contact him, but their usual go-betweens had grown suddenly scarce and a last-ditch call to his uncle's offices had elicited a chilly rebuff from the clerk who answered the phone. The family had left for Kuala Lumpur on business. That was all she discovered before Amelia's arrival downstairs cut short her phone call.

The drone of planes drew Lucy's gaze to the sky, where a skein of RAF Brewster Buffalo headed north over the straits toward Johore and Pahang. Last night, the shrill wail of an air raid siren and the krump of antiaircraft guns had roused her from sleep and sent her wiggling from under her mosquito netting and into the garden, where servants and family gathered to eagerly watch the sweep of searchlights as they hunted incoming Japanese bombers.

It had been a short-lived moment of excitement that amounted to nothing more than lost sleep, short tempers, and a ready-made excuse for her mother to plead a headache this morning and stay in bed, leaving Fortescue to accompany Lucy to the ship.

"Amelia promised to see me off."

Fortescue didn't even glance up from his newspaper. "She's indisposed but sends her best wishes for your safe trip."

"Of course. Wouldn't want her to overtax herself on my account." She inhaled a calming drag on her Sobranie in an attempt to chain her anger and subdue the unexpected ache in her chest.

"Don't be dramatic, Lucy. Your aunt will send someone to meet you when you arrive."

She ground the cigarette out in the ashtray, imagining it was Fortescue's thick skull. "Are you banishing me because I slept with Yoon Hai or because I didn't sleep with you?"

Other than a twitch of his upper lip, he remained unmoved. "You always were a vulgar young woman with a childish and tiresome urge to shock your elders."

"And you were always an arrogant prat with his brains in his cock."

His lip curled with distaste as he leaned forward to direct the syce where to park. The family driver got out to haggle with a wiry leather-skinned Tamil who proceeded to load Lucy's luggage onto his handcart.

"He'll see to it you're safely aboard and that you stay there until the ship sails," Fortescue directed.

"You think I'm going to sneak off? And do what? Run away with Yoon Hai into the sunset and live off coconuts and love? Not my style at all."

"Perhaps not, but you've had a rather nasty upset. No telling what the distress might do to your delicate feminine sensibilities."

"I'm not going to throw myself overboard in a fit of despair if that's what you're hoping."

The tide of boarding passengers swam around her. The carter tugged at her sleeve, beckoning her toward the gangway. "I suppose this is it then. Tell Amelia I'll write when I've arrived. I shall miss her."

"She'll be relieved once she knows you're safe with your aunt."

Lies on both sides, trite and meaningless. At least neither of them was so far gone as to embrace or—God forbid—kiss the other good-bye. That would have been taking hypocrisy a step too far.

The carter urged her on as he took up her luggage, and she followed him up the wide gangway. People thronged the decks, getting their last glimpse of Singapore and loved ones they were leaving behind. Lucy found herself near the bow, her linen traveling suit sadly crushed, the ribbon in her hat long since wilted in the high sun. She looked out over the wharf, but Fortescue's car was already gone, the crowd thinned as the great liner made ready to sail. A few lingered. A small blue Austin 7 pulled alongside a delivery van and a pair of ambulances, the driver emerging to stare up at the great liner.

She looked again. His black hair shone in the sun. His crisp gray suit was perfectly tailored to his lean body. It was Yoon Hai. He lifted an arm, though she couldn't tell if he'd picked her out of the passengers striving to shout their last farewells. Still, her spirits lifted at the gesture. Someone would be sorry to see her go.

The wail of an air raid siren sent the crowds shifting and heaving as every eye looked skyward. On the wharf, men scurried. The ambulances drove away. The lorries gunned their engines as the last soldier leapt aboard. Yoon Hai was lost amid the scramble for better cover or a better view.

Lucy leaned over the railing, craning her neck, as the ship inched from its berth. The water churned green and frothy as shirtless, brown-skinned men coiled great hempen ropes. The sirens seemed to grow more frantic, though the sky remained empty of planes. Her hat was torn free of its pins to blow away in the rising breeze. An elbow in the ribs knocked her off balance. She fumbled to catch herself, but the railing was slippery. A shove in the back pushed her closer to the edge. Just as she thought she must go overboard, someone grabbed the collar of her frock. Pulled her to safety.

"Careful, lass. It's a long way down."

Both feet firmly on deck, she started to thank her rescuer, freezing with the words still on her lips.

Corporal McKeegan smiled an infuriating good-natured smile, that same expression of amusement hovering in his carefree blue eyes. "Well hello there, Miss Stanhope. Fancy meeting you here of all places."

She almost wished he'd let her fall.

Chapter 3

After two weeks of shipboard life, Lucy would have traded a tidy sum for solid ground under her feet, edible food, and stimulating conversation. She shared a tiny cabin with an older widowed woman of a melancholy disposition and a penchant for weeping unexpectedly who, when awake, spent her time recounting stories of her dearly departed husband, Edgar, and when asleep, rattled the paint from the walls with her seismic snores.

"You must have a spare room somewhere in this behemoth. I don't need much. A clean bunk, preferably on the starboard side to catch as much of a breeze as possible. And one far enough away from the stairs that I'm not subjected to a steady clatter of feet up and down. Is that too much to ask?"

"I'm sorry, Miss Stanhope. Every cabin is full and every bunk taken. We're transporting not just paying passengers, but a large contingent of British and Commonwealth troops, and there isn't space to accommodate you."

She'd had a version of that conversation at least half a dozen times, the ship's bursar refusing to budge an inch and growing more short tempered with every request. It had gotten to the point where he avoided eye contact and about-faced when he saw her coming. She'd only managed to corner him this evening when he'd been caught up in sorting out an argument between a contingent of Dutch troops and Turkish sailors and couldn't disentangle himself before she pounced.

"Then what am I supposed to do?" she complained. "Remain awake for the duration of our voyage?"

"That's entirely up to you, miss." He offered her a clipped bow as he swung away, striding down the passage as if he couldn't escape her fast enough.

Muttering under her breath, she made her way up on deck. Swift-moving clouds threw shadows across the blue-green water and a warm salty breeze tugged at the ends of her scarf. Following the teeth-loosening rattle of a four-inch naval gun, she came upon a knot of soldiers and a half dozen young civilians taking turns firing at errant seabirds as if they were German dive-bombers. At the center of this laughing eager crowd stood Corporal McKeegan, his guinea-gold head silvered with spray, his face damp as he exchanged good-natured gibes with his fellow gun crew.

She quickly ducked back around the corner before he spotted her, then chided herself for a coward. What did she care if he saw her? Who did he think he was anyway? She was not going to tiptoe around this ship as if she didn't have as much right—if not more—to be here. Chin up and spine straight, she spun on her heel, determined to march right past that gun emplacement and to hell with all of them.

With her most self-confident air, she threaded her way through the group of admiring masculinity, smiling as she acknowledged the tip of a cap or a welcoming nod, warming to the heat of a half dozen gazes and the back-and-forth of murmured compliments.

Corporal McKeegan tossed her a friendly smile that she answered with an ambivalent dip of her head as she continued walking, eyes fixed on the golden haze of the western horizon in her most forbidding Queen Victoria inspecting the troops imitation.

That turned out to be a mistake.

Catching her heel on a warped seam in the plating, she lurched forward, but instead of regaining her balance with, at most, an embarrassing wobble, she skidded awkwardly along the slick deck. Arms flailing, she sought to catch herself, but momentum and gravity conspired against her. She landed on her backside in a puddle of oily water that immediately soaked through to her knickers, leaving her with a tender tailbone and a bruised ego.

Queen Victoria would not have been amused.

Smacking away the half dozen hands offering assistance, she scrambled to her feet with as much dignity as she could muster.

"You all right, lass?" That voice . . . that damned laughter-laden voice.

"If you value your life, Corporal," she replied through clenched teeth as she clutched the railing, favoring an ankle, heat burning her cheeks, "I would advise you to keep absolutely silent."

"Mum's the word." Laughter gleamed in his blue eyes and his shoulders shook as he struggled to keep a straight face.

Wishing nothing more than that the whole ship might choose this moment to sink, she continued her stately, and slightly drippy, progress down the deck, her ankle throbbing with every soggy step. Just as she thought gravity might win out over dignity, a hand steadied her under the elbow, scraped, dirty, and grease stained. She inhaled the reassuring scent of Yardley's and cigarettes.

"Let's get you somewhere you can sit down before you fall down—again." He just didn't give up.

"I'm quite able to—" She stumbled, a stabbing pain shooting from her ankle to her brain, biting her lip to keep from crying out.

"Of course you are." He placed a hand around her waist—cheeky devil. "Where's your cabin?"

"Nice try, soldier boy. As if I haven't heard that question a dozen times since this ship left port."

"Right, then. I'll take myself off and leave you to it."

His sudden abandonment sent her reeling in an undignified stagger. She swung drunkenly before latching on to him as if her life depended on it. He bore up under her awkward weight, his arms sliding down her ribs before she ended up on her backside a second time. He looked down on her with an I-told-you-so lift of his brows that made her want to knock him into next week.

"Perhaps I could allow you to assist me as far as the lounge," she said through a clenched jaw.

He grinned. "Whatever you say."

Together, they edged their way along the deck and through a doorway into a long pillared space where passengers sat to enjoy the ocean breezes out of the scorching sun. He helped her to a chair. She sank into it with a sigh of relief. "Thank you."

He seemed surprised at her manners, which only served to irritate her further. She wasn't a complete cretin.

"Look, lass, we got off on the wrong foot. Let's start over. Pretend we've never met." He stuck out a hand. "Corporal Michael McKeegan. Sapper with the Royal Engineers. Born and bred in Somerset, a little place called Charbury. Ever heard of it?"

"I'm afraid I've been denied that pleasure." Oh dear God. He was sitting down across from her. Waving over a steward. That would teach her to be polite.

"You're not alone. Barely a dot on the map. My family owns a garage there. We can fix anything on wheels."

"Sounds positively fascinating." Two glasses of lemonade appeared. She hated lemonade.

"Don't know about that, but it's a living. Not so much since petrol rationing took effect. Now we're more into scrounging and scavenging. A bit of a tinker's junk—all for the locals according to my mum. She's been holding down the fort while I've been away."

His persistence was really quite extraordinary. Few lasted this long when met with her wall of indifference. She was almost—mind you, almost—impressed.

"I'm sure the king is readying your knighthood even now."

"Damn." He leaned back with a sad shake of his head. "It must be bloody uncomfortable walking about all day with that bashing great stick up your arse."

"You dirty-minded bastard." Her face flooded with heat. "I'd scratch your eyes out if I didn't think it would be a marked improvement."

Rather than being offended, a corner of his mouth quirked upward, his eyes agleam with mischief. "That's better. I knew you weren't all priss and prisms. You've a bit of the fighter in you."

He was clearly not going anywhere. She couldn't escape on her sore ankle. Trapped, she chose to make the best of it. Tapping the rim of her glass with one polished nail, she surveyed him with new interest. "So, Corporal McKeegan, if you're a soldier, aren't you headed the wrong way? Seems like all you lot are headed toward Singapore, not away from it."

Was it her imagination or did he tense just a bit, his gaze narrowing as he stared into his lemonade, his thoughts clearly a million miles away? Then he smiled, and the moment passed. Perhaps it had never existed. "Malaria. Knocked me off my pins for weeks. Wouldn't have been so bad but it keeps coming back." Now that he mentioned it, he did have a sickroom pallor beneath the jungle tan, a bleakness to what she had to admit would otherwise have been a handsome face if one was into those boy-next-door kind of looks.

She was not.

"I didn't know they kicked you out of the army for malaria. Seems like they'd be down to scraps if that were the case."

"Suppose I'm special, then. The last bout in hospital nearly killed me. Doctors say it's damaged my heart. I've been marked as medically unfit and sent home. Just as things started getting interesting too."

What had Yoon Hai said? The Japanese *would* invade. It was not a matter of if, but when. The thought iced her blood.

"So, I've told you all about me. What's your story?"

"It's less a story and more a cautionary tale."

Obviously waiting for her to continue, he lounged in his chair with a rangy confidence as if he owned the whole damn ship. He eyed her untouched lemonade. Called the steward over once more and this time ordered her a pink gin.

That was more like it.

"If you must know, I'm going to England to stay with an aunt until events blow over."

"As in the war?"

"As in the gossip. My mother despises gossip—at least when it's not about her."

He surprised her by not asking what salacious horrors she'd committed. Perhaps he already knew. Or perhaps—and wouldn't this be a novel situation—he didn't care. His eyes never took on the curious malicious gleam she was used to seeing among Singapore's elite, nor did he take the opportunity to put her sordid reputation to the test with a leer and an unsavory suggestion. Instead, he studied her as he might a rather interesting equation.

"Are you always so prickly?"

"I don't know. Are you always so tedious?" she volleyed, the pain in her ankle and the curiosity in his gaze making her waspish.

Unfazed, he laughed and downed his lemonade, still making no move to leave, still watching her. The man was either dense or a glutton for punishment.

"Not that I didn't appreciate the assistance . . . and the drink, Corporal, but I'd really like to be alone."

He shrugged. "Keep it up, lass, and you will be."

The cloudless sultry days continued as the ship steamed toward the African coast. As if drawn like a lodestone on a string, Lucy found herself returning to the deck day after day to watch the men practicing on the ship's big guns. She told herself it was merely a way to pass the time, certainly not an excuse to catch a glimpse of a blond head and a quick smile. Just as well. Corporal McKeegan never reappeared, and she was left with nothing but ringing ears and innards scrambled as the powdered eggs she'd been served for breakfast.

"Do you suppose we'll really need them . . . the guns, I mean?"

Lucy turned at the question, before she realized she was not the one being addressed.

A teenage girl of about fourteen stood in company with what must have been her mother, an older woman wearing a shabby tweed suit and a harried expression. A younger child of no more than three or four clung to the woman's leg, a thumb corking her mouth. Her pink hair ribbon matched her frilled pink dress. All three watched soberly as the men exchanged good-natured boasts in between the rattle of gunfire.

"I'm sure it's only a precaution," the woman replied, though she chewed her lip as she did so, leaving red stains on her teeth. "They have to be ready for anything."

"Daddy be?" the child asked around her thumb.

"Daddy's at home in Johore with Uncle Allan and Auntie Jenny, sweetie."

"Want Daddy."

The teen scowled through thick glasses. "Don't be a baby, Iris."

"Not a baby."

"Sadie, please don't antagonize your sister. You know she doesn't understand."

"Neither do I." Sadie leaned against the railing and looked out across the water. "I don't want to go to school in England. I'll miss my friends, and I was going to be number one in singles tennis this term."

"It's only while things are so unsettled. Besides, you'll love Gloucestershire. Your grandmother can't wait to have us stay with her, and I'll show you all my old haunts. You'll go to the grammar school right in the village until we get you enrolled at Stonecase Academy. Won't that be lovely?"

"I suppose," Sadie conceded, albeit grudgingly.

"Of course it will. There's a stream that runs across the bottom of the garden and a delicious little wood where the bluebells grow thick as a carpet in the spring." Streams? Bluebells? Lucy cringed at the forced enthusiasm. "Daddy will write to us every day, letting us know how things are at home. And we'll write to him, telling him how well we're getting on."

Neither of the girls looked convinced. Lucy didn't blame them.

"Miss Daddy," the child whimpered.

"We all of us do, my love. But until we see him again, the important thing is that the three of us are together. As long as we're together we'll be fine. I promise."

The guns exploded in a flurry of sound that vibrated the plating beneath Lucy's feet, hummed in the metal railing, shot her heart into her throat. The child burst into tears. The mother knelt to soothe her with a peppermint, so perhaps only Lucy heard Sadie mutter, "I don't care how nice it is. It won't be home."

Lucy couldn't agree more.

After a lengthy stopover, the ship finally left Cape Town in early November, joining a convoy as it rounded the southernmost tip of Africa to begin the slow dangerous journey up the coast. A blackout was imposed and lifeboat drills became an almost daily occurrence. To take their minds off the perils they faced from German U-boats and bombers out of Senegal, the passengers organized a steady stream of entertainments.

Tonight's activity was a dance in the upper dining room. Most of the ship's sumptuous prewar furnishings had been removed, but the ceiling retained its elegant plasterwork and removable walls had been folded back to allow plenty of room for the couples swaying to a rather tone-challenged rendition of "Begin the Beguine." Lucy found a table by herself in a far corner, ignoring the raucous crowd shouting at her to join their shipboard game of hunt the slipper. From her seat, she watched three young officers pass a bottle between them, their voices loud as they assessed a giggling group of military wives traveling sans husbands—a heavy whiff of adultery hanging thick in the air along with the scents of whiskey and Jicky perfume. A pair of Wrens glared at the makeshift orchestra as if offended at this display of frivolity—or perhaps they were offended at the caterwauling mess they were making of Cole Porter's famous tune. It *was* rather bad, but what did one expect from two men from the Malayan Civil Service, a retired oil clerk, a businessman from Sumatra, and a soldier with three missing fingers?

Lucy sipped at her sherry and tried to decide how drunk she would have to become to be able to sleep through Mrs. Martin's eardrum-rupturing snores tonight. Probably somewhere between moderately cup-shot and out-and-out blind staggers.

The crowd of hunt the slipper participants grew rowdy in their eagerness, like hounds straining at the leash. They shoved their way past her table, knocking her drink and her handbag to the floor as they headed off to the game.

Her glass of sherry was a goner, but her silk clutch had her cigarettes, her traveling papers, and a few coveted Singaporean dollars tucked inside. She grabbed for it, but someone else got to it first, whisking it up before it was trampled. "Hello again, lass. Seems like I'm always swooping in to save the day, doesn't it?"

"You're a veritable knight in shining armor, Corporal Mc-Keegan."

"A couple of the lads heard the music and we thought we'd investigate. Pretty snazzy affair you have going on here."

She leveled him a quelling look, one that tended to send the less confident in search of an easier target. "It's obvious you have a very narrow point of reference."

As she suspected, her acid remark bounced off his armor-plated good nature. He laughed as if she'd made the best of jokes. Sliding in opposite, he produced a bottle of King George IV from some hidden fold in his jacket, borrowed two spare glasses from the table next to them, and before she knew how he'd done it, had poured a whiskey for her and one for him, and made himself at home. "Thought you might like something a bit stronger than lemonade."

The whiskey's heat warmed her all the way to her toes. "Was I that obvious?"

"Like a brick to the head, Miss Stanhope." He hooked an arm over the back of his chair. "How's your ankle?"

"It's better, thank you." She pulled a Sobranie from her handbag. "I haven't seen you about recently."

He offered her a light. "I've been in sick bay. Nothing too serious."

He did seem a bit gray around the gills, and despite having brought the whiskey he hadn't actually drunk any of it. More for her. She poured herself a second glass.

"I suppose your parents will be glad to have you safe at home."

"It's just my mother, but yeah, she's relieved. Lived through the first one, you see. Ambulance driver with the FANY. Met my dad over a gaping leg wound in Armentières."

"How romantic. A love story for the ages."

"Don't know about that, but they were happy enough together."

"Are you glad to be going home?"

He ground out his cigarette, his gaze sharpening, his lips thinning to a white slash in his pale face. "Don't know how I feel really. Bloody waste of a lot of training, and I'll miss my mates. But it'll be nice to see the old place again. Haven't been back in almost two years. Not that it'll have changed all that much. Charbury never changes. One of my favorite things about it." He leaned back, his expression softening. "How about you? Excited to see your aunt?"

"Not the first word I would pick. I barely know my aunt. The last time I visited Nanreath Hall, I was nine. I hated every moment of it. As did my mother. Amelia never possessed much in the way of familial devotion, and I spent my visit being pointedly ignored by the nursemaid put in charge of me in favor of a rather dashing footman."

"You call your mother by her first name?"

"Yes. What of it?"

"Isn't that a little strange?" Had she described his eyes as cloudless blue? That seemed to denote vacancy or naïveté. But Corporal McKeegan watched her with an unnerving shrewdness, those eyes of his like two blue spear points.

She shook off her discomfort with another drink. "Amelia always said being called Mama or Mummy made her feel old and dowdy. Lady Amelia Fortescue was the elegant life of every party, not some drab housewife who boiled nappies and wiped faces."

"A lady is it?" he scoffed. "Should have known."

"What's that supposed to mean?"

Instead of answering, he stood and offered her his hand. "Shall we dance, my lady?"

"I am not a lady, so stop calling me that."

"You prefer 'lass'?"

"I prefer Lucy. And I can't possibly dance with you."

"Of course you can. You said yourself your ankle is fine, the tune is one even this band can't slaughter, and you look like you could use some fun. I've not seen a longer face on a horse."

"Is that supposed to fill me with giddiness at your request?"

"No, it's supposed to make you smile." He cocked her an inquisitive glance that made him look like a ten-year-old with a bent for mischief. "You do know how to smile, don't you—Lucy? I'm no Astaire, but I promise your toes are safe with me."

She was about to offer him a venomous set-down that would have sent him scuttling back to his hole when an enormous bang and a series of deep thuds rocked the ship. A klaxon sounded. The lights flickered and went out.

They'd been torpedoed.

Lucy's teeth chattered, her shoulders and arms ached from endless hours of bailing, and her drenched skin was pebbled with more gooseflesh than a coop full of chickens. They'd been afloat for two days. The food was gone and the only fresh water had come from rain collected in a small tin pail. Last night's storm had separated the lifeboats from the sinking ship and one another. Every tiny knot of survivors had been left to manage the best they could as gale-lashed waves threatened to swamp them and the cold rain cut like knives.

A group seated near the back of the lifeboat kept up a steady stream of morale-rallying hymns. A thin, nervous-looking man vomited over the side. A party of Royal Navy Wrens huddled together in their heavy coats against the sapping cold that burrowed into one's bones until it was impossible to remember what being warm felt like. Lucy would have added her moans to the chorus if she'd had the strength. Instead, she stared out over the gray emptiness stretching in every direction, straining to catch sight of a ship or a plane. Hell, at this point she'd have been just as happy to see a passing U-boat with a sympathetic captain at the helm. She was too exhausted to be overly particular about their politics.

"Steady on," a seaman piped up, his face chapped with wind and spray. "The navy won't let us down. Betcha they're looking for us even now."

"*Shine through the gloom and point me to the skies,*" the singers in the back bellowed.

Forget a ship; Lucy prayed for eight simultaneous cases of laryngitis.

"Your mother ain't looking too good," the seaman commented with a concerned nod. "She all right, you think?"

"She's not my mother." Lucy glanced at the woman next to her. She seemed familiar, though so many did after three months living cheek by jowl. She wore a man's wool cardigan over what had once been a sensible blouse and skirt but were now sodden and dirty. Her salt-rinsed brown hair frizzed around her white face, and her large eyes stared unseeing as she worried at something in her right hand, fingers rubbing it like a talisman. She muttered what sounded like prayers under her breath.

"Here." A man in three layers of sweaters pulled a couple of soggy digestive biscuits from his woolly trouser pocket. "Ain't much, but it might help."

Lucy was tempted to snatch them for herself. She was ravenous. If she'd known she'd end up floating in a tin can on the open ocean, she'd have taken a second helping of dinner.

The woman ignored the offering and continued her nonsensical murmurings through blue lips, the gray skin of her face stretched nearly translucent, the artery in her neck fluttering with every phlegmy breath.

"Shut that bitch up already or I'm gonna go mad, I swear it," snarled a woman behind them. Lucy definitely remembered her. One of the military wives last seen dancing with a young RAF captain who was most definitely *not* her husband.

A rogue wave pushed them sideways, and the boat swung wildly as cold water poured in. Someone shouted, someone else screamed, the hymn singers trebled their volume. *"In life, in death, O Lord, abide with me."*

Lucy caught the woman as she toppled, her soft body collapsing against her. "Girls," she whispered. "Where are my girls?" Her breath barely warmed Lucy's cheek, her features slack as a deflated bladder. A pink hair ribbon fell from her limp fingers into the swampy water swirling around the bottom of the boat.

Of course. The gun battery. That's where Lucy had seen her. But where were her daughters?

"Christ all. What's her problem now?" the military wife snarked.

"Poor thing. Won't last much longer."

"None of us will if they don't find us soon."

"Keep bailing and your backs to the oars, lads. Stand strong."

"Who died and left you boss, eh?"

"Amazing Grace, how sweet the sound . . ."

The military wife's anger turned to wailing. "We're all gonna die. The old bat's just the first."

It would have been funny if it all weren't so horribly real.

"Shut up and get hold of yourself," Lucy snapped, her own courage hanging by a thread.

"Who the hell do you think you are to talk to me like that?"

"Someone who doesn't want her last moments on earth to be filled with your caterwauling, that's who." Lucy retrieved the ribbon, dingy and drenched, the pink now dull and waterlogged, before turning her attention back to the woman, who remained unresponsive. "Upsy-daisy, now. You lie here much longer they're liable to toss you overboard—and me along with you."

The woman's lashes fluttered. She looked up at Lucy with a bewildered expression. "Where are my girls?" Tears leaked from her eyes. "They'll be scared. Need their mum to tell them it's all right."

"I'm sure they're safe on one of the other boats, and we'll find them just as soon as we're picked up."

"Iris is only three. She'll be crying for me."

Lucy used to cry for her mother. Long ago when she'd been taken from the big house in Philadelphia and dumped in the care of a nurse, then later a governess, then finally a school headmistress. With each leave-taking, she'd wept and begged not to be left behind. Amelia told her she was being a spoiled, selfish baby. It didn't take Lucy long to realize tears were worthless and that if her mother had ever loved her, that emotion had died along with her marriage to Lucy's father.

The military wife harrumphed her displeasure. "Knew I should have stayed in Cape Town. Had my own house with a maid and a car and driver, but no, Ralph wants me with him in Scotland.

What's in Scotland? Furry men in kilts, smelly sheep, and haggis. Dear God, I'd rather drown in this bloody ocean."

"And so you might, so shut your bloody gob," the seaman growled. "Here, miss. Have my mac for the lady."

"I promised it would be all right. Iris will be scared, and none but Sadie to calm her."

Perhaps it was the way the woman clutched the ruined ribbon as if she clutched her small daughter's hand. Or perhaps it was the memory of Sadie's fiercely uttered words that so echoed Lucy's own sentiments. Or just maybe—though Lucy would barely consider it—Amelia's absence at Keppel Harbor as her daughter sailed away had something to do with what happened next. Perhaps it was all three. Lucy accepted the heavy oilskin mackintosh. "Let's get you warm. This kind gentleman has offered you his mac and I've a coat you can borrow."

"I can't take your coat, miss," she whispered, her voice soft as a sigh. "Wouldn't be right."

"Of course you can. I never liked it anyway. Green makes me look bilious, and it's so last season." The wind chilled her bare skin, but Lucy draped the plaid wool kimono coat over the older woman's shoulders, before tucking the mac around her as best she could. "It's waterlogged as everything else in the blasted boat, but another few layers should help. Can't hurt at any rate."

The woman's tremors subsided as she burrowed into the soggy wool as if curling beneath an eiderdown.

"Right, now let's see if we can get some food in you. Can I have those biscuits? And you there, a cup of that water if you please."

The military wife started from her glum study of the empty horizon. "Why waste it on her? She's half-dead and there's no knowing how long we'll be out here. We need it for those of us strong enough to survive. Not some sick biddy."

"Water," Lucy snapped in the same tone of voice she used on waiters, taxi drivers, and the occasional bounder trying to cop a fondle. "Now."

The cup was reluctantly passed over.

"Shut up and listen," the seaman shouted, shading his eyes as he searched the sky. "Is that an airplane?"

Everyone went silent, nerves on edge, senses straining.

"There!" someone shouted, pointing.

All eyes followed the track of the outstretched arm to where a plane circled and dipped its wings before heading east.

"They're leaving. They didn't see us."

"Wait! They're coming back."

"Look! It's a ship!"

Long and low, sprouting a single funnel amid a forest of thin spars, it steamed toward them, cutting the waves like a knife. A ragged cheer went up as the oarsmen bent their backs with new effort in hopes of narrowing the distance. The singers began a rousing if off-key rendition of Handel's "Hallelujah" chorus.

"Hear that? We're saved." Lucy swallowed down a cry of relief, her gaze never straying from the ship, as if it might disappear if she looked away. She counted the minutes that passed by the steady dip and lift of the oars and her own beating heart. "You'll be back with your girls in no time."

Bumping alongside, the merchant cruiser loomed over the little lifeboat, every wave smashing them against the hull. Lines were tossed to be made fast at stem and stern. The crew lowered netting, and one by one, the wet, exhausted, grateful survivors clambered their way onto the ship.

"We'll need some help," Lucy suggested. "A rope perhaps. We can tie her into it and they can lift her up."

"The lady won't need a rope, miss," the seaman said sadly. "Nor any other earthly aid. She's held in the best of hands now."

It was true. The woman's body had gone limp, her lips tinged blue, her face a waxy gray. Salt rimed her hair and seawater damped her staring eyes.

"Come along, love. You tried your best, but it weren't to be. Now, the men are here for you. Pull yourself together. It's war and not the first nor the last loss to be suffered."

She nodded dumbly, unable to pull her gaze away from the body even as the sailors helped her to wobble and wiggle her way up the side of the ship until hands reached out to take her under her shoulders and drag her like a landed carp onto the crowded deck. Her legs barely held her. Her arms felt like two noodles.

"This is the last of the *Strathleven*'s boats, sir. All the rest are accounted for. Twenty-five passengers lost. Ten in the explosion. Fifteen on the water."

A smelly blanket was draped around her shoulders. A cup of bitter coffee was shoved into her hands.

She couldn't have appreciated them more—or less—if she'd been wrapped in the softest cashmere and offered a glass of Veuve Clicquot.

"Where's my mother?" Sadie was pushing through the crowd at the railing. She wore an enormous coat over what had once been a pretty yellow frock. "Excuse me, sir, but was my mother on that boat? I've asked all around and no one's seen her."

Her words sliced through Lucy's raw nerves like a straight-edge razor.

"We were taking the air on deck when the ship was hit and somehow in the crush we were separated." Tears streamed down her cheeks. "Iris and I ended up in one boat, but Mother wasn't with us." The younger girl huddled close against her sister, her staring silence unnerving among the chaos of the ship's deck. Her right hand was bandaged, making thumb sucking impossible.

Lucy's heart turned over. She couldn't seem to breathe.

Sadie looked desperately from person to person. "She promised us it would be all right. She promised."

A head of shaggy blond hair and a pair of strapping rugby shoulders caught Lucy's attention. Her eyes met his. For the first time, no laughter lingered in his gaze. All she saw there was pity.

"Lass?" He started toward her, but Lucy turned away.

If Michael McKeegan so much as touched her, she would shatter.

Chapter 4

President Roosevelt called December 7, 1941, a day that would live in infamy. Lucy believed the same could be said of January 7, 1942. Or really any of the days that had passed since she'd disembarked at the Liverpool docks and into a boring existence of gray weather, gray food, and gray people. Now, two weeks, four trains, three buses, and a cab ride later, she had almost made it to Nanreath Hall, the rambling sandstone and granite house perched on the Cornish cliffs north of Newquay, principal seat of the Earls of Melcombe since the last ice age, and her mother's childhood home.

Almost made it—but not quite.

Pulling her collar up around her ears, Lucy stepped off the branch-line train at Melcombe village station.

"Whoever said Cornwall was England's Riviera ought to be sued for fraud," she muttered, huddling beneath the platform's overhang as cold rain poured from a leaden sky.

A porter dressed in everything but hip waders approached with a handcart. He gripped a toothpick between rubbery lips. "Any bags, miss?"

"Tragically, no," she answered through chattering teeth.

Her matched set of Louis Vuitton luggage had gone down with the *Strathleven*. In its place she'd been given a battered secondhand valise with a broken handle and a string bag. She didn't even want to think about the wardrobe she'd lost to the bottom of the ocean or she'd cry. Where on earth in this war-torn country of ration books and clothing drives would she ever find a little black Chanel to replace the one currently twenty thousand leagues under?

She tried to look on the bright side. At least she'd arrived, even if it was in a tatty blouse and ill-fitting skirt. She'd half the world behind her. Only three miles to go before this journey of unending hell would be over.

The porter checked his watch before removing his hat to scratch his thinning hair. "You must be headed to the hospital up Nanreath Hall way."

"I don't know anything about a hospital. I've come to stay with my aunt, Lady Boxley."

His eyes widened in recognition. "So you're the niece what's come from foreign parts." They remained wide as he took her in from stem to stern. "Not much of a look of the family about you, is there? Must come from being half Yank."

"I blame my father for my olive complexion, poker-straight hair, and horrible tendency to drive on the right-hand side of the road."

He grunted and moved his toothpick from one side of his mouth to the other. "Ever met that William Powell chap?"

"Can't say I've had the pleasure."

The porter seemed surprised. "Really? He's a Yank too."

"Is he? Then I can't imagine why we haven't bumped into each other before now."

Sarcasm was lost on him. He merely continued to gum his toothpick as he smiled fondly. "Now, there is a classy gent. Saw him in all them *Thin Man* pictures. Me and the missus love a good who-dunit."

"Really, not that I wouldn't love to hang about and chat," Lucy interrupted, "but my aunt is waiting for me. She said she would send a car to pick me up."

The porter's answer was lost as the wind gusted needles of rain in her face and the gutter overflowed, sending a river of icy runoff down the back of her neck. She yelped as the cold slithered along her spine, nearly leaping into the porter's arms.

Her spasms were met by childish laughter. Three boisterous young boys disembarked from the train at the far end of the platform, shoving each other in good-natured horseplay as they hooted and guffawed. A girl holding the hand of a rather grim-faced woman followed. Then came two older girls in pigtails and much-repaired pinafores. All the children carried satchels and gas masks. All wore tags pinned to their coats.

"Sam, keep your tongue in your mouth," the woman scolded. "Maude, don't scuff, and for heaven's sake stop scratching. George, you and Gerald need to keep your hands to yourselves. Come along, Daisy. Keep up, Susan. I know you're all tired and hungry, but we're almost there."

She felt instant empathy for the sullen, bewildered children. All Lucy needed was a label to be mistaken for one of them.

The porter cleared his throat, drawing her attention back to her own predicament. "No car from Nanreath, miss. Not that I've seen. But perhaps there was some muck-up and they forgot you was coming today. Wouldn't be surprised. It's all here, there, and back again since the government took the estate over for the war."

"When did that happen?"

Their conversation was interrupted by the arrival of a gentleman in a cheap suit and an ARP armband. His lips thinned as his gaze fell on the rowdy group of children, and he took an involuntary step back as if hoping to escape into the waiting room until the danger had passed.

The woman was faster. She collared him with all the determination of a quick-witted constable. "Thank heavens you're here. We'd arranged to billet the children in a village near Exeter, but, well . . . there were issues with overcrowding and then there was an unfortunate outbreak of measles. You were my last hope at seeing this group settled before I report back to my housing committee chairman."

The volunteer air raid warden took one more long gawk at the children, the boys aiming pebbles at a sign advertising Esso kerosene, the girls giggling over a dishy soldier making a call from the public phone box at the end of the platform. "Here for me wife," the man grumbled, shoving past to greet a white-haired housewife getting off the train with a day's town shopping to her credit.

The couple left, sharing an enormous black umbrella, the man casting a last backward glance at the children as if afraid they might follow him home.

Lucy's porter drew her attention back once more with a phlegmy clearing of his throat. "Let's see, now, when did the hospital move in?" He scratched his head again and leaned against his handcart. "Since summer '39, it's been. Government conscripted all sorts of places for wartime use without even so much as a by-your-leave. Just 'Thanks very much, but we'll take it from here.'"

"And Lord Melcombe and my aunt?"

"Oh, they still live there, leastways your aunt does. His Lordship's away in Plymouth working as an ambulance driver if you can credit that of a belted earl. Your aunt tries her best, but it's not like it used to be in the old days. Your mum would barely recognize it. People rushing about. Grounds torn up. Lorries and ambulances and cars whizzing up and down the lanes day and night. The pub full of wildness so you can't even get a relaxing pint of bitter and a game of darts. Countryside crawling with all types from every which place. Adults"—he eyed the children warily—"and sprogs alike."

By now, the woman's voice was rising as her shoulders sank. "Oh, dear. Sam, put those rocks down. George, you really must stop poking your sister. Maude, how many times have I warned you about scratching?" She dropped onto a bench, her face flushed, her grim scowl sliding toward complete surrender. She rubbed her temples as if her head hurt.

"A wild pub full of wild men?" Lucy replied over the growing ruckus. "That sounds promising."

"Suppose you're used to such goings-on. Probably used to living it up in New York City and Miami Beach. I hear it's awful nice there this time of year."

"Anywhere other than here would be nice this time of year."

Out of the corner of her eye, Lucy watched a kindly-looking man approach the woman where she sat nursing her migraine. "You for the village hall, ma'am?"

She straightened with a look of renewed hope. "Yes, we're to meet someone from the local Women's Voluntary Services. Is it far to Melcombe?"

"Just down the hill, ma'am."

She eyed the storm, which drummed on the shingles and plinked in the gutters, emerging in a bubbling muddy rush from the drains. Her migraine seemed to intensify if her grayish pallor was any indication. "Oh dear."

"Not to worry. I've got the shooting brake just by the siding there. I'll be happy to drive you and the children."

At this pronouncement, her earlier briskness returned. She rose with a gleam of renewed purpose and only a slightly manic expression. "That's wonderful news. Simply wonderful. Come along, boys and girls. Gather your things."

"You too, miss," he said, catching Lucy's attention. "I'm to take you on to your aunt after I've dropped off the kiddies and their teacher with the billeting officer."

Every eye swung her direction. Maude and Susan giggled and whispered behind their hands. Gerald goggled as he wiped his nose on his sleeve. Even George and Sam left off biting one another to stare.

Lucy felt like an exhibit at the zoo.

"Hurry, children," the woman caroled in a singsong voice that grated on Lucy's fast-fraying nerves. "No dawdling."

They trooped like soldiers out of the station, where they were shoehorned into an already crowded shooting brake that smelled of wet dog and boiled cabbage.

"It's so hard to find suitable accommodations. I've rehoused this batch twice already," the woman complained as she took her seat up front with the driver, Daisy on her lap, Susan wedged against the gear lever.

Lucy was trapped in the backseat between George and Sam, who decided to thumb-wrestle over the top of her while Gerald hovered at one shoulder complaining he was carsick and Maude at the other whinged into her ear that a great bloody spanner was jammed under her bum.

Lucy had traveled nearly twenty thousand miles since leaving Singapore.

The last three might be the longest.

Here is your room. It's small, but at least we're still in the house. Lord and Lady Astruther are reduced to residing in their old gatekeeper's lodge now that the government has decided their estate would be better suited for German prisoners. May as well set up housekeeping in a stable if you ask me."

If Lucy had entertained hopes of a jolly doily-making, biscuit-baking aunt to take the place of her mother, they'd been dashed as soon as she'd been shown into Aunt Cynthia's sitting room by a mousy village girl who bobbed up and down like a cork on the waves. Lady Boxley's youthful beauty and dimpled softness had boiled away over the years, leaving a sharp-edged manner and a tongue like a scythe.

"The military hospital takes up the rest of the house. They're a loud, blundering bunch of heathens with no sense of the irreparable damage they're doing to this once-grand lady, but I can assure you I'm noting every instance of destruction and shall ask for proper compensation when this war is over. I'm related to Lady Turnbull, whose son serves on the War Damage Commission. I shan't hesitate to call on him if needed."

Lady Boxley pushed open a door to reveal a small musty wood-paneled chamber stuffed to the gills with at least two centuries' worth of clutter. A great curtained four-poster that looked like something Good Queen Bess might have died in took up most of the space with little left over for a dressing table, an armoire, and one threadbare armchair pulled up to a writing desk. A stuffed badger glared at Lucy from the mantelpiece while a pair of mounted ibex and a wildebeest sneered at her with lip-curling disdain.

Lucy assumed the fire in the grate was meant to be a cheerful addition rather than a necessity—a clanking hissing radiator belched steam in a corner—but the flames barely flickered above the minuscule heap of coal, and the shadows they cast crawled like fingers over the dark paneled walls and burned red in the eyes of the trophy animals.

"The hospital's staff does not appreciate the family's interference, in fact they're quite testy on the subject, so I would suggest you restrain yourself from visiting the wards—despite the obvious lure." Aunt Cynthia studied Lucy as if she were a modern-day Mata Hari, making her wonder how much Amelia had passed along about her transgressions. "I was not expecting to have you thrust upon me in such a harum-scarum way, but you *are* family and I know my duty. In return, I expect you to behave, be mindful of the family's dignity in all ways, and keep your own things tidy—the char we have has far too much to keep up with as it is."

Lucy had thought her last school dormitory was bad. This was worse. There she had friends . . . or, at the least, comrades in crime. Here she was completely on her own. At the mercy of her aunt for every scrap and crumb. An aunt who made it clear Lucy would be tolerated but never welcomed—the story of her life.

When Lucy didn't answer right away, Lady Boxley continued on in the same overburdened tone of voice. "My son, Hugh, has the chamber at the end of the passage, but he's away working as an ambulance driver if you can countenance such a thing."

"You make it sound as if he's serving time."

Lady Boxley arched one perfect brow, a simple twitch guaranteed to cut one down to a more squashable size. "My son lost a leg serving in Norway. Apparently, he feels one limb is not enough and wishes to risk the other three in some misguided attempt at patriotism." She sniffed into her handkerchief. "Ah well, water under the bridge. And I've learned to keep quiet; a mother can only say so much before her opinion is ignored, her years of thankless labor dismissed."

Seemed to Lucy that Aunt Cynthia said rather a lot, but she chose tact—for once—and kept her own mouth shut.

"My rooms are around the corner and up the small stair. But you shouldn't have any need to seek me out there. I will see you at meals and perhaps in the evenings for a small glass of sherry and a listen on the wireless, but other than that you are free to amuse yourself as you wish." She made a final look round the room before offering Lucy one more skeptical glance. "I suppose it's just as well you got out of Singapore when you did. No telling what's going to happen now the Japs have officially entered the war."

"Do you suppose Amelia is safe?"

Lady Boxley sniffed. "I shouldn't worry. Your mother is like a cat. Always lands on her feet."

Lucy recalled describing herself to Yoon Hai in just those words, and an angry flush climbed her throat to heat her cheeks.

Her aunt didn't seem to notice as she adjusted her suit jacket and straightened her cuffs. "I'm headed into Newquay for a meeting. I won't be back for dinner, but there's some leftover haddock in the icebox and I believe Mr. Deevers at the Home Farm has brought us a cabbage and potato pie."

"My favorite."

Aunt Cynthia shot her a stern glance. "I agree it's not Escoffier, but we make do. You'll learn to do the same." With a final once-over of Lucy that clearly transmitted her complete disappointment and irritation, she departed in a rapid clicking of heels down the corridor, her jaunty fox stole smirking back at Lucy with one beady glass eye.

Alone, she paced out the perimeter of her cell. Rain rattled against the tall windows. In the muddy yard below, two mechanics wrestled a lorry into a shed out of the weather. A trio of nurses stood in a doorway sharing a cigarette. A leather-clad goggled messenger arrived in a cloud of smoke, his motorbike spraying gravel as he skidded to a stop, his great bag slung over his shoulder.

Beyond the house, brown fields stretched away to a belt of leafless trees. The sea was hidden by a veil of rain and cloud, but she could hear it like a deep rolling bass note and feel it vibrating up through her feet like a second heartbeat.

One of the mechanics spotted her at the window. He whispered something to his mate and the two of them looked up at her, the nurses giggling.

Lucy drew the curtains closed, shutting out the ugly yard, the sodden landscape, the sneering soldiers. The radiator gave a great belch of steam. A mouse scrabbled in the wall. One of the ibex leered at her.

"Welcome bloody home."

She promised us it would be all right. She promised.

Lucy came awake on a terrified gasp. The meager fire had gone out, throwing the room into deep and chilly shadow, and for a heart-crashing moment she was back among the *Strathleven's* survivors. A steadying breath. Then another. Her pulse slowed. Her grief subsided. She was left merely groggy and stiff.

And very hungry.

Her watch had run down and the clock on the bedside table only possessed one hand—hardly instructive. It must be late. The house was quiet, no grind of ambulance gears or shouts from lorry drivers. No babble of conversation and slamming doors. Just the sea's low purr infiltrating through the heavy folds of the dusty blackout curtains and now and again the call from some lonely bird.

"What do you think? Should I search out something to eat or ring for room service?"

The two ibex maintained expressions of complete imbecility, the badger sneered, while the wildebeest merely offered her a reproachful look but no advice.

"Right. Maid's day off. We'll find the kitchen on our own."

Throwing a cardigan over her rumpled clothes, she followed the carpeted corridor until it opened onto an enormous oak-paneled gallery. In the shaded light of a table lamp, she saw walls full of men in Restoration curls and Georgian periwigs, women in elaborate hoops and high-waisted muslin. Normal families might have an album with a few grainy photos. Leave it to hers to have an entire room dedicated to every ancestor dating back to Adam and Eve.

As she passed through the gallery, shadows moved along the far wall. A breeze curled past her legs. A whispered word echoed from among the clusters of comfortable furniture. Shades of Nanreath's exalted past passing judgment on the new arrival? Or . . .

She peered over a camel-backed sofa upholstered in rather careworn cream silk. "Is that for medicinal or recreational use?"

Two young men froze crouched in the space between a Chinese cabinet and a set of tall chintz-covered armchairs. They both wore robes over their army-issued pajamas. One had his arm in a sling.

"Bugger all, miss. You took five years off our lives. We thought you was Nanny Goebbels."

"Who?"

"Sister Murphy. She's worse than a bloody prison warden. Treats us lads like we're still in nappies. Lights out at ten. Eat all your veg if you want your pud. No fraternizing with the nurses—"

"And no liquor on the wards," they repeated in unison.

"So you came up here to do your tippling?" Lucy asked, making herself comfortable.

"It was the safest place we could think of."

"You won't turn us in, will you, miss?"

A matching pair of young soldiers with a bottle of Barclay's lager was far more interesting than cabbage and potato pie and a plate of haddock. She eyed the bottle expectantly. "Well . . . I don't know . . ."

The chap with the sling passed it over. Lucy took a hearty swig.

The beer fell into her empty stomach with a thud, but the buzzy warmth that followed banished the last of her ghosts. "What alcohol?"

They grinned.

"This here's Nate," said the one with the sling, who seemed to be the bolder of the two. "He's recovering from pneumonia. I'm Tom. Busted the arm in a bailout over the Channel."

"If you ain't a VAD nurse or one of the sisters, what are you doing here?" Nate asked, taking his turn with the bottle.

"I'm Lord Melcombe's cousin."

Tom's brows lifted in pleased surprise. "You're the bird from Singapore. The one who . . ." He stammered to a halt. "That is . . . we heard you were expected."

"My reputation precedes me. Just as well. Makes everything that much easier."

"Did you really—"

Tom jabbed Nate in the ribs and shot him a warning look. "Good thing you sailed when you did. Looks like there isn't much stopping the Japs now that they've sunk our battleships and trapped most of our lads between jungle and sea. I'd not be one of those poor bastards for all the tea in China."

Lucy followed the bottle around until it came back to her. "Poor bloody bastards is right," she murmured, ignoring the tremble in her hand and the wash of fear across her shoulders. This time the beer didn't come anywhere near warming the cold place in the pit of her stomach.

"There you two are!" Light shattered their dark little corner as someone snapped on a switch and four chandeliers blazed into blinding life. "I should have known I'd find you up here."

Nate scrambled to his feet while Tom fumbled to hide the bottle behind his back.

Lucy grabbed it before it slipped through his clumsy fingers.

A sour-faced nurse wearing the scarlet-edged cape and crisp veil of Queen Alexandra's Imperial Military Nursing Service bore down on them with purpose in her long mannish stride. The acrid hospital odors of disinfectant and bleach followed in her wake like a noxious cloud. "Peasham, Lisk—you both know the regulations."

Sister Murphy, Lucy presumed.

"They're not to blame." Instinctively, she stepped in front of the young men, though she had no idea what she might do to defend them. The QA sister looked more than capable of snapping Lucy like a twig. "The beer's mine. They were just explaining the hospital's rules on alcohol consumption. Very proper rules they are, too."

Sister Murphy sized Lucy up with a long look from her beady little eyes and snorted her disbelief. "You must be Her Ladyship's niece. We were warned about you." She pointed a finger at the young men. "You two—back to the wards." They shuffled off, slump shouldered and chastened, leaving Lucy alone to face the sister's full wrath.

"And you, Miss Stanhope—you'll keep away if you know what's best. We don't need your type disrupting the men."

Lucy supposed most people would have been quaking in their boots, but this was hardly the first time she'd been raked over the coals for breaking the rules. "What type would that be?" she asked with a casual quirk of an eyebrow and an evocative half smile. "Cousin to His Lordship, you mean?"

Sister Murphy's face purpled as she chewed and swallowed whatever threats she'd been tempted to issue. "I'll say no more, but you'll heed me if you know what's what. You're not the pampered young miss anymore. Those days are done."

She turned on her heel and departed the gallery in a flap of skirts like a great gray storm crow.

With the departure of Sister Murphy, the dusty scents of rose petals and sandalwood settled once more like leaves after a whirlwind. The sudden silence roared in Lucy's ears like the incessant pound of the sea. She matched it breath for breath until the hollow ache against her ribs eased, though her cheeks still burned as if she'd been slapped.

With a harsh bark of angry laughter, she polished off the last of the Barclay's, wiping her mouth with the back of her hand before staring around her at generations of pedigreed breeding and aristocratic arrogance. "Some help you lot were."

Chapter 5

Lucy might not possess many attributes her aunt would find valuable in a proper young lady, but what she lacked in modesty and kindness, she made up in adaptability and resourcefulness. It didn't take long for her to learn the house's routine and take full advantage of any official lapses, much to the patients' delight and the staff's annoyance. It became her greatest game to irritate Sister Murphy to the point the nurse's face purpled with rage and she sputtered and spat like a teakettle on the boil.

As Singapore fell and the Japanese island-hopped across the Far East unchecked by either the British or their new American allies, Lucy was caught sharing dirty magazines with a lieutenant in the RASC recovering from a bad case of influenza.

As Malta in the west and Leningrad in the east both withstood deadly sieges by the Germans, Lucy was caught canoodling with a dispatch rider in the back of a Bedford lorry.

And as U-boats picked off merchant ships in the Atlantic like punters in a shooting gallery, Lucy was caught being pulled through a downstairs window after a late drunken night with a corporal from St. Eval airfield.

These adventures generally led to a trip down the hall and up the stairs to her aunt's boudoir, nearly the only interaction she had with Aunt Cynthia, who led a nonstop life of volunteer work in the time not devoted to the running of the estate in her son's absence.

Lucy almost began to look forward to these little family tête-à-têtes. Other than her occasional wander through the Nanreath gallery, it was the only time she was reminded she actually had family.

"Are you even listening to me?" Aunt Cynthia sat at her dressing table applying a fresh coat of powder, her unyielding expression no less powerful in reflection. "I've had complaints from Sister Murphy about your behavior—again. She says she found you dancing in the salon in an overly provocative fashion, much to the men's lascivious delight."

"It's called the jive, Aunt Cynthia. Everyone's doing it." Under her breath, she added, "Everyone who isn't an old boring fogy, that is."

Her aunt barreled on, undisturbed. "And twice she's caught you drinking with patients behind the petrol sheds."

"Amelia taught me it was impolite to refuse a gentleman's offer of a drink."

Aunt Cynthia turned to eye Lucy down her long straight aristocratic nose. "Your mother never refused a gentleman anything, which is why she's already on husband number three."

Lucy didn't even try to argue with that.

Rummaging through her jewelry box, Aunt Cynthia clipped on a pair of pearl earrings and fastened a slender choker around her neck. "You're not a child, Lucy. There are consequences to your actions. You can't continue to behave in this unbridled manner."

"I was boosting morale. Isn't that what Churchill wants us to do? Keep our boys' spirits up?"

"Those boys' spirits will have to survive without your assistance."

Aunt Cynthia gave her hair a final pat and rose from her chair. Lucy would have loved to ask her how she managed to make the green-and-red uniform of the WVS look like something put together by the finest Parisian couturier, rather than Father Christmas run amok, but even her boldness had limits. "Now, I'm due at the village hall in ten minutes. Can you try and behave yourself until I get back? And refrain from further upsetting Sister Murphy? The last thing I need is for you to goad the woman into an aneurysm. As spiteful as she is, she's liable to haunt us, and, heaven forfend, we'd never be rid of her."

Her deadpan delivery made it impossible for Lucy to determine whether Aunt Cynthia was joking, but the thin-lipped glare caused her to swallow back an unexpected bubble of laughter. "I could always take a flat in London. That would solve everyone's problems."

"Out of the question. I'll not have my niece swanning about town on her own. Aside from the obvious dangers, it's not seemly. The place is awash in soldiers, and not just solid dependable British officers, but these rowdy swaggering Americans"—eying Lucy, she positively sneered the word—"with the savage manners of Billy the Kid."

Lucy suspected Aunt Cynthia still held a grudge against the United States over that whole revolution thing and regarded the arriving American troops more like an invading army than a welcome ally. "It's not the Middle Ages. Plenty of single women are living and working in the city. I met all sorts of wealthy businessmen through Fortescue. I'm sure one of them would give me a job."

Her aunt eyed her warily. "Yes, but doing what exactly?"

Lucy almost had the grace to blush—almost.

"Though I do think an occupation of some kind is a good idea—something besides your one-woman ENSA crusade. The WVS are always looking for volunteers. Or what about the MTC? You certainly seem to know how to spark an engine." She placed a lipstick, three fresh handkerchiefs, her compact, and a tin of licorice allsorts in her purse. "Or is it the backseat you prefer?"

Once again, Lucy was struck by the brilliance of Aunt Cynthia's poker face. The woman could deliver the most scathing insult in the same dignified tones one might use to address the queen. Amelia had never been so proper or so precise.

"Now, I really have to run. If I'm not at the meeting on time, Loretta Stanley will volunteer me to head up the new children's home." She grimaced with distaste. "My life would be consumed by unending head lice and bed-wetting. I'd rather face Hitler's worst than that."

On that final complaint, she ushered Lucy out as she headed to her meeting with a ruthlessly efficient gleam in her eye. Poor Loretta Stanley didn't stand a chance.

Neither did Lucy. If she wasn't careful, she'd be spending this war mucking pig shite in the WLA or serving endless cups of tea with the NAAFI.

Making for the back stairs that would take her down to the west terrace entrance, she grabbed an old raincoat off a peg and stuffed her feet into a pair of battered rubber boots. A few orderlies stood about in the yard by the side terrace doors. Two Red Cross VAD nurses chatted with a sentry. Sister Murphy pushed a young man in a wheelchair toward a waiting ambulance.

"Where are you hurrying off to, Miss Stanhope?" she asked, looking as if butter wouldn't melt in her mouth.

"Nowhere in particular."

Sister Murphy's mouth curled in what passed for a smile. "It must be pleasant to be exempted from conscription and do nothing but laze about. Enjoy your afternoon for the rest of us, won't you?"

The soldier in the chair winked, and Lucy flashed him a wicked grin before addressing the sister with a straight face. "Why don't you come with me? I'm off to meet with black marketeers for silk stockings and whiskey, then over to Neville's farm to make mad passionate love to their dairyman in return for a glass of real milk. I'm sure his brother would love to meet you. He has a thing for women in uniform . . . and out of them."

The soldier nearly choked. Sister Murphy's face blanched the color of cold porridge, and Lucy passed on with a private smile of triumph.

Take that, Nanny Goebbels.

Her satisfaction barely survived the time it took to leave the graveled path beside the motor pool and shove her way through the scrubby privet hedge separating the old kitchen garden from the park. By the time she'd walked off her frustration, she was miles from the house and regretting her impulsive words. Sister Murphy would waste no time tattling to Matron, who would go to Aunt Cynthia, and Lucy would be up to her neck in it all over again.

What made it worse was that Lucy knew she was behaving like a pampered, self-centered bitch and yet couldn't seem to stop. It was as if she needed to push everyone away before they pushed her away. Well, she'd certainly accomplished that. She was officially persona non grata with everyone at Nanreath Hall and probably in a ten-square-mile radius. Nicely done, Lucy, old bean.

She shoved through the narrow path's thick underbrush, sinking up to her ankles in a muddy puddle.

"Damn godforsaken island!" she cried, pulling her boots out of the slimy muck with a slurping squelch.

The whole place could go to hell for all she cared. It was too damn cold and the damp drilled right into her bones. The three months she'd been here may as well have been three years. A gray

unending existence marked only by moments of irresistible spiteful-
ness she immediately regretted.

Still cursing, she emerged from the stunted, wind-bent trees of
the spinney and onto the moor stretching up to the western cliffs
where the remnants of an ancient stone watchtower stood sentinel
and the sea frothed with the chop of whitecaps. Empty bottles and
old newspaper littered the ground around the tumbled stones
and graffiti blemished the crumbling ruins, but she didn't care.
She'd found this place on her very first ramble. Yes, that was what
she'd been reduced to for entertainment—long walks. The irony
was not lost on her.

Sadly, she'd yet to come across any fresh-faced young men loi-
tering beside stone walls. More's the pity. What she had found was
the tower, and since that discovery, her hikes had always led her
back here. She started thinking of it as hers, a place she could come
to be alone with her thoughts—and her dreams. Or what was left
of them anyway.

She climbed the last distance to the ruins, taking a seat on a
comfortably eroded boulder out of the wind, lit a cigarette between
cupped hands, and inhaled the soothing tobacco deeply into her
lungs.

Low cloud and drizzle kept the German bombers at home,
though it sounded as if the ack-ack gunners farther south weren't
taking any chances. The boom bounced over the water, mingling
with the growl of the surf and the lonesome almost-human moan of
the wind through the rocks.

No wonder Amelia had left as soon as she could. The place was
like something out of a Brontë novel.

She took another drag before tossing the butt away to hug her
arms to her body in a vain attempt to conserve heat. Singapore
might be just as soggy as England, but at least it was warm. She

hadn't properly appreciated that steamy equatorial humidity when she had it.

She hadn't properly appreciated a lot of things.

Lucy pulled Amelia's last letter from her pocket. A hasty scrawl dated the end of January, it was taken up almost completely with Government House rumors and the latest complaints about shortages and inconveniences brought on by the war. Only in the postscript had she imparted anything of interest—a comment regarding the Yoon family's cowardly escape to Chunking. *Like treacherous rats from a sinking ship* was her caustic turn of phrase.

Good for them.

Lucy could only hope Amelia and her stepfather had decided to be as gutless. But there had been no word since this last letter. No way to know whether they were dead, imprisoned by the Japanese, or still trying to make their way to the relative safety of Australia.

She leaned back and closed her eyes, lifting her cheeks to the pinching wind.

How many of those polished young officers she'd danced with at the Tanglin Club had died in the jungles north of the city fending off Yamashita as he marched south? How many of those preening self-satisfied tuans and their mems sipping cocktails at Raffles Hotel had lost everything they owned in the disastrous retreat south across the Straits of Johore? She would have been one of them had her affair with Yoon Hai not come to light. He had wanted her out of Singapore, and she had been banished. Funny how it had all turned out.

There were moments, usually when she lay sleepless in bed at night, when she questioned their last meeting. Had Hai chosen the department store knowing that in such a public place there was a good chance someone would spot them and report the affair to his uncle or her stepfather?

Or was she attributing selfless devotion where there had only been unthinking carelessness?

Either way, she prayed Hai and his bride were living happily ever after in Chunking. Though was there really such a thing in the face of the unstoppable might of the Japanese?

The cry of a seabird pulled her from her reverie.

An odd, almost yelping sound like a macaw with its foot caught in a snare. Nails on a slate made a more dulcet tone than this aggravating bird.

It came again.

She sat up listening. The soft moan of the wind. The sharper almost-shout of the bird.

Both a bit odd now that she was paying attention.

"Hello?" she called, a prickling shiver rippling up her spine.

The moaning snared-macaw yelp turned to a hiccup of gasped breath. "I'm down here."

The boy clung to a small outcropping of rock about six feet below the edge of the cliff. His face was smudged with dirt, his sweater was torn and muddy, and his hair—an indeterminate shade of brown—stuck up around his thin pale face like a rooster's comb. All elbows and knees, he looked to be about twelve, though he was skin and bones, with the same hunger-pinched look possessed by most of his countrymen.

"What on earth are you doing down there?" Lucy asked.

"Mostly holding on for dear life, miss."

"I meant how . . . oh, never mind. Wait a tick." She looked around for help, but there was nothing but open meadow and moorland. The closest habitation was an old cottage on the far side of the spinney. She hadn't seen anyone at home when she'd passed, but there might be a telephone she could use. In a pinch, perhaps they kept a ladder or rope in their shed.

"I'll be right back."

"Don't leave. Please. I"—his voice broke—"I can't hold on much longer. My arms are awful tired, miss."

"But I have to get help."

His bottom lip quivered.

"Oh, all right, I'll stay. Just let me think a moment." She knelt at the edge of the cliff, mud seeping cold through her stockings as she reached as far as she could. "Can you take my hand?"

The boy stretched his arm toward hers, his fingers still a foot or two away. "It's too far."

Soggy clumps of brown grass stuck out of the otherwise rocky ground. Patches of thick mud oozed like chocolate.

"Right." She grimaced as she lowered herself down until she lay flat, a stone jutting into her hip, another scraping her side. Dirt smeared her borrowed mackintosh as she reached again. "Any better?"

Even now, he was too far below her. "I can't, miss."

"Of course you can. Jump if you have to. I'm not asking you to vault ten feet. It's barely a few inches. If I can cover myself head to toe in filth, the least you can do is try a little harder."

He bent his knees and gave a little spring in the air. His fingers grazed hers. He tried again as she fumbled to catch him, but once more he slipped through her grip. He was crouching for one last attempt when a small landslide of rock and dirt peeled away to fall the hundreds of feet to the shale below.

He screamed and dug his hands into the side of the cliff, his face white as bone beneath the mud and the tears accentuating the brightness of his wide brown eyes. Lucy blinked and swallowed back an unconscious cry of alarm, clenching her jaw with renewed determination.

"Come on. One more jump will do it."

"Please, miss. I'm scared. I can't."

Lucy rolled over and up onto her knees. This wasn't going to work. She needed a rope or a vine, something to drop down to him. She didn't have anything like that—her hand paused as she brushed the dirt from her laddered stockings. Or did she?

"I've got an idea. Give me a minute."

"I ain't going nowhere, miss."

She scrambled to her feet and kicked off her boots. Then with a quick glance around, she hiked her skirt to her waist. "My name's Lucy by the way, not Miss."

"I'm Bill."

"Nice to meet you, Bill." She unclipped her right garter and rolled off her stocking. Did the same with her other leg. Gooseflesh prickled her skin, and she lamented losing a perfectly serviceable pair of stockings, but she was all out of ideas. Tying the two of them together, she stretched them out and tested her knots. Hardly Royal Navy approved, but they'd have to do. "I'm going to drop you a rope. Tie it around your waist and I'll pull you up."

She tossed the end of the stocking over the edge. A smothered giggle floated up to her. "This ain't no rope, miss. It's your unmentionables."

"It's all I've got. Now do it. I'm freezing up here and it's starting to rain."

"Right, miss . . . I mean Lucy. Just a tick." A moment later, he tugged on the end. "All set."

"Hold on, and whatever you do, don't look down." She looped her end of the stockings around and around her hand, braced herself against an outcropping of rock at the edge of the cliff, and heaved.

The stockings stretched, but the knots held. She pulled again, hand over hand, inch by inch. "Almost there."

A hand appeared over the edge, grabbing into the soil. Another hand. Then a head. She made one last lung-burning effort, and the boy slithered up and over onto the turf at her feet. Eyes squeezed shut, he rolled over onto his back, gasping as if he'd run a marathon.

"Are you all right?" Lucy asked.

His eyes popped open, and he tossed her an impish grin. "Ta. You wouldn't have a fag, would you? I'm dying."

Chapter 6

Look who's taking London by storm—Hollywood's own version of King Midas. Mason Oliver, renowned producer of such well-known pictures as Blood and Passion, The Taming of Tammy, *and last year's Oscar nominee* Thistledown Manor *is in England until the end of this month as part of a morale-lifting goodwill tour. But don't despair, stars and starlets to be. He's also on the hunt for fresh faces and fresh talent for an upcoming cinematic production rumored to begin filming this very summer in sunny California. Looking to be the next Clark Gable or Greer Garson? He's your man. Just one touch could turn your future golden.*

Lucy nearly choked on her popcorn as the Pathé newsreel reported the latest entertainment news. There he was, flickering up on the screen of the Victoria cinema: a handsome man, wearing a young woman on each arm, being helped from his limousine by an umbrella-carrying Dorchester hotel doorman. He gave a nod to the camera as he flashed his best world-premiere smile before hurrying out of the rain and into the lobby.

The announcer moved on to extolling the virtues of the British transport system, but Lucy had lost interest in the sweet story of a London railway porter and his best gal. Mason Oliver—a name she'd forgotten until now—brought Singapore back with startling clarity: the relentless midday sun, the chatter of battling languages, the sleepy ennui broken by spurts of frenzied rebellion. Her affair with Yoon Hai fell into that category. She imagined it had been the same way for him, an attempt to break free of stifling expectations, a diversion from the scripted content of their monotonous lives.

They should have known to be careful what they wished for.

Snatching up her raincoat, she left the cinema for the pub on the corner. The bus for Melcombe didn't arrive for another hour. She would have a drink while she digested the bittersweet taste of memory.

The pub was Saturday-night crowded. At the long polished bar, where a balding man with furry brows and a bellowing laugh polished glasses and pulled pints, flyboys from the airfields at St. Eval and Malvern flirted with Land Girls from Whitecross Halt and the farms around Portnance. Seated at the crush of tables surrounding a tiny dance floor or hovering by the dartboard, staff and the occasional up-patient from Nanreath Hall rubbed shoulders and traded stories with boys working the harbor's fishing boats and shopgirls from the village.

She shucked free of her raincoat, enjoying the approving glances tossed her way. Her dress had started life as a rubbish-bin castoff at the last Women's Institute village jumble. Alter the sleeves, place some tucks along the side seams to cinch the waist, and add a matching belt discarded by Aunt Cynthia, and no one would ever know it hadn't been hand stitched in a Paris fashion house.

As she found a table, ordered a pink gin, and lit a Sobranie, she eyed a delicious young flying officer on the other side of the room. He possessed the RAF's prerequisite cocksure posture and aristocratic good looks, his wavy brown hair just begging to have fingers running through it.

Lucy leaned forward to crush out her cigarette in the ashtray, letting her figure speak for itself. Immediately, she felt attention focus her way. The handsome officer even glanced over with his dark bedroom eyes. She offered him a careless smile in passing.

"You still owe me a fag, you know."

Lucy stiffened, her gaze flicking to the boy sliding into the seat across from her. With his face scrubbed clean and his hair combed, he almost looked presentable, though a devil's gleam remained in his eyes. She sympathized with his poor parents. "You're too young to smoke."

"So are you." He pulled a cigarette from the pack lying on the table. Started to reach for her lighter. "Let me stand you a drink, miss. What's your poison?"

She snatched the lighter back. "A bit too short to play Humphrey Bogart, don't you think?" She glanced around to see who might be watching. "What are you doing here, Bill?"

"I got tired of hearing nothing but wind and frogs so I hitched a lift into town for a spot of fun."

"Do your parents know you're haunting the pub?"

"Ain't got parents. Got me mam, though."

"Look, I'm flattered, Bill, but you need to go home."

"I would if I could, miss, but the blighters won't let me."

"If you spend your evenings at the pub chatting up older women, I'm not surprised, you little delinquent."

"It's not that . . ."

"Here, boy. Haven't I told you before not to come in here?" The barman stood over their table, his thick wiry brows drawn into a scowl. "Shove off before I call a constable to toss you in stir."

Bill's jaw jutted in defiance. "Bus-nappers don't scare me. Naught but a bunch of thick-headed chubs."

"None of your sass, brat. Out you go before I take the strap to you myself. And don't think I won't. You city brats might swagger round big as brass at home in London, but down here we know how to handle young'uns that don't mind their elders." The barman grabbed Bill's left ear in a tight pincer hold and dragged him to his feet. "You should be happy you've got a nice place to stay 'stead of causing trouble."

"Lay off, mate. I ain't doing nobody no harm," Bill shouted.

"You can do the same somewhere else, cheeky bugger."

Trapped in the man's grip, Bill was dragged away shouting curses and threats, much to the delight of the pub. The flying officer leaned over to whisper to a tableful of his friends.

A group of RAF gunners began an obscene chorus of "Hitler Has Only Got One Ball." The pub relaxed back into its groove, the night's entertainment over.

No doubt about it. Jasmine-scented Singapore and the company of Yoon Hai were a lost dream. Her reality was this provincial corner of England, where the highlight of her week was being hit on by a twelve-year-old. Yet up there on that movie screen for a brief moment, those two worlds touched.

Perhaps—just perhaps—she wasn't as trapped as she thought she was.

On that unexpectedly cheerful note, Lucy moved to the bar to order another gin.

"Allow me." A hand reached past with the shilling for payment.

"I can buy my own drink, thank you very much," she said, pulling another cigarette from her case.

"I'd wager you can bathe and dress yourself too." He lit her cigarette with a monogrammed lighter. "But isn't it so much nicer when someone else is there to help?" Up close, that electric smile was about a million watts, dazzling after months of blackout restrictions. His hair shone soft in the light and he smelled of sandalwood and bay rum. "Flying Officer Samuel Parsonhurst at your service. What brings a pretty American pigeon to our little corner of the world?"

Oh dear. Normally, an opening line like that wouldn't even merit a response, but she was feeling unexpectedly generous. Perhaps a result of the tantalizing glimpse of a possible future beyond cold baths and warm beer. She relaxed her face into a slow sultry smile. "If you fly as poorly as you flirt, Mr. Parsonhurst, the Jerries don't have a thing to worry about."

He shrugged. "A chap can try, can't he?"

She inhaled the tang of the cigarette. "In war, you don't get a medal for trying, though, do you?"

His smile widened, and he ducked his head sheepishly. "Look, I know you must think me an awful cad, but you see, the boys over there . . ." He gestured to a corner by the dartboard where RAF blue congregated. "They bet me I couldn't get you to give me the time of day."

"How much?"

"A half crown off each of them for every minute you don't toss your drink in my face."

"I'll take that wager and that drink."

He ordered her another gin. By now, her body tingled with a honeyed warmth and the world had softened to a fuzzy glow. Even the singers seemed to have improved. The airmen's amateur fervor had been replaced by a coin-operated phonograph whose rendition of "Stardust" had her swaying gently to the beat.

"Let's dance," Mr. Parsonhurst said.

He took her in his arms and they moved onto the crowded floor, the couples jostling for space, her feet fumbling to keep up. His gaze seemed to suck her in, the scent of him drowning out the harsher odors of sweat, wool, and stale beer. Memories seemed to hover close tonight. She was unexpectedly reminded of another dance and another soldier.

Then the tempo slowed, and Parsonhurst pulled her close. His buttons bit into her stomach. His breath was hot against her neck. She stepped wrong. An elbow caught her in the ribs. A woman's laughter made her wince and stumble. The image faded, and with it, her optimism.

She drew away. "You're a lovely dancer, but if it's all the same to you, I think I'll head home. This evening has fallen rather flat."

"One last drink for the road. I mean"—he shrugged his shoulders in a gesture of forbearance—"I could be dead by tomorrow. Shot down in my prime."

"Continue in that vein and I may be the one to do it. Good evening, Mr. Parsonhurst."

Lucy grabbed an abandoned newspaper off the end of the bar, held it over her head, and with a final pause like a diver before she leaves the blocks, she dashed out of the pub into the rain in a race for the bus stop. A soldier whistled. A car splashed mud all over her legs and coat. A trio of WAAF offered smug—dry—smiles from under their regulation umbrellas.

Lucy reached the stop just as the paper disintegrated, smearing a county-wide scrap-metal drive and a hospital damaged by bombs in black newsprint over her hands.

She tossed the soggy dregs of the *Western Morning News* away, wiping in vain at her inky hands and her muddy coat with a handkerchief, but only managed to leave streaks of gray from her wrists to her elbows. A slick of greasy gutter water dripped down her legs and into her shoes.

A long, dark green Packard pulled to the curb. Parsonhurst leaned out of the driver's-side window, his white scarf and white teeth gleaming. "Want a ride home?"

"You don't take no for an answer, do you?" she said while eying the comfort of American automotive engineering. He was pushy, but she was familiar with pushy, and it was better than drowning while waiting for the bus. She got in.

He gunned the engine, and the long car sped up the dark street, quickly leaving Newquay behind. The darkness beyond the town was complete, barely a line between land and sky, the fold of the rising hills and shallow valleys a blur beyond the worn wipers and the shuttered headlamps. At a crossroads, he took the turn in a spit of gravel and a squeal of brakes. Something in the backseat fell to the floor with a heavy thud and what sounded like a grunt, but Lucy was too busy holding on to the door handle for dear life to investigate.

"Slow down, flyboy. You're not piloting a Spit."

"Wish I were. The brass hats have me flying damned Blenheims. Now, I tell you, is that a waste of my talents or what?"

She looked back to see a cyclist cursing them from the middle of a hedge. "You certainly have evasive maneuvers down pat."

By now, the rain had stopped and the moon peeked in and out of the breaking clouds. She recognized the road they were on. Another mile and they'd be at Nanreath's gates and she could get off this roller-coaster ride. But instead of continuing on, he drew into the grass and cut the engine.

"Out of gas?"

Parsonhurst grinned like a Cheshire cat. "I've always held a soft spot for our colonial cousins." He leaned close. She smelled the beer on his breath and saw the way he swayed even without the band. It was a miracle they'd made it this far without crashing. "I thought you and I could enjoy our own private transatlantic alliance."

She tried and failed to stop her laughter. "I'm flattered at the offer—but I've had more than my share of British hospitality if it's all the same to you."

She started to get out, but he grabbed her wrist. "I don't give up until I get what I want. And you're the prettiest thing I've seen since I enlisted."

"I don't doubt it, but you're really not my type. So let me go—or else."

"Or else what?" Without warning, he pulled her into his arms, pressing his mouth on hers. His tongue pushed between her lips. She tried to break free, but his hold on her tightened. He grabbed her breast, fumbling at her collar.

"You'd better ease off the throttle, airman," she protested, attempting to ooze her way free of his clumsy advance. "It's not a dogfight."

"You want it. I could tell back at the pub."

"I wanted a drink. Not a grope from a sweaty pilot desperate to have his cherry popped so he can crow about it to his friends."

"Little tart." He pushed her back against the seat, ripping her collar. She made to slap him but he caught her wrist and dragged it behind her back until she cried out in pain. With his free hand, he squeezed her breast until she winced. "Think you're so damned clever, don't you? Won't be so quick to joke when I'm done with you."

Knee poised, she was just about to strike a blow for outraged womanhood everywhere when Parsonhurst folded like a tent on top of her.

"My mam told me you never hurt a girl or make her cry."

"Bill." Her voice emerged shaky with adrenaline. "What are you doing here?"

"It was raining, and the car was unlocked." The boy sat in the backseat, a spanner in his hand, his face set in fierce lines. "Come on, miss. We'd better hop the twig before he wakes up."

She grabbed his hand and together they left the Packard with its unconscious driver behind.

Name's Bill Smedley. My mam and me live in Bethnal Green. That's in London. She works as a maid for a swanky gent up the West End during the day and takes in washing at night."

"Where's your father?"

He shrugged, kicking a stone farther up the track. "Gone for a sailor, I reckon. Least that's what Mam says. She says he's a jolly fella but not a reliable one and I shouldn't expect him to be around much even if he comes back alive . . . which he probably won't on account of her bad luck. 'If I love 'em, they leave or they die, Billy boy. That's my lot.' That's what she says. Then she lays down with a wet rag on her forehead and sings sad songs."

"If she's in London, who are you staying with?"

"Mr. and Mrs. Sayres. I'm a sore trial to good Christian folks like them, but a cross they must bear for the war effort," he parroted in a doleful voice.

Lucy tucked her torn collar up and pinned it with her brooch. It didn't look completely right, but it kept her slip from showing. Damn that bloody airman. She should have known the arrogant jackass was too good to be true.

"I expect you must have the same problem as my mam," Bill said as he turned down a narrow rutted track. A thin bar of light could be seen in the distance, a gap between the curtains that would have sent any passing air raid warden into a frenzy.

"Unreliable or dead?"

"Aye . . . or rotters like that bloke back there."

"I think you're right."

"It's a good thing I was there. Now we're square. You saved me at the cliff and now I saved you."

The house Bill led her to was a long granite cottage with a mossy slate roof and a squat chimney at either end. Small square windows flanked the front stoop, where a scrawny man with a chinless face and a pair of bulbous eyes stood smoking a pipe.

"Is that you, Bill? Where you been, boy? Mrs. Sayres has been worried sick."

Bill's hand slid into Lucy's. She found herself giving it a reassuring squeeze. "He's been with me. I hope we didn't worry you."

A plump woman in a flowered housedress and bedroom slippers appeared at the door, her dimpled face anxious. "That you, Father?"

"Aye, Mother. Bill's home."

"Not before time neither. Well come on. I've kept your supper warm for you." Bill looked like he was being led to the gallows as he followed Mrs. Sayres into the house. Gone was his tough-guy swagger. For the first time he looked like the child he was. "Then straight to bed with you. Mr. Lewis stopped in. Said you've missed three days of school and not turned your lessons in for a week. And Mrs. Bitter tells me you've been at her chickens again. I'll not have that kind of nonsense in my—"

The door closed on her harangue, plunging Lucy and the old man back into gray darkness.

Mr. Sayres continued his puffing. "Hope he weren't any trouble."

"Not at all," she said, her own bravado reasserting itself in the face of this dour, disobliging man. "In fact, Bill was very helpful. He saved me when a . . . a nasty dog tried to bite me."

Barely lifting an eyebrow, he chewed on the end of his pipe. "Did he now? I can barely credit it. The youngster's a wild one; slick as a Gypsy. Shoulda seen him when he arrived. Naught more than the clothes he stood up in and the manners of a wild animal. Mrs. Sayres and I took him in out of the kindness of our hearts and he's repaid us with nothing but mischief and back talk."

She had a feeling their kind hearts were tied directly to the ten shillings a week they received for his care. "I assure you in this instance Bill acted quite the hero. You'd have been proud of him."

He snorted his disbelief. "Well, there's a first for everything." He tapped out his pipe on the side of the house and, without more than a nod, left her standing in the dark of the swept yard, a bolt sliding home to signify the end of her visit.

Lucy turned to leave, but not before a last glance up at that barely parted curtain, where Bill stood watching her. She made to wave good-bye, but the curtain was wrenched closed, dousing that last sliver of comforting light.

A fitting end to a dreadful night.

She arrived back at Nanreath Hall as the case clock in the hall struck two. By now, her dress was sadly rumpled, the heel of one of her expensive pumps had broken off, and she'd a long painful weal on her upper arm she'd received crossing the stile at the bottom of the water meadow. This added to her bruises from Parsonhurst's rough treatment, and she ached for a drink. Something strong that would render her unconscious until at least noon tomorrow. Nodding a passing good night to the sleepy sentry, she headed for the family wing, where a decanter of expensive brandy with her name on it waited on the sideboard.

"Enjoyable evening, Miss Stanhope?"

Lucy sighed and turned round, broken pump in hand, to face Sister Murphy, harpy in training. She lurked in the telephone alcove, her eyes glittering with an unreadable expression.

"Enjoyable? I don't know if I'd go so far as that."

"I suppose we must all seem rather dull and ordinary to you after your glamorous life abroad. I don't wonder you laugh at us behind our backs."

"Not that I don't love our little heart-to-hearts, but I've had a wretched evening, so if you'll excuse me, I'm going to bed." Anything to escape a lecture on the proper decorum for ladies. Hadn't anyone figured out yet that she wasn't a proper lady and didn't aspire to be one?

"Of course. I really only stayed up to deliver this. It came while you were out. I thought you should have it immediately rather than wait until morning." Sister Murphy handed Lucy a telegram. "I'm sorry, Miss Stanhope. I know you may not believe me, but if there's anything I can do to help . . ."

. . . inform you that Lady Amelia Fortescue . . . Reginald Fortescue . . . sinking of Diamond Star *. . . torpedoed off coast of New Guinea . . . missing, presumed dead . . .*

"I think you've helped enough for one night, don't you?" Lucy said quietly.

Sister Murphy's dark eyes gleamed in a face that would have cracked at anything remotely resembling a smile. "It must be rather a shock. You'll want to be alone. I know I would in your situation."

"And what situation would that be?" Lucy crushed the telegram in a fist. Took a step toward the QA nurse, who seemed to suddenly realize she was alone in a dark corridor with a potentially unhinged woman. "My mother's death? Amelia was barely a mother when she was alive. I doubt death will change the tenor of our relationship much."

After the initial hesitation, Sister Murphy recaptured the high ground, her expression suitably sympathetic with a touch of superiority thrown in for good measure. "You're overwrought and lashing out. I've seen it a hundred times in the men on the wards. It's very common in those who suffer such a tragedy. It takes time to heal, to truly comprehend the enormity of the loss."

Despite her compassionate patter, it wasn't pity Lucy saw in the nurse's eyes. She knew pity. She'd seen it often enough from teachers at her various schools, or parents who invited her home on holiday breaks when Amelia didn't bother to show up, though that was usually pity mixed with self-righteousness. No, Sister Murphy waited for the collapse, the moment when Lucy would be vulnerable and open. Then she would pounce. That was the way of women like her. They saw a weakness and exploited it. But Lucy wasn't anyone's pawn, and she'd plated herself in chain mail years ago. "If you're expecting me to fall to my knees rending my clothes and bawling hysterically, it won't happen. Not for her. Not for either of them."

"You're a selfish, heartless girl," the older woman muttered under her breath.

"Are you just now realizing?" The companionable hours she'd spent with Bill were forgotten as the familiar anger that simmered beneath her skin erupted. "Yes, I'm afraid my lack is well documented."

Lucy headed for the stairs. If she didn't get to that brandy decanter soon, a violence would occur.

"I feel sorry for you, Lucy Stanhope, but I don't know why I should. You're nothing but a common slag." Sister Murphy's words slithered up the stairs after her.

"I may be a lot of things," Lucy tossed over her shoulder as she concentrated on putting one foot in front of the other, the pin she'd used to repair her dress cold against her collarbone, her pump pinching her toes from the long walk, a painful bruise forming on her rib cage from her tussle in Parsonhurst's car, "but common has never been one of them."

Chapter 7

This wasn't the first time Lucy had watched the sun rise after a sleepless night. It *was* the first time she'd been stone-cold sober and all alone.

Okay, to be honest, she was only mostly sober, but definitely by herself.

Light inched its way up the mossy stones of the ruined watchtower, spread across the wide cliffs to gild the far green wood with gold. The sea danced with a million diamonds and gulls rose and fell on a soft salty breeze. Even the ugly line of pillboxes and ribbons of deadly razor wire took on a rosy glow in the dusty gilded air. It would have been a completely glorious morning if not for the fact that she felt like something the cat coughed up.

She closed her eyes against a thudding headache that pushed down into her neck and shoulders. Her beautiful red dress was damp and stained, and her arms prickled with cold. She should have brought a sweater with her, but she'd assumed the decanter of brandy she'd snatched from the sideboard would keep her warm. With the dawn, its numbing effects were quickly wearing off.

She tried to weep, but tears were impossible. Her face burned hot and her throat ached, but her eyes remained traitorously dry. Instead, she heard Amelia's voice telling her to stop sniveling. Crying made one's nose red, one's eyes puffy, and almost never solved the problem. Move on with one's best face forward, and when the chips are down, look for the main chance. Survival had been Amelia's motto. Look out for number one at all times. Everyone else was expendable.

Even her only child.

Lucy had always known she was superfluous to Amelia's life, detritus from a marriage forgotten as soon as she had signed the papers and dumped her daughter in the first of a string of boarding schools stretching around the globe. As a child, Lucy fantasized about her father arriving like a hero on horseback to whisk her home to the big house outside Philadelphia. Early on, she made excuses for his lack of letters and gifts. He was too busy to keep in touch. Correspondence was lost in the mail. The school and her mother were keeping them apart out of spite. Then when she was twelve she'd seen a newspaper clipping of Carlton Stanhope's departure for France as an ambassadorial envoy. He stood proudly with his new wife and his new son. No mention of the daughter he'd left behind. No place for Lucy within the happy family portrait.

She burned the newspaper in the dormitory grate, and those dreams stopped.

Now, with Amelia missing, for all intents and purposes, she was an orphan.

Alone. On her own. Free of them all.

Just the way she wanted it. To hell with Sister Murphy's gloating sympathy.

She took a swig of brandy, hoping a little hair of the dog would help soothe the worst of her hangover and prepare her for the storm to come. Aunt Cynthia would be furious. She'd laid down an ultimatum after Lucy's last run-in with the hospital staff. Once she heard about this latest to-do, it wouldn't be a question of whether Lucy wanted to volunteer but how soon she could be signed up and shipped out.

What else was new?

A shadow slid across her legs followed by a quick frightened gasp. She looked up to see Bill frozen at the edge of the ruined tower wall, a knapsack slung over his back. "What are you doing here?" she growled, far more belligerently than she intended.

His chin took on a mulish jut, his eyes narrowed suspiciously. "What's it to you?"

"Nothing at all, but don't expect another rescue. That was my last pair of good stockings you ruined."

He kicked at a stone. "Don't need rescuing. Don't need anybody. I can take care of myself."

That sounded familiar. Lucy smiled despite the clanging in her head and the taste of cotton coating her tongue. "I'm quite sure you can, but that's not what the authorities think."

"They can all go hang, the whole bollocksy lot of them with their rules and their talk and their noses in the air. Don't need 'em. Me and my mam did fine before 'em and we'll do fine after 'em."

"Right, then. Well, it's been lovely talking to you, Bill. Cheers and all that." She took another pull from the bottle before lying back to look up at the sky. A circling hawk made her dizzy.

"You feeling all right, miss? You look sick as a hooked cod, if you don't mind me saying."

She laughed harshly. "It's just a large dose of self-pity mixed with a larger dose of Hennessy."

He sat on the grass beside her and rummaged in his knapsack, pulling out two cigarettes. He lit one and offered the other to her. "I have an extra fag. You can have it if you like."

"Keep it, but thanks."

He leaned back against the rocks, knees up as he settled in with his smoke.

"You're not going to go away, are you?" she asked.

His lips pressed in a tight angry line. "I'm going away all right. For good and all. I'm going home to London. Home to me mam."

She finally focused her blurry gaze, her brow furrowing. Bill wore a dark purple bruise around his right eye and the corner of his mouth was split and scabbed over. "Maybe I'll take that cigarette, after all."

He handed it over and even dug in his pocket for a pack of matches. She accepted both, settling herself to face this unexpected crisis. At least Bill's problems took her mind from her own. "So, let me get this straight—you're running away."

"Aye." His features grew positively defiant. "Mr. Sayres has an old atlas. Some of the pages are missing or torn, but I traced out a route on a piece of paper. London's east. If I follow the sun, it shouldn't be too hard."

"They'll come after you."

"Nah, they won't bother. Mr. and Mrs. Sayres don't like me, and I don't have any friends to notice if I'm gone."

"I don't believe that."

"It's true, but who wants to be friends with a bunch of namby-pamby mama's boys anyway? They can rot for all I care."

"Hear hear. To hell with the world of goody-goodies. Damn them all!" She downed the last of the brandy.

"Damn Mr. Sayres and his stinky pipe!" Bill echoed.

"Damn Aunt Cynthia and her lists of rules!"

"And Mrs. Sayres's wooden spoon!"

"And Sister Murphy's sympathy!"

By now they were shouting at the top of their lungs. Bill rocked

up on his heels, dimples flashing. Lucy took a last drag on her cigarette and tossed the butt away.

"... teachers who yell ..."

"... cheeky soldiers ..."

"... boiled parsnips ..."

"... cabbage and potato pie ..."

"... mean sheep ..."

"Mean sheep?" Lucy fell into a fit of giggles. Bill joined her until
they were both rolling in the grass laughing hysterically. But what
goes down must come up, and with a retch, Lucy threw up all over
the grass, her stomach spasming until there was nothing left. She
collapsed on her side, wrung like a sponge.

"Better now, miss?"

"Much," she answered, though her head still swam and the
world continued to tip and fall. "Are you really set on getting back
to London, Bill?"

"I been away too long. My mam needs me. She don't like to be
alone."

Was that what sent Amelia hurtling from man to man and marriage to marriage? She didn't like to be alone? Would things have
been different if she'd kept Lucy with her instead of packing her
off to boarding school? Would they have been different if Lucy had
remained in Singapore? Or would she have died in the torpedoing
of the *Diamond Star* like the rest?

A wild, crazy thought struck her. "What if I went with you to
London?"

"You're soft in the head. You can't leave, miss."

"Why not? If we take the train, we could be there by tonight."
Now that she said it, it sounded perfectly reasonable. And as with
Bill, who would care if she left? Certainly not anyone at Nan-
reath Hall. They had made their feelings perfectly clear. In Lon-

don, she could finally do as she wished. London, a proper city with proper shops and fancy clubs, and—her thoughts slid into place—Mr. Oliver. Hollywood's very own King Midas was staying in London. The man with the golden touch who could make a star out of anyone. The man who had once offered her his card and an invitation to look him up.

All she needed to do was get there, and she could be one of those fashionable women on his arm, staying at the Dorchester, being wined and dined, and—if she was lucky—being whisked away to California and away from her aunt. It was a long shot, but one couldn't hit the barn without first taking aim. "What do you say, Bill? You and me? Traveling buddies?"

"A train does sound better than hiking all that long way, and these shoes the Sayres found me crunch my toes something fierce. But I don't know . . ."

"Try to make the journey on your own, you'll be noticed for sure. The police will be on the lookout for a boy traveling by himself. But a sister and brother won't be remarked on at all."

"That is clever, but I still think you're soused, miss."

"Really?" She stood, dusting off her grass-stained dress. Picking up the empty brandy decanter, she heaved it as far as she could out over the cliff. It made a satisfying smash as it shattered against the rocks below. She lifted her face to the wind and drew a deep fortifying breath. "For the first time in a long time, I feel I can finally see clearly."

She snapped her suitcase closed, plumped up the bank of pillows she'd hidden beneath her coverlet so they more closely resembled a sleeping body, and gave a final glance around her cluttered, musty bedchamber. She fit right in. One more unwanted item no one knew what to do with but didn't quite have the heart to toss out.

"Cheers, lads. I'd say it's been fun but I'd be lying." She saluted the menagerie as she lugged the heavy case out the door.

She had at least until dinner before she'd be missed. Aunt Cynthia would more than likely have a plateful of meetings and appointments that would keep her busy all day. By the time she realized anything was amiss, Lucy would be long gone. But she couldn't turn up at the Dorchester dressed in the sensible tweeds and cheap Woolworth's outfits she'd been reduced to.

She weighed the coins in her purse. Not exactly a pirate's fortune. Barely enough to conjure a pair of silk stockings and a bottle of Arpège from the black marketeers. If she were to succeed, she needed to look the part. Oliver wouldn't glance at her twice otherwise.

Lucy followed the threadbare runner to her aunt's apartments. Her stomach jumped, and she found herself starting at every creaky floorboard as if Aunt Cynthia would pop out from behind a curtain with a big "gotcha," but the maid-of-all-work from the village had finished her cleaning hours ago. The hospital staff was prohibited from entering this part of the house. No one would catch her.

Lifting the latch, she stepped into Lady Boxley's rooms. Her aunt's lilac perfume hung heavy in the air, and dust motes danced in the golden spring sunlight streaming through a set of tall windows. For a moment, Lucy imagined Amelia living here, pictured her dressing for a party or curled on the bed with a magazine. Laughing with her sister. Getting teased by her elder brother. Those images shifted and blurred until it was Lucy enveloped by brothers and sisters, Lucy dressing in a frilly bedchamber peppered with cherished photos and childhood souvenirs. Lucy coming home to a warm embrace and a cozy chat over cocoa.

A horn sounded outside followed by the shouts and rushing feet that meant an influx of new patients. The images popped like soap bubbles almost as soon as they formed. Amelia wouldn't have recognized her home as the luxurious country house of her youth. Nanreath Hall was no longer a serene bastion of the idle rich. It hummed with efficiency and hard-nosed management. Even Aunt Cynthia, staunch defender of the status quo, had begun to fall under the power of work schedules, production charts, and timetables.

And Lucy hated cocoa.

Crossing to the enormous wardrobe, she pushed aside her aunt's daily wear, the scent of old roses and cedar chips heavy among the tidy folds of jackets and skirts, silken blouses and matronly frocks. Shoes lined up like soldiers along the wardrobe's floor. At the very end of the rack hung two elegant evening gowns wrapped in linen bags to keep away the moths and the mildew until they might emerge in happier times.

Lucy passed these by, hunting the recesses of the wardrobe for forgotten treasures. Every woman had them: clothing too out of fashion or made for a younger, slimmer version of herself and thus no longer wearable. Aunt Cynthia was no exception. Long flat dress boxes—dented, worn, and dust covered from years tucked away and forgotten.

The first one Lucy opened revealed a sleeveless dress in chiffon with a floral silk underslip. The second was a green taffeta, jet beading at the collar and cuffs. There was a steel-blue satin evening gown she could just imagine being worn to a Downing Street dinner party, and a rather frisky cream-colored frock perfect for kicking up one's heels at a Soho jazz club.

All of them leftovers from Aunt Cynthia's glittering youth, some frayed, others with torn stitching, or rips where the fabric had grown fragile and thin with age. Here the odor of neglect was almost eye watering. They would all need a proper airing. Oliver was hardly likely to be seduced by the smell of camphor.

A pang of conscience twisted beneath her breast, but Lucy shoved it aside. Too chic to wear them in public, but too frugal to toss them out, her aunt would never miss a few old clothes.

In Lucy's hands, they'd be perfect.

Let me go. I ain't done nothing wrong."

Lucy emerged into the yard just as a sentry dragged Bill by the collar of his sweater out from behind a stack of petrol barrels. So much for an inconspicuous exit.

"What's going on here, Private"—she fished her memory for his name—"Banks, isn't it?"

His eyes brightened. "That's right, miss. You and me met last month in the cellar during the last air raid when . . ." He blushed a refreshing shade of pink.

Lucy did not.

Bill looked from one to the other with a calculating expression.

Private Banks cleared his throat and resumed his official bearing. "I caught this lad snooping about by the mechanic's sheds. Up to no good, I reckon."

"I was just looking, guv. No law against that, is there?"

"There is in wartime, lad. Looking where you shouldn't can get you shot."

"I'm sure he didn't mean any harm," Lucy said, casting Bill a grim look.

"I didn't see nothing anyway. Just a lot of tools, and a bloke taking a piss."

"Watch your tongue in front of a lady, lad," the sentry growled before turning a mild face to Lucy and smoothing his hair back from his forehead. "He might be all right, miss, but I'm to report all intruders to the duty officer."

Lucy fought back the urge to huff and instead smiled indulgently. "Look at him. He's no Nazi spy. He's a mischievous little boy, and if you report him to the duty officer, you'll be laughed right out of his office."

That struck a chord, as she knew it would. Banks's gaze grew cautious. "I don't know, miss . . ."

"Well, I do. Why don't you hand him over to me? I'll see he gets home. I'm heading into the village now."

"Well, if you think it'll be all right."

"Of course it will. I know the couple he's living with—he'll not dare sneak onto the property again once they're done with him. And if the duty officer cuts up stiff about it, you tell him to come see me."

Private Banks tipped his hat. "I do appreciate it. I'm not in the sergeant's good graces right now. Won five quid off him last night at backgammon. I'd rather not show my face if I don't have to."

"There. Problem solved all around."

"Not to be bold, miss, but . . . that is . . . I'd be honored if you . . ." Banks stumbled over his words, his eyes somewhere near his boots.

Lucy gave him no chance to stammer out his invitation. "Must run if I'm to get him out of here before your sergeant finds him. Ta, Private." She took hold of Bill and, with one last icy glare for the benefit of the sentry, frog-marched him toward the old buttery.

"Here now," he whinged. "That hurts."

"Good." Once in the buttery and away from prying eyes, she released him. "Are you trying to get caught before you even get a mile from home?"

"You was taking too long, and I got bored." He pulled his knapsack out from behind a stack of old barrels. It clanked as he slung it over his shoulder.

"What on earth have you got in there?"

"A box of matches, my ration book, three fags I swiped from Mrs. Sayres, a deck of cards, a map I traced on a page out of my composition book, a torch, and four apples . . . well, three now. I ate one while I was waiting for you."

"Not exactly Boy Scout approved." She took hold of a corner of a heavy canvas tarpaulin. "Help me with this."

He grabbed another corner and together they pulled it back, revealing a cherry-red roadster. "Crikey. That's a beauty. What is she?"

"I've no bloody idea in the world. It belongs to my cousin."

"Does he know we're—"

"Of course he doesn't, but the keys are in the desk in the study. While my aunt's away, no one will question if I take his car."

"We could drive it all the way to London."

"Afraid not." She pushed open the heavy wooden shed door. "There's barely enough petrol to get us to the train station. And I've no coupons for more."

She took the wheel as Bill slid in. He stroked the leather seats, pushing every button, opening and closing the glove box. She smacked his hand away from the gear lever. "Sit still. Don't touch anything. And hold on. I might be a bit rusty." With a growl and a puff of black smoke, the car sprang to life. She shoved it into reverse and inched her way backward out of the shed, praying she didn't scrape the paint.

Under the painful scrutiny of two orderlies, a group of up-patients out for a stroll, and a VAD taking a smoke, she lurched and jolted her way out of the yard and onto the tree-lined avenue that would take them to the main road. Rifle slung over his shoulder, a sentry tipped his cap as he waved her off. She raised a hand in response, her heart lifting as the house grew smaller in her mirrors.

"And we're off. I feel better already, don't you?"

"No," Bill groaned, holding his stomach. "I think I ate too many of Mr. Sayres's apples."

"You said you only had one."

"It was more like four, but they was small and kinda wrinkled."

"Don't you dare get sick in this car, Bill Smedley."

"No, miss. I won't." He pursed his lips tight and cradled his stomach. "Isn't the station that way?"

"Yes, but we're headed to Newquay."

"That's miles from here."

"It's also crowded with soldiers. No one will notice us among so many. If we leave from the village, we're bound to be seen or remarked upon. I can park the car somewhere in town and when we get to London, I'll ring and tell them where to pick it up."

"I'd never have thought of that. You're right clever."

Was she? She was even now driving a stolen car in company with a runaway boy to meet with a man who might not even remember her. Not exactly signs of intelligence by any normal measure. She clenched her hands tighter on the wheel as she fought back the urge to turn the car around and forget this folly.

"Miss?"

"What now, Bill?"

"I'm glad you're coming with me."

She smiled and took a deep breath. "I am too."

Chapter 8

ou're a liar,' said the third one, 'for mine's as big as the moon. A
man went up in October, and didn't come out until June,'" Lucy
and Bill sang at the top of their lungs, their voices carried off by a
salty sea wind that buffeted the little roadster.

Bill waved at a man walking with his dogs.

The man waved back—or was he gesturing angrily? Difficult to
tell at this speed.

Lucy shoved the car down into second and took the bend, praying she'd not meet a military convoy headed the opposite direction.
She'd already squeezed over into a hedge once to let an ambulance
pass, and that had ended in the veriest teensiest of scrapes along the
passenger door. Barely noticeable—she hoped.

Bill leaned back against the seat, a flush of pink in his cheeks and
his eyes alive with excitement. "That's a ripping good song, Lucy."

"I thought you might like it."

The seaside town of Newquay had transitioned from a holiday
destination to a military bivouac with barely a blink. Beachfront
hotels now acted as billets for thousands of RAF cadets. Palm-lined
streets were crowded with khaki, and dance halls, cinemas, pubs,

even the tea shops all did a spanking business from the influx of staff and personnel. Surely, no one would notice them among such a crush.

Lucy followed Cliff Road to the station, parking the car on a side street away from traffic. The railway station was just across the road.

She checked her watch. "We have an hour until the next train."

"I'm hungry." Bill looked with longing toward the ABC tea shop across the street. "Can we get a sandwich?"

"I thought you said your stomach hurt."

"It doesn't hurt for a sandwich."

"All right, but this has got to hold you until we reach London tonight."

She purchased two cups of steaming hot tea and two ham sandwiches—refusing to look too closely at the meat involved—which they devoured out on the sidewalk. A group of soldiers strolled past, their corn-fed faces and broad flat accents marking them as fellow Americans. Since the bombing of Pearl Harbor last December, troops had begun flooding into the country. Most of the locals welcomed them with open arms, though some resented their generous salaries and the women those generous salaries enticed. Lucy didn't hold it against the poor girls seduced by promises of Coca-Cola and chocolate bars. She'd done a lot worse for a lot less.

Bill hopped off the wall to follow the group, shoulders hunched, features slack, and glassy eyed. She'd not be surprised if he feigned a limp. "Got any gum, chum?" he said with a woeful tremor in his voice. The ridiculous boy could go on the stage with that Oliver Twist act.

"Sure, kid." A skinny redhead with freckle-sprinkled cheeks dug in his pocket.

A young man with a crooked nose and slick dark hair caught sight of Lucy, finishing up her sandwich. "Well now, does the young lady want a piece of gum too?"

"I'll leave chewing cud to the cows, thank you. But a light would be divine." She held out her Sobranie.

"My pleasure, doll." His eyes drank her in from head to foot with a look universal to all men on the make and one that instantly set her teeth on edge. "The name's Roger."

"I'll bet it is," she said, blowing out a thin stream of smoke.

"Me and the boys just arrived a few weeks ago. Sure is different from back home, I can tell you. Kinda dingy, you know?"

For some reason his criticisms struck a nerve. "Two years of bombing will do that to a country. I'd like to see how the good people of New York or Boston would fare under the same circumstances."

"Calm down. I didn't mean anything by it."

"Then keep it to yourself."

"Hey, Lucy," Bill called out. "Look what I got. A stick of Juicy Fruit."

Roger's smirk was back and smarmier than ever. "Lucy, is it? That's a pretty name for a pretty girl. You from around here? You don't sound like the other girls."

"Not much gets past you, does it?" She remained unmoved by his aw-shucks routine. She'd seen too many variations on the same theme to be taken in by such a rank amateur. She rose from the wall, crumpling her paper wrapper and dusting crumbs from her skirt. "It's been lovely meeting you boys, but we have to go."

"Do we have to, Lucy?" Bill asked plaintively. "They was going to buy me a lemonade."

"Sounds a treat, but you and I are in a bit of a hurry. Remember?"

"You don't want to deny the kid a lemonade, do you?" Roger

coaxed. "Besides, we're still learning our way around, and we could sure use a friendly face. Why don't you and Bill join us? We'll treat you both to lemonades. No chewing involved."

"A tempting offer, but we really can't."

"We're going to London," Bill piped up. "To see me mam."

What she wouldn't give for a nice hefty gag. Lucy shot Bill a nasty look as she grabbed him by the elbow. "Good luck battling the Hun, boys. Thanks for the candy."

"But—" Roger protested.

"Cheerio!" She tossed the men a finger wave over her shoulder as she marched Bill into the station.

"What's got your knickers in a twist?" Bill complained.

"The idea was to be inconspicuous. Not broadcast our plans to the entire US Army."

"I didn't."

"They know who we are, they know we're headed to London. Why not just tell them we stole a car and a . . . a bag of apples . . . in the process?"

His face fell as he scuffed the curb. "I'm sorry, Lucy. I didn't mean to give it away. They were just being so nice."

"Men are always nice until you get to know them."

"You don't like men much, do you?"

"Unreliable rotters . . . remember?"

"I'm a man." He puffed out his chest.

"Then you, sir, are the exception that proves the rule."

"What's that mean?"

"It means, William Smedley"—she hooked her arm through his—"you're the only man for me."

So far, so good. With a blow of the whistle and a chuff of steam, the train moved slowly out of the station. Lucy let out the breath she didn't know she'd been holding. If all continued to plan, they'd be in London by this evening. That gave her four days to insinuate herself into Mason Oliver's good graces. If she couldn't get herself "discovered" by then, she'd lost her touch.

The train was full, but Lucy managed to find two rather stained and musty-smelling seats in the third-class compartment across from a middle-aged gentleman reading a newspaper. Seeing his privacy being invaded, he made dismissive harrumphing noises that Lucy chose to ignore as she made herself comfortable.

"You suppose they have a restaurant car on this train?" Bill asked as soon as they were settled.

"You just ate a sandwich. And a candy bar. And four apples. You'll survive."

Bill grumbled and looked out the window.

The businessman grumbled and rattled his paper.

Lucy chose to ignore them both.

The train inched its way through the lush green Cornish countryside before pulling into a siding outside Luxulyan and coming to a lurching, steam-filled stop.

"What now?" the gentleman growled, glancing up from the stock reports. He checked his watch. "This better not take all day."

Lucy couldn't have agreed more. She was already beginning to regret her impulsive departure. Given a bit more time to plan, she would have found a better way to reach London—some officer's chauffeured car perhaps? She pictured herself whizzing past a blurry landscape in dark sunglasses and a trailing scarf with a handsome colonel at her side. Betty Grable, eat your heart out.

She glanced at Bill, who was writing his name in the soot on the train's window.

Not exactly a traveling partner on par with a dashing Don Ameche.

"Look, Lucy. A Spitfire." He grinned, dimples carved into his narrow face as he showed off his drawing.

She felt a sudden stab of empathy. She knew what it was like to be thrust into a strange new world, alone, frightened, and homesick. One learned resourcefulness and self-reliance in order to survive. One also learned skepticism and to remain detached lest one get one's heart stomped on.

Lessons difficult to forget.

Lessons Bill might have learned all too well had he remained with the Sayres much longer.

She smiled back.

Don Ameche was overrated anyway.

As they sat, goods trains rattled past on their way south toward Falmouth. Line after line of cars with barely a break between one train and the next. The compartment grew stuffy. Sweat trickled down Lucy's back and her heavy stockings clung uncomfortably to her legs. What should have been an hour's journey had already stretched to two.

"Rummy?" Bill had his cards out, shuffling them with the skill of a Monte Carlo dealer.

Anything was better than sitting and stewing. But after three losses in a row, it was clear her concentration wasn't up to games of skill. Refusing to be bested by a twelve-year-old, she forced herself to focus as Bill dealt out a new hand.

"Hold on." She smacked her palm on the top card. "What's this?" The upper right corner had a slight crease. "Let me see these cards." She fished through them: a nick here, a smudge there. Subtle, systematic, and highly dishonest. "You're playing with a marked deck."

"A bang-up jug, ain't it? The boys at the Lion back home taught me how to do it."

The newspaper twitched in agitation, and Lucy thought she heard a distinct snort of repugnance.

She handed the deck back to Bill. "I think we're done playing cards for today, thank you."

That entertainment lost to him, Bill grew squirmy and impatient. He fiddled with his seat, the latch on the window, the scab on his knee. He knocked over the man's briefcase, squashed his hat, almost coldcocked him in a monkey-like attempt to inspect the luggage rack.

"If you can't keep that damned hoodlum under control, I'll call a conductor to throw you both off this train."

It was one thing for her to have fantasies of gags and handcuffs, but quite another for some stuffy middle-aged bore to start spouting threats. "He doesn't mean any harm. He's bored."

"I don't care. Keep him quiet and chain him to his seat or I bloody well will."

Bill puffed up like a cockerel, his long face drawn tight into a scowl. "Oi, guv. Don't talk to her like that." He turned to Lucy, a vision of injured pride. "He can't say those things to you. It ain't proper. You're a lady."

"There are those who may dispute you, but your gallantry is noted." She dragged Bill back into his seat, where he decided to kick at the wall while humming a monotonous tune that grated on her nerves.

The gentleman's grip on his newspaper became increasingly white knuckled.

Bill's humming became singing. "*There were four old whores from Baltimore—*"

"Bill!" Lucy swung around. "Maybe now's not the best time for a song."

He dipped his hand back in the soot, smearing pictures in the window glass. "How much longer until we're in London?"

"We only just left Newquay."

"I know, but I'm bored."

"We'll get there soon enough."

"Where you suppose that train over there is going?"

"I don't know."

"How many cars you think one engine can pull? Fifty? Hundred?"

"I don't know."

"You think—"

"Not while you're pestering me with all these blasted questions, I can't," she snapped.

Bill's face took on a mulish cast.

The gentleman tossed aside his paper on one long disgusted harrumph, got to his feet with further grumblings under his breath about the shortcomings of the next generation, and left the compartment, probably hoping to find some peace and quiet with the ten RAF lads whooping it up farther down the carriage.

The shadows lengthened. Bill's stomach growled. Lucy would have sold her virtue for a cold martini if she'd still had it to sell.

Bill draped himself over the seat like a fainting diva and sighed dramatically. "I'm positively gutfoundered."

"Hush. You've eaten plenty. We shouldn't be much longer." As soon as she said this, another train bumped its way past their siding. She could imagine the engineer smirking as he sped past the poor stranded passengers with a blow of his whistle. Bloody cheek.

Bill pulled out his deck of cards. Lucy checked her watch—again.

Finally, with a grunt and a huff, the train moved on, slowly creeping into the station at Par. It had taken them three hours from Newquay, but saints be praised, through the grime and soot of their window, she spied their London connection on the opposite platform. It must have been held up by the same delays on the line that kept them stranded. Maybe someone upstairs *was* looking out for her.

As they gathered their belongings, the compartment door slid open with a crash. The gentleman was back and towing a portly conductor with him.

"That's the thief," he growled.

Lucy's heart skittered alarmingly, but a lifetime of youthful indiscretions had hardened her to accusations of crimes and misdemeanors. She barely twitched when the man pointed a wrathful finger at Bill. Instead, she flashed them her most innocent smile. "Is there something the matter, sir?"

"You better know there is. That lad there stole my money."

"I ain't never," Bill argued, the slightest tremble in his squeaking voice as his panicked gaze swung between Lucy and his accuser.

The conductor cleared his throat. "Mr. Emory here"—he nodded toward the businessman—"believes the lad might be responsible for the disappearance of a half crown from his change purse."

"Then Mr. Emory is mistaken." Lucy squared her shoulders and lifted her chin, channeling Amelia's version of upper-crust-y outrage. "William Smedley is one of our most well-behaved boys at the evacuee home."

"And I suppose he got that shiner polishing his good-conduct medals," Mr. Emory sputtered. "I heard him acting the card sharp on you earlier, miss. He's a sly customer." He glared at Bill. "Turn out your pockets, boy, or I'll shake you until your teeth rattle."

"I ain't done nothing wrong, guv," Bill whinged. "Honest. You believe me, don't you, Lucy?"

"Of course I do. We'll get this sorted."

She cast a swift glance across to the London-bound train making ready for departure with much slamming of doors and the shouts of harried rail guards. If she didn't comply, she may as well wave her one-way ticket to Hollywood good-bye.

"Do as he says, and we'll prove to this odious man that we have nothing to hide," she said, praying that if Bill was stupid enough to steal a man's money he was clever enough not to get caught.

"But . . ." Something in her expression must have warned him it was no use arguing. "I'll do it if you say I must."

Two rounded beach pebbles, an apple core, a wadded handkerchief, a pencil nub, a bit of string, a fuzzy peppermint stuck to an equally fuzzy button.

"Satisfied now?" she asked when Bill stood with all his pockets pulled inside out.

"He's hidden it." Mr. Emory's face had gone a violent shade of red, as if he might explode on the spot. "Or you have. You're both in on it."

The London train gave a long blast of its whistle. It was now or never. Lucy played her last and riskiest card. "I've been polite until now, Mr. Emory, because I sympathized with the loss of your belongings, but my patience has come to an abrupt end. If you wish to continue this interrogation, you may call my cousin Lord Melcombe and explain why I was unable to meet him in London for a dinner honoring the king of Norway."

The conductor began to look distinctly uneasy. Mr. Emory was a tougher nut to crack. "I don't care if your cousin's bleeding Churchill and you're headed to London to visit George VI, I want my brass and I know you two had something to do with it."

"Would you mind awfully, miss?" the conductor asked, his expression one of apologetic long-suffering.

Lucy watched the train depart with a last wistful sigh. What had she told Bill? They'd be in London as quickly as tonight? Together, they'd not draw attention to themselves? She should have known better. This wasn't the first time she'd made a bad decision after a night drunk on brandy. The last time she'd ended up with a tattoo on her . . . well, that was neither here nor there.

She cleared her throat. "I would and I do mind, sir, but if it will stuff a sock in Mr. Emory, I'm happy to oblige."

Lucy opened her handbag for inspection, counting out the change in her purse. Then the conductor searched the entire compartment. No half crown.

He offered Mr. Emory a beseeching look. "We've done all we can and no sign of it, sir. You can fill out a lost form in the office if you like." He turned to Lucy with a tip of his cap. "I apologize for taking up your time, miss. And my regards to your cousin and His Royal Highness."

Mr. Emory was not to be placated. "That's a load of bollocks. I want them arrested . . . questioned . . . I demand . . ." The conductor all but picked him up by the seat of his trousers and carried him out the door, his newspaper left behind in a flutter of wilted pages.

Bill let out a whoop of success. "You showed him, miss. The old windbag."

Her headache sinking into her spine, her nerves frazzled down to a nub, Lucy finally exploded. "All right. What did you do with it?"

Bill's smile faded. "I didn't take his blunt, miss." His voice cracked and trickled into a lip-wobbling silence as his eyes flashed to her clenched hands. "Honest."

Damn Mr. Sayres and his quick fists. Lucy fizzled like a deflated balloon. There was no point in taking out her frustration on Bill. It was her own fault.

What made her ever think she could help him?

She could barely help herself.

Chapter 9

Exeter—finally.

It had only taken most of the day and half the night.

Just twenty-four hours after German bombers had let loose their high explosives on the city, the waiting room at the train station bustled with life. Harried soldiers on leave. Impatient civilians sporting official-looking armbands. A few dazed families, most with sleepy, petulant children in tow.

Posters and notices firmly reminded civilians that food, shells, and troops came first, unnecessary travel impeded the war effort, and housewives should leave buses, trams, and trains free for war workers.

The list of rules Lucy was breaking seemed to grow with every placard. She needed a smoke or she'd go stark staring bonkers.

"A pack of Sobranies."

The pair of middle-aged ladies running the Salvation Army canteen wore their official armbands like generals' pips. "We've none of that here, miss. Just coffee and jam rolls."

"Fine. I'll take two—extra jammy."

She had ten short minutes before their train pulled out of the station. Lucy took advantage of the time to stretch her legs and escape Bill's incessant prattling. Were all children so bloody chatty, or was Bill a special kind of irritating in that regard? She'd seriously contemplated a muzzle—or earplugs. Hopefully, stuffing his mouth—or her ears—full of sticky jam roll would work just as well.

This had been the longest day of her entire life. Hours of sitting cramped in uncomfortable seats on overly hot trains relieved only by hours of sitting cramped in uncomfortable seats in drafty waiting rooms. It was nearly midnight, and they weren't even halfway to London.

As she waited for her change, a pair of station employees entered from an office at the back. Both looked grim and businesslike. ". . . air raid east of Taunton, track's out and a bridge is damaged. Breakdown train's on its way, but we're looking at a twelve-hour delay at the least . . ."

"Bloody Krauts," the station official grumbled. "Don't they know I have a schedule to keep?"

"Least they ain't bombing us tonight. Give thanks for small blessings that some other poor sod is getting his."

Twelve hours? What happened if it took longer than that? Was she just supposed to kick her heels in Exeter while Mr. Oliver found some other young woman to star in his next picture?

The railway officials passed her by, still deep in conversation, and headed out onto the platform.

Lucy followed, making her way down the line toward the passenger car where Bill waited.

Amend that—where he should have been waiting. Instead, the seat was empty and Bill's knapsack was gone. The tiny blue interior lights allowed during the blackout made the gloom thick as cobwebs, but she checked each compartment down the car, hoping he'd ducked in for a chat or a game of cards. No sign of him.

She collared a passing rail guard. "Excuse me. I'm looking for a boy. About twelve. Gangly. Brown hair, brown eyes. He was wearing a blue sweater and a pair of brown trousers."

"Don't know, miss. Sorry."

After another ten minutes of fruitless searching, she decided he must have scampered. Maybe he'd grown scared or suspicious or figured he was better off on his own after all. Maybe he'd received a better offer. Fine. She didn't want him hanging about cramping her style anyway. And if he was better off on his own, so was she, damn it.

She pulled her case down from the upper rack and sloped off the train, which remained idle in the siding. The platform's crowds had thinned now that news of the delay had spread. Just a few passengers milled about, and the stalwart Salvation Army ladies with their cups of strong tea and jam rolls.

She made her way down the platform and out of the station onto the road, feeling her way through the blackout by the light of a bomber's moon. She tripped over a curb. Smacked into a pillarbox. Nearly broke her nose on a lamppost before a torch flared the ground in front of her.

"Lucy?" The torch's light slid up until it shone in her face, blinding her. "It *is* you."

"Bill?"

"I been looking everywhere for you."

"That's rubbish. You left when I specifically told you to stay put."

"I was hungry as a kicked dog and you were taking ages. So I decided to poke about to see what was what."

"And?"

"I found a bang-up shop selling fish and chips just on the corner. Here, I saved you some." He held out a greasy cardboard box covered with a paper napkin.

"How did you pay for it? You only had a few pennies."

His grin was triumphantly wicked.

"Please tell me you didn't steal that man's half crown."

"The ugly old sod deserved it for talking to you like that. Mam says a true gentleman treats ladies with respect. Course she likewise says true gentlemen are rare as hen's teeth, but she has hope."

"Your mother is a wise woman and Mr. Emory had the manners of a baboon, but that doesn't make it right. And what's worse? You lied to me. You looked right at me with that wobbly chin and those great cow eyes and lied to me and, fool that I am, I fell for it."

"I had to lie. You'd have made me give the money back otherwise."

"Of course I would have."

"Then we wouldn't have fish and chips."

"That's not the point."

"I had to take the money, Lucy. I knew it was wrong and I shouldn't have done it, but it was only a half crown, and I might need it just in case."

"In case of what?"

He scuffed the toe of his shoe in a crack in the paving, his narrow shoulders hunched in a defensive shrug.

"Bill? In case of what?"

He glanced up, his eyes like two great hollows in the pale disk of his face. "In case Mam isn't there when I get home."

Lucy led the way down the street assisted by Bill's torch, which she'd shielded with the napkin off the fish and chips. The last thing she needed was to draw the attention of a nosy air raid warden. The small pool of greasy yellow lit a road pocked with craters and scattered with trash and bits of rubble. A breeze moaned through a broken window and set a metal door to banging. A piece of torn sheeting flapped white like a ghostly arm beckoning to them.

Bill pressed closer to her side. "Aren't we going back to the station, miss?"

"A bomb's hit the line and the train's stuck here until tomorrow morning at the earliest. We'll find a detour around the damaged track and pick up the train again closer to London."

"Was there dead people? Did a train blow up? I'd'a liked to seen that. Ned Hollis saw a dead person once. He was with his mam in Padstow when a bomb fell on a house. Killed a man and a baby. Ned boasted that he saw them taking the bodies away. I don't know if I believe him. Ned Hollis is a awful liar."

"What bloodthirsty creatures you and Ned Hollis are."

They rounded a corner. Soot and dust choked the air. Bill pulled the collar of his sweater up over his mouth. They passed a building buckled on its smashed foundation, its windows blown out. Another had toppled into the empty lot beside it, plaster and bricks and lathing all jumbled up with an old steel sink, a pair of upholstered chairs, a splintered bed frame.

She'd heard about the raid on the wireless. Snug in her room at Nanreath Hall, she'd barely paid the boring BBC newsman any mind as he reported on scores dead and hundreds injured and displaced. Instead, she'd snapped over to hear Harry Roy and his orchestra play their hearts out from London's Embassy Club while she polished her nails. Now, surrounded by the broken, ugly ruins of bombed-out buildings with the specters of those who'd died hovering at the edge of her imagination, the war seemed closer than it had at any moment since the *Strathleven* had been struck.

To fight the bleak turn of her thoughts, she hummed the bouncy refrain from "She Had to Go and Lose It at the Astor."

"Look 'ere, Lucy." Bill held up a doll in a frilly pink organza dress. Her porcelain face had been smashed, leaving only one sight-less blue eye and a few strands of blond hair that streamed from the crushed head in a sodden tangle.

"Put it down, Bill."

"But—"

"I said put it back. Now!"

"All right, miss." Bill set it down at the curb. Lucy grabbed his hand and they hurried on. At the corner, he glanced back over his shoulder. "You suppose they'll come back for it?"

Lucy took a breath, feeling the scratch of cinders and ash in her throat. "No, Bill. I don't suppose they will."

The raids had left the city skittish and on edge. The streets were nearly empty. An ambulance headed to a call. Two fire wardens made their rounds. A soldier pedaled by on his bicycle.

"Maybe we should go back," Bill suggested, a slight wobble to his voice. "It might be better to wait for the repairs. It's terrible black out here, and who knows how long the batteries will last in the torch? If it dies, we'll be blind as beggars."

"You wanted an adventure, didn't you?"

Bill nodded doubtfully.

"Well, you got one."

High above them came the growl of bombers. Lucy tensed, but the sound soon faded back into the night and they were left once again with only the crunch of their shoes on the road and the la-bored hiss of their breathing.

"You suppose they're headed to London?" Bill asked quietly.

"I doubt it."

"The Sayres said the cities are what's getting hit worst, and Lon-don's the biggest city of them all. They said they'd not be surprised if it was bombed flat before the end."

"The Sayres are a bunch of cranky old codgers who don't know what they're talking about."

"That's true," he replied, adding sadly under his breath, "but that don't mean they're wrong."

By now, her shins ached, the court shoes that had looked so darling when she saw them in the store blistered her heels, and she felt as if she'd stashed anvils in her damned traveling case. As the thick air became a misting drizzle that clung with wet fingers to her skin, her zeal for hoofing it waned. Another of her bad ideas? She was racking up quite a list so far.

"Do you have a mam, Lucy?"

"I didn't emerge fully grown from a clamshell," she said, more sharply than she intended. "Of course I have a mother."

"What's she like?"

Lucy swapped the case to her other hand. It gave her pause to consider. "Glamorous and witty and everyone who knows her falls in love with her."

"She sounds lovely. My mam's got a dimple in her chin and hair the color of caramel, all soft and shiny. Mostly she wears it up under a kerchief on account of work, but on Saturday nights, she does it up right. Sometimes she lets me comb it out for her after she's had her bath. She says I have the gentlest hands, better than one of them West End hairdressers what charge a whole shilling just for a trimming." His voice grew soft with memory. "I used to love Saturday nights."

"In a few days, you'll be back home with your mother. Maybe in time for Saturday night."

"What about you? Where's your mother?"

Perhaps because so much of their lives had been spent apart, the truth of Amelia's death was easy to push aside. It was an absence she recognized. A void long callused over. She was able to answer Bill without any hint of darker emotion. "I don't know."

Bill put his hand in hers, glancing up at her through wet hair. "Don't you worry, miss. We'll find my mam and yours. You wait and see. It'll be all right once we get to London."

That was supposed to be her line, but she offered him a quick smile of thanks and when Bill sought to let go, she found herself holding on just a moment longer.

"If the trains ain't running, does this mean we have to walk there after all?" Bill asked.

A van passed them before pulling into a gated loading yard. Lucy picked up her pace. Maybe her luck was turning after all. "Not if we can hitch a ride."

Chapter 10

It was a small brown-and-white scrap of a dog with ears that pricked and a curious nose constantly on the prowl for new scents. Currently, it was engaged in searching out the jam roll Lucy had wrapped in a handkerchief and stuffed in her handbag for later, its tail wagging like a metronome beating out bebop time. Bill giggled—he actually giggled—as the dog turned its attention to him, its little tongue licking him in a frenzy of excitement. For a moment, the streetwise toughness slipped, and he was a little boy.

His face was almost pleasant when it wasn't screwed up in that jaw-jutting wary scowl of his.

"Let me have a look at that map of yours."

Bill fished it from his knapsack. Lucy propped it against the delivery van's steering wheel to study. The paper smelled like pilchard and the pencil marks were faint, but the important bits were all marked. The train headed north toward Bristol before turning east. A more direct route would be to head for Salisbury and from there east again to London. She traced a path through villages and towns:

Honiton, Charbury, Yeovil. She paused, following her finger back the way it had come—Charbury . . . Charbury . . .

Where had she heard that name before?

"Here, you!" The driver's-side door was wrenched open with a meaty fist, and a blunt round face, pockmarked and flat nosed, squinted in at her. "What do you think you're doing mucking about in my van . . . and with my dog?"

At the first syllable, the dog left off biscuit hunting, his bright button eyes sparkling with excitement. "We're not mucking about," Lucy replied tersely, snapping off Bill's torch and folding the map. "We're waiting—for you. We began to despair you'd ever come back. Your pup here was growing quite antsy, the little beggar."

The driver jerked a thumb. "Out."

His wrestler's body spoke of a lifetime of hard labor. He'd no neck to speak of and his forearms under the grease-stained coat he wore were like tree trunks. He looked to be anywhere between thirty and fifty. His light brown hair was thin but held no touch of gray, and his face, while jowly and weathered, was as yet unlined. She'd need to tread carefully with this one or they'd be in front of a magistrate by dawn.

She tried to look irresistible. Hard to completely nail with Bill giggling beside her and the dog's tail wagging in her face, but she did her best. "We were hoping you'd give us a lift. It's an awfully nasty night and we've got a long way to go. It would be jolly nice of you, Mr. . . ."

"Teague, though it's no business of yours."

"A pleasure to make your acquaintance, Mr. Teague."

Just then, finished with its cleaning of Bill's face, the dog swung round to Lucy, its paws on her shoulders, its slobbery tongue scraping across her cheeks like a soggy flannel.

"Uh . . . dog breath," she groaned, trying to push the interloper away. "Yuck."

Bill laughed. "He's taken a shine to you, Lucy. Dogs know who's a right one and who's not. Don't they, guv?"

The dog crawled into her lap, curled into a brown-and-white ball, and stared up at the driver with big sad eyes. She sighed. It was impossible to exude an aura of glamour covered in dog hair.

Mr. Teague's belligerence relaxed. He even managed a tight smile. "Aye, dogs know the truth about a person, all right." He slid into the cab beside her and slammed the door. "Off the young lady, Dex. You'll ruin her nice frock."

The dog whined but didn't budge. Its soft heavy weight on Lucy's thighs was almost reassuring. She ran a hand through its wiry fur. "He can stay. My frock is a lost cause at this point anyway."

"Right, then. My run is to Honiton and on up through Cullompton way if that's where you're headed."

"That will do splendidly for a start. Thank you."

"Thank Dex. If he vouches for you, that's good enough for me."

He started the van's engine and pulled out with a great grinding of gears, managing to jolt his way through every rut until Lucy had to brace a steadying hand on the dashboard to keep herself from falling onto the floor. The dog merely yawned as if used to this sort of rough travel.

They hit the edge of town and the empty A30, but the van's shuttered headlamps barely illuminated more than a few feet of macadam, making anything over ten miles per hour impossible. Lucy gritted her teeth to keep herself from stomping on the accelerator.

"Where you two headed?" Mr. Teague asked, breaking the silence.

"London," Bill piped up before Lucy could come up with a suitable lie.

"What you want to go to that dirty place for? As likely to rob you blind as give you the time of day."

Bill bristled, and Lucy clamped a hand over his mouth before he took it into his head to defend Bethnal Green's dubious honor.

"I have a job offer," she supplied, "but if I don't get there fast it'll be gone."

"You never said nothing about a job." Bill looked as if he wanted to question her further. She quickly changed the subject.

"Your dog is an interesting breed, Mr. Teague," she said, scratching the mutt under the chin. "Terrier of some sort?"

Mr. Teague smiled broadly, taking his hand off the wheel long enough to pat the dog on the head. "I found old Dex half-starved in a ditch two years ago. Suppose somebody decided what with the war, it was too much trouble keeping a pet. Just dropped him off on the side of the road to fend for himself."

"That's horrid."

"Yeah, well, better than what most of 'em got, isn't it? Millions of the poor blighters done in on account of the invasion panic. Makes you sick thinking of John Bull doing such a black thing to a poor innocent animal, but there you are . . . the world goes mad in wartime."

The cab was warm, the windscreen foggy with their steaming breath. The springs in the seat poked Lucy's legs and there was a decided odor of wet dog and sour milk. Bill dozed, his head on her shoulder, his mouth, at last, blessedly closed. Fields and farms flashed past, their shapes picked out in black on black against the midnight ink of the sky. The moon hung low behind them, a pale disk in the rearview mirror.

"You have a dog growing up, miss?" Mr. Teague asked, breaking the companionable silence.

"My mother thought they were too much trouble. She didn't

want the responsibility." Lucy dug her fingers into Dex's thick fur. "Didn't want to be tied down."

The van rattled over a cattle grid and into a village, houses closer together. Strings of shops. Teague turned into a side street and parked outside a dairy. Men were already hard at work loading and unloading trucks. Lucy roused Bill, who yawned and stretched. They climbed out of the cab; the rain had stopped but the chilly air brought her back to the present like a slap to the face.

"Thank you for the ride. We can walk the rest of the way from here."

"Are you sure? Those clouds are thick. Rain's not through yet, I'm thinkin'."

"We don't melt, and we've a long way to go yet."

Teague was being summoned by a man with a clipboard. The loading dock was crowded with milk cans ready for transport. "Right, well, careful as you go, miss. Not everyone who'll offer a lift is as nice or as respectable as I am."

She gave Dex a final pat on the head and in a moment of weakness kissed him on his cold wet nose. "I'm neither nice nor respectable so I'm sure whoever it is, we shall get along swimmingly."

They made their way east as best they could. Away from town, thick hedges rimmed the winding road. A wooden gate stood open to a gravel lane. A path led away through a leafy fern-scented wood. "Why's the countryside so bleedin' quiet? And dark," Bill complained.

"Everywhere is dark these days, but go ahead and turn on your torch if it makes you feel better."

The narrow beam of light wobbled ahead of them as they walked. No road signs to offer them guidance. She couldn't even use the moon to mark her way. Clouds covered the sky, a wet wind pushing at their backs, rain threatening to return. The jam rolls were devoured. She smoked her last cigarette.

"What did you mean about finding a job in London, miss?"

She'd had a feeling Bill would bring that back up. For some reason she couldn't explain—even to herself—she found herself prevaricating instead of answering the question directly. "I couldn't tell him I was helping you run away, could I? It was the first thing that popped in my head."

Bill fell silent as if mulling this over. Then he gave a quick little laugh. "I'd not have thought it about someone what has the gingerbread you do, but you're a right swindle, Lucy. The boys at the Lion would think tops of you."

"I'm flattered—I think. But we should probably come up with a better story in case anyone else asks."

The lane they followed was thick with wet grass and rabbit holes that dragged at their legs and turned their ankles. Twice they made wrong turns that left them stranded. The rain resumed, soaking their clothes and making every footstep a squelchy dreary mess.

"Damn and blast," Lucy finally said when they'd come to their third dead end. "We'll be drowned if we stay out here much longer."

Bill swept his torch in front of them. Off to their right was a gravel track lined by a double row of elms. "Look. A farm. I always wanted to sleep in a barn." He took off running, and Lucy could only follow as fast as she was able, muttering under her breath the entire way about inconsiderate children with no respect for their elders.

The track widened as it neared a wooden gate opening onto a farmyard. "What d'ya think, Lucy?"

"I think we need to find somewhere out of the way. All of these buildings are too close to the house."

They continued along a grassy swale that led into a wood. A

church stood on a far rise, but down below the copse was thick and the way looked little traversed. "There."

A small stone-and-timber shed set into the side of a hill. As she predicted, it smelled, but the odor was faint and not unpleasant, and, best of all, it was dry. An old vine-covered tractor sat alongside rusty broken bits of mechanical equipment and ancient farm machinery. Rungs nailed to a pair of wooden beams led to a small loft above.

Bill poked his head over the side. "Look at this, Lucy."

She climbed up, flinching as she encountered the drift of a spiderweb.

"It's perfect," Bill said, sweeping his torch back and forth to reveal low, cobwebbed eaves set with pegs upon which hung coils of rope and moldy bits of harness. Sacks of grain rested against one wall alongside a stack of mismatched lumber, obviously left over from a variety of jobs.

"A veritable Shangri-la," she grumbled.

Bill curled up on a pile of old tarpaulins with his knapsack as a pillow. He gave a great sigh. "What a lark. The boys at the Lion won't believe it. They'll think I'm telling a bouncer."

"It's like a story out of *Warne's Book of Adventure*, all right." She pulled an old boot from underneath her sore bum. "We'll rest for a few hours, but that's all. We need to be on our way if we're to find a ride."

Rain drummed on the shingles above her head. Lucy counted her money. After two train tickets and meals, her small savings had dwindled. How was she ever going to stretch it to last until she'd hooked Mr. Oliver?

Her stomach's growling was her only answer.

Well, that and a scurrying in the walls that left her rigid and smothering a scream.

Rats.

She should have bloody well known.

Squeezing her eyes shut, she fought to remain calm. Of course there were rats. She was sleeping in a damned shed in the middle of bloody nowhere. Had she once complained about the humdrum monotony of her life? If she had a smidgen of sense, she'd march right into that farmer's kitchen, demand the use of a telephone, and be back at Nanreath Hall in two hours tucked up in her comfy bed, boredom be damned.

She could just hear Sister Murphy's gloating and Aunt Cynthia's withering disapproval.

Forcing herself to ignore the pitter-patter of rodent feet, she leaned back against a lumpy feed sack.

No. She'd rather be boiled in oil than give up and go back and face those two. Instead, she took off her coat and tucked it around Bill, who curled asleep beside her. He flung an arm across her legs, nestling his head against her hip, his lashes fluttering as he dreamed.

She closed her eyes.

Ah well, she'd never claimed to possess a smidgen of sense and she certainly wasn't bored now.

Below the cliff-side nightclub, shimmering seas lapped at wide beaches fringed in ferns and thick groves of rain trees. A band played a sad, smoky jazz number. Amelia, stunning in a floor-length Vionnet gown of royal purple, vodka martini in her hand, sat among a group of sycophantic hangers-on. She laughed and tossed her auburn head, the emeralds and diamonds at her throat catching and refracting the light.

"Bath caught it last night, poor buggers. Over four hundred dead."

The tropical air hummed with the steady whirr of cicadas, loud

as fighter planes. Lucy stood at the edge of the dance floor, awkwardly gauche in her old school uniform, unnoticed by everyone
while Amelia held court.

"Heard one of them gun batteries was manned by the ATS.
Shot a bomber down and everything. What do you think of that?"

Her skin prickled and the hair lifted at the back of her neck. She
left the party, following a set of wooden steps to the beach, where
the soft rush of the waves was punctuated by the sudden air-raid-
siren shriek of a macaw or cockatoo. Still, Amelia's voice and the
clink of glasses was caught on a monsoon breeze, thick and hot as a
steam-filled bath.

"Killing Jerries sure sounds more exciting than killing vermin.
That's a quarter of a sack gone to the filthy buggers, Stella. When's
the rat catcher due to arrive? The bloody things are eating us out of
half our seed."

At the shoreline, sand oozed gritty between Lucy's toes, and a
cool wash of foam licked at her ankles. Golden glimmers flickered
on the ocean, reflections from the strings of fairy lights decorating
the club above her, where dancers clung to one another against the
coming dawn.

"Not until next Thursday. I could have joined the ATS, but
me mum wanted me somewhere safe out of it. Join the Land Girls,
Stella, she said. You might find yourself a nice handsome farmer,
she said. Huh! I'd punch her in the nose if she was here."

Light speared the heavens to the east, the sky an opalescent rain-
bow of color. Lucy lifted her face to it, impatient and excited.

"You go on. I can manage. I'll grab what I need from the supply
in the loft."

The sun burst from the sea, red and orange licking the horizon
like flames. Lucy put up a hand against the blinding glare, blinking
away tears. The band fell into a ragged silence. She spun away, but

the nightclub, the cliff, Amelia, had all vanished. There was nothing left of the once-familiar landscape. A silhouette wavered in and out of focus as she wiped the tears from her eyes.

"Mother?" she whispered. "You promised."

"Crikey!" a shrill voice demanded. "Who the blazes are you?"

Chapter 11

"A good thing it was me that caught you in Mr. Ennis's machine shed."

Patsy Dean was a big-boned young woman with limp mousy hair under her brown felt WLA hat and regular no-nonsense features weathered by sun and wind. Lucy had known Land Girls around Nanreath, bold, plainspoken creatures rumored by the locals to be fast and immoral. Lucy had felt an immediate affinity. This one, though, looked anything but a kindred spirit. She eyed Lucy with obvious suspicion.

"He doesn't abide trespassers."

"We weren't trespassing," Bill piped up. "We were sleeping."

"To him, it's one and the same. He nearly took a shot at a Yank officer scouting out sites for airfields last month."

"Why would you shoot at a Yank?" Bill said. "They're a bunch of rum bluffers, and they're always giving out sweets."

"It's what they want in exchange that's the problem," Patsy said, swinging one last sack into the barrow by the barn door.

Bill's frown cleared in understanding. "Oh, you mean—"

Lucy clapped a hand over his mouth as she threw him a deadly stare.

"Well, come along back to the house," Patsy offered. "There's no sense in leaving before you've had a bite of breakfast. And we can dry those clothes of yours before you catch your death. Stella's gone to the Coppages' about borrowing an Allen scythe, but Judith will be finishing up with the cows and want a bite before she heads out to the lower meadow."

Breakfast sounded positive bliss, and their clothes were a bit clammy. She and Bill followed as Patsy gripped the barrow and headed back up the track, barely staggering under a weight that would have had Lucy on her knees. "I suppose you want to know what we were doing in your loft. We're not spies if you're wondering."

"If I thought that, I'd have taken a shot at you myself," Patsy replied quite matter-of-factly.

Bill squeezed in between them, his gaze wide and puppyish, his smile engaging. Even his half trot seemed intended to give an air of fresh-faced innocence. "My sister Lucy and me are going to visit our aunt. She's feeling real poorly and needs us to nurse her. If we don't, there's no telling what might happen. She don't have no other family but my sister Lucy and me." He gave Lucy a broad wink.

"Your aunt is fortunate to have someone to help her while she's under the weather. Where does she live? Is it very far away?"

"Miles and miles. That's why my sister Lucy and me slept in your barn. But once we get there, it'll be all right. You see, she lives in a big house with a hundred rooms and a fleet of motorcars, and a chuffer and a maid, even one of them butler gents what opens the doors." He ended his tall tale with the flash of a grin. "Ain't that right, sister Lucy?"

"Couldn't have explained it better myself," she replied while praying for a stray bomb to put her out of her misery.

Clearly incredulous, Patsy merely nodded and led them onward. Either she didn't care enough to call them on their lies or she planned to lull them into a false sense of security and pounce when they least expected it. Hopefully, any potential ambush would wait until after breakfast.

In the yard, a lean, long-jawed girl with her wispy blond hair tied in an oily scarf tinkered with an ancient tractor. She too wore the standard WLA uniform of coveralls and a scratchy green sweater, though hers was liberally grease stained and smelled like cow.

"Fancy a cuppa, Judith?" Patsy asked, dropping her load by the barn door.

"What I'd fancy is for Mr. Ennis to get back here with the gasket we need for this old bucket of bolts or it'll be Wellington in harness to clear that lower meadow, and he'll not last ten yards before he collapses in the traces."

"Ennis'll turn up."

"Aye, but before or after he's pissed away half a day in the pub?"

"Don't listen to Judith. Ennis isn't that bad. He likes a pint now and again and he's a bit gruff, but there are worse farms to be billeted on." Patsy brought them into the house and up a narrow back stair to a cluttered room overlooking a long sloping field; the church tower they'd seen last night was off to the right beyond the trees. Three beds took up most of the space, but a wardrobe had been jammed in one sloping corner, a dressing table in another. "Most of the other girls stationed round here have quarters in old sheep barns or converted cider sheds. The three of us get this room and run of the kitchen as long as we cook for the old man too. Since his wife left him for an RAF lad from Newcastle, the poor chap's been all but living on boiled eggs and toast." She pulled a skirt and blouse from a chest of drawers.

"Put this on and bring your wet things down to the stove to dry." She sized Bill up. "There's some old bits and pieces in the jumble bag we could make do for you. Come along. I want to hear more about your aunt. You say she lives in a great big house?"

Before Lucy could advise or threaten, Bill scurried after Patsy, his high reedy voice spinning ever more elaborate and implausible yarns. By the time he came to the end of his story, they'd be the lost heirs to an empire, kidnapped by Gypsies and sold into slavery. As she wriggled into a skirt (too big) and a blouse (too tight), worry snaked its way up her spine and clenched at her stomach, but short of snatching Bill and making a break for it, there was nothing she could do. At one point during the burble of conversation, she heard Patsy laugh. Hopefully, that was a good sign.

Back in the kitchen, she modeled her outfit for Patsy and Bill. "What do you think?"

"Crikey, sis, you look a fright." He was dressed in a pair of men's overalls rolled at the ankles and an old fisherman's sweater. He had his cards out, moving three of them back and forth and in and out in an elaborate dance she could barely follow.

"Brat," she said, giving him a playful cuff to the head before watching him switch and swap the cards on the table. "Three-card monte? Another game those boys at the Lion taught you?" She leveled him a stern glare.

"Aye, miss," he said, sliding the cards back into the deck and all of them into his pocket.

If Patsy caught his slip of the tongue, she continued to keep silent as she poured hot water into a teapot to steep. "Lay your things by the stove there. They'll be ready in a trice."

"Is that what I think it is?" Lucy peered into the skillet on the stove, every sense overtaken by the mind-altering aroma of frying bacon.

Patsy grinned as she put toast on to brown and set a jar of blackberry jam on the table. "I knew that pig club would pay off. Ennis thought I was mad, but he's as happy for a chop now and again as anybody."

Lucy nibbled an end as it singed her fingers. "Can one feel lust for a slice of pork belly? I think I would gladly let a chap have his way with me if he could promise me a ham dinner afterward." Patsy nearly dropped a plate, while Bill smirked into his sleeve. "Did I say something amiss?" she asked innocently.

"It's hopeless. Bloody hopeless." Judith banged into the kitchen, wiping her greasy hands on a rag. "There's only so much I can do with bits of twine and the odd cannibalized bolt."

"Don't get hysterical," Patsy replied, recovered from Lucy's remarks enough to shovel up eggs and bacon onto plates and set them at the table. "You know Ennis will find what he needs at that garage in Charbury. McKeegan has all sorts of salvaged bits and bobs."

Lucy nearly choked on her tea. Charbury—now she remembered why that name sounded familiar—a garage in Charbury. The pieces fell into place with a thud that dropped straight into her gut while the hair at the back of her neck prickled with something almost like anticipation.

"Not to interrupt, but might you have a telephone?"

Breakfast over, Judith and Patsy dumped their plates and mugs in the big stone sink on their way back to work.

"Care to come along?" Patsy asked Bill, who was sliding a finger across his plate to lap up the last drop of bacon grease. "We'd be glad of an extra hand."

"Crikey, can I?" He leapt up from the table, nearly knocking over his chair. "That sounds brilliant."

"What am I supposed to do while you're gadding about like a farmhand?" Lucy asked.

"The washing up, I expect." Patsy chucked a dishcloth at her on their way out the door.

"Should have known bacon with my breakfast was too good to be true," Lucy grumbled as she turned on the taps full blast and rolled up her sleeves.

She fumed through the breakfast dishes, muttering under her breath as she scrubbed until her hands went pruny and the paltry few suds dissolved in the dingy gray water. But at the end of the hour, the drain board was full, and every plate, mug, bowl, and pan sparkled.

Work worth doing was worth doing well. Wasn't that the old chestnut? Now, where had she heard that? Certainly not her mother. Amelia and work would not have been mentioned in the same sentence, though if she wanted something, she stopped at nothing to achieve it. Did that count?

By now, the damp clothes that Patsy had hung in front of the Aga to dry had crisped up nicely. Lucy pulled them stiff and warm off the rack, shaking each piece out before folding it for later. Her frock had come through without too much suffering, but Bill's trousers had sprung a great leak in the backside. That wouldn't do. A bit of shabbiness seemed to be de rigueur these days, but she drew the line at wearing actual rags.

Upstairs in the girls' bedroom, she found a sewing basket. The house was stuffy as the day grew warm and the small deep-set windows let in little light. She'd do much better outside in the bright morning sunshine, and it would be easier to keep an eye on the road. If all went to plan, it wouldn't be long before the farm would be a dwindling dot out the rear window.

Finding a corner of the yard upwind of the cowshed and not too close to the dung pile, she made herself comfortable on a low stone wall with needle and thread, watching Patsy drag large corrugated sheets of rusty metal from various outbuildings into the middle of the yard and dump them in a pile. Her face grew shiny and red with exertion, and at one point she discarded her sweater, but her breathing remāined steady as she labored under her heavy awkward loads.

Lucy finished mending Bill's trousers and began on a pair of dungarees with a hole in the knee, then a skirt with a ripped hem and a blouse with three missing buttons.

Patsy dropped a bundle of long metal poles onto the ground with a clang that echoed in Lucy's ears for minutes afterward.

"You do this—voluntarily?" Lucy asked after the ringing stopped.

Patsy wiped her hands on her oil-streaked coveralls. "I grew up on a farm so I'm used to the hard work. Judith's the same. Stella, now, she's a town girl. Joined the WLA to get away from the bombs. Soft when she started, but you look at her now. Hands as callused as mine and a dab hand with the dairy cows."

"So, you think a few months here and you could turn me into a farmer?"

Patsy paused to watch as Lucy stitched a popped seam on a pair of trousers. "Not sure if farming would be to your liking, but you're right clever at the fiddly work."

"Being a very bad girl at St. Hildegarde's School for Young Ladies meant becoming a very good seamstress." She bit off a thread.

"Not that it's any of my business, and you can tell me if I'm butting in where I shouldn't"—Patsy cleared her throat, looking all at once self-conscious and almost embarrassed—"but it's clear you and Bill aren't brother and sister."

Lucy tried to pass off the allegation with a joke. "Really? What gave it away?"

It seemed to work. Patsy's grim countenance relaxed. "The boy's got the gift of gab, I'll give that to him. But when he started describing how he's got the job of feeding the alligators that live in your esteemed aunt Dorothy's moat, I had to stop him right there. Then I had to reassure him I had no intention of turning him over to the scabby beaks—his words, not mine—before he would agree to come back with me to the house."

"Bill seems to have a rather strong aversion to the police. If I had to guess, he's had more than his share of run-ins with them over the years."

"So you're not brother and sister and you're certainly not WVS or Red Cross. So who are you? And if you're not headed to a moated castle to wait on your sick aunt the duchess, where are you going?"

"I'm nobody, really. Just someone who wanted to help Bill get home." Lucy spread her palms across the surface of the soft workaday wool. "And maybe in the process, find one of my own."

Well, I'll be damned." Corporal Michael McKeegan emerged from an estate wagon, MCKEEGAN'S GARAGE stenciled on its wooden door panel. His blond hair was darker now, barring a few bleached streaks courtesy of the Singapore sun, but his lopsided choirboy smile still made her ache to throw something at him.

She'd never been so happy to see anyone in her life.

Not that he needed to know that. He was confident enough without encouragement.

"Lucy Stanhope?" he said, coming round to stare at her as if she were a phantasm.

"Don't gawp. It attracts flies."

He laughed, any lingering stiffness melting away. "It *is* you.

Blimey, I almost thought it was a joke when my mum told me you called."

"If it's a joke, the laugh's on me. We didn't exactly part on friendly terms." She rubbed her arms, suddenly chilly. She'd forgotten the way he seemed to stare right through her. And the way she hated it. A girl needed some secrets.

"You were upset."

"If by 'upset,' you mean 'mad as hell,' you're right. But it wasn't your fault. You didn't sink our ship or cause Mrs. Pratchett's death."

"Neither did you, lass."

There it was again. That damned perceptiveness. She needed to be on her guard around him. "It was good of you to come. I'm not sure if I would have done the same in your shoes."

"What are you doing here?" He looked around. "And why do you look as if . . ." He seemed to think better of whatever he was going to say, falling back on a feeble shake of his head. "Last I heard you were going to take London by storm. The city would be your oyster and every gentleman at your beck and call."

"And so I shall—with your help. I need a lift, you see."

Her mother had perfected the art of twisting men round her little finger. It didn't take much: a smile, a look, a careless touch. They fell like skittles at her feet. When Lucy was eleven, Amelia had thought it amusing to see her daughter emulating her methods. When Lucy was eighteen, Amelia found it rather less so. But by then, it was far too late, and her daughter proved more than adept. Lucy employed those skills now with a subtle sway that brought her all too comfortably close. "I know it's asking a lot, but you were the only one that I thought might help. Doesn't that make you feel special?" She lifted a hand to caress his cheek.

He grabbed her wrist, his face hard, the smile gone. "It makes me feel like I'm the only man left in England who doesn't want to strangle you on sight, though I'm not sure why that surprises me. You never were someone interested in making friends, only collecting followers."

She tore away from him, feeling suddenly cheap and ugly. Humiliation burned her cheeks. "You don't have to be rude. It was a notion I had, that's all. If you don't want to help, I'm sure I can find someone who will."

She started to walk away, but he reached for her hand and swung her round to face him. "Hang on. I didn't say I wouldn't help. I just wish you didn't . . ." He spread his hands. "All you needed to do was ask."

"Very well. I'm asking. Can I get a lift? The trains are stopped between Exeter and Bridgwater while they repair the tracks, and I need to get to London as soon as I can."

"Hot date?"

"Something like that. I'm meeting an old friend about a job. Now, will you please help me?"

He gave his chin a thoughtful rub. "I don't know. The last time we spoke, you treated me as if I were muck under your dainty foot. Now I'm your Prince Charming. It's a lot for a simple country lad like me to swallow."

"Prince Charming? Let's not get carried away. I'm in need of a lift, not a fairy tale."

There it was, that damned insolent amusement again. Oh, how she wanted to clobber the cheeky sod. "Well? Yes or no?" she snapped. "I haven't got all day."

"Right, then. I may be the biggest fool in Christendom, but when a beautiful young woman asks me for a lift, who am I to refuse?"

"Really? You're an absolute lifesaver." She grinned before putting her fingers between her lips and giving a quick blast. "Come on, Bill. It's on."

"Wait a minute. Who's Bill?"

She kissed him on the cheek, whispering in his ear, "Our chaperone, of course."

So since I was going to London anyway, I thought I'd offer my services as chaperone. Bill's going home to his mother in Bethnal Green," Lucy explained before Corporal McKeegan could ask. The back of the estate wagon was loaded with toolboxes, empty gas cans, coils of rope and chain, a folded car rug covered in dog hair, and three bushel baskets of ripe strawberries.

Lucy was squashed hip-to-hip and thigh-to-thigh against Corporal McKeegan. Every shift of the gears, his left hand brushed her knee. She noted the long squared fingers, grease under the nails; the glow of blond hairs sprinkling his wrist; a livid white scar across his freckled knuckles.

So different from Yoon Hai's sleek beauty and courtier's polish.

A proud feline compared to an affable sheepdog.

But for some reason, she imagined the sheepdog's strong capable hand caressing the slope of her shoulder, the length of her rib cage, and her body warmed uncomfortably. To hide her humiliating reaction, she turned her attention to Bill, who was hanging out the rear passenger window.

"Get back in here before you knock your head off," she scolded. "Or end up with a mouthful of bugs."

"You sound like an old mother hen," McKeegan said.

"Go faster," Bill urged as he waved to a passing bicyclist. "Faster."

"Any faster and this old rattler will bust a hose. She's held together with Sellotape and string as it is. Besides, there's a sentry post on the other side of the bridge. Don't want old Mr. Bonnie or Dr. Carr to panic and take a potshot at us."

Lucy's stomach tensed. "Sentry post?"

If they checked her papers, they might realize she'd done a bunk and call the authorities. Aunt Cynthia was sure to be hot on her trail by now. It wouldn't take a fortune-teller to figure out where she'd gone or a genius to trace her route. She'd only just managed to elude disaster. Was she so quickly going to be up to her neck in it again?

"Nothing to worry over," McKeegan explained. "They built pill-boxes and tank traps all up and down this stretch of the county when they thought the Germans might invade. Home Guard took it over last winter. If you ask me, it's more an excuse for the lads to escape their wives so they can drink a few pints in peace. I mean, Mr. Bonnie couldn't hit the side of a barn if he were standing five feet from it."

"Drunk, blind, and armed. You fill me with confidence, Corporal."

He looked over, his blue eyes crinkling with silent amusement. "It's Michael. I'm not in the army anymore."

"Maybe not, but I prefer to keep our relationship on a more businesslike footing."

They dropped over the crest of a hill. Below them, a river tumbled and curled over slick rocks as it made its way south toward the Channel. A pair of ducks paddled in the shallows. A willow trailed green like a curtain beside a mossy bank. Just before the bridge stood a squat cement structure, an ominous slit peering at oncoming traffic. A spectacled man in the tin hat and khaki uniform of the Home Guard sat on a folding chair reading a paper. Another wearing an old LDV armband smoked a pipe, his rifle leaning against the bridge's parapet. Hardly what one would call a deterrent to crack German paratroopers.

The estate wagon gave an asthmatic cough and rattle as McKeegan ground the gears down to idle. The man in the hat wandered over to them, leaving his rifle behind. "Morning, Michael. You're out and about early this fine day. Feeling better, are you?"

"Much."

"Well, don't overtax yourself. A heart condition is nothing to sneeze at."

"I'm fine, Dr. Carr. Really. The boffins have said it's just a murmur. Nothing fatal." Crushed against his side, Lucy sensed his growing impatience in the jump of taut muscles, the tightness in his frozen smile.

The good doctor was not so observant. "So you say, lad, but little problems can grow into big ones if we don't take care." He finished with a jolly laugh that was not returned.

"You have me there, sir."

In the meantime, the second sentry wandered up, making no attempt to even look as if he were remotely concerned about invasion. He leaned on the butt of his rifle as if it were a walking stick. "Thought that was you, Michael. Didn't see you down at the pub last night. Shoulda come. Martin beat that Frobisher lad from over Crewkerne way in shove ha'penny. A real nail-biter. It came down to the final point."

Watching grown men toss pennies all evening sounded like one of the inner circles of hell to Lucy, but McKeegan brightened immediately. He relaxed back against the seat, his fingers loose on the wheel. "Sorry I missed it," he answered with absolute sincerity.

"There's to be a rematch tonight. You should come and lay money down. Could pick yourself up enough for a trip to the pictures, maybe. Martin's got a real flair. Not as fine as Tommy Bowen down at the chemist's shop, mind, but then few can match Bowen for the skill."

"I might just do that, Mr. Bonnie. I hear they're showing *Here Comes Mr. Jordan*. That's one I'd like to see."

Mr. Bonnie leaned against the car, and any idea Lucy had that they might make a swift getaway was lost. "Sylvia went last night with that lad working out at Turrell's sawmill. The one with the finger missing."

"Harris?"

"Aye, that's his name. Good lad. Got the use of that cottage up by Simmer's Wood since his grandfather passed. I went to school with his aunt—Harris's, not the old duffer's. Name of Ruby. Pretty as a dream. Kissed her behind the coal shed. She slapped my face for my troubles."

"I remember his cousins from Sunday school picnics. They were always driving the vicar mad with their antics. Mum said they'd both joined up with the merchant navy."

"Aye. It was that or a stint in Dartmoor for 'em both."

Dear God. Would this torture never end? Not that she wasn't interested in Sylvia and her nine-fingered sweetheart or curious about what sort of antics those Harris cousins got up to at Sunday school, but . . . well . . . in point of fact . . . she wasn't.

Just as she thought they might effect an escape, the doctor shoved his way back into the conversation. "Where you headed so early this morning and in such a rush anyway? It's barely half nine."

"Mum sent me to pick up the WI's strawberries. They're canning at the village hall this afternoon."

"Looks like you picked up more than that." Mr. Bonnie peered across at Lucy as if only now realizing McKeegan had company—and thus a new source of gossip. He tipped his hat. "How do you do, Miss—"

"Stanley. Sarah Stanley."

"Pleased to make your acquaintance, Miss Stanley. Headed into Charbury for the canning, are you?"

"Passing through. The corporal was kind enough to give my brother and me a lift."

"He's a kind boy, is our Michael, especially to pretty girls," Mr. Bonnie said with a wink and a smile.

"That's a fine thing to say, Henry Bonnie." Dr. Carr gave a grandfatherly harrumph. "You'll scare the poor girl. Go on, then, lad. Your mum will be waiting for those berries, I expect."

"And be sure to come to the pub tonight," Mr. Bonnie interrupted. "Martin's a sight to behold when he's on top of his game."

"Will do." With a final wave, McKeegan accelerated over the low stone bridge.

"Oh my God, I thought we'd never escape," Lucy commented with a roll of her eyes.

"I wish we could stay like they said," Bill said with a bookmaker's gleam in his eye. "I'd like to see that Martin bloke take on Frobisher. Might be worth a bob or two if the odds is right."

Around a curve toward the village, McKeegan pulled over to the side of the road out of sight of the post, the tension back in the rigid bracing of his spine, the squaring of his shoulders. "All right. Spill it."

"What do you mean?" Lucy stalled.

"I mean the fake name. What's going on?"

Bill left off writing his name in the dust of the back window. "Tell him, Lucy. Michael's no double-crossing whiddler."

"His name is Corporal McKeegan."

"He told me to call him Michael."

"Since when do you do what people tell you?"

"Tell me what?" McKeegan interrupted. "And why do I think I'm not going to like the answer?"

"Well, you know how I told you that I was escorting Bill back to his mother in London?"

His brows crinkled to a confused frown.

"Well, that much is true. It's just that maybe . . . just maybe . . . I'm doing it a bit more unofficially than I let on."

"What's that supposed to mean?"

"We've done a bunk, Michael," Bill said proudly. "Lucy and I are on the lam."

"You ran away? You kidnapped him and ran away?"

"Don't be so dramatic. I didn't kidnap anyone. Bill was already running away. I just decided he might be more successful if he had someone with him—a sort of guardian, if you like."

"You, a guardian?"

"Don't sound so shocked."

"'Shocked' doesn't begin to cover it." He looked at her long and hard, but beyond a flicker of displeasure, his face gave nothing away. "What's in it for you?"

"Can't someone help someone else without having their motives questioned?"

"In the normal run of things, I'd say yes. Where you're concerned, I hedge my bets."

"That's a terrible thing to say."

He put the car in gear and pulled back onto the road. "So prove me wrong."

"Maybe I will . . . Michael."

Chapter 12

McKeegan's Garage turned out to be an old converted smithy, a stone water trough to one side of the petrol pump. An Austin 7 and an older-model Buick, both in various stages of repair, stood in the two main bays, while a motorbike lay in pieces below a rusted red, white, and green sign for Castrol motor oil. A wooden outside stair led to a set of sparsely furnished rooms above the garage with a small kitchenette and bath at the far end.

Michael snatched two pairs of drying socks from a line strung across the small sink, which he shoved into his trouser pockets. "Mum lives across the way, but the garret is my own little paradise."

"Lucky you," Lucy replied, eying the drab set of rooms.

"I like it," Bill declared.

"You would."

Automotive magazines and a week-old newspaper proclaiming *First Bombs on Tokyo* lay scattered across a lumpy, stained couch, while a row of empty Bass beer bottles stood on the scratched and scarred end table alongside a few rusted engine parts. Someone had attempted to pretty up the place with a colorful rag rug and curtains at the dormers, but it wasn't nearly enough to combat the general air of neglect. Michael might live here, but this was a temporary billet at best. Not a home.

She was reminded of Nanreath Hall and felt an immediate stab of empathy.

"Guess this isn't exactly the rich digs you're used to," he said.

"Not even close. For one thing, it's decidedly lacking in dead animals."

He cocked her a puzzled look, but she merely smiled enigmatically.

"I'm only staying until I can save enough for a place of my own. There's a cottage just beyond the millpond I've my eye on. It's been empty for a few years, needs some work, but the bones are still good." He grabbed a dirty bowl and glass from a table and hid a pair of flannel pajama bottoms under a couch cushion. "There's even a cowshed out the back."

"You've sold me. What right-minded person wouldn't jump at the chance to own his own cowshed?"

He laughed, her comment bouncing off his impenetrable good nature. He gave one more despairing glance around at the mess. "Right. Well, there's a bath just through there. You can wash up and I'll be back to collect you in twenty minutes."

"Wash?" Bill shuddered. "I don't need a wash. Tell him, Lucy."

"You'll bathe," Lucy answered. "No ifs, ands, or buts about it."

Bill looked mutinous, a stubborn jut to his jaw.

"If you hurry, you can be clean and still have time to explore the village. I thought I saw a sweetshop at the end of the lane."

"Right. I'll only be a tick." He made a dash for the bathroom, where loud sloshing and humming soon followed.

"I can't believe I'm saying this, but you have a real knack with him," Michael commented.

"I'm making it up as I go. But he's not bad, only a little wild. He's had to grow up too quickly and on his own."

Michael caught and held her gaze. "Something you might know a little bit about." Her heart skipped a beat and a twinge of something electric curled up her spine. Then he went and ruined it. "But are you certain helping him run away is wise?"

"I asked for a lift, not a lecture. If I'd wanted to be told off, I'd have stayed with my aunt in her horrid mausoleum."

"Is your aunt that bad?"

"No, in fact she's irritatingly good, which is even worse."

"Only you would hold someone's virtue against them."

"It's not her virtue that rubs me the wrong way. It's that she expects me to be virtuous as well." My God, how Lucy hated his look of patient understanding, as if he knew anything about her and her life. It was almost as bad as his usual expression of patronizing amusement. "Not that I don't appreciate these little chats of ours, but why don't you stick to carburetors and leave the psychoanalysis to the experts? Okay?"

He leaned against the table, crossing his arms. "Very well. No psychoanalysis. Just the honest truth—what's really going on?"

"I told you."

"You told me some cock-and-bull story about helping Bill find his mother, which is well and good, but what's waiting for *you* in London?"

"I don't see how it's any of your business."

"You rang me up out of the blue on a busy Wednesday morning. That makes it my business. So spill it or else."

"Or else what?"

Michael shrugged and began tidying. A discarded pair of half-darned socks. An old greasy newspaper. A dirty plate. Slowly . . .

Methodically . . .

As if he had all the time in the world . . .

"You'll refuse to help me? Is that it? I should never have telephoned you. It was a daft idea."

"You said it. Not me."

She fumed inwardly, but he continued his snail's-pace spring cleaning—a pair of battered work boots, a stain on the end table. All while that glimmer of laughter crinkled the corners of his blue eyes, and his mouth twitched as if he were at the edge of laughter. It was as if even when he was being completely serious, there was a part of him that couldn't help but see the absurdity of the situation. Despite her best efforts, she felt a betraying smile tugging at her own lips. How did he manage to make her want to scream and laugh at the same time? It wasn't fair. "Fine. If you must know, I'm meeting an important man about a job. He'll only be in London for a few more days and then he leaves for the States, so I have to get there as soon as I can."

That brought his amusement to a full stop. His arms dropped to his sides in obvious astonishment. "America?"

She rather liked rendering him speechless. It made a nice change from being lectured or being quizzed. "Yes. California to be exact. Palm trees and movie stars, dinners at the Brown Derby and Hollywood parties that last all night. Doesn't it sound dishy?"

"I admit it wasn't what I expected." He turned away rather abruptly to pace the length of the room.

"Nor I, but Mr. Oliver's here looking for his next leading lady and I intend to be her."

"Oliver? The chap in Singapore. The one who interrupted your little tête-à-tête with the Chinaman?"

Cocking a hip against an enormous draftsman's desk, she ran a finger through the layer of dust. "I knew you were eavesdropping that day. Mason Oliver is my ticket to a perfect life of champagne and caviar dreams. What girl wouldn't jump at the chance?"

"None, I suppose."

"You bet your best set of wrenches. So will you take us to Yeovil or not?"

"Are you certain it's what you really want?"

"It's not a cottage complete with cowshed, but we can't all be so lucky."

Michael released a small breath, as if coming to a decision. "Right, then," he said with the flash of a distracted smile. "I suppose we'd better get cracking." He headed toward the door. His back was straight as a pike, an odd unreadable expression on his face. "Wouldn't want you to miss your big chance."

"Michael . . . ," she called after him. She'd no idea what she planned to say, only that she didn't want to leave things between them like this.

"I'll be downstairs when you're ready." He closed the door behind him.

Why did she feel as if she'd disappointed him and somehow diminished herself? And why did she care what Michael McKeegan thought? She tried to laugh off his criticisms as she'd ignored so many previous lectures from well-meaning do-gooders, but the sting of his words remained like a splinter.

Pulling a cigarette from her bag, she sank onto the creaky swivel Windsor pulled up before the desk. She fished for her lighter but came up empty. Odd. Had she left it at the farm? Had it fallen out in Michael's car?

Perhaps he had one squirreled away amid his stacks of accounts ledgers and piles of correspondence. She carefully moved the clutter aside as she searched—the man was a positive magpie. Just as she was about to give up, she moved a folder of receipts to discover a full ashtray with a lighter propped next to it, and more interesting still, a half-burned piece of paper wadded up amid the ash.

He'd eavesdropped on her at Renee Ullman's that day with Yoon Hai. Turnabout was fair play. See how he liked being spied upon.

She smoothed the paper out to discover it was a piece of stationery. Expensive by the look and feel of the page, with a whimsical border of curlicue blue flowers. The top third had been burned, leaving a ragged singed edge. Below, the remnants of a note penned in a hasty scribble.

> *... sorry if I hurt you, Michael. Come to London. I'm throwing a birthday party for Daddy at the Dorchester at the end of the month. There will be dancing and drinking and lots of dark corners where we can talk.*
>
> *We need to talk.*
>
> *Arabella*

From the bath, Bill's voice was raised in a rather enthusiastic rendition of "Roll Out the Barrel" accompanied by the occasional groaning pipe.

Who was Arabella? And what might she and Michael have to talk about?

Perhaps the answer lay in one of the half-open file drawers beside the desk. Glancing over her shoulder, she dismissed her prick of conscience by telling herself if he meant his correspondence to be private, he'd have closed and locked his cabinet. It was weak reasoning, but enough to satisfy the worst of her guilty pangs.

The top drawer yielded a few pads of lined paper, pencils, pens, nibs, a bottle of half-dried ink. The second was more interesting: a catalog from the British Empire Exhibition Scotland and sketchbooks filled with page after page of architectural details—windows, doors, rooflines, gables, brickwork, interiors. Modernist in influence, yet here was a touch of Oriental styling, there an old-fashioned cottage garden look. Halfway through the last book was a folded letter from his mother.

The rest of the pages in the sketchbook were blank.

All but for the final page, which was littered with hasty drawings done in dull pencil. A simple stone cottage exterior from the front, sides, and back. The margins littered with notes and measurements, a quick sketch of a gabled addition, a floor layout of a modern kitchen. She smiled to see a whimsical drawing of a cow in the upper corner of the page.

She put all the books back in the drawer, but some obstruction kept her from closing it, no matter how hard she pushed. She slid her hand behind the sketchbooks, hoping to work the drawer free, only to catch her breath on a sharp stinging pain.

"Damn!" Wincing, she snatched her hand free. A thin line of blood beaded the skin of her upper wrist. Not a deep gash, but enough to hurt like the devil. Pulling the drawer out farther, she moved the sketchbooks aside. There, stuffed at the very back, was a framed photograph, the glass smashed and jagged. It was a snapshot of Michael and a pretty, dark-haired young woman, both in uniform as they lounged on a blanket in the grass. He had his arm around her. They looked happy. Arabella?

"I'm finished, Lucy. Even scrubbed my feet and behind my ears and put on an almost clean pair of socks." Bill stood damp and pink in the bathroom doorway.

Startled, she shoved the photograph back in the drawer. "Then enjoy your freedom, but don't swindle anyone out of anything, no cadging a smoke, and stay out of the pub."

"Yes, miss." He slammed out of the door and clattered down the stairs in a heedless gallop. Charbury had better brace itself.

The tiny bathroom was as stark and charmless as the rest of

the flat—and awash in at least three inches of water. It dripped in steamy rivulets off the small mirror, overflowed from the tiny corner sink, and soaked the shelf above the toilet containing a shaving kit, tooth powder and brush, and a pillbox containing a half dozen little yellow pills—*Atabrine*, the soggy label read. Every towel had been used and now lay in a drenched pile on the floor.

It wasn't possible. A mess of this magnitude couldn't have been created in ten short minutes by one small boy.

Where was a housemaid when you needed one?

Wading through the shallows, she plucked the towels up as she went, wringing them out and hanging them up to dry. She found a washrag, surprisingly the one thing in the room to escape the deluge, and sopped up as much of the water as she could before it leaked into the garage below. She even rinsed out the sink, which bore a scum of tooth powder and soap. The place still didn't sparkle, but at least it wasn't the forty-day flood she'd found upon arrival.

Her quick shower in lukewarm water quickly cooled to frigid and the sliver of soap for washing smelled like antiseptic, but by the time she was dressed in a clean blouse and skirt, coiffed, and dusted with powder she almost felt like herself again.

Coming down the stairs to the garage, she heard a woman's voice.

". . . can't just rush off with a strange girl and not let me meet her, Michael. Invite her for dinner."

She peeked around the door to see Michael tossing tools into a metal chest, screwing lids onto jars of bolts and washers. He'd changed his shirt and combed his hair, and the clean scent of Yardley's battled for dominance over the rather acrid odors of grease, brake fluid, and exhaust fumes.

"She's in a hurry, Mum. Besides, you two wouldn't have anything in common to talk about."

"What's that supposed to mean?"

"She's a fancy girl with grand relations. She's not used to the way we do things."

"How do you know what she's used to? You've only just met her."

"I know her type."

Ouch! Somehow Lucy didn't think he referred to her amazing brilliance and incredible beauty, but he didn't have to sound so adamant.

His mother either didn't notice his tone or chose to ignore it. "You show me a body that turns up their nose at my plum charlotte and I'll show you a body what's soft in the head. Mrs. Moseby at the post office raves over it, and you know how grudging with her praise she is."

"It's nothing to do with the food, Mum. Miss Stanhope . . . well . . . she can be . . . rude." He quickly added, "I don't think she means to be. It's how she's been raised."

"To be rude?"

"To come out swinging."

Lucy's face heated at the brutality of his statement, and a lump formed in her stomach, but she forced her shoulders back and lifted her chin. And if there was a quiver in her limbs, she refused to let it take hold.

It wouldn't be the first time she'd been subjected to a verbal scything of her character. Merely the first time it had hurt.

Ignoring the sting, she stepped off the bottom riser and into the garage. "Never let it be said I ignored an endorsement from Mrs. Moseby."

Fancy me, having a real American in my kitchen. The girls at the sewing circle won't believe it when I tell them."

"I don't know if I qualify as a real American, Mrs. McKeegan. My mother's British."

"Is she now? Well, we'll keep that to ourselves. Don't want to disappoint the girls, do we, love?"

Michael's mother was a tall, robust woman with a snub freckled nose, brown hair threaded with gray pinned in a bun at the back of her head, and the same mild blue eyes and dimpled smile as her son. Her accent bore traces of an Irish childhood beneath the solidly middle-class English enunciation, and from the moment she'd welcomed Lucy into her cozy kitchen, she had bossed her about with well-meaning high-handedness. For some reason, this overbearing attitude didn't lift Lucy's hackles as it normally would have. Maybe because it was born out of kindness rather than censure.

They sat in her kitchen, the table draped with a fine tatted lace cloth yellowed in places, but obviously laid out for Lucy's benefit. The air smelled of baking and more faintly of carbolic soap. Morning light shone watery across the scrubbed flagstone floor and lit the copper pots hanging above the stove.

She poured hot water from the kettle into a teapot. "You wouldn't happen to have met William Powell, would you? He's American."

"Mum . . . ," Michael groaned.

"Don't Mum me. It doesn't hurt to ask, does it?"

"Afraid I haven't had the pleasure, Mrs. McKeegan."

"Ah well, you never know. The girls and I saw him in *Love Crazy*. We do love a good comedy."

All through the visit, Michael had watched Lucy with a wary tightness in his face and an edge-of-his-seat nervousness. His uneasy strain would have been funny if not for the very real concern she caught in his gaze every time she opened her mouth. Did he really expect her to insult his mother at her own kitchen table? She might be a bit . . . sarcastic . . . at times, and on occasion she could be outright nasty, but she didn't go about snarling at strangers unless given a good reason, and so far Mrs. McKeegan had been nothing but welcoming.

In fact, she couldn't have been more perfectly maternal if she'd been plucked from central casting for the part.

"Can I have some more?" Bill asked, shoving the last bite of cottage pie into his mouth as he spoke.

"Don't talk with your mouth full," Lucy instructed.

"How'm I supposed to ask for more if I can't talk?"

"Wait until you've swallowed."

"She might change her mind if I do that." He scratched his head. "Or some other bloke might get dibs ahead of me."

"What other bloke? There's not exactly a queue," Lucy pointed out. "Besides, you'll get sick if you eat any more. That's your third helping."

Bill stretched his neck out, pulled his shoulders back, lifted his head. "I'm going through a spurt. Ned Hollis says a bucket of beans and a pound of snuff is guaranteed to put hair on your chest."

"And what would you want with a hairy chest?"

"It would keep me warm in the winter."

"He's got you there," Michael intervened.

"You eat as much as you want, love. Makes me happy to see someone enjoying their food so much." Mrs. McKeegan placed a plate of warm soda bread fresh from the oven on the table. "Should have seen Michael at that age. The boy had a hollow leg."

Bill examined his appendages with a careful eye.

The brass clock on the sill chimed twelve. Lucy sidled toward the edge of her seat, trying not to look eager to escape.

Mrs. McKeegan planted herself in a chair opposite, pouring a cup of tea, which she slurped comfortably. "A shame you have to run off so soon. The ladies at the WI have managed to get their hands on a few of the canning machines the Americans sent over, and it's all hands on deck. Sure I can't tempt you to help us try them out?"

Michael looked as if he'd swallowed a fly.

"We're to meet at the village hall. Ethel Mortimer wanted it at her house, but her husband is laid up with the gout and a terrible grouch he is when he's feeling poorly. You'd blush to hear some of the words what come out of that man's mouth. I don't know how poor Ethel stands it. I'd have booted him out on his backside years ago."

By now, Michael's expression was one of silent and incomprehensible horror, as if witnessing a train wreck in progress with no possible way to stop the catastrophe unfolding in front of his eyes.

"Have you ever made jam, Miss Stanhope?"

Lucy actually saw Michael brace himself, awaiting what he must assume would be a crushing set-down from Lucy. Perversely, this made her want to deny him the satisfaction. "I've never made jam, Mrs. McKeegan, but I always seem to be in one."

Her face broadened in a cheerful smile. "Well now, don't you have a little bite under all that sugar."

"I've the teeth marks to prove it," Michael mumbled under his breath, his shoulders no longer up around his ears.

The phone rang, sending Mrs. McKeegan scurrying into the hall to answer it.

Alone together, Lucy kicked Michael under the table.

Michael threw Lucy one of those irritating smirks.

Bill helped himself to a chunk of soda bread.

All felt right with the world.

And then it didn't.

Michael shucked on a jacket as he headed out the kitchen door. "I won't be long, but I have to repair Miss Maude and Miss Ruth's radio before they come completely unglued."

"Are they directing bombers with it?"

"Only slightly less crucial. *Music While You Work* comes on soon. It's their favorite."

"Never let it be said I stood between two old ladies and Eric Winstone."

"Can I come, Michael?" Bill pleaded eagerly. "You'll be faster with help."

"Take him." Lucy shooed them both toward the door. "Anything to speed things up."

"Mum's gone round to the vicarage, so make yourself at home. I won't be long."

"Is that a promise?"

"More like a hope," he said on his way out the door. "But it's the best I can do."

Alone, Lucy checked her watch. Paced the kitchen, glancing through the curtains at a neighbor repairing a gate, another hanging out her wash. Checked her watch again. Thumbed through a well-leafed copy of *WI Life*. If the bookmark was any indication, Michael's mother was interested in keeping bees. Checked her watch. Counted the number of drips from a leaky tap. Seventeen in sixty seconds. She knew that because she'd checked her watch again.

Having exhausted the kitchen's cornucopia of delights, Lucy took Michael at his word. Make herself at home, he said. Very well. She would.

Imagining herself the owner of this snug little house, she climbed the twisting crooked staircase to the upper floor. Three doors led off a narrow passage. The first opened into a large airy bedroom with an enormous cherry sleigh bed complete with quilted counterpane and a bank of frilly pillows. Two dormered windows curtained in dotted poplin looked out over the road and the garage just across the way. A dresser held an assortment of bottles and jars along with a framed photo of a proud young Michael in a university gown.

The second room was smaller and looked out over the garden. Obviously Michael's, it was a shrine to an idyllic boyhood. Ribbons; prizes; certificates; an old cricket bat propped in a corner; postcards from such exotic locales as Lyme Regis, Blackpool, and Scarborough stuffed in the edge of a mirror; lead soldiers lined up across a desk amid a clutter of family photographs. A shelf displayed a row of metal cars and trophies from various sporting events, and a few tattered books: *Treasure Island, Twenty Thousand Leagues Under the Sea, The Count of Monte Cristo.*

The third door opened into a bathroom painted a cheerful canary yellow. The ceilings sloped low to either side, meaning one had to hunch to see oneself in the mirror over the sink, while the elaborate claw-foot tub took up so much space one had to sidle past it to reach the loo.

Back downstairs, she browsed a rather workaday study. Relics of the late Mr. McKeegan's presence remained in the pipe stand on the desk and the fishing rods in the corner, though these had been incongruously augmented by bright floral cushions on the chairs and ruffled chintz curtains at the windows. The kitchen hadn't changed since Michael and Bill had banged out the back door on their mission of mercy—she checked her watch—fifteen minutes ago.

What was taking them so long? Marconi invented the blasted thing faster than they were fiddling with a few dials.

She had only one room left to explore. If Michael didn't return in five minutes, she'd search him out and remind him not-so-subtly of his promise of a lift to the train station. Miss Ruth and Miss Maude would just have to find another repairman. She had dibs.

Quite determined and not a little perturbed, she lifted the latch on the front parlor. Here, Mrs. McKeegan's influence reigned supreme. Braided rugs and spotted dimity curtains. Polished beeswax-scented furniture and copies of *Woman's Weekly* and *Tatler*. More photos of Michael standing in pride of place on the mantel along with school medals and certificates of merit, and calling out to Lucy where it stood gleaming in a patch of bright morning sunlight, the pièce de résistance: a glorious Singer 66.

A smile of delight and then inspiration crept onto Lucy's face. She left and returned with her suitcase, setting it on the sofa and snapping open the clasps. She removed each of Aunt Cynthia's gowns, laying them out to examine them with a designer's eye.

The taffeta's beading would make it difficult to repurpose without more time, while the cream-colored lace was lovely and light but not exactly what she had in mind. The steel-blue satin, while a bit on the severe side, draped beautifully and had plenty of extra material that might be used to add a bit of flair to the neckline, but it was the chiffon that won her heart.

The floral motif of the underskirt gave it a peacock brightness when so much of the world seemed sapped of every color but khaki and the material flowed through her hands like water. She could imagine half a dozen ways in which to make the old dress not only new again, but better than before. Her earlier impatience faded as she sketched possible ideas on a scrap of paper she found in a drawer.

Just five minutes more.

Chapter 13

Would you look at that? It's like an advertisement from out of a *Vogue* magazine, isn't it?"

Struggling with her artistry, Lucy hadn't heard Mrs. McKeegan come in but there she stood, the cherries on her hat wobbling as she took in her front parlor's current disarray.

"I'm so sorry," she said, reddening. "I was waiting for Michael to get back and got a bit distracted."

"I can see that, love."

Mrs. McKeegan took in the deconstructed chiffon. Putting her handbag down on a chair, she circled the gown, fingering the fabric.

Lucy tensed in expectation of a lecture, and she'd had quite enough of those to last a few lifetimes. "It's in my head clear as day, but it's not turning out the way I planned."

Mrs. McKeegan glanced at the hastily penciled design sketch, then studied the results of Lucy's labor for the past half hour. "Did you come up with this all by yourself?"

"That depends. What do you think?"

"I think you've a real eye, that's what. It's a rare few that can look at something and see the possibility. My Michael is the same. Give him a view and it's not five minutes before he's penciling it in with all sorts of pretty little buildings."

"I don't think your son would appreciate being compared to someone of my . . . type."

"You heard that, did you?" She gave a good-natured laugh. "Don't pay him any mind. No girl could ever measure up to Michael's standards. The boy's looking for a cross between Nurse Edith Cavell and Sylvia Pankhurst."

"With a splash of Carole Landis?"

"What's that, love?"

"Just thinking out loud."

"He'll learn soon enough that he can't build the perfect girl from the ground up. It just happens."

"Or doesn't, as the case may be." Exhibit A, the mysterious Arabella.

"Right. Enough about that son of mine," Mrs. McKeegan declared with a bracing snap to her voice as she shed her jacket and hat. "We've work to do."

"We have?"

"Mrs. Forrester and her niece are fabulous at fine work. Miss Mason is a whiz with measuring. And Mrs. Buskin has a dressmaker's dummy left over from when she used to do alterations at the local milliner's shop. I daresay that will come in very handy."

"Handy for what?" Lucy asked in a slightly dazed voice as she wondered where she had lost control of this conversation.

"Sprucing up this dress of yours, of course. Oh, you wait. We'll have it looking smart enough for tea with the queen."

"But all those strawberries . . . you're supposed to be canning today."

"Don't fret yourself, love. The girls and I will have you kitted out long before we're needed at the hall. And just between you, me, and the lamppost, the sewing circle could use a wee bit of a pick-me-up after all the camouflage netting we've been making recently. Useful, but not exactly aesthetically satisfying, is it?"

What followed was a miracle of organizational planning and execution as Mrs. McKeegan gathered her troops and explained the situation. "Now, Lucy dear, tell us what you're thinking of and we'll get to work."

Soon enough, Miss Mason studied Lucy's sketches with a careful eye. Mrs. Forrester and her niece pulled apart seams, marking and saving each piece for use later, while Mrs. Buskin arranged the gown shell on her dressmaker's dummy.

Mrs. McKeegan worked the Singer, and Lucy moved from woman to woman explaining her ideas and listening to suggestions in her turn. Someone switched on the radio. Someone else threw open the front windows to the spring breeze scented with lilac and viburnum. The group worked and talked with equal fervor.

"What do you think if we were to take the hemline here . . ."

"Did you ever try that recipe for Spam casserole that I cut out of the *Woman's Weekly* for you?"

"I've some lovely lace left from my old wedding gown that would be perfect for this bit here by the collar . . ."

"Elaine's mother hasn't left her bed since news came of her brother missing in Borneo. Nasty Japs. Knew we couldn't trust 'em."

"Careful of that ruching at the waistline. You don't want it to bunch up by the hip there . . ."

"I substituted cauliflower for the Spam. My Henry said it tasted like dirt, but I noticed he had three helpings."

"What do you think, ducks? Would it be better up here . . . or down here . . . ?"

"Did you see that new girl they got working at the telephone exchange? Talk about cheap goods."

"Pass me that spool of pink thread, would you, dear?"

Like the men at the sentry post, the women were happiest as they traded gossip about neighbors and friends. Lucy was reminded of the backbiting and innuendo traded over Singapore's tennis courts and dance floors, yet as she listened, she realized this was different from the smug rumors and nasty scandals that were the bread and butter of Malay's expatriates. There was no ugliness or spite in this endless river of chatter. These women cared about their little community; the triumph of Hazel Clapper's new job as a secretary and the tragedy of Norma Askey's boy gone missing over the North Sea were as important as the Russian army's attempts to break through the German lines or the US Army's retreat in the Philippines. The war for the ladies of the Charbury Sewing Circle wasn't being fought on battlefields far away. It was being fought by people they knew. People they loved.

Despite the grim talk and the forced delay, Lucy experienced a bubble of unexpected happiness. She was usually the outsider looking in: new school, new home, new father. Never staying in any one place long enough to make close friends or put down roots. She'd always called it freedom. It had a better ring than "isolation."

Outside, a bicycle bell chirped. All work paused and all eyes focused on the window as the telegram boy passed. Mrs. Buskin watched from the window to see where he stopped. "He's knocking at the Wagstaffs'. Don't they have a son in the air corps?"

"And a daughter working in Birmingham."

The room fell silent but for the ticking of the clock and a static-laced duet on the BBC Forces Programme.

Mrs. McKeegan gripped the Singer's hand crank in her fist, her face white as chalk. "Too many telegrams," she said softly. "Too many of our good boys lost to this fight. And too many left to die."

Old sorrows shuttered her face, but Lucy glimpsed an unexpected oaken strength beneath the double chin and flour-coated apron.

The Wagstaffs' front door opened. The boy passed over his telegram.

The women waited, watching, listening.

A shriek ripped the eerie stillness. "Sam? Sam! It's Davy!"

Lucy's nerves tightened as if they'd been stretched in a winch. The room held its breath.

"Sam? Did ya hear?" came the feminine shouts from across the street. "Our boy's got a week's leave. Davy'll be here tomorrow."

The room exhaled on a sigh. The Singer ticked over slowly, then built up steam. Miss Mason laughed at something Mrs. Forrester said. Her niece hummed around a mouthful of pins. Mrs. Buskin went into the kitchen to put the kettle on. The room settled. The work resumed. Their earlier fear and anxiety were pushed aside by a prattle of village gossip.

Lucy had always assumed independence equaled strength. But these women displayed a different sort of strength, and a courage found only among friends. As she passed by Mrs. McKeegan, Michael's mother reached out and gave Lucy's hand a quick squeeze. Her simple gold wedding band gleamed with a patina of decades, and she smelled of sugar and flour, lavender and soap.

"A shame you've got to run off to London, love. We could use some fresh blood among the ranks. The sewing circle hasn't been so energized since we helped Maude Caskell turn an old parachute into a wedding dress."

"I wish I could, Mrs. McKeegan, but—"

"You look at London and see the possibility. I understand, love. Wasn't I just the same when I was young? Eyes on the horizon and not on what was under my own nose." She winked, and in that moment, Lucy felt included. Like she was one of them.

Like she belonged.

Then Miss Mason leaned close to Lucy, her voice a conspiratorial whisper. "Mrs. McKeegan says you know William Powell."

W hat do you think? I like the way the . . ." She swung around to find Michael, not Mrs. McKeegan, standing in the bedroom doorway. "Oh. It's you."

"Sorry. I didn't realize you were in here. I came up to retrieve my old crystal radio receiver. I thought Bill might like to have a go at it." He sidled past her to the wardrobe, where he knelt and began rummaging through crates and old cardboard boxes. "Wow! I'd forgotten I still had this." He held a wind-up tin car painted bright red and yellow. "And look here. My old building blocks."

"Really?" She did a little twirl, the skirt breezing round her legs. "Is that all you have to say?"

He sat back, his gaze traveling over her refashioned gown. "That's right. Nearly forgot."

She preened, awaiting his comment.

"Car's gassed and ready to go whenever you are."

The first pillow struck him in the back of his thick head. The second caught him square in the face.

He laughed. "You know good and well you look smashing with or without that fancy dress on."

It was her turn to arch a mischievous eyebrow.

"You know what I mean," he grumbled, stuffing his head back into the dusty closet of old toys.

As he resumed his search, she picked up a framed photograph of Michael in a school uniform beside his mother puffed up like a baker's loaf with pride. "You're a lucky man, Corporal McKeegan."

"What do you mean?"

"The few times my mother deigned to show up at my school,

she'd turn the place inside out—all the teachers and staff jumping to do her bidding, wanting to be the one the perfectly perfect Lady Amelia singled out for her regal smile. The girls thought she was some kind of princess. They'd no idea how I envied them their dull, plain, sensible-shoed mothers with their care packages of clean underwear and stale cake." She paused. "Mothers like yours."

"There's a compliment in there somewhere, but damned if I can find it." Michael stood up, a long, dusty wooden box in his hand, the label half-peeled away.

She put down the photograph, running a finger over the glass as if tracing the outline of mother and son beaming proudly into the camera. "Do you know I don't have a single photograph of Amelia and me? We may as well have been complete strangers." She shrugged. "I suppose when it came to what counts, we were."

Before he could answer, she turned her back to him, pulled her hair from her neck. "Would you mind? The zipper sticks." When he hesitated, she sighed. "I'm not going to attack you."

He put the box down on the bed and stepped close behind her. She felt his breath against her skin and smelled the tobacco-and-soap scent of him as he tugged at the hook and eye. The shallow jump of his breathing sparked an answering hitch in her own.

Cool air splashed across her back as Michael slid the zipper down as far as her hips. He paused for a moment, his body absolutely still, his deep voice close against her ear. "Is that a tattoo?"

She could almost hear his jaw snap closed over the word and laughed softly. "What you get when you mix three bottles of brandy with one very bad boy." Holding the front of the gown against her chest, she started to pivot in the circle of his arms, but he released her, his hands dropping to his sides. "Does that shock you?"

His face remained impassive, but his eyes gave away the storm of his thoughts. His pulse leapt at the open collar of his shirt.

"I see." She turned away. "I guess you were wrong, Michael. You don't know my type at all."

The estate wagon was loaded and gassed. Mrs. McKeegan dragged both Bill and Lucy into lavender-scented, bosomy hugs. "Take care of yourselves. Keep your papers and your gas masks close. See that you stay together and send word just as soon as you're safe in London."

"We will. And thank you"—Lucy gripped the suitcase that held her new and improved chiffon—"for absolutely everything."

She was rewarded with a final kiss on the cheek and a maternal gleam that seemed to dance with the promise of orange blossom.

Oh dear.

Lucy hid her chagrin in a last check of her watch as the car sped away.

Michael spotted her frown and quickly defended himself. "Don't blame me. Bill and I have been waiting for over an hour."

"I know. It's completely my fault."

This seemed to confuse him. He glanced over not once but twice with a bewildered expression. "Who are you and what have you done with Lucy Stanhope?"

"Hardy har har."

Lucy didn't know what had come over her in those few lightning-charged moments in his bedroom, but she was relieved any lingering awkwardness between them had dissipated in the flutter of last-minute preparations for departure. Michael was back to his usual genial self and she . . . she was fully clothed. He'd not surprise her into exposing herself like that again.

"Laying aside blame for the moment, you're certain you can still get me to the train station in time, right?"

He gave a wry grunt of what she chose to take for laughter as he shoved in the clutch and changed gears, but they'd only driven a few miles before he pulled to the side of the road and shut off the engine.

"What are we doing?" Lucy cried. "Did we forget something? Don't tell me you need to . . . Why didn't you take care of that before we left?"

Michael's left arm was flung along the back of the seat, his right draped loosely against the wheel. He motioned with a jerk of his chin. "What do you think?"

She followed the track of his gaze to find herself staring at a shabby stone cottage, the whitewash faded and mildewed. Chimneys sprouting weeds squatted at each end of a slate roof slick with moss. Birds flitted in and out from under a small covered porch flanked by wide mullioned windows, one of which was shattered. Smaller upper-story windows looked out on a back garden overgrown with wildflowers that sloped down toward a meadow and the green shore of a pond rimmed in tall grasses.

It was the sketch in Michael's book.

"It's not a big estate or a grand mansion, but it'd be mine."

"A questionable privilege." As they sat there, a mangy cat climbed out of the broken window. "Could you really be happy burying yourself out here where the highlight of the social calendar is watching two men play shove ha'penny in the pub?"

"That's what I thought you'd say."

Bill leaned over the seat and pointed toward a long stone shed with a caved-in roof. "Is that where you'd keep your cow, Michael? I been to Smithfield Market once. There was blood and guts everywhere. And the butcher marched around with a big hammer what smacked 'em right between the eyes."

"Bill!"

Michael laughed and pulled back onto the road. "My cow would be for milk and live a long and happy life up to her waist in meadow grass."

Lucy tried to look at the view and see the possibilities. She imagined herself living in a cottage by a millpond. Chatting with Mrs. Buskin and Miss Mason outside the village shop. Walking her dog on the village green and running into Old Man Yancy, who would bend her ear over the RAF officers billeted at the vicarage and the scandal over Louisa Dunlop's elopement with a conchie of all things. Waving to Miss Jervis, the pretty new schoolteacher, whom all the boys were sweet on.

It wouldn't take two weeks before she was bored out of her mind. Six months and the men with the butterfly nets would have to take her away.

Yet still she found herself glancing back at the little cottage as it fell behind them, watching through the rear window until it was swallowed around a bend in the road.

Michael glanced over. "Penny for your thoughts."

Caught off guard musing over cows and cottages and a life bordered by one's own garden walls, Lucy ventured what she hoped was an expression of cheerful interest, though she'd little experience at such a combination of facial features, and blurted out the first thing that popped into her head. "Your mother said you won a scholarship to university. I'd no idea I was in the company of such an accomplished academic."

Clearly her look of cheerful interest needed practice if Michael's response was anything to go by. He shot her a sardonic smile. "I read and write and even do sums. I'm a veritable savant."

"Don't be sarcastic. It doesn't suit you. What did you study?"

"Do you really want to know?"

"I wouldn't have asked if I didn't. Stop being so defensive, or is it to be name, rank, and serial number the rest of the trip?"

"Suppose I'm still not used to the Lucy Stanhope who cares what I have to say." He dodged a slap that sent them swerving across the narrow road and nearly into a ditch. "Steady on. All right, if you must know I went for architecture, but my father took ill so I left my job in the city to come home and help out."

"Will you go back now that you've been invalided out?"

"Don't know. It really wasn't my cup of tea."

Bill started a loud and very flat version of "Aiken Drum," which almost drowned out the car's ominous rattling chug.

"Funny," Michael continued, "but I spent my entire childhood wanting to escape this place. I was lucky. Got good marks. Was singled out to attend a posh prep school in Hampshire. Then off to university. I had dreams of being the next Edwin Lutyens."

"So what happened? Why give that dream up?"

"I guess somewhere along the way another dream took over."

After a swift assessing glance, he cleared his throat and resumed his scan of the road while she, suddenly self-conscious, focused on Bill—namely fantasizing about stuffing his face with a sausage roll before he could squeeze out one more verse of "Aiken Drum." The boy couldn't hit an F-sharp to save his life.

The car dropped over the crest of a shallow hill and the road fell into green shadow, a lattice of trees above, heavy thickets of fern and rhododendron perfuming the air. Lucy closed her eyes, the filtered flash of sunlight beating against her eyelids. Even blind, she sensed Michael beside her and her skin prickled with something that, were it any other man, she might have called expectation. She'd no time to consider this rather horrible and unnerving idea when a honk of the horn had her sitting up as they passed a line of military trucks. Lucy was reminded of the telegram boy, the women's taut silence, Mrs. McKeegan's quiet rage against the war.

"Must be headed to the army camp near Lufton," Michael suggested.

A young man waved to her out of the back of the last truck, his cap pushed back on a face round and smooth as a child's. Her chest ached with an odd sadness. "Do you ever wonder what might have happened if you hadn't fallen ill, Michael? If you hadn't been discharged?"

"Don't you start fussing at me about my health. I've had enough of that from Dr. Carr."

"Do I look like someone who fusses? I just . . . started thinking . . ."

He didn't answer, but a sadness entered his usually carefree gaze. He reached for a cigarette, fumbling to light it as he drove. He took a long drag, his eyes intent on the road, though she wondered if he was really seeing the bends and turns or if his mind was miles away.

"You'd be dead like the rest of them," she said quietly. "Or imprisoned. Or missing with no way to know what had happened but only a constant questioning that goes nowhere." She looked away across the gentle hills, seeing her own ghosts in the movement of sun and cloud against the green. "I'm very glad you got sick, Michael."

He slid his eyes from the road toward her, and their stares caught and held. They were back in his room, his fingers barely touching the curve of her hip, his breath warm on her cheek. In her imagination, this time when she turned to face him, he did not step away. Her stomach clenched and a strange fluttering started in her chest until Bill shouted, "Oi! Watch the tree!"

Michael jerked his hand hard on the wheel, the estate wagon swerved and steadied, and the moment was lost.

His voice, when it finally came, was—as always—laced with laughter. "Is that a perverse way of saying you might actually like me?"

Shaken at this bewildering ache of reckless desire, Lucy conceded with a grim smile of her own. "Let's just say I don't not like you."

Their eyes met once more, his seeming to scorch a path straight through to her spine. Her skin prickled as if she'd touched a live wire while her stomach lifted and swooped as if she were back on the *Strathleven*.

No. This was all wrong. He was all wrong. She didn't care how relaxed she felt in his company or what crazy notions entered her head when she looked at him, the sooner she nipped these ridiculous feelings in the bud, the better for everyone. Turning away, she choked free words guaranteed to make him despise her. "After all, if you were dead, I'd have no one to give me a lift to London."

"That's a rotten thing to say." He laughed it off as he'd laughed off all her other caustic remarks, but she was ready for him. She knew where to place the knife.

"Did you think it might be something more than that? Don't flatter yourself, Corporal. You're sweet, but I need a man who can do more for me than change a tire."

Bull's-eye. There was no hint of amusement—or warmth—in his gaze now.

Michael maneuvered the car off the road and onto the edge of a long sloping field.

"Sellotape and string, I believe you said?" Lucy chided as the estate wagon sputtered, coughed, and died, steam spewing from under the hood.

Below them, a meandering belt of trees revealed the cut of a creek bed. In the sudden quiet, the trilling squawk of a blackbird sounded from the wood, and there was the far-off chuff of a tractor.

Bill tumbled out, eager to stretch. Michael opened the bonnet, the steam escaping in a great heated cloud. "Damn. I just fixed this yesterday."

"Anything I can do?" Lucy asked.

"Not unless you've got a set of hose clips in that handbag of yours." She lifted her arm and pushed up her sleeve. "And don't bother checking your bloody watch. You'll get there when you get there. I can't do anything until the engine cools." He retrieved a toolbox from the back of the wagon, muttering under his breath the whole time.

If there had been any flutter of mutual attraction, her nasty comment had squashed it flat. No more quiet confidences. Only a stony uncomfortable silence. She should be relieved. Instead, she merely felt disappointed it had taken so little to drive him away.

Perhaps a little fence-mending was in order. She just needed to be sure that once she mended the fence, she made very certain it remained high and wide enough to keep Michael on the far side, where he couldn't hurt her—and she couldn't hurt him. She got out of the car to stretch her legs before leaning against the door. "Architecture wouldn't have been my first guess."

"I'm well aware of your first guess," he answered from under the hood. "You made it clear when we met."

"Sometimes, first impressions can be wrong."

He glanced over, his expression unreadable. "Well, in this case, yours was right. I'm a backwater provincial who'd rather spend an afternoon jawing with the gaffers outside the pub than with a bunch of stuffed shirts at the Savoy Grill."

"Doesn't it get dull?"

"Depends on what you consider dull."

"Doing the same things with the same people in the same place day after day until you're old and gray with nothing to show for your life at the end but a mossy stone in a churchyard."

"When you put it like that, it's no wonder you run from it like the plague. But turn that on its head. Knowing who you are and who you can count on, and knowing no matter how far you travel, you always have a warm hearth waiting. No questions asked. No judgments made."

"You make it sound almost bearable," she said, using flippancy to mask the sudden tightness in her chest.

He finally looked up, his mouth thin, face unusually taut. "Small doesn't mean less, Lucy. Then again, quiet doesn't mean trouble-free. Sorrows find you no matter how you try to escape them. I learned that one the hard way. I imagine you will too."

"Michael—" she started.

"If we're going to make it to the station, I need to concentrate." He burrowed himself back under the hood, effectively dismissing her.

"Of course." While his attitude didn't surprise her, his opinion did. She'd pegged him as a glass-half-full type. So, did this morose outlook have anything to with the hidden photograph and the crumpled letter? Could the choirboy have a dark side?

Was something burning?

Bill knelt beside the car, charring bits of dried grass. A small thin flame caught and flared.

"Is that my lighter?" Lucy asked.

Bill struggled to look innocent and failed miserably. "It was down in the seat of the car, miss. Honest. I didn't know it was yours."

"No, and I'm sure the engraved initials weren't any help at all." She grabbed her handbag and the old car rug from the back of the wagon. "Let's go for a walk."

"All right." Bill rose from his knees, dusting himself off before plunging his hands in his pockets.

"Aren't you forgetting something?"

He grinned, dragging the lighter from his pocket.

She put it back in her handbag and snapped it shut. "You'll end in stir before you're thirteen, Bill Smedley."

"Naw, not me. I'm too slippery for the coppers to be snabbling. Besides, they got bigger fish to fry than a runt like me."

"I bet your boys at the Lion told you that too."

She and Bill set off toward the trees, the grass pulling at their legs and throwing up insects that fluttered and whirred around their heads. The day was warm and still, thick clouds spreading and breaking in a pale sky. Thoughts of war were impossible as sheep grazed a far hill and a kestrel rose and dove above them. Distant as a dream. But if she woke from such a dream, would she be back in Singapore staring down another endless empty day? The idea was enough to clench at her chest, and she nearly caught herself thanking the fates for their deadly intervention.

"Look, Lucy. A fox." Bill ran ahead, disappearing into the thick underbrush, but was soon back with muddy shoes. "Come see. There's a stream up ahead and a little clearing with flowers."

The war had turned her life inside out, but it had dropped her here, at this spot, at this hour, with Bill. She couldn't count it as all bad. "Show me."

Together, they picked a path through the tangled thicket of briars to reach the earthen rooty bank. Bill was right. Yellow kingcup bordered a stream that meandered sluggishly, eddying around the dying branches of a fallen beech tree, before creeping in a muddy froth southward, taking with it twigs, leaves, and the occasional paper wrapper and old bottle. "Here, grab me that dead limb there."

"Whatcha gonna do with that, Lucy?"

She reached out with the limb, dragging the bottle in to her at the shore before taking pencil and paper from her handbag. "'To whomever finds this note: we are trapped on a desert isle. We're living on bananas and coconuts . . .'"

"And bugs . . . put in bugs."

"Right. 'Please rescue us.'"

She rolled the paper and stuffed it down into the neck of the bottle.

"Now what, miss?"

"Now we throw it back in the water. It follows the stream out to sea and someone somewhere far away finds it and reads it."

"That's all?"

"What did you think was going to happen?"

"I don't know, but seems mighty tame, don't you think? We won't even be around when it's read."

"That's not the point."

"Then what is the point?"

"I don't know really." She spread out the rug. The ground beneath was soft with moss and fern, and she lay back to stare up into the thick-laced canopy of branches. "It's something I did when I was a child."

Bill sat cross-legged beside her. "Did anyone ever come to your rescue?"

"No." Her one word, a weight she couldn't rid herself of despite a lifetime of frivolity.

His hand stole into hers. "I'd have rescued you, miss."

The sun slanted through the leaves, warming her face. A maiden fly hovered above the surface of the stream. Bill found a bit of string in his pocket and dangled it over the water, hoping to catch a trout.

Lucy closed her eyes despite her best intentions. She knew she shouldn't. She should be marching straight back to the car and standing over Michael to hurry him along, but a restless uncomfortable night followed by restless uncomfortable feelings kept her where she was. She leaned back, her head propped on her arm, and let the chuckle of water and the hum of bees carry her away.

"I wish my mam could see this place." Bill's murmured hopes roused Lucy from her half doze. She glanced up through heavy lids to see him lying on his stomach at the stream's edge, staring out over the water, head in his hand, string forgotten. "In the summer when it's too hot to sleep and it feels like the whole of the city is pressing in on you, we pack a thermos of tea and go sit out on the grass in Vicky Park. I dig my bare toes into the dirt where it's cool and she tells me stories she makes up right out of her head." He swatted at a fly. "She says the park is pretty enough in the daytime but she likes it better at night. She says the dark is better for pretending. It's easier to see the pictures in your head that way."

"Your mother's right."

A fish jumped, followed by a rattle of pebbles as Bill lunged for it. "What do you do with your mam, Lucy?"

"Nothing if we can help it."

Once more she felt that odd drowsy contentment, her limbs sluggish, muscles loose, lungs filling slowly and deeply as her mind slipped from thought to thought like the insects from flower to flower. In that moment between wakefulness and sleep, an image surfaced, delicate as the wild columbine growing along the stream bank. A bright memory buried under a lifetime of slights and disillusionment. "She took me to a fair once."

As she spoke, the memory at first hazy with the dust of time took light like a match had been set to it. "I couldn't have been more than five. Father was away on business. Amelia was bored.

She was always bored when my father was out of town, and he was always out of town. She burst into the nursery like a whirlwind and whisked me away with her. I still remember Nanny's face, like she'd been struck by lightning." Lucy caught back a swift breath, her pulse drumming so loud in her ears, she no longer heard the spill of water or the trees' leafy whisper. "It was nothing fancy, a few colorful tents along a tiny midway, but she held my hand as we strolled among the stalls. We shared peanuts from a cone of newspaper." She swallowed, but her mouth was dry, the words like ash against her tongue. "There was a minstrel show. I remember sitting in the dark and watching her laugh at the juggler and the magician. Even in the smoky stage light, she shone like a diamond . . . or an angel. At the end after the applause, she turned to me, and . . ." Tears burned Lucy's eyes and swam on her lashes. Her voice dropped to a whisper as if she were fearful the spell might be broken and the images disappear like popped soap bubbles. "She told me it had been the most perfect day she'd ever had."

"It sounds grand."

The deep baritone voice sent Lucy's heart stuttering into her throat before it dropped like lead into her shoes, leaving her dizzy and a little sick.

Not Bill.

Michael.

She rolled up onto her knees, ignoring the dirt and the bits of grass in her hair. She faced him, her face hot, her jaw locked against her humiliated anger.

"How long have you been standing there?" she demanded.

He twirled a stem of grass between his fingers. Troubled sympathy swam behind his clear blue gaze, and she waited for the hollow platitudes.

"It took some doing, but I got the car up and running." He tossed away the grass and shoved his hands in his pockets. "We should get a move on. No telling how long she'll last."

She began to realize he wasn't going to fill her ears with well-meaning if clichéd inanities. That she might be able to scrape together the remnants of her dignity. Relief flooded her, and she hurriedly rose to gather up the rug. "Where's Bill?"

"I thought he was with you."

"He was. He must have wandered off."

She picked her way down the riverbank, where she found Bill's piece of string crushed into a small muddy boot print at the water's edge.

"Bill?" she called.

There was no answer but the spill of water over a half dam of rocks.

"Certain he didn't do another bunk?" Michael had followed her and now stood watching from the top of the bank.

"He wouldn't just leave me."

"People leave all the time."

An air kiss. A careless wave. A car's taillights receding into the darkness as a strong hand gripped her shoulder when all she wanted to do was chase after. One perfect afternoon hadn't been enough to make her stay. "People might, but Bill wouldn't. He needs me to look after him."

Michael seemed to consider her, his features unnaturally serious, his gaze almost quizzical. "I'm beginning to wonder who's really looking after whom."

Chapter 14

Michael and Lucy split up to search. Not only could they cover more ground that way, but it gave her time to pull herself together.

Still a bit wobbly-kneed, she headed upriver along a footpath. Trees dipped their leaf-heavy branches into the swirling water, the air pungent with the sharp scents of mud and dead leaves. A startled fox dashed across the trail. They both froze, eyes locked in a mutual moment of surprise, before the fox plunged back into the woods.

That's when Lucy heard Bill.

Following his laughter, she rounded the bend to find him sitting cross-legged in a place where the creek widened and slowed to a pool. A young man sat with him, an unheeded fishing pole clamped between two large rocks, its line limp, bobber motionless.

Bill had a cigarette between his lips and a pair of dice in his hands, which he tossed onto a piece of brown paper that looked as if it had once held someone's sandwich. A small pile of pennies lay in a pile in the middle of the paper.

"Seven out," he crowed. "I win."

The man groaned good-naturedly as Bill raked in the coins.

"There you are!" Lucy scolded. "Should have known you'd be waist deep in trouble." She eyed his trousers. "And mud, by the looks of it."

The man scrambled to his feet as he dragged his cap from his head.

"Hiya, Lucy," Bill shouted. "Look who I met."

She bent to snatch the cigarette from Bill's mouth and ground it beneath her heel. "Michael and I have been looking everywhere for you."

"I've been right here with Enzo the whole time."

The man offered her a small continental bow. His large hands were at odds with his bony wrists and the scrawny set of his shoulders, and his thick black hair brushed his coat collar.

"He works at the mill and lives at Barwick House camp." Bill paused before adding in a stage whisper, "He's an Eyetie."

"Thank you for pointing out the obvious. What's he doing here?"

"Playing craps. Enzo was winning, but then I bested him for ten pence and four fags."

"The boy is a very skillful player." The man's accent was thick enough to cut with a knife.

"Skillful, yes," Lucy replied. "Trustworthy is still up for debate."

"Allow me to introduce myself. I am Sergente Enzo Raneri."

His manners were impeccable. No self-consciousness or discomfort. She might have been meeting him at a house party in Florence or a soiree in Rome. She'd known prisoners of war in England were allowed a certain amount of freedom. They were put to work on neighboring farms or anywhere a strong back and willing hands were needed. But she'd never come across any face-to-face. And certainly not handsome charmers with the grace and airs of a Medici prince.

He nodded toward a fishing pole and a basket lying in the

grass. "I was given leave to fish this afternoon. But the only thing I am catching today is Guglielmo here, who took a tumble into the water."

"There was a frog, Lucy."

"Of course there was."

"I meant the boy no harm. I am sorry if I worry you."

"I should be the one apologizing. If I hadn't come along, Bill might have emptied your pockets of everything, including the lint."

"You are not from the village," Raneri suggested.

"How do you know that?"

"I have been at the camp long enough to know most of the villagers, and I would remember having seen someone as enchantingly beautiful as you." He smiled, a dimple winking at the edge of his mouth.

"You're Italian, all right." Even scruffy and malnourished, the man could probably *piacere di conoscerti* the clothes right off a woman.

Bill started to gather up his ill-gotten gains. Catching Lucy's sharp eye on him, he sheepishly handed them to Raneri.

"Is that all?" Lucy chided with a lift of a brow.

Bill offered another two pennies.

"I should not," Raneri objected. "The boy won fair and square, as you would say."

"I doubt that. Bill's not exactly a model of British sportsmanship."

Raneri smiled and pocketed the returned loot. "Then I very much thank you. I would hate to admit I was swindled by a child."

"You wouldn't be the first, though hopefully the last"—she speared Bill with a hard stare—"if I have any say in the matter."

Bill had the grace to blush, but only for a moment before he recovered with a shake like a duck sluicing water off its back. "I told

Enzo about me mam, Lucy. About the bombs and . . . well . . . she'll be all right, won't she? You said she would, but . . ."

"Of course she's all right." She and Sergeant Raneri exchanged a long measuring look.

He knelt beside Bill with an arm around his shoulder. "I too am missing my mother, young Guglielmo. She remains in Campione del Garda—that is the village where I am from—and it is difficult for news to reach me here at the camp. But every morning as I lay in my bed, I am very still and I reach out with"—he tapped his temple—"you see? I seek to touch her spirit and open myself so that she might touch mine. In that way, we know we have survived another day and are closer to being together again. You try this. Close your eyes and reach out."

Bill shot Raneri a sideways skeptical look.

"Do it. Tell me what you hear and what you feel."

Bill sighed and did as he was told. "I hear the birds and the stream and you breathing. You whistle through your nose."

Raneri chuckled. "You have smart ears, but do you not hear your mother's voice, her song?"

Bill nodded once slowly before his eyes sprang open, a suspicious shine shimmering at the corners. "I did hear her. It was 'Billy Boy.' That's her favorite."

Raneri offered Bill a comforting pat on the back. "There, you see? She is safe. You would know if she were not. You would not hear her voice, you would hear only a great rushing wind, a hollow place."

"You try it, Lucy," Bill said. "See if you can hear your mother. You said you didn't know where she was. Maybe you can ask her."

An icy chill slithered up her spine to curl cold around her shoulders. "We don't have time."

"Go on," Bill urged. "Try."

"Stop it. Please, just stop." Lucy's breath came in a hot painful rush, her earlier emotions scraped raw and bleeding. "Do you hear me? I don't want to close my eyes or hear my mother. All I want is for you to quit your damned chattering. Now, are you coming with me, or am I leaving you behind?"

Raneri watched her carefully, compassion in his sloe-dark eyes.

Bill's chin wobbled. Perfect. She might as well pluck the wings from a butterfly and kick a puppy while she was at it. Her anger drained away, leaving her achy, temples throbbing. Her cheeks burned hot and tight. "I'm sorry, Bill. I didn't mean it. I don't know what came over me."

"It's all right. My mam scolds too," he answered bravely, though his gaze shone overbright. "She says, 'Bill, you could test the patience of a saint with your palavering.'"

Lucy gave a small pained laugh. "I'm no saint and you can palaver all you want."

There's Michael," Bill shouted, leaping through the grass like a gazelle.

The estate wagon sat where they'd left it on the verge with its hood up and Michael bent once more over the engine.

He straightened, wiping his hands on a greasy rag, his lopsided smile dispersing the lingering tightness in Lucy's chest. Had he always looked so ruggedly capable, or was there just something about men working on cars that screamed raw masculinity?

"The lost sheep finally found their way home." His gaze flicked questioningly toward Raneri and back to her, his smile fading. "Everything all right, lass?"

"This is Enzo." Bill tugged him forward. "He lives at the POW camp."

"Good afternoon, signor," Raneri said politely. "You must be

Guglielmo's father and this beautiful woman's husband. You are very fortunate."

"That wouldn't be the first adjective that sprang to mind," Michael countered. "But no, we're not married."

Raneri took in the open toolbox and the open hood. "You are having automobile problems?"

"Afraid so." Michael shot Lucy a pained look. "I managed to repair the clip, but now the hose itself has burst. There's a village a mile or two back. You can probably catch a bus there to take you on to Yeovil."

"What about you?"

"I'll stay here and work on the car. I wouldn't want you to miss your chance for a perfect life."

She flushed with anger, but before she could put sharp words to her hurt, Raneri rescued her with a low whistle of approval. "My father had an automobile like this one." He gazed at the battered Ford with a nostalgic shake of his head. "As temperamental as a woman but loyal as a dog. That is what he would say. May I look?"

Michael stood back with a wave of his hand. "Help yourself. I've about had it with the old banger."

Looking a touch wistful, Raneri put down his basket and pole and leaned over the engine.

"Can I see too?" Bill anxiously hopped from foot to foot as he sought to crane his neck above the two men. "I want to see."

Michael hoisted Bill onto the bumper to join them. "Right there. That's the problem."

What was it about engines that invited such manly camaraderie? The three of them were like kids in an oily, metallic candy store. Lucy tried to imagine any of the men of her previous acquaintance up to their elbows in motor oil and enjoying it. Impossible. The closest she could come was an old boyfriend of Amelia's who'd been a grand prix driver. She'd been sixteen and spending the summer with her mother in Monaco. He'd been French and fast. His car *and* his hands.

When she clocked him with a tire iron, Amelia decided to send her back to school early. It had been one of the few times Lucy hadn't complained about going.

"I never seen inside an engine before." Bill reached out with a hand. "What are all those wires and things there?"

"That's called a ring gear," Raneri replied. "It can catch little fingers if you are not careful."

"Grab me a pair of pliers from the toolbox," Michael instructed.

Bill hastened to follow orders; his light enthusiastic chirp was a melody to the mellow baritones of Raneri and Michael as they bonded over gearboxes and drum brakes.

Soon, talk of clutch release bearings and gudgeon pins became just talk.

"Enzo fought in Africa," Bill volunteered eagerly. "Did you fight in Africa, Michael?"

"No, I missed that particular fun."

"Just think, if you'd been in Africa with Enzo, you might have had to shoot him or he might have had to shoot you and then you'd both be dead. I'd be sorry if you were dead."

"Not half as sorry as we would be. That's right. Connect it there."

"Ever wonder what it'd be like if there weren't any war? I did all the time when I was with the Sayres. I'd be home with me mam right now. What about you, Enzo?"

"Ah, I would be working in my family's cotton mill with the beautiful Sophia Maria by my side and many plump happy children. There would be food and singing and wine and the stars would scrape the tops of the mountains and glitter across the lake like diamonds."

"Crikey, that sounds nice. What about you, Michael?"

"If there'd been no war?" He never looked up from his work. "Let's see. I'd be running my Dad's garage, doing errands for my mum, and playing darts with the lads at the pub."

"But that's what you do now," Bill said.

"Exactly. Hand me that clip, would you?"

"When I am back home in Italy, the first thing I plan to do is ask my Sophia Maria to marry me. Will you two . . ." Enzo nodded toward Lucy with a sly smile.

"Me and Miss Stanhope? You must be joking."

He didn't have to sound quite so shocked at the suggestion.

"She's on the hunt for a toff with a fat wallet who'll keep her in the style to which she's become accustomed. That leaves me out of the running."

"As if you ever wanted to be in the race," she shot back, shading her tired eyes against the sun.

"I don't know," he replied with a cynical smile somehow only improved by a smear of grease on his cheek. "I've always liked a challenge."

"Arabella might not be pleased to hear you say that."

His smile froze, his body completely still but for a jumping tightness in his jaw.

Lucy swallowed around a mouth suddenly gone dry. Why on earth had she blurted out mention of Arabella? It must be this blasted headache, making her feel muzzy and thick. She waited for the explosion, but after the initial shock, he seemed to collect himself. He drew in a long breath and tossed her the keys. "Give her a go."

Oddly let down, she slid behind the wheel to crank the starter. It sputtered, coughed, groaned, and died with a belch of black smoke.

"Again."

This time, the engine caught with a roar and the car shuddered to life.

"Woo hoo!" Bill danced around the front of the car like a wild man. "We did it."

Michael and Raneri exchanged smug looks of success as they slammed the hood closed.

"She is not so temperamental as she appears." For a moment, Raneri's eyes met hers. "Nothing that a little care and attention would not fix." Was it her imagination, or did he just wink? There was a new liveliness in his thin face, an energy that lasted as he gathered his gear. "I must say good-bye now. It is late, and the guards will begin to question my absence."

"Thanks for your help." Michael shook his hand.

"It is for me to be thanking you. For a few moments, I was back home and working on my father's . . . how you say it . . . old banger, and the war was forgotten." Raneri squatted in front of Bill with a hand on his shoulder. "Good luck in your travels, Guglielmo. I hope you and your mother will be together very soon."

"I'll do just what you said, Enzo. Maybe I'll listen for you too."

"I would like that." He straightened and turned to Lucy with another of those small continental bows that gave him an air of authority despite his incarceration. "I hope you find who it is you are looking for too, signorina."

"I'm not looking for anyone."

His dark eyes seemed to bore right through her until she squirmed under his examination. "Are you not? She is there. Locked away. You have only to listen to hear her voice."

"My mother?" she whispered.

"Yourself."

It took a few miles before Lucy recovered from Raneri's rather odd parting remark. The man was Italian but no Gypsy fortune-teller. Then again, he'd told Bill to listen to his heart for the song of his mother. He might not know better than to fall for such soul-searching, sentimental claptrap, but she certainly did. The only person she looked for was a gentleman wearing a tuxedo and a Pepsodent smile.

"Well?" Michael broke into her thoughts with a voice ominously mild. "Care to explain yourself?"

"Explain what?"

"You know perfectly well what." A flash of irritation hardened his expression. "That was a private letter."

She should apologize for prying—she really should—but knowing she was in the wrong only made her want to defend herself more. "I didn't mean to read it. I was searching your bear's nest of a desk for a lighter, and as I was moving things around I sort of came across it accidentally."

"And sort of read it accidentally?"

"You can't blame me for wanting to find out what I can about the almost complete stranger to whom I've entrusted myself and a young, impressionable boy. You might have been a crazed maniac for all I knew."

"Do you generally ring up potential crazed maniacs?"

"Yes, well, you were readily available. Standards tend to slip when one's desperate."

She risked a glance from under lowered lashes. A pulse beat under his jaw, his eyes stabbing the road like daggers, but in no other way did he give vent to any emotion greater than slight exasperation. It was like battling a feather pillow. Every blow he turned aside, causing her to hit harder. What would it take to get that iron control to shatter? To see what lay behind his always-even temper? No one was that content. Everyone had something to hide.

"I was merely trying to understand what made you tick. You're a puzzle, and I've always been mad over puzzles."

"I always thought I was pretty straightforward. I treat others with respect. I expect them"—he swept her a pointed glare—"to do the same."

"Well, there's your first mistake."

His hands white-knuckled the wheel. "I'm so glad you find the situation amusing, but steer clear. Arabella is none of your business."

Finally. She'd landed a solid hit. Anger blazed up within his untroubled blue gaze, his voice a harsh growl. She should claim the win, shake hands, and retreat while retreating was still an option. Then he made the error of adding, "Besides, what would a spoiled little rich girl like you know about it anyway?"

That did it. She'd a lifetime of being summarily dismissed and uncounted. She was not about to let Michael starch-in-his-shorts McKeegan push her away like an afterthought. "If by 'it' you mean having someone stomp all over my heart, then the answer would be plenty. The poor girl just wants to talk. Where's the harm in a conversation?"

Michael gave an ugly little laugh that somehow seemed all the uglier coming from him, his eyes alive with some dark emotion. "I've asked myself that question a thousand times since Singapore."

Lucy frowned but otherwise chose to ignore his dig. "If you love her, you should fight for her."

"You've seen too many movies. Not every romance has a happy ending."

"That doesn't mean they shouldn't."

"Lucy?" Bill said quietly from the rear seat.

Michael drowned him out. "Why don't you figure out your own life before you start arranging mine?"

"I have."

"That's right. I forgot. You think you're the next Bette Davis."

"Sorry for having aspirations beyond pumping petrol."

"You have aspirations, all right." Michael clenched his jaw so tightly it was a wonder his teeth didn't grind down to nubs. Maybe peeking beneath that placid exterior hadn't been her smartest idea. "You think you can hide out in sunny California and attend your swanky parties as if the world tearing itself apart is just some big inconvenience to be endured."

"That's a horrible thing to say."

"Lucy?" Bill said in a quavery voice. "I don't feel so good."

"Can you tell me I'm wrong? I saw you in Singapore. You behaved as if the war were a Saturday matinee put on for your amusement, and the soldiers bit actors barely worth your time. It's real, Lucy. Good men are dying. Cities are being destroyed. Just two years ago, everyone around you went to bed at night not knowing whether our little part of the world would still be ours when we woke. But what would you know of that? What would you know of anything more serious than the strength of your next cocktail?"

So much for feather pillows. His words struck her like a slap to the face. She'd poked the sleeping bear once too often. And he'd made her pay dearly.

Shame heated her cheeks. Perhaps once his words might have been true—all right, they were all too damningly true—but not now. She clamped her hands in her lap to keep herself from slugging the bastard. "If you'll remember, I was on the *Strathleven* when it was torpedoed. A woman died in my arms. Amelia . . ." She turned away, throat burning.

"What about Amelia?"

"Nothing. Forget it. Forget this whole horrid conversation."

"I'd love to." He gave a disgusted snort, eyes pinned to the road, anger thrumming in the space between them.

"Lucy, I need to stop," Bill said more loudly.

"What's wrong?" She turned to look into the rear seat, where Bill was curled in a ball.

"I'm gonna be sick." He clutched his stomach.

"Pull over, Michael."

He drove onto the grass and cut the engine. Lucy opened the door and helped Bill out. She felt his forehead. It was cool to the touch but clammy, and his face was a sickly green. "What did you eat?"

"Nothing."

She lifted a brow.

"Well, there was these . . . these uh . . . mushrooms. I found 'em by the side of the stream."

"Are you out of your mind?" She bundled him back into the wagon. "Get us to a doctor as quickly as you can, Michael. Bill's gone and poisoned himself."

Chapter 15

The doctor's office was in his home, a great brick behemoth just a few streets off West Hendford in Yeovil with a shiny brass plate by the front door. Michael carried Bill up the porch stairs swaddled in the car rug, Lucy a step behind. "Careful with him. You're joggling him. Watch the door there. You're joggling him again."

"You try holding him. He's heavier than he looks. Five stone, easy."

What had once been the house's double parlor had been transformed into a small waiting area with an exam room behind. A few bored-looking patients sat in a row of wooden chairs while an elderly woman worked at a desk by the door. She looked up, her horn-rimmed spectacles taped at the bridge slipping down her nose. "What's this, then?"

"An emergency," Lucy said, trying to keep the panic from her voice. "Where's the doctor? Michael, stop for God's sake, you're joggling him."

"Please, miss," the secretary scolded. "If you would just settle down."

"How can I settle down when he could be dead within minutes and you're just sitting there doing nothing?"

The patients stirred in their seats, looking much less bored. Bill's arm fell from the blanket swaddling him to dangle uselessly.

"Oh my God!" Lucy cried. "He's dead."

"He's not dead," Michael responded patiently. "He's alive and looks as if he plans to stay that way."

"Are you the boy's mother?" the secretary asked, clearly disapproving of this chaotic intrusion into her well-ordered office.

"No, I'm not his mother," Lucy snapped. "I'd have had to be nine years old when I had him, wouldn't I?"

"She's just clarifying matters, Lucy," Michael soothed. "Take a deep breath and relax."

"Don't tell me to relax. This is all your fault."

"How do you figure that?"

"He'd not have had a chance to eat those mushrooms if your car hadn't broken down."

"Well, you're the one who let him wander off."

"I didn't *let* him wander, thank you very much."

"My belly hurts, Lucy," Bill sobbed.

"I know, Bill." She threw Michael a final glare as she smoothed the hair back from Bill's forehead. His cheeks were flushed, and he shivered as if he was cold. "We're going to get you fixed up quick as a wink." She turned her attention to the secretary. "Where's the doctor? Why isn't he here already?"

The secretary drew herself up in agitated dignity. "Dr. Ellison is just across the hall finishing his tea. Bring the boy back to the surgery, and I'll send the doctor through to you."

Michael carried Bill through to a spotless room equipped with a cot, a long glass-fronted cabinet stocked with medical supplies, and a shelf of dusty medical books. The lino floor had been softened by the addition of a small rug, and there were framed watercolors of noble stags on craggy mountaintops and rugged-looking men in beards and kilts hanging on the wall. Insipid and amateurish, but supposedly there to take one's mind off the worst.

It didn't work. The worst was all she could think about.

Michael laid Bill on the cot still bundled in the old blanket. His lashes fluttered now and again but his eyes never opened.

"Is he breathing?" she asked.

"Yes, he's breathing."

"His skin is flushed. Does his skin look flushed to you?"

"Not particularly."

"What's all this, then?" Dr. Ellison was a whippet-thin white-haired man in a suit dusted with crumbs. He paused sharp eyed in front of Michael. "Miss Pursley says we have a very sick boy in here."

"Not him," Lucy griped. "Him." She pointed to Bill, who rolled over, face to the wall, his arm curled over his head.

"Don't feel good," he mumbled.

"He's eaten some mushrooms," Lucy explained. "He's barely breathing and his skin has gone splotchy and red and he's complaining of a stomachache."

The doctor cocked a last surmising stare at Michael before settling his glasses on his nose and turning his attention to Bill. "Let's have a look, young man. Tell us where it hurts."

"It hurts real bad right"—Bill twisted around suddenly, his small body spasming as vomit splashed onto the doctor's coat and down one sleeve—"here," he ended weakly.

The doctor never flinched, just wiped himself off with an enormous handkerchief he pulled from his pocket. "Yes, I begin to see the problem."

"Lucy?" Bill's voice was weak and shaky. "Are you and Michael mates again?"

"Of course."

The doctor studied Bill's skin, his eyes, palpated his stomach. "Did you see him eat these mushrooms?"

"If I'd seen him, I'd have stopped him," Lucy replied. "I'm not completely daft."

"Will he be all right, sir?" Michael cut in politely before Lucy could say anything more.

"Why don't you two wait out in the parlor while I complete my exam?"

"I can't leave Bill," Lucy said. "He needs me."

Dr. Ellison drew himself up. "He needs some peace and quiet. I'll come find you as soon as I know what's what." He ushered them out and closed the door firmly behind them.

By now, almost every wooden chair in the waiting room was full. Miss Pursley was trying to simultaneously soothe a crying child, calm an agitated mother, and broker a peace between octogenarians debating the merits of cricket over football. By the harassed look in her eye and the shrill tone to her voice, she was losing the battle for order on all fronts.

Lucy and Michael took the last two remaining seats, he beside a pretty young mother with a little girl of about three on her lap, and she next to an old man smelling of peppermint and mothballs with a cough straight out of a tubercular ward.

"That doctor didn't look like he knew one end of a stethoscope from the other," Lucy grumbled. "And did you see how thick his glasses were? Probably blind as a mole. No wonder he mistook you for the patient."

"Is that your doll? It's a lovely doll." Michael turned to Lucy. "I'm sure Dr. Ellison is more than qualified."

"If Bill dies, it's all my fault."

"It's no one's fault. It was a stupid accident, that's all." He smiled at the little girl. "Her name is Nettie? I had an old auntie whose name was Netitia, but we called her Aunt Nettie."

Lucy punched him in the arm. "Are you even listening to me? Oh God, I would kill for a gin and soda right now." Catching herself, she waited for Michael's I-told-you-so, but he was busy sweet-talking the child. Thank God. If he wanted to scold her about her bad habits, he needed to stand at the end of a very long queue. She reached into her handbag for a Sobranie, but the pack was empty. She snapped the bag closed with a sigh and an oath before dropping her head in her hands in complete surrender. "What am I going to do?"

"There's a newsagent's down the street. You could buy a pack there."

"I'm talking about Bill. I didn't mean for him to get hurt."

The little girl giggled at something Michael said. "You got her for your birthday? Many happy returns of the day. Lucy, you did what you thought was right."

"Did I?" She pushed herself to her feet.

"Where are you going? Wait, listen . . ." By now, the little girl had oozed her way onto Michael's lap and her pretty mother was looking at him as if he'd hung the moon. "I should have told you, but . . . well . . . you're going to think it's funny . . . I know I do . . ." The little girl's chubby arms flung themselves around his neck and latched on in a python hold. The pretty mother looked as if she wanted to do the same.

How the hell did he do it? How did he manage to charm his way into people's affections until they all but flung themselves at him in needless adoration? He was one of those irritating individuals who skated through life untouched, comfortable in his own skin and thus able to make others comfortable as well. People like that made her sick.

She'd never had that facility for friendship. Instead, she hung on the fringes of others' relationships, not quite able to break through, not quite sure she wanted to. Laying oneself bare came with risks. Safety was found behind walls; one couldn't be hurt if one couldn't be touched.

Still, she felt a pang of something nearly like jealousy when she watched Michael's easy savoir faire.

By now, the young woman was well into some sob story that had Michael nodding his head in sympathy. He broke off to wave her over once more. "Lucy—wait."

"Be right back," she replied, hurrying away before jealousy at his easiness with people became jealousy of a different and far more personal sort.

A telephone sat on a stand beside a large draping fern. A directory was tucked in a drawer beside a pencil and a pad of paper. Should she? Would it make any difference?

Lucy's stomach fluttered as the call was put through by the operator, but she fought it back until her breathing was even and her hands were steady as they gripped the receiver.

There was a click at the other end of the line. "Nanreath Hall. This is Lady Boxley speaking."

As if Lucy needed to be told. She'd recognize that stiff disappointed tone anywhere.

"Aunt Cynthia?"

"Good heavens, child. Where are you?"

"I'm somewhere in Somerset."

"Somerset? Do you know how—"

"Stop! What are you doing?" A hand smashed down on the phone, cutting the connection.

Lucy swung around to confront four and a half feet of quivering child.

"Bill?" His hair stuck up at odd angles, strands of it plastered to his damp forehead, and his shirt was buttoned up wrong so that one side hung low on his narrow hips. He was an absolute mess. She wanted to kiss him.

"He made it up." Michael's blue eyes danced with silent laughter. "That's what I was trying to tell you."

"I don't understand," she said, replacing the receiver in its cradle. The fluttering in her stomach had become a knotted weight quickly sinking into her toes.

"He wasn't poisoned by any mushrooms."

"But he threw up. He was flushed and his hands were clammy."

"He held his breath, licked his palms, then stuck his finger down his throat," Michael explained. "The boy's a con artist of the first degree."

She stared at Bill. "Why on earth would you pretend to be sick?"

He stuck out his chin, his face screwed into an expression of defiant bravado. "You and Michael were fighting, and I thought if you were worried about me, you'd stop yelling at each other. Wasn't that a dashed clever rig?"

The pair of them awaited her answer with identical expressions of sad-eyed contrition. She could have sworn Bill braced himself. Michael definitely possessed a slight nervous twitch. She tried summoning a white-hot rage that would leave both of them wishing they'd never been born. It should have been easy. She should be furious at them for wasting her time and making her look like a fool. Yet, what boiled up through her was laughter. Catching her breath against a further attack of the giggles, she shook her head. "Now I know how the Artful Dodger's mother must have felt."

Miss Pursley shut the door on them with something akin to relief.

"You're really not angry, Lucy?" Bill asked, still looking a bit shamefaced. "I wasn't meaning to frighten you."

"No, I'm not angry. Not even a little bit. I'm too happy that you're all right."

"Are we still going to London?"

"Why? Have you changed your mind?"

"No. I was worrit you might have."

She gave him a reassuring smile. "Not a chance." She dug into her purse. "Now, here's a shilling. Run up the street to the newsagent's and fetch me a pack of cigarettes."

A picture of blooming health, he snatched the coin and dashed off, only pausing to press his nose and dirty hands against a five-and-dime store window.

"And I expect change back."

Her smile drained away as she leaned against the porch railing, checking her face and hair in her compact mirror, touching up her lipstick. She felt Michael's eyes upon her; he was almost as shamefaced as Bill had been. "How did you know he was faking it?" she asked.

"I guessed. He's good, but I was a boy once. I know all the tricks." He paused. "Will your aunt come looking for you?"

She gave a grim little laugh. "The oh-so-dutiful Lady Boxley is too busy running the estate and everyone on it to spare a bother for one wayward niece. Maybe I'll drop her a postcard when I reach Hollywood. She can say she knew me when."

"Look." He scrubbed a hand over his face. "I'm sorry for losing my temper. I didn't mean what I said back there . . . about you not caring."

"Didn't you? I've found that the truest words are born in anger or alcohol." Satisfied she was, if not impeccable, at least presentable, Lucy snapped her handbag shut and checked her watch—half three. God, it seemed years since she'd been startled awake in the old grain shed on Mr. Ennis's farm. If she was lucky, they'd bypassed the damaged tracks and from here on out, the trains would be running on schedule. But she and luck hadn't been particularly cozy the last few days. It was more likely she'd be hoofing it all the way to Trafalgar Square. "While we're exchanging mea culpas I will concede that maybe—just maybe, mind you—I might have been wrong to read your letter."

"Might have been?"

"I don't see why you're making such a big to-do over the teen-siest of indiscretions. You'd think I'd absconded with government secrets or something." A provocative smile played over her mouth as she shoved off the porch rail and came down the two steps to the sidewalk. "Unless 'Arabella' is the code name for a German spy and her invitation to London is really a cover for your nefarious doings."

He closed his eyes as if asking for patience. "Can we forget Arabella?"

"Of course," she replied sweetly. "She's none of my business."

"No, she's not."

"I couldn't care less if you spend the rest of your life miserable and alone."

"That's a bit harsh."

"Bent and wrinkly with a cane and an ear trumpet and all the while pondering what if—what if I had listened to Lucy? What if I made that trip to the city all those decades ago? How different my life might have turned out."

"I'll take my chances." The slightest hint of a smile broke through his somber gaze. "What about you? What if you get to Hollywood and find out it's not all bright lights and big parties? What if Mr. Oliver turns out not to be the key to your happiness? Will you keep running? Or will you finally trust someone enough to take a chance?"

Lucy felt suddenly awkward. Unsure of how to behave, what to say, who she was. A sensation she'd only ever experienced while in Amelia's presence. She'd hated it then. She didn't understand it now.

Before she had to answer, he took her hand. "Come on," he said with a fond if exasperated look on his face. "If you're ever going to make your train, we'd best find Bill before he uses that shilling to buy himself a tin of snuff."

Hoping to return to familiar ground, she answered with a beguiling half smile and a toss of her head. "Dipping tobacco? He'd better not. A gasper now and again is one thing, but I do have standards."

Sorry, luv. Not a single seat to be had. Damaged rails. Overcrowded troop trains. Maybe the six fifty-three this evening. Next, please."

Yeovil.

Marston Magna.

Sparkford.

Castle Cary.

It was the same tired answer at every ticket window up the line.

But desperate times called for desperate measures.

"Are you certain you want to take the bus?"

The three of them relaxed under the trees above the village, sated and sleepy after a picnic of Spam sandwiches and a thermos of cold milky tea. Lucy reclined on the car rug while Bill and Michael played cards.

"Do I look as if I can't handle a few hours on a smelly bus with a bunch of farmwives and factory workers?"

He and Bill exchanged dubious looks.

"I've made it this far, haven't I? Besides, you heard that last chap. It's hopeless to try and find a seat on the train until tomorrow morning at the earliest. We haven't time to wait."

Bill glanced up at her over his cards. "Your aunt won't find us, will she, Lucy? She won't make me go back. I won't do it. I'll run away again."

"They won't take you back. I promise."

This seemed to relieve his worry, and his face cleared before he tossed down his cards. "I'm tired of playing brag. Can I go feed the rest of my sandwich to the sheep?"

"Just don't wander too far off. We have to be at the depot soon."

"Ta!" He scrambled to his feet and headed toward a herd of black-faced woolly sheep huddled against a nearby stile.

Only the sound of a dog barking down in the valley and the drone of an airplane's buzz as it landed at a nearby airfield over-lapped the birdsong and Bill's laughter as he leaned precariously over the stile to twist his fingers into the thick wool. Lucy rucked her skirt up to her thighs, enjoying the warm sun on her bare legs.

Michael lit a cigarette and stretched with his back against a tree. The sun through the branches gilded strands of his blond hair, throwing shadows along the strong line of his cheekbones and in the angled hollows beneath his eyes. "Not to be the voice of doom, but what happens if the authorities catch up to you? Surely they must be searching for Bill by now. Or if you can't find Bill's mother? Worse—what if she's not alive to be found?" He stubbed out his cigarette in the grass, his features unnaturally grim. "Be careful what you promise, lass. It could come back to haunt you."

She promised to see me off.

She promised us it would be all right. She promised.

Lucy shuddered, pain scissoring its way along her nerves, but she shoved the memories away before they took hold. Pasted on a brilliant smile. "Don't be such a worrywart."

"I don't want to see Bill disappointed."

"Neither do I."

Michael's words rankled like a sore tooth—what else was new? The man was a positive irritant. Had she thought a moment of soppy weakness would change that? Before she could think of a suitable scathing response, Bill scurried toward them, his hands cupped ahead of him.

"Oi, Lucy. Look." A little gray-and-yellow bird with a black cap nested in the bowl of his palms. "I think its wing is broken."

"That's a siskin," Michael instructed.

Lucy sat up, pulling her skirt back down and dusting grass from her hair. "Best put it back where you found it. We have to get a move on if we're to make the bus."

"But he'll die if he can't fly. Can't I take him with us to London?"

"Him?"

"I named him Rufus."

"Wonderful. He has a name."

"I can't just leave him here all by himself. What'll happen to him?"

"I think I've an old basket in the wagon," Michael suggested. "You can put him in that."

"Can we?" Lucy asked. "That's a great help." What she'd like to do was beat him over the head with it. She let her thoughts be known with a cold dead stare.

He grinned, his earlier solemnity banished back to wherever he kept it hidden away in his incessant need to remain always optimistic. Perversely, now that she knew he didn't spend every waking moment in a dazzle of good humor, he was far more likable.

"Please, Lucy," Bill persisted. "I want to show Mam. He's just about the prettiest bird I ever saw and he's so soft. Ain't got nothing like him on Mansford Terrace."

"There's a reason for that," Michael explained. "Siskins like trees and meadows. Not smoke and traffic."

Bill held the bird gently. His eyes were big and wide, and there it was—right on cue—the lip wobble. "But Rufus needs me."

Lucy was a sucker for the lip wobble. She caved like a house of cards. "Bring Rufus. Bring a whole flock of Rufuses if you like. The more the merrier."

Ignoring her sarcasm, Bill retrieved the basket. "It don't look very comfortable. You think he'd like a bed to lie in? Maybe some grass and leaves and such? What do siskins eat, Michael? I should get him some food for the trip."

Bill wandered off again in search of furnishings and dinner for Rufus.

Michael reclined back on one elbow, watching Lucy with bemused curiosity. "You moan and complain, but you really do care for him, don't you?"

"Rufus?"

He laughed and tossed a conker at her. "Bill, you idiot."

"Do you think I'd have put up with him this long if I didn't? I'm not completely cold and unfeeling."

"No, but on first inspection you don't strike one as particularly maternal."

"Okay, I have to ask—how did I strike you on first inspection?"

A corner of his mouth turned up in malicious delight. "The honest truth?"

"I'd expect nothing less."

"Very well. I thought you were rude, immature, conceited, selfish, and a spoiled little girl who should be taken over someone's knee."

Her eyes danced with wickedness. "Are you volunteering for the job?"

He shook his head. "You never miss an opportunity, do you?"

"To make you squirm? Where would the fun be in that?" She

smoothed her hands down her skirt, all too aware of the picture she must make in her wrinkled hand-me-downs. No wonder he looked on her with amusement. She'd become no more than a figure of fun. "So, if you held such a low opinion of me, why agree to help me reach London? You could have just as easily told me to bugger off."

"Maybe I held out hope my first impression might be wrong."

"You must be sorely disappointed."

Their eyes locked and held for the space of a heartbeat. "Not completely."

To hide the excitement blooming in her cheeks, Lucy leaned back to stare up at the sky, a pale blue bowl streaked by dingy white clouds. It would rain before nightfall, probably one of those English misting drizzles that made everything smell like an old shoe. But now, this very moment, the air was fragrant with the musty scents of earth and new budding leaves. Birds rattled the hedges, calling in a spring matchmaking frenzy, and there was a sense of rebirth, of hope, and for the first time in a long time the chance that tomorrow might not arrive wearing jackboots and singing Wagner. It made her feel as if anything were possible. As if all her dreams were an arm's length away, and all she needed was the courage to reach for them.

"Look here, miss!" Bill held up a juicy wriggling worm. "It's a beaut!"

Her body lighter than it had been in weeks, Lucy still couldn't help her pained smile. "An avian gastronomic delight, I'm sure."

Bill's brow wrinkled in momentary confusion.

She clarified. "Rufus will love it."

He dropped the worm in the basket and returned to digging.

Lucy stood and shook out the rug before folding it away. "We should be leaving for the bus station. Bill has a date with his mam and I have a date with Mr. Oliver. Neither of us wants to be late."

Michael's gaze traveled between Bill and Lucy and back again. "You can't tell me you won't be a little sorry to see him go."

She glanced at Bill, who was placing meadow grass carefully in the basket. Despite his age, there was no soft roundness of boyhood in his cheeks, no childish plumpness to be outgrown. Beneath a thatch of ragged brown hair, his face was lean and narrow. And there was too much knowledge in those quick, darting brown eyes.

"Are you kidding?" she scoffed, the lightness in her chest sinking into her stomach, where it mixed uneasily with a Spam sandwich. "I can hardly turn up at the Dorchester with a twelve-year-old in tow, now, can I?"

"No, I suppose not. I just thought when it came right down to it, you might find it hard to say good-bye."

Did he speak of Bill now? Or himself? She hardened her resolve as she hardened her heart. Sentimentality didn't figure into her future plans. She tossed her head, chin set, throat tight, stomach knotted. "Don't worry about me, Corporal. I'm an expert at saying good-bye."

Chapter 16

The bus depot was crowded with soldiers heading out on leave and sailors returning to their ships after a few precious days at home. A trio of Red Cross nurses with their blue gabardine uniforms and air of efficiency thumbed through a rack of magazines; an older couple weary after a day trip, faces tired and shoulders hunched, sat on a wooden bench beneath a poster advertising the latest war bond campaign.

Bill poked a stick into a drain while Lucy scanned a paper someone had left on the bench. *Devastation in Malta*, screamed the headline.

Normally, she skipped past the war news with barely a second glance, but this afternoon not even an announcement of what movie was playing at the Metropole, an advertisement for a dance contest to raise victory funds for the Red Cross, or a story about a two-headed dog in Shropshire was enough to drag her attention away from every page and column.

The nightly destruction meted out on Britain's rocky Mediterranean island outpost.

Tit-for-tat air raids by Germans on the ancient spa city of Bath.

British air raids on the cultural center of Rostock.

Japan's seemingly unstoppable advance through Burma.

For a moment, Michael's warnings had her doubting her ability to find Bill's mother as easily as she'd boldly proclaimed. Years of overnight raids on the city had displaced thousands. It was just barely conceivable Mrs. Smedley might be among them. What then?

She tossed the paper aside. This was why she avoided the news. There was only so much one could take in one go, and borrowing trouble wasn't her way. There was nothing she could do until they arrived. Either Bill's mother was fine and Lucy worried for no reason or Bill's mother was not fine and all the worrying in the world wouldn't change the fact. They'd find out soon enough.

"Did you mean what you said back there?" Lucy was jolted from her thoughts to find Bill watching her, head cocked to the side in suspicious observation. "About going to London for a job?"

"You heard that, did you?"

"Hard not to when you and Michael was hollering." He jammed his stick in and out, in and out. "When I asked you before, you told me you made it up, that it was all a hum. Why did you lie, Lucy? Didn't you trust me? I wouldn't rat you out. We're mates, you and me."

"I know we are, Bill. Best mates. It wasn't that, but you were so excited at first and then as we went along, it felt nice to be . . . looked up to for a change."

"But you're rich and you live in a great big house and your aunt's a real lady, the kind what knows the king and queen. Don't people look up to you now?"

"Some might for those reasons, but I liked that you looked up to me for . . . being me. Does that make sense?"

"I suppose." He seemed to ponder this riddle. "So, I guess Michael was right."

"I'm sure he'd be gratified to hear it. Right about what?"

"That you're running away."

Her hands tightened on her bag. "Maybe he's got it backward. Maybe I'm running toward instead."

"Toward what?"

She tried conjuring a picture of palm trees and Pacific breezes but found the images as blurry and ill defined as the rain-streaked landscape beyond her Nanreath windows. "I suppose I'll find out when I get there."

Michael approached with their tickets. "Here you go. Two seats on the next coach."

"I wish you'd let me pay my own way," Lucy replied.

"It's money well spent if it gets you out of my hair once and for all." His smile took the sting from his words. It wasn't one of his cocksure grins either, but sweet, almost wistful.

It made her want to kiss him—or pinch him. Either response would prove whether he was real or just a strange hallucination. She was leaning toward the latter because nobody in her jaded experience was this Andy Hardy wholesome.

Michael could be depended upon to do the right thing in any situation.

Michael could be depended upon—period.

She found that a novel and disconcerting experience and envied Arabella, though any girl who held this man's heart and let it go couldn't be the sharpest knife in the drawer.

The coach approached with a crank and grind of gears. The waiting passengers fidgeted, heads up, bags and parcels clutched more closely in expectation. Bill dropped his stick. She gripped her suitcase. A few more minutes and she'd be stepping aboard.

There would be no better time to speak her mind than these final moments.

"Michael, I—"

"Lucy, I—"

They spoke one over the other. He motioned for her to continue.

"Pardon, miss. Are you taking this bus?" A policeman had approached while they were locked in stilted conversation. He wore a friendly smile but his posture and the shrewd gleam in his eye told a different story.

"That depends," she hedged with a swift sideways glance for Michael. He gave the barest hint of a nod in answer, but it was enough to reassure her. He'd not give her away.

The policeman sized her up from top to bottom as if committing her to memory. "We've been told to be on the lookout for a young woman fitting your description. We have reason to believe she might be headed this way."

Golly. Aunt Cynthia worked fast.

Lucy scrambled for an explanation, but her mind had gone frighteningly blank.

"A pretty dark-haired young woman of slender build, that's what we were told."

The passengers headed for the coach, all of them pointedly ignoring the scene playing out before them while straining to catch a whiff of possible scandal.

"I appreciate the compliment, Constable, but you see—"

"Oi, Lucy." Bill rushed over, his eyes bright with triumph. "I found a whole tuppence dropped down that drainpipe there."

The policeman's friendly gaze narrowed. He rolled up on the balls of his feet as if preparing to strike. "Your name is Lucy?"

"That's right," she answered, forcing her voice to remain calm and her smile to remain ambivalent. Not an easy task when her insides were churning and her tongue seemed glued to the roof of her mouth. "Lucy Stanley."

Spotting the policeman, Bill's face drained of color and his mouth sagged open. He took an involuntary step back. As if sensing his panic, Michael put a comforting hand on his shoulder. Or perhaps it was a restraining hand. Either way, it worked. Bill looked like he was going to neither faint nor scarper.

"My sister and I are taking this child back to London," Michael offered. She almost expected him to clamp a hand on *her* shoulder. "He's an evacuee who's been staying with our family in Charbury, but his mother's taken sick and wants him home with her."

Lucy could almost see the first crack in the policeman's confidence. Faced with a trio rather than the lone woman on the lam he was expecting, he lost his single-minded bluster. "And you are, sir?"

"Corporal Michael McKeegan." He dug in his wallet for his identity papers. "Formerly of the Royal Engineers. It's good to make your acquaintance, Constable . . ."

"Grantley."

"Pleasure to meet you." Michael's handshake was accompanied by one of those disarming smiles of his that never failed to ease any situation. They should paratrooper the man into Germany. He'd have Hitler eating out of the palm of his grease-stained hand.

"McKeegan?" the man pried, his nose buried in Michael's particulars. "She said her name was Stanley."

"Half sister. Call McKeegan's Garage at 25430 if you need to verify it. My mother is there. She can explain the situation."

The policeman continued to eye them suspiciously, his gaze lingering longest on Bill, who seemed to have shrunk in on himself, his eyes unfocused, his face the color of chalk as he gripped his prize tuppence.

"Hey! You ridin' or not?" the driver shouted, anxious to keep to his timetable.

The policeman handed Michael his papers back. "Go on, then. Get the lad home to his mother."

"Will do." Michael quickly shepherded Lucy and Bill ahead of him onto the coach.

"What are you doing?" she hissed under her breath.

"Saving your bacon," he muttered as he followed her up the steps.

With a gasp of brakes, the coach moved out, still under the policeman's eagle eye.

"Well that didn't go quite to plan, did it, brother dear?" Lucy commented as town gave way to hilly countryside.

Michael gave a bark of dry laughter. "At this point, I'd have been surprised if it had."

The coach lurched and rattled, the young ticket-taking chippie balancing easily as she passed from front to back like a seasoned sailor on a heaving deck, her leather bag slung over her shoulder, whistle round her neck swinging back and forth.

"'With superb skill, Flight Lieutenant Wood rolls the Lysander . . . ,'" Bill read aloud over the shoulder of the man in the seat ahead.

The man turned round to glare, and Bill sank back into his seat.

"Will your mother back up your story?" Lucy asked as Michael handed over his tuppence and was issued a ticket for as far as Pitcombe.

"I have no idea, but by the time they ring her, you'll be long gone, so it won't matter."

"You could get in trouble."

"I'll take my chances."

By now, Bill had sidled up once more, peering over the seat

in hopes of learning Buck Ryan's fate. "'Battling with the ice-cold waves, Ryan struggles ashore. "I'd better stick to the rocks . . ."'"

The man cleared his throat as he shot Bill a "do you mind" look through thick horn-rimmed spectacles. Bill pretended to be studying the flowers on a spring hat three rows to their left.

"Why are you doing this, Michael? Why are you going out of your way to help me when you don't even like me?"

"I never said I didn't like you."

"You never said you did."

He glanced out the window. "I suppose you looked like someone in desperate need of a friend."

"I thought I didn't make friends . . . only collected followers," she answered tightly.

He ducked his head, swiping a hand across the back of his neck in embarrassment. "I did say that, didn't I? Guess there's a first for everything." A corner of his mouth curved up, his blue eyes laughing—but at her or with her, she couldn't tell.

Bill's feigned interest in women's hatwear waning, he'd once more oozed his way forward, nose pressed against the seat ahead. "'"Hm . . . there's Gull Island and it was about here that we flew inland this morning . . ."'"

The man spun round, but instead of giving Bill a piece of his mind, he gave him his paper. "Here you go, lad. I've finished the crossword anyway."

Bill grinned his delight as he curled up to pass the time with the comic-strip exploits of Popeye, Buck Ryan, and Ruggles.

"Thank you for not saying anything to the policeman back there. I know you disapprove," Lucy said.

"I can't make you behave . . . much as I'd like to. I'm not your mother."

"Amelia never cared what I did as long as it didn't inconvenience her." She gave a bitter laugh. "I don't think she'd have given two hoots about Yoon Hai if it hadn't affected my stepfather's finances. That was the unforgivable sin in her eyes."

Michael seemed startled at her mention of Hai. She could sense his desire to question her further and tensed, expecting the usual disapproving interrogation. Yet a part of her yearned to speak aloud Hai's name, if only to acknowledge his existence. To prove that her life in Singapore had not been a dream. That once she had almost been happy.

"You must have loved him very much to flout social convention," Michael said.

She wanted to agree to his romantic narrative of star-crossed lovers. To be Juliet ripped from her Romeo by class and race. But she couldn't lie. Not now.

"Hai was a good man. Kind. Honorable. Generous. He looked at me as if he truly saw me. He listened to what I had to say. It was refreshing after so many years of being invisible."

"You and your mother don't get on?"

"That's a very civilized way of putting it, but accurate as it goes. If you hadn't noticed, I don't get on with most people."

"Now that you mention it, you do seem to be a bit . . . shall we say . . . unsociable. It's as if you want people to dislike you."

"Maybe I do. Saves the bother of disappointment."

"On whose end?"

She gave a sniff of resigned laughter. "Both, I expect."

She had once thought of Yoon Hai as overly observant. He was a rank amateur compared to Michael, whose shrewd stare peeled her like an orange. She lit a cigarette as a way of putting distance if not space between them. "You asked me about Hai and I told you. So you owe me an answer in return—did you love Arabella?"

"Yes." He didn't even pause.

She took a breath and ignored the prick beneath her breast where her heart was supposed to be. "Then why won't you go see her? Don't you owe it to yourself to make absolutely sure before you close that door forever?"

"Awfully philosophical about matters of the heart all of a sudden."

"I just know if it were me, I'd be hoping you'd give me a second chance."

His gaze grew shuttered, his features giving nothing away. The bus slowed as it approached a crossroads. Michael gathered himself to disembark, their moment of shared intimacy over.

Bill dropped his paper, comics forgotten. "Are you leaving, Michael?"

"'Fraid so, mate. But keep your head down and your mouth shut and you should make it to London all right."

"You could come with us," Bill suggested.

"Wish I could," he said, his gaze shifting from Bill to fall on Lucy, "but I'm already where I belong."

"I know you don't approve, Michael, but Mr. Oliver is my chance at finally getting what I want."

"What *do* you want, lass?" His gaze locked with hers, steel rimming the blue of his eyes. "Do you even know?"

"Of course I do." An insolent comeback formed on the tip of her tongue, a quick shot that would put him firmly in his place and release her from his questing gaze. But she found herself unable to turn the knife as she would normally have done. It wasn't that she couldn't. Oh, there were plenty of sarcastic comments in her repertoire, and all humdingers guaranteed to crush anyone foolish enough to attempt to see beneath her veneer, but Michael had become more than a target for her put-downs. She didn't want their last moments to drip with acid. "I know you think I'm an opportunist at best and a tart at worst and I wish it weren't that way.

But when you only have yourself to count on, you learn to count yourself first."

"What if you found you could count on someone else? That you weren't as alone as you thought?"

He never cracked a smile, and she found her own features sobering, her chest tight.

The bus jerked to a stop and the doors clanked open. Michael rose from his seat. "Good luck. I hope you find what it is you're looking for." He started up the aisle.

"Michael . . . wait." She chased him down, grabbing his sleeve just before he reached the top of the steps and pressing a kiss on his cheek. "I couldn't have made it this far without my knight in shining armor."

"I thought you didn't believe in fairy tales."

"No," she said sadly, "but I wish I did."

Chapter 17

Michael's seat was taken by an older couple. She carried a knitting bag. He read a copy of a James Joyce novel, using his bookmark to follow the page. Quiet people minding their own business who wouldn't task her with painful soul-searching. Lucy liked them already.

She settled back with a sigh of relief that started somewhere near her toes. She wanted nothing more than a hot bath, a soft bed, and a stiff cocktail—not necessarily in that order. Hopefully one, or all of these things in combination, would set her firmly back on a track that seemed to grow increasingly muddled with every mile she put between herself and Nanreath Hall.

It was all Michael's fault. She wasn't sure exactly how, but leave it to a man to confuse what should be a completely straightforward endeavor.

"Candy bar?" Bill asked, holding out a rather melted corner of Hershey's chocolate.

"Where did you get that?"

"A soldier give it to me back at the depot."

"Thank you, no."

He popped the chocolate in his mouth before digging in his bag again.

"Was that a gift from the soldier as well?" she asked, eying the cigarette he'd retrieved.

"Naw, it's one of Michael's. I found it down between the seats of the wagon. Only a little crushed."

"And now it's mine, thank you very much." She snatched it away from him.

"That's not fair."

"Who said life was fair?"

Bill's face grew mulish, but he bit back whatever argument he thought of making and instead turned his attention to the basket perched on his lap. Cracking the lid, he crooned softly, "'Ere now, fella. It's all right."

He was answered by a series of distressed burbles and chirps and a fluttering that rattled the basket.

"What have you got in there?" The woman's knitting needles clicked as she worked on the sleeve of a lumpy sweater. "A kitten?"

"A bird. He's got a bum wing. Want a look-see?" Bill leaned forward to show her.

The woman gave a sad tsk and a shake of her head. "Ah, the poor wee mite."

Bill stroked the bird's head with a finger while it lay on its side surveying him from one beady black eye. "He won't eat the worms or the beetle I found for him, and I weren't able to find him any seeds."

"Do you think he would eat currants?" The woman offered Bill a bun from a bag on the seat beside her, which garnered her a forlorn look from her husband but wide-eyed delight from Bill.

"Crikey!" he gasped. "If Rufus won't eat it, I sure will."

A dusting of crumbs spread across the front of his shirt as he slowly dissected the bun for bits of currant, which he placed in the basket close to Rufus's beak. It flapped its broken wing pathetically but otherwise remained unimpressed with this gift.

"My boy Darren used to bring home strays all the time," the woman offered with an indulgent softening of her weary features. "Never knew what he'd turn up on the doorstep with next. Kittens, puppies, you name it. Once he even brought home a fox kit, raised it until it was tame as a house cat."

The gentleman lifted his head from his book to give his wife a long look somewhere between irritation and bewilderment. She ignored him, continuing to smile wistfully, needles clicking as a sweater grew from the ball of thick blue yarn in her bag. He cleared his throat before returning to his Joyce, but Lucy could tell he'd begun splitting his attention between his book and his wife.

"He's in the army now, of course—the tank corps. I was relieved when I heard. Can't get hurt rattling around in a metal can. I told Mr. Britt our Darren's safe as houses. That's what I said." The man's face grew longer. His hands on the book whitened. He hadn't turned a page in at least ten minutes.

"I'd like to drive a tank," Bill exclaimed, momentarily distracted from feeding Rufus by thoughts of military derring-do. "Or maybe a Spitfire. That would be brilliant. I'd shoot up those Jerries what come over to bomb London. I'd be an ace, and they'd give me a medal for it."

"Darren's elder brother Alistair flies planes," Mrs. Britt said with a proud smile. "Hurricanes. He's somewhere up north, though he can't tell us where, of course. Security, you know." She put a finger to her lips and gave a furtive glance around her. "All four of my boys are serving. The twins are in the navy. I tell the gals at the WI, the Britts of Blythe Street have done their part to beat the Hun. And Mr. Britt did his bit in the first war, didn't you, dear?"

Her husband grunted, but his face had gone quite gray. He looked as if he wanted to be sick. Lucy moved her bag subtly out of the line of fire, just in case. Hopefully, his nausea wasn't a result of his wife's currant buns.

"I couldn't have asked for four better boys. So handsome and so smart. Futures bright as four copper pennies. Growing up, the girls buzzed round them like bees, and now they're in uniform, why, they have to beat them off with a stick."

So much for Lucy's peace and quiet. At least she didn't seem to have to do much more than look interested and nod at proper intervals. Mrs. Britt seemed quite capable of holding up both sides of the conversation.

"I'm knitting this sweater for Alistair. He's told me the weather is horrid. He's never liked the cold, poor thing. Used to have to put two hot water bottles in his bed to keep the chilblains away. Blue's his favorite color. Matches his eyes."

"Stop it, Gladys," Mr. Britt shouted, his voice strained, the color bleached from his face. "Just stop it now, do you hear? I don't want to hear any more. Not one more word."

He yanked the sweater from her grip, unraveling the threads. A knitting needle slid under the seat. His book fell to the floor, the bookmark fluttering loose to settle between the seat cushions. He tore at the seams, the sleeve unraveling, the sweater losing its shape until there was nothing left but a jumbled knot of unshapely yarn. He tossed it in the bag.

Mrs. Britt's face crumpled into her handkerchief. Her shoulders shook. Her husband huffed as if he'd run a race; his face was red, his eyes large, the pupils dilated to near-black.

Bill moved closer to Lucy. She cleared her throat and grew extremely interested in the edge of her skirt.

Hours passed. Shadows lengthened. The countryside trundled

past as the bus made its slow but steady way east, stopping to add and subtract passengers at every rural crossroad and village green. Bill's stomach growled. Lucy bought them each a packet of crisps.

At an unidentified depot in an unidentified town that looked much like every other depot and town they'd passed through, the bus hissed to a stop. The lack of signposts and markers might be vital to the war effort, but it was a damn nuisance. She checked Bill's sad excuse for a map. If she was reading his illegible scribble right, they were in Hungerford—or perhaps Faringdon.

Wherever they were, Mr. and Mrs. Britt stood up. He grabbed a battered leather suitcase. She took up her knitting bag. She shied when he put his hand up to assist her. He dropped his arm back to his side as if she had burned him. His fingers opened and closed. His face tightened.

She smiled her farewells. "You take care, miss. Little boys are experts at finding trouble. But I'd not trade my four for any prim and proper daughters, no sir." She gave Bill one last pensive look before passing down the aisle, her face drawn and gray with age as if she'd grown older in the few short hours they'd been traveling.

Mr. Britt hovered as if biding his time. Lucy clutched her handbag and met his hard gaze head-on.

When his wife was safely out of earshot, he cleared his throat and his thin-lipped frown now seemed anxious and unhappy more than angry. "I wanted to apologize for Gladys."

"Apologize for her? That's rich."

"It's our boys, you see," he carried on. "She natters on and on about them. She won't stop. Bends everybody's ear whether they want to hear about them or not."

"She's proud of them. Any mother would do the same." Amelia probably not, but this was a normal mother. "You should be proud of them too, I should think."

"They're dead, miss. All of them."

"I don't—"

He pulled his bookmark out of his book. It was a much wrinkled and dog-eared photograph. Four uniformed young men standing arms linked in front of a nondescript terrace house. They were mugging for the camera. No hint of fear or misgiving, just cocky smiles and swaggering confidence. No idea of the horrors they would soon face.

The grief they would experience.

The losses they would suffer.

War had been something distant, a game to win, not a fight to be survived. If Lucy had thought of it at all, it was only as an endless bounty of dashing men in smart uniforms queuing up to take her out for the evening. She'd had her pick of the services' finest; anything less than a lieutenant need not apply.

Was it naïveté that had blinded her to the truth? Or had she simply refused to see what stared her in the face?

Even after Singapore fell and the reality of war became her reality, she continued to push aside what she didn't want to feel, didn't want to face. At Nanreath Hall, among the sick and injured, she ignored the devastating physical evidence of battle's cost and called the oversight compassion. Made fun of those who talked of responsibility and duty and selflessness.

She looked at those four laughing men, unbearably young and incredibly earnest, purpose etched in every grinning visage, and felt shame like a lance between her ribs.

"The twins died last year," Mr. Britt explained, his voice quiet but containing only the hint of a tremble. "Alistair's plane went into the North Sea this past January. We received word just this week that Darren's been killed. She won't believe it. She keeps on about them as if they'll be home for Christmas. And they won't." He tucked the photo lovingly into his jacket pocket. "She knits socks. She sends care packages. She writes them letters and then harasses the postman every afternoon. She acts as if all's right. It's not. It won't be ever again. I try not to say anything. I'm afraid I shall lose her too, but sometimes it just grows to be too much."

"I see." Lucy hid her shaking hands in her skirt, her fingers curled tight into the leather of her handbag.

"Well, I don't know why I'm telling you all this. I suppose I just thought you should know after the way I behaved. I wanted . . ." His shoulders slumped. "I don't know what I wanted." He clutched his book. Like his wife, he seemed to have aged before her eyes. "Take care of the lad. He does have the look of Darren at that age, Gladys was right about that." He wiped his eyes with a great handkerchief as he left, shoulders hunched within his raincoat.

"Is the old lady cracked?" Bill asked. "There was a lady lived below us on Marvin Street. She was bats. Used to run around the streets in her nightgown screaming little men was after her. They took her away in a Black Maria."

"Mrs. Britt's not cracked. She's unhappy, and so she . . . she dreams."

"She wasn't dreaming just now, was she? I mean she was awake and talking to us. She even gave me a bun. Someone asleep wouldn't do that. Unless they were sleepwalking, I suppose."

"Some people don't have to be asleep to live in dreams. They simply pretend to themselves things are one way when in reality life is really quite different."

"Why would they do that?"

Lucy stared past him to watch Mr. Britt's hunched body disappearing down the aisle.

If her stay at Nanreath Hall seemed like a lifetime ago, Singapore seemed like another life altogether. A life she would never see again.

She swallowed around the sudden ache in her throat. "Because it hurts less that way."

The light grew purple and gold across the far hills before graying into spring twilight and then night. The coach slowed to a crawl as the driver fought to see the road with the weak glimmer of light his painted headlamps gave off.

Bill lay curled against Lucy's side like a puppy, the basket containing Rufus on the floor at his feet.

"I don't remember what she looks like." His voice was soft, almost frightened.

"I thought you were asleep."

"I was, but I got to thinking. I can't remember my mam. She's all faded and jumbled in my head. What if I get home and I can't recognize her? What if she don't recognize me?"

"Of course she'll know you."

"I ain't seen her since the start of the fighting when all us kids was evacuated."

"You haven't been home since then?"

"Naw, I wanted to, but Mam wrote to say it weren't safe and I should stay put and be a good boy. I tried. I tried something awful, but the Sayres didn't think anything I did was good."

"So you stopped trying?"

His lips pressed to a flat line, his eyes hard as he stared out the window into the dark.

"I've found it takes a lot less effort to live down to someone's low opinion. The trouble comes when it doesn't take any effort at all. Then you've let the Sayres of the world win."

The slop of the coach wheels against the macadam acted as a bass line to the murmur of quiet conversations. A group of soldiers near the front joined together in a chorus of "The Rose of Tralee," but the tired passengers, stiff and impatient in their seats, didn't have the heart or the energy to sing along. The attempt ended with a stern warning by the chippie.

Lucy lit a cigarette and leaned back to exhale a thin stream of blue smoke. She knew all about low expectations. She'd made it her life's work to sink to the bottom. People didn't expect anything after that. They left you alone.

She knew alone.

Preferred it.

What do you want, lass?

Michael's question lingered at the edges of her mind as his face hovered before her eyes, that quizzical mobile choirboy face.

Excitement. Attention. Fun. That's how she might have answered him once. Now she wasn't so sure of her response. She wasn't sure of a lot of things.

A new and uncomfortable feeling.

"Maybe your mam is in London too, miss. Maybe she's in London looking for you just like you're looking for her."

"A pleasant thought, but highly doubtful."

Bill continued to watch her expectantly.

"I spent most of my life away at school. When I was home, my mum was always very busy with other things. She didn't have much time for child raising."

"Is that why you want to go to America?"

"I suppose it's one of the reasons. There's nothing for me here in England. I was born in the States and went to schools all over the world. Then I was in Singapore until last year, when I was sent to my aunt's, where you met me."

"Were you evacuated like I was because of the war?"

"In a way, though at the time no one really thought war would come to us there."

"Michael said I needed to look after you."

"He did, did he?"

"He said it would be hard because you don't think you need looking after, but that you really do."

"Well, you can tell Corporal McKeegan that I'm a big girl and don't need him or anyone else sticking their nose in. And another thing you can tell him—"

"I can't tell him nothing." He frowned, perplexed. "Michael's gone back home. Remember?"

She sighed and crushed out her cigarette. "So he has." She turned to look out the window, but there was nothing to see except the hollowed cheeks and eyes of her own cheerless reflection.

M iss, it's a raid." A hand shook Lucy free of a slightly risqué dream featuring Michael in a starring role. He crossed a rain-drenched field in a rain-drenched shirt, ready to sweep her into his strong arms, when—

"Lucy, we have to get to a shelter before them Jerries smash us to smithereens." The hand came again, more firmly this time, and the last streamers of pleasurably misty unconsciousness evaporated with a crash of ack-ack fire and the moan of sirens.

"Where are we?" she asked thickly, her tongue feeling as if it had become glued to the roof of her mouth and her eyes scratchy and dry.

"The city, miss. Leastways, close enough it makes no difference."

That brought her upright and awake. "London?"

"Aye, miss. Now, please come on."

She peered out of the coach window to see a sky burning smoky red, great gouges of yellow and orange flame piercing the clouds each time the gunners sent up their fire. Explosions vibrated in her chest and along her bones. British. German. It didn't matter to her heart, which lurched with every air-rushing whump, or the hair at the back of her neck, which prickled and rose at the scream of incoming HEs and incendiaries.

She checked her watch. It was just past midnight. "How long have I been asleep?"

Bill shrugged. "Dunno. I got bored and went up front to sit by the driver. He's from Wandsworth. That's south of the river."

A few straggling passengers were filing out of the coach. No one panicked or shouted. Instead weary resignation seemed to be the order of the day as they gathered belongings, grumbled about the inconvenience, and made their way onto the pavement, where the driver nudged them along with brisk instructions. "Shelter's down the alley and off to the right, folks. Double quick like."

Lucy took her case down from the overhead rack. "Have you got your knapsack?"

"Aye, miss."

"And Rufus. Where's Rufus?"

"I've got him."

"Where's my handbag?"

"It was right in your lap."

"It was, but I can't find it now." She laid aside her case to look on the floor, felt under her seat, checked the rack above. Checked under the seat again. "It's gone."

"Hurry, folks," the driver scolded. "It's getting worse. Them planes are right on top of us."

Indeed they were. The drone of engines, roar of explosions, and return fire from the guns became a wall of sound that pummeled Lucy's eardrums and made her stomach loosen. The air was punched from her lungs and tears sprang unbidden to her eyes. Or maybe they weren't completely unbidden. If she'd lost her handbag, she was buggered but good.

"Lucy, we've got to go."

"Not until I find my handbag. Every cent I possess is in that bag." She knelt on the floor of the coach and reached to sweep under all the seats. "It has to be here somewhere."

Bill tried pulling her onto her feet. Rufus squawked and fluttered in his basket as if he were being pulled apart feather by feather. The driver finally grabbed her by the back of her coat and yanked her to her feet.

"Found it!" She waved it in the air above her head like a prize.

A street over, a bomb sent a plume of fire and shrapnel in all directions. The coach lurched sideways. Bill grabbed her arm, his eyes wide, mouth a frightened O. Lucy's legs jellied, but she managed to swallow the terrified shriek jagging its way up her throat.

The driver ushered them to the rear of the alley, where a flight of steps led down to a doorway. Inside, they pushed through a canvas curtain and followed a corridor into a room filled with a double row of bunks, all of them occupied. The place smelled of sweat and drains and boiled cabbage. Blinking owlish eyes in pale weary faces stared at the new arrivals. Some rolled over and tried to go back to sleep. A baby wailed. An old man grumbled and broke wind. A family sat on the floor, the children wrapped in blankets, sleeping, their mother engrossed in the latest edition of *Tatler*, all of them unmoved by the cacophony outside the shelter.

The room was already crowded but with the addition of the coach's passengers there was nowhere to sit that wasn't uncomfortably close to one's neighbor. Lucy found herself a few inches of floor space crushed between Bill and his basket, which dug into her rib cage whenever she tried to move, and an old woman smelling of stale urine who coughed her way through a pack of Player's cigarettes.

The shelter warden passed out cups of tea with a bright, determined smile. "Nasty night out, but a nice hot cuppa should do the trick. Warm you inside and out, it will."

"Ta." Bill took the mug in both hands.

Lucy sipped at the tea, which scalded all the way down to her stomach lining. Mouth on fire, she gulped, coughed, and choked her way through half the mug, but it seemed to ease the jittery sick feeling making her teary eyed and trembly. "Is it like this every night?"

"Worst was the autumn of '40. They'd come up the river every night and flatten anything what stood in their way. It's better now. They still come, but not near as often."

Down in the subterranean bowels of the shelter, the noise dulled to only a hurricane growl, but it still seemed to pulse along Lucy's veins like small jolts of electricity.

"One . . . two . . . three—"

The shelter rocked, plaster sifting down on them like powdered sugar.

"One . . . two—"

The lights flickered, went out for a gasp of a second, and came back on with a blink of fluorescence.

"What are you doing?" Bill asked.

"When I was a child during thunderstorms, we'd count between the lightning flash and the thunder to see how close the storm was."

"But this isn't a storm."

The walls seemed to shudder with the force of the attack.

"Isn't it?"

Chapter 18

The next morning Lucy woke from a broken sleep with a crick in her neck and a body stiff from the cold floor. The shelter was alive with activity as people took turns washing up in the one tiny lav at the back of the corridor before heading squinty eyed into the gritty daylight to assess the damage. The old woman was gone, the only evidence of her existence being an overloaded ashtray. But the squalling baby remained, and the family stood near the entryway, the mother in her printed cotton dress surrounded by her stair-step children chatting with the warden about the laundry merits of Oxydol versus Rinso.

Despite the acrid aromas of dozens of grubby people trapped in a space the size of her aunt's drawing room and the mysterious stains on the lumpy mattress, Lucy gazed with longing at an empty bunk. An hour of uninterrupted sleep. Maybe two. That was all she asked.

"Lucy!"

It was not to be.

Bill stood over her with a revoltingly cheerful expression on his face. "I've brought you a piece of toast and marg."

Not exactly the breakfast in bed she envisioned, but it was the best on offer.

Her tidying consisted of a sponge-off with a handkerchief dipped in the lav sink and a quick swipe of powder from her compact. The outfit was a dead loss, but that was easy enough to fix once she booked herself into a hotel, while her hair would need at least an hour under the hot rollers to look even halfway decent. If she was going to make it to the Dorchester in time for a pre-dinner aperitif, she needed to get cracking.

She found Bill in the alley outside the shelter, shuffling his deck of cards. "Are you ready to go?"

"Aye. Mrs. Driscoll, she's the shelter warden, she says we should take the 116 as far as Wellington Road, change to the 657 and ride that to Shepherd's Bush, change again to the 17 to Holborn, and then there's a trolley bus that will take us along to Hackney Road. Isn't that smart?"

"I hope you wrote that algebraic equation down because I lost track somewhere among the fractions."

"She done it for me," he said, holding out a piece of paper. "She give me some sesame seeds as well. Rufus hasn't eaten them, though."

"Maybe he's not hungry."

"I hope he's not taken sick. I've done everything Michael told me and I've bound up his wing but he just lays there. He don't even cheep anymore."

"You wait. Once he's out in the sunshine of a spring day, he'll feel much better." She slung her coat over her shoulders and took up her bags. "And so shall I."

The air stank of cordite and gas from a ruptured main while smoke and ash swirled in eddies like low-lying mist. But above the gray cheerless streets, the sun rose bright, clouds high and fine across a blue spring sky. From a shrubbery nearby, a resilient thrush sang its lungs out just as if the world hadn't been about to end a few short hours ago.

Lucy felt her spirits lift as they climbed aboard the 116 per the warden's instructions. Funneling in from the suburbs were shopgirls in faded print dresses and painted-on nylons and clerks in practical tweeds and tailored jackets, worn shiny at elbows and cuffs. Factory workers in serviceable wraparound overalls or bib dungarees hung upon the straps jostling for balance with what seemed like a battle array of women attired in the ranks and uniforms of half a dozen government agencies. Everyone rushing to be somewhere, moving with studied purpose and habit.

They rattled up Holland Park Avenue, past Notting Hill Gate. An ambulance nosed its way through traffic. A street was roped off where a building had been sliced open, its contents tumbled into the street like scree off the side of a mountain. Another, nearly as damaged, sported a hand-painted sign: STILL OPEN FOR BUSINESS. A mobile canteen served a queue of fire wardens and shelter staff. Sidewalks full of grim-faced, war-weary soldiers from every country in the empire rubbed shoulders with starry-eyed, gawp-jawed GIs fresh off the transports and as yet unbloodied by battle.

Bill pressed his nose against the glass, his eyes darting everywhere, Rufus's basket balanced between his legs. "Crikey, miss." His voice sober and almost afraid.

"Crikey is damned right," she breathed in agreement.

This was not the London she recognized from the few shopping expeditions she'd made here with Amelia. The dull colorless conformity she'd experienced in Cornwall had infected this once-vibrant city, leaching the beauty from its stones and its people until the very air seemed bone white and ash dark. Pinched faces, hunched gaits, no-nonsense clothes sapped of style and worn with sensible shoes.

If she noticed an occasional splash of color, it inevitably belonged to some WVS do-gooder in her gaudy red sweater.

There was a head-down, shoulders-squared, back-straight, gritty determination that gave jaws a sharper angle and eyes a more sober glint. Even their humor bore a darker edge after years of facing the almost certainty of invasion.

The bus traveled up Bayswater Road past Hyde Park, bristling with giant guns pointed skyward and sliced through with sludgy trenches dug during the first panic of war, now sandbagged pits of mud and debris. Barrage balloons hovered ominously over the churned turf while a lone agitator stood at Speakers Corner, his gas mask hanging from one raincoated shoulder as he prophesied doom to a crew of soot-blackened firemen heading home and an ATS driver leaning against her car as she waited for her high-ranking charge.

A spark of a thought had Lucy pulling the cord to be let off. "Grab your things. Let's go."

"Where are we going?" Bill followed after. "This ain't Holborn. Mrs. Driscoll said—"

"You've heard of reconnoitering, haven't you? What soldiers do when they want to check a place out before an attack?"

"What's that got to do with us?"

"I need to do a little reconnoitering of my own before I attack."

After the first burst of morning rush-hour bustle, the leafy sidewalks of Park Lane were relatively quiet. Lucy felt herself standing a bit taller, slowing her gait to one less rushed and more beguiling. She even tossed her hair off her shoulders with a practiced flip of her head.

"You all right, Lucy?" Bill asked. "You got a sore neck or something from sleeping in the shelter? You're all twitchy-like."

"I am not twitchy."

She slowed her pace. There it was just ahead. Its famous front was hidden behind a wall of sandbags, but still recognizable—the Dorchester.

"Is that grand place what we're reconnoitering?"

"It is." She didn't cross the street. There was no way she was going to suffer the humiliation of being seen in a dingy outfit she'd worn across half the country. She'd save her big entrance for to-night, when she'd had a chance for a scrub and a primp. "I've got a job for you, Bill."

"What's that?"

"Here's a sovereign. I want you to ask around. See if you can find out if a Mr. Mason Oliver is staying there."

"They'll call the coppers on me."

"That's what the money is for." He stared skeptically at his palm and back to her. "Oh, all right. Here's two sovereigns. If you can't finagle some information with that, you don't deserve to call your-self a sharper."

He continued to eye her cautiously, his cheeks pale but for two high spots of color. "I don't know . . . remember what Michael said? Keep our heads down and our mouths shut?"

"The police aren't looking for you. They're looking for me."

He swallowed, kicking his toe against the curb as if still uncertain.

"I'm sure the boys at the Lion wouldn't be put off by a little dan-ger," she cajoled.

That did it. His narrow shoulders lifted in a deep breath. Then he clamped his jaw, his gaze hardening with purpose. "You'll look after Rufus?"

"As if he were my own," she replied.

"Right," he said firmly. "Be back in a tick."

He dashed across the street, dodging the liveried doorman to disappear inside the hotel.

Lucy waited beneath the greening plane trees, letting the grumbling bus engines and squeak of car tires wash over her drowsy brain. Funny, maybe it was Bill's worry, but she could almost make herself believe she was back in Cornwall listening to the growl of a storm surf and the squabble of seabirds. She glanced over her shoulder, half-expecting Aunt Cynthia to pounce from out of the bushes reciting all the ways in which she was a horrible disappointment.

She didn't know Lucy was used to being a horrible disappointment.

It was being looked up to that was a new—and somewhat terrifying—experience.

The minutes passed. Lucy tapped her watch to make sure it was still working. What was Bill doing? Going room by bloody room?

As she watched, a young woman in a rumpled dress and fur stole slipped through the swinging doors. Head down, she carried her shoes, and there was a definite look of morning-after remorse about her posture.

Lucy knew that look. She'd worn it more times than she could count. It was the look of someone who'd begun the evening sipping fancy cocktails while listening to a crooning tuxedoed jazz singer and ended it swilling bathtub gin while listening to the squawking serenade of sloppy drunks. Of someone waking dry-mouthed with a hammer pounding between her eyes and gaps in her memory, gathering the shreds of her dignity, and making a discreet exit, hoping she'd not done something too humiliating, but knowing she probably had. And trying to brazen it out anyway.

Unease squirmed in the pit of Lucy's stomach—and, for some odd reason, embarrassment. Not just for this poor girl, but for herself.

She had gleefully broken every rule and boldly crossed every line, heedless of those who sought to curb her intemperate excesses. Hell, their opinions only made her further test the riskiest waters.

Some had called her courageous for flouting convention so boldly, but courage had never entered into her decisions. Nor even hedonistic enjoyment. What was there to enjoy in kneeling over a basin spewing your guts up? Or popping seltzer tablets like candy allsorts?

She had used her excesses as a blunt-force weapon.

A way to hurt as she hurt.

Somewhere along the way, it had simply become habit.

Now, with Amelia gone, that chronic need to outrage and appall seemed less—necessary. Less appealing.

The woman drove off in her cab, taking Lucy's second thoughts with her. Faint heart never won fair lady—or anything else for that matter. And she'd not come this far to fold like a bad hand of poker at a passing hint of uncomfortable doubts. She had to find out what was going on even if it meant being seen in togs no self-respecting charwoman would wear.

Juggling her suitcase and Rufus's basket, she stepped off the pavement to the frantic ring of a bicycle bell and a surprised shout just before a sharp pain caught her behind the knees and she was knocked to the ground, luggage one way, she the other. Her hands scraped along the roadway, her elbow struck a curb, and she ended up with the heavy steel frame of a Raleigh SF Model 11 lying on top of her, a pedal digging into her ribs.

"Oh dear, I'm frightfully sorry. I didn't see you standing there and then my brake went wonky and I lost control. I hope you're not hurt. Please tell me you're not hurt. I'll feel just awful if I've damaged you."

The bicycle was lifted away, and Lucy was helped to her feet by a fine-featured pixie of a young woman in slacks and a tunic, under a raincoat with the ARP badge prominently displayed on the breast. "Golly. Look at your knee. I really am very sorry."

Blood slid warm into Lucy's shoe and her knee stung like the devil. She tried dabbing at it with her handkerchief. "I'll live, but where's Rufus? Damn it all, where's that blasted bird?"

"Is this what you're looking for?" The woman set the basket beside her, from which sad little warbles could be heard. "A bit tossed about, but all present and accounted for."

"Thank heavens. Bill would kill me if anything happened to him."

"I do hope you'll forgive me. Daddy says I'm a threat to the general public on this thing, but it's so much handier for getting about in the city. I brought it up with me from Kent last time I was home. It was my younger brother's, you see, he's in the navy, following in Daddy's footsteps and all that. Daddy's an admiral, don't you know, and, well . . . are you sure you're all right? You look a bit pale around the lips. You're not going to faint on me, are you?" She turned to Bill, who'd just come running up and was standing in silent awe at the stream of consciousness. "She's not going to faint on me, is she?"

"Crikey," whispered Bill, staring goggle eyed at Lucy. "She's hinged both sides, miss."

"Golly. I'm talking too much, aren't I? I tend to babble when I'm nervous. I've always done it. Can't seem to help myself."

She was indeed talking too much—with a voice straight out of the ranks of the upper ten thousand. Amelia had that same drawing-room drawl. She'd once tried to have Lucy taught those regal tones, but no amount of elocution lessons could impart the sense of entitlement that rolled off the tongue in clear vowels and crisp consonants.

Right now, it made Lucy's head pound.

"Are you certain you're not limping? That gash looks terribly deep. And your frock has a horrid rip in it."

"No bones broken and this outfit could only be improved by tire tracks."

"I feel terribly dreadful about that. It's so hard to find decent clothing nowadays." The girl surveyed Lucy with pained sincerity. She could almost see her totaling the cost of blouse, skirt, cardigan, and shoes down to the last ha'penny. "My flat is just a few streets over. I've an entire cabinet full of gauze, sticking plaster, and iodine. Positively swimming in the stuff. We can fix you up and have you back on your way in no time."

"I'm fine. Really," Lucy demurred, unable to decide whether it was the fall or the stream of conversation making her head throb until her brains felt as if they were oozing out her ears, but lights swam across her vision like fish and the world had taken on a strange shimmery halo.

"I insist. That's what I do . . . well . . . one of the things I do—first aid. I'm a bit of an odd-jobber, really. I'm ARP officially, I work in a response center on the other side of Green Park, but I do a bit of ambulance driving and fire watching on the side when I'm needed, which isn't so much these days, thank heavens, but I like to keep my hand in, and since I bowled you over the least I can do is patch you back up again."

Somehow the young woman was moving them along without any conscious effort other than the force of her words. Lucy had a feeling the Pied Piper must have had this sort of mesmerizing effect on his audience. "It's actually my parents' flat, but when Daddy went to sea—did I mention he's an admiral—Mummy closed it up and retired to the house in the country. She wanted me to join her in Lower Stokenoor, but I ask you—what happens in Lower Stokenoor? Nothing. So I moved to London. Mummy was furious but Grand-mère was on my side, and if she's on your side, you know the battle's half-won." She smiled, revealing an endearing gap between her two front teeth. "She lives on her own in Kensington with only Mr. Pidge for company. I think he's her butler, but there are rumors . . ." She gave a delicious lift of her eyebrows. "Grand-mère is terribly bohemian. It gives poor Daddy palpitations."

"We really have to be on our way. Bill's anxious to—"

"But you're limping."

Lucy did feel as if she might be listing to port just a tetch. "Yes, but—"

"And you really are awfully pale."

The pavement did move under Lucy's feet in a rather disconcerting way.

"She only ate a piece of toast for breakfast," Bill said with a worried glance.

"Then that settles it. I'm perfectly useless in the kitchen, and while my parents allowed me use of the flat, they didn't actually allow me use of any of the staff, so I don't prepare much but beans on toast and an occasional bread pudding if I'm feeling particularly ambitious, but I can fix a cup of tea, and I have some egg-and-cress sandwiches left from a luncheon I attended with Grand-mère yesterday. She was scandalized when I asked them to wrap up the scraps for me to take away, but honestly, it would be a waste to just throw it out. Please say you'll come."

"Much as we'd love to, Bill and I are on a very tight schedule."

Bill piped up. "I've got time for a sandwich."

"How did I know you were going to say that?" Lucy grumbled.

"Then that's settled," the young woman replied briskly.

"But, Bill," Lucy said, grappling for control of this roller coaster of a conversation, "what about that very important errand I sent you on? We should really be getting on so that we can discuss it."

"Errand?" He goggled blankly at her.

"You know . . . the visit to the . . . place . . . with the man . . . and you were going to find out . . . things . . ." She tossed him a wink-wink, nod-nod pointed stare.

He glanced innocently over at the woman. "I'm afraid she's awful poorly, miss. You think she might have taken a crack in the head?"

"It's entirely possible," she replied.

"I did not take a crack in my head, and I feel perfectly fine," Lucy argued, though the effort cost her in a renewed wave of stomach-lurching vertigo.

Bill gave a mournful shake of his head. "That's what people always say right before they topple over stone dead. I knew a bloke what tripped coming out of the pub. Thought nothing of it. The next day they was measuring him for a box."

"I'll be measuring you for a box in a minute if you don't stop this madness."

"He has a very good point," the woman answered. "Head wounds can be devilishly tricky things. And your leg really is a mess. I'm sure your errands can wait ten minutes."

"Ten itty-bitty little minutes, Lucy. That's hardly no time at all," Bill wheedled.

"Who's in charge here anyway?"

His face lit up with puckish satisfaction.

"That's what I thought," Lucy grumbled, admitting defeat.

"Right. All settled," the woman said. "You're coming home with me. No more arguing. I'm Irene Turnbull, by the way." She stuck out a friendly hand for Lucy to shake.

"Lucy Stanhope. And this little con artist is Bill."

"Nice to meet you, miss." He grinned. "What kind of sand-wiches did you say?"

Irene's flat turned out to be a palatial set of elegant rooms taking up the top two floors of a converted town house just off Clarges

Street. Only the ground floor had been let out, and this, according to their hostess, was currently inhabited by a Jewish couple originally from Munich. "Grand-mère knew the Fleischers from her time wandering the Continent. He played cello in a chamber orchestra there and she taught at the conservatory, but of course that all ended under Hitler's horrid laws. They left everything behind, poor dears, and now he sweeps floors and she gives music lessons to nasty little children who bang away night and day with no sense of rhythm."

Horrible noises did seem to be coming from beneath their feet, compounding Lucy's mounting head-thumping nausea.

Irene tossed her keys on the table and shucked off her coat onto a chair. "There's a bathroom at the end of the passage. You can wash up while I rummage through my first aid kit and then I'll see to that cut on your leg. Despite my poor bicycling skills, I'm a whiz with iodine and a gauze pad, I promise." Bill was peering round him with a hopeful hungry look. "The sandwiches are in the icebox. There might even be some cake. Help yourself."

Now that she was here, Lucy had to admit a sponge-off and a few sticking plasters might not be a bad idea. Her knee ached, her palms stung, and there was a knot the size of a golf ball on the back of her head from hitting the sidewalk. She hoped Mason Oliver had a soft spot for the walking wounded. Splashing water on her face, she wiped away the worst of the road dust. Any makeup she might have worn was long gone, leaving her with smudges beneath her eyes and a jaundiced pallor reminiscent of an underbaked tea biscuit.

"I look a positive fright," she stated as she dragged her aching body back into the drawing room.

"No worse than you did before," Bill offered cheerfully.

"Thanks . . . I think."

"Here." He shoved a glass in her hand. "Miss Irene made you a drink."

"A bit early for cocktail hour, but under the circumstances, don't mind if I do." Lucy tossed it back, nearly choking on the sugary tang of—vegetable. "Sweet mother of pearl, are you trying to poison me?"

Bill frowned. "It's carrolade—carrots and rutabaga. What did you think it was?"

"Something suitably medicinal and numbing to help me recover—a Bloody Mary wouldn't be out of the question."

"It's not even lunchtime."

"Since when did you join the temperance league?" Lucy set the glass down. "Thank you, but unless there's Worcestershire, horseradish, and vodka involved, I'll pass on the veggie juice if it's all the same to you."

Irene entered just then, shooting both of them an odd and somewhat alarmed look before motioning toward the couch and a table full of various mystery potions in dark pharmacy bottles, squares of gauze, and enough bandages to wrap a pyramid full of mummies. Even a small sewing kit, though it looked rarely used. "Sit, and let me take a look at that knee."

"You're not planning to stitch me up, are you?"

"This is for your skirt, silly." She retrieved the glass of carrolade and handed it back to Lucy. "You may not like it, but you need to drink it."

"I don't want—"

Hard to believe, but that pixie face became positively stern. "All of it. If nothing else, it'll distract you."

"Why do I need distra—criminy! What is that? Sulfuric acid?"

"It's just iodine. Hold still and don't be a baby."

Ignoring Bill's smothered laughter, Lucy focused on the carrot-and-rutabaga juice through Irene's ministrations. Her knee still hurt, but oddly enough her stomach felt better, the odd bursts of light fading after not one but two glasses of the homemade orange brew. Who knew?

Both eyes pointed in the same direction, she was finally able to properly study her surroundings, which were like something out of *Country Life* magazine. All the place needed was its very own Jeeves offering pearls of wisdom with his extra-dry martinis. "You've landed in the clover, haven't you? Living on your own in urban splendor with a sea of lonely homesick men right outside your door."

"Not quite on my own. Grand-mère has a tendency to drop in unannounced every few days to 'see how I'm getting on.' I'm not sure if she's relieved or disappointed that she's never caught me in flagrante delicto with a man. But I have five loud, smelly brothers. The last thing I need is another male in my life." Irene sniffed. "Besides, I've seen too many of my friends taken in by the thrill of a wartime romance. Next thing they know, they've a row of nappies on the line and they're trapped in a marriage with a man they barely know. I didn't want that before the war. I certainly don't want it now."

"Who said anything about marriage? A nice evening out. Dinner. Dancing. A few laughs. Then sayonara, sailor, and you're on your merry way."

"I suppose," Irene said, obviously unconvinced.

"Carpe diem. Isn't that what the poets say? Seize the day."

"My days are bally well full already." With a stern grimace, Irene jerked tight the bandage round Lucy's knee. "What about you? Are you staying at the Dorchester?"

"Do Bill and I look like people who would be staying at the Dorchester?"

Bill looked rather like a delinquent casing his next target, but that seemed to be his normal expression. As long as his attention was taken up with egg-and-cress leftovers and kept off the priceless Lalique glassware, Lucy decided he was safe to leave to his own devices.

"Hard to say anymore," Irene said. "We're all looking a bit faded and worn round the edges. If one's bang up to the fashion mark, it usually means they're buying from the black market or gaga over some American GI with a fat pay packet."

Lucy bent her knee, hoping to return circulation to her toes. "Desperation can be a powerful force."

"For shampoo and nylons?"

"For normal. Or as close a facsimile as we can find right now."

"But when everyone else is muddling through, it seems wrong to pretend that nothing's changed, don't you think? Almost cowardly in a way."

Drawing in a breath, Lucy focused on the ache in her elbow and the sting of the antiseptic on her knee. Was she a coward? Michael had accused her of running away. But she wasn't. She was merely being practical. Making the best out of a bad situation. England wasn't her home no matter Amelia's nationality. But then neither was Singapore . . . nor Australia . . . nor Switzerland . . . nor France . . . nor any of the places she'd settled for a year or two at the most before moving on. She'd called herself a citizen of the world. Maybe that just meant she didn't fit in anywhere.

Irene wiped her hands on a towel. "There. No permanent scars but keep that gash clean and change the plaster daily."

"Feel better, Lucy?" Bill asked, his plate empty, his belly full.

"I expect I'll live, no thanks to you and your garden juice."

They were interrupted by the door buzzer, which sounded as if someone leaned against it. Irene hadn't even risen to her feet before a key rattled in the lock.

"Irene, darling. Are you at home?"

"In here, Grand-mère!"

"I just stopped by to bring Mrs. Fleischer some fresh eggs and real butter your mother was kind enough to have shipped up from Lower Stokenoor this morning, and thought I would pop up to ask you about that wretched invitation to Sir Reginald's birthday. You know I hate going to these dreary engagements alone, darling, and if I ask anyone else, they'll insist I act my age. You know how I dislike to do that. Acting *your* age is much more jolly."

A vibrant butterfly of a woman floated into the room, a silken patterned jacket billowing out behind her like a sail and a bright Liberty scarf tying up her hennaed hair. She had a slightly wrinklier version of Irene's pixie features, but her eyes shone with the same brilliance as the string of beads at her throat, and her lips and nails were touched in unapologetic scarlet.

"Oh, I say, darling. I didn't know you had company?" It was said in the form of a question, as if she was unsure whether Lucy and Bill were on a social call or here to scrub the floors.

"Not company so much as a patient," Lucy commented wryly.

"This is Miss Stanhope, Grand-mère," Irene said, delightfully pink. "I knocked her over with my bicycle outside the Dorchester and brought her back here to—"

"Mummify her? The poor lamb is practically suffocating under all that sticking plaster." Up close, the impression of masquerade ball meets operatic grande dame was only enhanced by an almost overwhelming aroma of patchouli. "How do you do, Miss . . . you did say Stanhope, didn't you? I'm a bit hard of hearing."

"Yes, ma'am. Lucy Stanhope."

The woman's plucked and painted brows drew close, her amused gaze sharpening for a moment before she turned to Bill with a shake of her head. "And you are?"

He left off picking a scab on his elbow to swallow and smooth a nervous hand over his hair, which refused taming. "Just Bill, mum."

The woman's frown deepened. Not enough to alarm. But it put Lucy on edge. As if cogs and wheels were slowly grinding into motion.

"Well, just Bill, mum. I am Lady Turnbull, Irene's esteemed grandmother." She sat heavily in a rather flimsy armchair Lucy was worried might collapse in an explosion of gaudy floral silk, but other than a few creaks—of chair or old bones she couldn't be certain— all stayed put. "I apologize for Irene. She only has to say the word and I'd have Pidge drive her anywhere she needs to go, but she insists on riding that calamity on wheels."

"Pidge is too busy looking after you to spare the time," Irene interrupted.

"Then I suggest you invest in some lessons before you kill someone—or yourself." She focused her attention back on Lucy. "You have a lovely accent, but I can't seem to place it. It's not American and certainly not Australian. Are you from Canada by any chance?"

"I'm not from anywhere really."

"Pfah!" She waved a dismissive airy hand. "Everyone is from somewhere. You didn't drop from the heavens or spring into being like a soap bubble."

"My father's American. My mother, English."

"There, you see? Puzzle solved." Her probing gaze slid from Lucy to Bill and back, the cogs gaining traction. The wheels whirring.

Lucy's insides knotted. Lady Turnbull was onto her. Another few moments of glancing interrogation and she'd have the entire unvarnished truth.

It was time to go.

"It was lovely meeting you, but Bill and I really must dash," Lucy explained, uneasy, as she sidled toward the door.

"What about my cake?" Bill whinged.

Lucy flashed Bill a look. He scowled right back.

"You say your mother is English? Would I know the family?" Lady Turnbull asked, completely ignoring Lucy's attempt at a dignified retreat.

"It sometimes seems as if Grand-mère's related to half of England and friends with the other half," Irene interjected, equal parts pride and exasperation in her face as she said this.

Lucy subtly backed toward the door while keeping up a steady stream of conversation. Maybe they wouldn't notice. With one arm behind her back, she fumbled for the knob. "Yes, well, we Stanhopes are all tediously dull and make it a habit never to come to London . . . one has to practically pry us from our little corner of the country like turtles from our shell."

By now, Lady Turnbull's frown of confusion was beginning to look like a frown of consideration. "Stanhope . . . Stanhope . . . why does that name sound so familiar?"

"It's a very familiar sort of name. There are positively scads of us about." Lucy grabbed up her suitcase. "Come on, Bill. Thank you for the first aid."

"Wait," Irene called after as Lucy clambered down the stairs, Bill at her heels.

"TTFN!"

Back on the sidewalk, Bill laughed as they hurried down the street toward the bus stop, but Lucy felt as if she were running away all over again.

We're almost there, Lucy. Look, it's the Odeon." Bill wriggled in his seat, nearly clambering over Lucy in an attempt to see out the window as the trolley bus rumbled up Hackney Road. "You think she'll be home? She usually works until half four."

"Let's hope she took a rare day off."

He wiped at the grime of the glass and peered with great hungry eyes. If the West End had been a gritty jigsaw of cordoned-off streets and bombed-out buildings, the eastern reaches of the capital looked as if a giant foot had smashed flat whole neighborhoods. A knot of ragged children clambered over piles of bulldozed scrap for bits of shrapnel while a pair of women in aprons and scarves smoked cigarettes as they watched from fresh-swept marble doorsteps across the way. A district nurse cycled past in her prim blue cap and coat.

Bill's fevered giddiness seemed to falter with each exploded alteration to the world he remembered. His body took on an almost nervous tension, bottom lip caught between his teeth.

"Look at you. You're a positive mess, Bill Smedley," Lucy said, seeking to distract him as yet another bombed-out building came into view. "At least run a comb through your hair."

He allowed himself to be tidied, though without pomade or water, there was no taming the rooster's comb he sported at the back. "There. That's a little better. We don't want your mother thinking I haven't taken proper care of you."

"She wouldn't think that. I'd make sure." Lucy was relieved when the sparkle returned to his otherwise pinched and sallow features. "I can't wait to show you our street. I'll introduce you to everyone in our building, even Mr. Purslip what some think done away with his missus. Not me. I think she run off with that salesman was selling toasters from out the back of a lorry. Mam always said Mrs. Purslip had airs above herself and a toaster salesman from Hutton-on-Tilby was just what she deserved."

"I'm sure Mr. Purslip is well rid of her."

"And there's the canal where us boys used to swim in the summer, and the old schoolyard. My teacher Miss Blessing was pretty as the pinup girl in the back room of Mr. Tate's butcher's shop. All the boys used to make eyes at her." He put his hands out in front of him, palms cupped. "She had bazoombas—"

"Got the picture. Enough said about Miss Blessing."

Bill turned back to the window. "You wait, Lucy. We'll have a cracking time."

"It sounds wonderful, Bill, but you know I can't hang about once I've delivered you."

His face fell. "Oh, right. Mr. Oliver from America."

"You did say he's still registered at the hotel, right?"

"That's what a baggage porter told me. Said as how he's got a whole string of girls chasing after him. All wanting to star in his picture. Is that what you want to do, Lucy? I mean, this bloke could turn out to be a rotter like all the rest."

"A chance I'm willing to take."

"But you'll be all alone once I'm gone. Won't you be lonely?"

"I don't plan on being alone long, Bill . . . and if I play my cards right, definitely not lonely."

"That don't sound half-proper."

"The way I do it, it won't be." She tried to cajole him with a sly wink, but he only gave a halfhearted smile. "Come on. You know me. I'm like a cat . . .'"

"You always land on your feet," he recited in a dull monotone as he played with a bit of bent metal trim. "I suppose."

She nudged him with an elbow. "Buck up. You're back home where you belong. No more Mr. and Mrs. Sayres. Just you and your mam together again."

A dimple winked at the edge of his mouth, his mood lifting. "You think she'll be surprised to see me? You don't think she'll cry, do you? I'd hate to have her cry. It makes her eyes all puffy. She don't like it when she looks puffy. Says it's not elegant-like."

"I have a handkerchief if the waterworks start."

Bill turned back to the bus window with a jiggle in his legs like a puppy at the door, so he didn't see Lucy's smile fade or catch a glimpse of the wad of crumpled linen twisted between her hands.

They were set down halfway up the road by the gutted abandoned remains of what once must have been a pretty garden square. Bill strained against her slower pace, his breath shallow and quick, his eyes everywhere at once as if drinking in this bitter taste of home.

"How much farther along?" Lucy asked, hurrying to keep up.

He looked around as if gauging his bearings. A barrage balloon floated above the rooftops to the east of them. Another farther along loomed sinister to the north. "It's another street over and then down the way past the school."

Lucy followed, nearly colliding with him as he drew up short at the end of a street—or what had once been a street. They stood on the corner beside a dented phone box, a scarlet gash against the destruction beyond. Tidy shops and busy warehouses, grubby tenements and neat rows of terrace houses were nothing more now than jumbled piles of scattered rubble, splintered timbers, and gaping glassless windows.

He took a few steps up the street before turning around. "This ain't right. Can't be. Must have passed it somehow."

They retraced their steps, not once but twice, ending at the same point of destruction each time.

She looked about for someone to ask the way and spotted a man in cap and suspenders wheeling a barrow. "Pardon me, but is this Mansford Terrace?"

He gave a doleful shake of his head. "It were until last year."

Chapter 19

"E at something. It will make you feel better."

Bill shook his head as he pushed his mushy peas about with the tip of his fork.

"Then do it because it will make me feel better. You look pale as a ghost and I haven't had to shout at you once in the past hour. It's positively terrifying."

Bill just stared at the scratched marble-topped table, kicking his chair in a steady rhythm that set Lucy's teeth on edge.

She was at a loss. Sarcastic banter tended to be her way of dealing with anything unpleasant. Never take life too seriously. Never let them see they could hurt you. But Bill's crumpled silence called for more than a clever quip or a droll comment. It called for empathy and compassion. She was out of practice at both.

"I'm sure they would have sent a telegram to the Sayres if something had happened to your mother. She probably moved in with nearby relatives."

He shivered and there was a sickly sheen of sweat across his brow. "Ain't got none."

"What about friends or people she worked with?"

He picked at his food.

"Well, if you're not going to eat your lunch, why not offer it to Rufus?" she said, hoping caring for the bird might take his mind off his grief.

Bill tore a palmful of crumbs off a piece of uninspiring brown grainy bread. He peered into the basket, chewing his lip. "Go on, Rufus. Eat." He looked up, his expression bleak. "What's wrong with him? He won't eat. He don't even chirp no more."

"Sounds like someone else I know," she said with a pointed look.

"You think he misses his mam like I miss mine?"

Lucy joined Bill in examining the bird. It lay unmoving, its broken wing spread like gray lace across the newspaper lining the bottom of the basket. The crumbs from this morning were soggy and smeared across the newsprint. "I think you're doing all you can, but sometimes that's still not enough. Sometimes bad things just happen and there's nothing we can do about it."

His eyes glistened, his face twisted now with anger rather than sorrow. "I shouldn't have brought him. I should have left him in the hedgerow like you said. Now he'll die and it's my fault. And me mam's not even here to see him."

A couple at a nearby table looked over. A waitress paused in pouring a cup of tea.

"What if she's"—he swallowed hard—"dead, Lucy? I got what's left of that half crown and the tuppence I found in the drain. Think that'll be enough?"

"For what?"

"For going on with until I can find a job. They might hire me at the gasworks, mightn't they? I can lie and tell 'em I'm sixteen."

"Don't even start talking like that."

"But I'll have to be doing something if . . ." His words petered out in another shove of peas with his fork.

"I know exactly how you're feeling and it's completely beastly."

He offered up a ferocious look of hostile disbelief.

"It's true. I was younger than you when my parents split up." She drew in a breath to steady herself and clenched her hands until her nails dug into her palms. "I still remember driving away from our house in Philadelphia. Seeing everything I'd ever known getting smaller and smaller out the back window." The memories were drawn from her like splinters with a needle. She licked her lips and cleared her throat before she continued, but at least Bill watched her now with interest rather than rage. "For months, I woke each morning expecting to be back in my old bed with Nanny rocking beside me and light streaming through the lace at the windows making patterns on the floor. It was like a part of me was left in that moment before, when my life was humming along just as I wished, and the moment after, when the world shifted and cracked under my feet, and no matter how I wished it, nothing would ever be the same again."

Bill's fork had paused, tines deep in his mash, and his jaw clenched and unclenched as he fought back tears. "It's not the same. Your mam is still living."

She felt her own jaw clenching, her throat closing around her words even as she spoke them. "No, of course it's not the same." She swallowed back the swamping rush of emotion threatening to consume her. It would do Bill no good and turn her into the kind of sniveling drip she despised. Amelia wasn't worth her tears. "I have an idea. I don't know why I didn't think of it before. Remember what Sergeant Raneri taught you? Close your eyes and listen for your mother."

"But—"

"Go on. Open your mind and your ears and tell me what you hear."

He scrunched his eyes shut. His screwed-up little face looked on the verge of tears, pale and pinched and unspeakably young. He sat still but for the shallow rise and fall of his chest for what seemed an eternity.

Lucy felt herself leaning forward in her chair, palms dry, shoulders damp from nerves. "Well?" she asked finally.

His eyes snapped open. "I heard her, Lucy. I did. Just a few words, mind you, but it was definitely her. She was singing 'Billy Boy.' She's alive. I know it." He smiled through his shining eyes and his cheeks were flushed.

"Of course she is," Lucy replied, tartness back on her tongue. "I never doubted it for an instant. One small question, though—amid all that singing, did she happen to mention an address?"

They started their search for answers on Bethnal Green Road. The woman selling eels said she knew of the bombing at Mansford Terrace and wasn't it a crying shame. Last she heard, some of the families had moved south into tenements nearer Whitechapel.

A butcher selling offal and "C" sausages from the back of a cart cursed the bloody Jerries whose bombs had killed his sister as she made her way from the bus stop on Cable Street, but no, he didn't know nothing about the residents of Mansford Terrace. Best try the local ARP first aid station.

A warden there sent them to a shelter near Liverpool Street, which in turn sent them to Town Hall, a very official building full of very official people, none of whom seemed to either know what happened to Mrs. Matilda Smedley of Mansford Terrace or particularly care.

One rather condescending clerk suggested they try the shelter near Liverpool Street or perhaps the local ARP first aid station, at which point Lucy finally gave unladylike vent to her frustration that had even young Bill goggle eyed at her invective.

Unfortunately, while completely satisfying, her colorful—if physically impossible—suggestions as to what the toffee-nosed upstart could do with his advice landed her and Bill on the corner with a stern warning not to come back. The bright spring day had taken a decidedly gray turn. Slow-moving clouds thickened black-rimmed across the sky and a dank wind carried with it the sour greasy odors of the Thames at low tide.

"I'm sorry, Bill. I shouldn't have lost my temper."

"Crikey, miss. That bloke inside went red as a boiled crab."

"Serves him right, but it's left us no better off than when we started."

"Maybe so, but it was worth it to hear you give him what-for. Where to now? Back to the shelter like the man said, or maybe down toward Cheshire Street or Brick Lane? Mam spent a lot of time down that way."

"I say we try the police. We passed a station five minutes ago."

"The coppers, miss?" Bill's eyes flashed in alarm. "We can't."

"They're not my first choice either, but I've run out of ideas. And they could help."

Bill's chin firmed. "They won't do nothing but poke their noses in and ask a lot of questions. They'll find out I ran away. They'll make me go back to the Sayres to live." He folded his arms across his chest, his legs spread in a fighter's stance. "I won't go, and you can't make me."

"I wouldn't let them send you back to the Sayres. Even if they can't find your mother, I'm sure they'd find you a better place to stay."

"It wouldn't matter where I went. The people wouldn't want me. Not really. They'd only be doing it because they had to. Because it was their duty."

The Sayres. Aunt Cynthia. Bill might have come from the tenements of Bethnal Green while Lucy was born to power and position, but they were more alike than different. Her defiance faded. "Fine. No police, but what do you propose we do?"

"We could try down the Lion. Mam never missed a Saturday night there. Maybe someone will know where she's gone."

"Fine. I could use a drink, and my feet are killing me. To the pub it is."

The Lion stood on the corner of St. Peter's Avenue and a more uninviting place could hardly have been dreamed up. Its front window had been blown out at some point and replaced with a large piece of muslin tacked over the gaping hole. The door, once a cheerful red, was now a chipped and weathered grubby brown, while a drunkard sat on the pavement just outside with a jug in one hand and a watery toothless gaze for all who entered.

"That's Joe. He always sits there. Hiya, Joe."

The man squinted at Bill but gave no other sign he acknowledged the salutation or even comprehended it.

The pub's interior was barely more appealing. It was dim and smoky with a floor scarred and warped from years of abuse and a drab air of wartime neglect. In the public bar, a few hardy souls nursed their pints as they exchanged gossip with the barman while a young couple, the boy in uniform, the girl dolled up in lipstick and a victory roll, sat at a table in the saloon staring into each other's eyes over two glasses of cider.

She'd get nothing sensible out of those two lovebirds.

Ignoring the disapproving looks, Lucy bellied up to the bar alongside the men. "A gin if you have it."

Her accent sparked curiosity, her looks admiration, but it was Bill who roused the men to attention.

"Is that you, Mr. Leonard?" he said with a gum-cracking grin. "How's the missus? She still suffering from weak nerves?"

A broad-shouldered man with a face like a platter eyed Bill with new interest.

"It's grand to see you too, Ginger Jack," Bill continued. "Is your boy Frank still in Scrubs, or did they let him out for good behavior?"

A scrawny underfed gentleman in a flat cap and a pair of dungaree coveralls blearily sat up and took notice.

"Why, Billy Smedley, as I live and breathe." The barman put down Lucy's gin with a smile of recognition. "What are you doing here?"

"And with her?" Ginger Jack thumbed at Lucy. "She one of them Salvation Army birds come to tell us off over our evil ways?"

Lucy tossed back her gin. "I wouldn't dream of it."

Ginger Jack pushed his way between her and Bill, looking her over from bleary, red-rimmed eyes. "She's a Yank. I can tell by her talking. Hey, you know William Powell what was in *Evelyn Prentice*? That's my favorite. Love me a good thriller."

"This is Lucy, Sean," Bill explained to the barman. "She's helping me find my mam."

"You try the shelter over—?"

"If you say on Liverpool Street, I shall strangle you with your own snakeskin belt." Lucy pushed her glass back across the bar for a refill. "Think harder."

"She always came here on a Saturday," Bill supplied. "Never missed a evening out unless she was poorly."

"True, Tilda Smedley always did like to dress smart and enjoy a song and a drink of a weekend."

"That's not all she liked." Mr. Leonard cackled knowingly into his foaming tankard until Ginger Jack slapped him on the back of the head. The barman glared at both of them like a schoolmaster subduing two urchins before turning to Bill with a sympathetic shrug of his shoulders.

"Tilda was always one of my better customers, but I ain't seen her lately, Bill. Not for maybe two or three months."

Lucy perked up. "But it *has* been in the last two months. You're sure of that."

The barman scratched his scalp as he considered. "I'm mostly certain. Seems like it was just toward the end of February."

"Aye, that it was," Ginger Jack interrupted. "I remember she was wearing a pretty red scarf, and she'd a winter shine to her cheeks. Come in with a bloke I never seen before. Big fella. Sailor maybe, or a docker from down Poplar way? I never seen him round here before. Two of them were drinking and carrying on, even singing songs along with Wilkins on the piano. Always did have a nice voice to go with that pretty face of hers, did Tilda Smedley."

"A mite too pretty for her own good, if you ask me." Mr. Leonard continued to smile like a baboon.

"Well, no one was asking you, was they?"

"She'd do better to find a nice man and settle down 'stead of walking out every Saturday with a different bloke. Why don't she find a nice man and settle down, eh, Bill?"

"She ain't found the right one yet, I expect, Mr. Leonard. But Mam always says, you got to be kissing a lot of frogs before you find your prince."

"That leaves Leonard out. He's all frog."

"I'm more of a catch than you any day, you old coot."

"Don't be daft. Tilda's young enough to be your daughter."

"You're the one who's daft. I'm only thirty-five."

"You ain't seen thirty-five for a score of years at least, Crandall Leonard. And don't even try to tell me otherwise."

Lucy felt like a spectator at a tennis match before she cut through the back-and-forth. "Hear that, Bill? She was alive and well in February. Now all we have to do is find out where she's gone."

Every freckle on Bill's face seemed to quiver with excitement. "Would any of you know where she might be living?"

The men shook their heads, their earlier animation dimmed. But then, Ginger Jack straightened with a light bulb look on his weedy features. "Ace'd know where she's off to."

The others agreed with nods of their heads. "Aye, that's probably true. He's an ear at every keyhole, does the lad. He'd know for sure."

"Ace?" Lucy asked.

"His real name's Valentine," Bill answered, "but your life ain't worth a tuppence if you call him that. It's just Ace. He's cracking. Taught me everything I know."

"A dubious distinction." Lucy lifted an eyebrow in skeptical recognition. "He's one of the boys at the Lion, isn't he? One of the boys you're always on about?"

"He's *the* boy. Everyone knows Ace. He's grand."

Lucy just bet he was. Grand in a larcenous kind of way.

"Where can we find this Ace?" She addressed the barman as he refilled her glass. He seemed to be the only one even halfway sober.

His gaze grew shuttered. "Dunno where he might be this time of day, but he and his mates usually turn up here for a pint most evenings."

"If you see him, let him know Miss Stanhope is asking after him. We'll be back tomorrow evening."

"I'll tell him, but you want to be careful of Ace, miss. He and his boys, they ain't exactly what you'd call gentlemen."

"All we want is news of Bill's mother. Surely he can't grudge us that."

"He might know or he might not, but either way it'll cost you. And his price ain't always in pounds and pence if you take my meanin'."

"I appreciate the warning."

"Ta, Mr. Leonard." Bill scooted off the stool with a last freckled smile, his earlier grief evaporated. "Tell Fred I said hello, Ginger Jack."

"Will do, Billy. Next time I visit him in stir I'll pass on your regards."

"Remember me to your mam, Bill. Tell her we miss seeing her pretty face here at the Lion," Mr. Leonard said, smirking, which elicited another slap to the back of the head.

Lucy lingered to finish her gin before following Bill, but she was held up by the barman's hand on her arm.

He seemed to study her closely. "It's good of you to take an interest in the lad, miss. He's not had a lot of proper raising up. More like t'other way around. It's always been just the two of 'em, and he looked after his mum better than most boys twice his age. Tilda shouldn't never have sent him away like she did."

"I'm sure she thought she was doing what was best for Bill."

"Maybe so. But doing what's best ain't always doing what's right, is it?"

Put it on Mr. Fortescue's account."

It had been a long time since she'd used that particular phrase—and frankly, she wasn't certain of its current efficacy—but the result was the same as always. An obsequious bow and a rush to do her bidding, even ahead of the elderly woman in the fox fur and the man wearing general's tabs. Lucy had forgotten how nice it felt, especially after a day of tramping from pillar to post and back again. If Bill's mother had vanished in a poof of magic, she could not have disappeared more thoroughly. Lucy could only hope Ace might offer up some clues. Bill might be content enough for now, but it wouldn't take long for the worst of the what-ifs to reemerge. If history served her, these usually occurred between three and four in the morning when life was at its blackest.

"Crikey, this place's bigger than the Sayres' whole house," he said, exploring every inch of their hotel suite, including drawers, closets, cupboards, and even under the bed.

Lucy quickly closed the door on the porter before he realized their deception and tossed them back out on the street. "My step-father always stays here when he travels to London. My mother prefers Claridge's. The Connaught doesn't suit her sense of conspicuous consumption."

"You sure they won't mind us staying here?"

His question gave her pause for only a moment. "Quite sure."

"If they turn up, we could share. There's plenty of room. I can sleep in the bathtub. It'd be jolly. Almost as good as sleeping in a shed."

Stretching out on the enormous sofa in the opulent sitting room, she gave a contented sigh. "The shed was definitely the high-water mark of *my* trip so far."

Bill began a tour of the bathroom while Lucy fantasized about rolling herself in a soft blanket for a twenty-four-hour nap with no interruptions.

Sadly, reality meant dragging herself off the couch to assess the damage.

What she met in her mirror did not inspire optimism: rat-tailed hair and wet, rumpled clothes more suited by style—and smell—to a Somerset dairy farm than a Mayfair nightclub. She shooed Bill out of the bathroom. "I'm going to scrub myself from top to bottom. Don't bother me unless there's fire or blood involved."

By the time she emerged from a long leisurely soak, lulled nearly to a stupor by gallons of steaming water and scented soap, she felt almost human again.

Now for the heavy lifting.

She sat at her dressing table, staring blindly at her reflection as she listened to the radiator clank and an attentive maid knock on a door farther down the corridor, the muffled sounds of Mount Street traffic underpinning the dulcet voice of Vera Lynn coming from the Ekco radio on the credenza. Past and present mingled and overlapped like inrushing waves and ebbing tides on the beach below Nanreath Hall. She felt disoriented, as if she were standing outside herself looking at an intimate stranger.

"Lucy?" Bill held her hairbrush. "I can comb out your hair if you like."

"I don't . . ." She paused when she saw the solemn, almost crestfallen look on his face. Perhaps he too found himself haunted by memories tonight. "Thank you, Bill. I don't think I've had a nicer offer all day."

He drew the bristles through her damp hair. If Lucy closed her eyes, she could imagine it was her Chinese amah wielding the brush, and she was back in Singapore with the promise of a jazz-filled night drenched in champagne and caviar ahead of her.

As she applied her carefully hoarded cosmetics, Lucy felt her nerves dissolving like a sugar cube at the bottom of a champagne flute.

"You really do have a gentle touch, don't you? Better than any high-end hair salon."

Bill grinned.

She'd not realized how long her hair had grown since she'd arrived in England. She'd always kept it closer to shoulder length and arranged in elaborate pin curls or tight waves. Now it hung nearly to the middle of her back, straight, thick, and treacle dark.

She'd always envied Amelia her shining mass of auburn curls. Loosed of its pins, it was a wild tangled cloud that fell to her hips, though it was rare anyone saw her like that. Not even Lucy had been allowed to see past the artistic perfection to the real woman beneath. Perhaps after so many years of playing a part, the attention-seeker within had forgotten how to be artless and unbound. Or perhaps there was simply nothing beneath the Max Factor façade to reveal. Perhaps Amelia really was thin as the newspaper society page and shallow as a looking glass.

The excited tingle of anticipation sank to the pit of Lucy's stomach like a bad oyster.

What a horrible epitaph—to leave nothing behind simply because one gave nothing of oneself away.

What if you found you could count on someone else?

"Are you all right, miss?"

She was recalled to the present and her watery blurred reflection staring back at her, unblinking, from the mirror. She dabbed at her mascara with a tissue. "Of course. Why do you ask?"

"'Cause you're crying."

A sharp knock at the door broke her from the depressing turn of her thoughts.

A maid with her gown, freshly cleaned and pressed, followed by a porter bearing room service: finger sandwiches, scones warm from the oven, and an aromatic pot of Darjeeling to wash it down. But it was the bottle of wine that some particularly astute waiter in the bowels of the Connaught kitchens had provided that made Lucy smile.

As Bill hovered over the platter with an imploring glance her direction, she laughed. "Go on. Have as much as you want. You've earned it."

"Crikey, miss. Ham, chicken, even cheese. The cream's thick enough to stand my spoon up. And look at the berries. I've died and gone to my reward. You sure it's legal?"

"So far restaurants are exempt from rationing."

Bill's response to this information involved downing two more sandwiches and another jam-covered scone. She'd never seen anyone take such pleasure in the simple act of eating, but then she'd never known anyone who'd lived without the guarantee of a next meal. "Don't seem fair, do it? That those what got the money can live just as if there ain't no war on."

"No, but it's always been that way. The rich can afford to wear blinders."

"Maybe so, but that don't make it right." She was saved from answering when, seemingly sated, Bill collapsed across a chair clutching his stomach. "Blimey, I'm stuffed fatter than a Christmas goose."

"Then you can go wash up. And that means more than hands and face. I want every inch of you to touch water, do you hear?"

"But I washed yesterday."

"And if I have my way, you'll wash tomorrow as well. You reek of adolescent male."

"You're like one of them medusas; ain't that them women with snakes coming out of their mouths?"

"Not quite, but your point is taken and I'm flattered." She pointed. "Bath. Now."

He puffed himself up as if he might argue but, recognizing the steel in her gaze, chose to slink off, muttering under his breath about the unfairness of life.

Alone, she found herself unable to eat but fortified herself with a tumblerful of liquid confidence before completing her toilette. No hot rollers available, she arranged her hair in a simple up-twist fastened off her face with a jeweled comb and finished her transformation with a liberal application of red Tangee lipstick and a spritz of Shalimar.

She smiled in satisfaction at her reflection. Not exactly Dorothy Lamour but definitely second-glance worthy.

Drawing off her robe, she oozed into the refurbished gown.

The cool slink of the underskirt against her newly lotioned skin after days of rough wool and scratchy cotton immediately lifted her spirits. She fingered the expensive chiffon, the shimmering sequins along the bodice, the sleek cascade of material that skimmed her hips before flaring just above her knees. The ladies of the Charbury Sewing Circle had surpassed even her wildest imaginings. They had taken her ideas and improved upon them, turning Aunt Cynthia's mothballed castoff into a unique and daring original design.

She admired herself from every angle in the mirror, trying to imagine Aunt Cynthia—solidly middle-aged, duty-driven Aunt Cynthia—hot-footing the night away with some tuxedo-clad tulip of fashion at Café de Paris or the Kit-Cat Club.

Bill emerged before her head exploded with the effort.

"What do you think?" She pirouetted.

"Crikey, miss. You look a real treat."

"Now if only Mason Oliver thinks so."

He sat on the edge of the sofa and watched her as she primped. "What if we found your mam too? Then you wouldn't have to go to the States."

His words stole her breath like the punch of a fist.

"I figured it all out while I was washing up. We can get Ace and the lads at the Lion. They got mates all over the city that tells 'em what's what."

"Why does that not surprise me?"

"You done for me, Miss Lucy, and now I do for you. Just like last time, eh? If you find her, you can stay here in England, maybe even in London, and we can still see each other. What do you say?"

The BBC announced the hour, echoed by the faint sound of Big Ben's chimes. A newscaster came on reading the headlines of the night. Bombs. Sinkings. Advances. Retreats. Death. Death. Death.

Lucy sank back into the chair, her earlier pleasure gone. Instead, anger burned up her throat and pounded at her temples.

It was so damned typical of Amelia to leave without saying good-bye. Would it have killed her to toss off a last farewell wave before leaving Lucy with one more nanny, one more governess, one more headmistress? Or better yet, turn around—just once—to see Lucy standing alone? All she'd ever wanted was a smile, a hug, a "good show," or a "well done."

Was that so impossible?

"Lucy?" Bill said quietly.

She smiled until her cheeks felt as if they might crack. "I think that's a brilliant plan, Bill."

Chapter 20

She made a show of emerging from her taxi, though she'd only hailed him round the corner after hoofing it most of the way from Mount Street. But appearances were everything and to be seen walking to the front entrance to the Dorchester as if she were queuing for a job would put her at a disadvantage right from the start.

Lucy was down to her last seven shillings. If she played her cards right, she'd never have to use them.

Being sure to ignore the attentive doorman, she swanned through the crowded lobby as if she owned it. She imagined herself as a pilot on a bombing raid. Target selected, route mapped out down to the smallest detail, taking into consideration every possible obstacle.

As she left her wrap with the cloakroom attendant, she sensed the eyes and the curious whispers that followed her, though she'd die before she acknowledged them. With a regal tilt to her chin, Lucy passed through to the sumptuous promenade, where men, young and old, in uniforms from every country in the empire, mingled with glittering women in evening gowns. A babble of conversation underpinned the smoky romantic music being played by the orchestra in the ballroom next door. A pair of working girls plied their trade in a darkened corner with a couple of staff officers. Men in deceptively bland suits with deceptively bland faces met with others of the same ilk as big business was hashed out and secrets were bought and sold. A liveried waiter passed with a tray of drinks. A manager in a frock coat chivied a set of overworked porters.

She smiled to be back among her own cutthroat kind.

Sideways glances became stares. Conversations dwindled, picking up again once she moved on. Whispers from nearby followed her. She disregarded them all while committing every dropped name to memory and accepting every second look with a sultry flick of her lashes and a surreptitious curve of her lips. Mystery would be her calling card tonight.

Stepping into the hotel's grill, she paused for a moment to survey the evening crowd of diners. A few faces she recognized from the newspapers. A few more looked as if they actively avoided being photographed. She dismissed them all, her attention firmly riveted on the man holding court at a table near the bar.

Bookended by a slender round-faced redhead and a healthy bubbly blonde who looked as if she'd be more at home with a hockey stick in her hand than a champagne flute, Mason Oliver was much as she remembered him. Still handsome in a well-fed, preening way like a prized Persian cat.

In place of an elegant dinner jacket or a sharp uniform, he wore a sober three-piece suit, though she noted canary-yellow socks peeking from beneath his trouser cuffs. Observing him from the far end of the room, she watched as the redhead leaned across for the bottle of champers, allowing Oliver a view straight to the South Pole. To his credit, he seemed completely oblivious to the ploy. The blonde gushed at something he said, her eager enthusiasm and horsey laugh drawing looks from the nearby tables.

Lucy snagged a whiskey from a passing tray. It burned a path from her gullet to her knees but fortified her against a mad desire to turn tail and flee. She'd come too far to back out now.

Seating herself at the bar—perfectly situated so that Oliver's gaze would casually fall her direction—she ordered a gimlet, heavy on the gin. As hoped, the handsome young bartender winked and waved away her money as he pushed the drink across to her.

"Miss Stanhope?" A light tenor voice interrupted her appreciation of both the delicious bartender and his delicious gimlet. "Is that really you?"

She turned on her stool, her expression one of aristocratic ennui. "I'm sorry, have we met?"

He was standing with a jovial, toothy smile, much to the dismay of his dinner companions. "Mason Oliver—we met in Singapore last year. Don't pretend you don't remember. I never forget a face, and certainly not one as striking as yours."

She lifted her brows in slow recognition. "Of course, Mr. Oliver. It's wonderful to see you again, though I'm surprised to find you in London. Last I heard you were headed home to the good old US of A."

"I'm here visiting as part of a USO mission. Now that our boys are joining the fight, we have to have some good clean American entertainment to remind them of what they're fighting for."

"I've met some of those boys. Are you sure clean is what they're after?"

Laughing, he conceded, "We can lead a horse to water, Miss Stanhope. We can't make him drink." He glanced back at the blonde, who looked as if she'd like to knock a hockey ball right between Lucy's eyes. "Scoot over, Pamela. That's right, Lizzie. Make room for an old friend from the exotic Far East. What's your poison? The girls are drinking champagne, but as I recall you like your alcohol with a little more kick."

"Another gimlet would be divine." Lucy gracefully slid into the chair vacated by the disgruntled Pamela. "I never did ask you how that evening at the *bangsawan* theater went."

He gave a friendly laugh. "I couldn't have been more delighted, though, as I recall, your mother seemed rather unwell and we had to leave partway through. How is Lady Amelia? Did she accompany you to London?" He scanned the room expectantly.

"I'm afraid not." Ignoring the lurch of her stomach and unable to meet his eyes, she reached into her handbag and artistically removed a Sobranie from her cigarette case. "She and Fortescue made arrangements to remain in Australia. I suppose he wanted to be as close to his investments as possible in case any news of them reached the Allies."

His dazzling cap-toothed smile faded, but only for a moment before it returned a thousand watts brighter than before as he offered her a light. "London's loss is Melbourne's gain."

She leaned close, not in a vulgar "look at me" way as that tart Pamela had tried, but just enough to show she was interested. "I hope I can make up—at least in small part—for Lady Amelia's absence."

"Are you kidding? It's like old times seeing you again."

"I saw *Thistledown Manor* four times when it came to town a few months ago. I got goose bumps it was so good."

"You're sweet to say so, and I suppose the academy agreed, but I could have done better. With this next one I'm planning—"

"So there's a next one?"

Oliver reclined in his chair with tycoon smugness. "Soon as I get back. We're still searching for just the right actress, but we've got our leading man all lined up."

"Really?" Lucy couldn't help herself. "It wouldn't be William Powell, by any chance, would it?"

The evening was perfect—well, almost perfect. Damn it, it should have been perfect. Everything was progressing according to plan. The mirrored ballroom reflected back a dazzling kaleidoscope of dancers clinging to each other in the dim lamplight, a heady buzz loosened her limbs and hazed the world in a gentle glow, and the handsome man in her arms had the power to sweep her far away from Aunt Cynthia and the dreary, disinfected corridors of Nanreath Hall. Yet, something felt wrong. No, not wrong exactly, but definitely uncomfortable, like a pebble in one's shoe. She could ignore it for so long and then the pang would strike, and her pleasure would dim, her evening's perfection fraying at the edges.

It wasn't Mr. Oliver's fault.

He couldn't help that his wavy cinematic hair wasn't that certain shade of sun-touched barley gold. At least he had a full head of it.

She closed her eyes and held him close.

Or that he was a bit padded round the middle. Really, what was so special about those lean, athletic types anyway?

Ignoring his slight paunch, she glanced swiftly up at Oliver, who was as blandly handsome and innocuously kind as ever, his manner still brimming with over-the-top joie de vivre.

He'd never scold with boy-next-door provincial morality or offer sharp-edged Sunday school criticisms of her principles. But then neither would she catch a fleeting glimpse of something hot and dark in his superficial gaze or experience that zing of unexpected anticipation when he offered her his lotion-soft hand.

He didn't spend his evenings down at the pub with his mates. Or help little old ladies dial up their favorite radio show.

He would never ever own a cow.

Mason Oliver might be her rescuer.

He wasn't her knight in shining armor.

Lucy gave herself a mental slap. What was wrong with her? She needed to get a grip. She'd not hitched halfway across England to hesitate now. Not when she was a foxtrot away from a California future.

". . . Bass if you have it . . ."

That voice. That beer. Was this someone's horrible idea of a bad joke?

She risked a glance toward the bar.

Slicked-back blond hair. An angular face, all teasing eyes and quirky mouth. He chatted with the bartender over his pint as if he were down at the local public house with the lads, dimple flashing. The only one in this damned hotel not playing a part.

". . . not really my crowd . . . more a beer-and-skittles type . . ."

He'd refused the invitation. He'd told her flat out he wanted nothing to do with Arabella. So what in God's name was he doing here?

". . . lost ten bob on Manchester City in the third round of the War Cup . . ."

Did he still think he could convince her to stay in England? Was that his intention by following her here? Who did he think he was, telling her what she should and shouldn't do? What gave him the right to boss her about?

Maybe if she simply pretended she hadn't seen him. The room was crowded, it wasn't out of the realm of possibility that she wouldn't notice. The refrain of "Day Dream" and Oliver's fancy footwork sent her spinning out of range. She could breathe again.

"May I cut in?" A tap on Oliver's shoulder brought them stumbling to a stop.

No, no, no. This wasn't happening. Her evening was not about to be sabotaged.

"Of course," Oliver conceded—damn him. He might have put up a little more of a fight. She didn't necessarily want a scene, but now and then it was gratifying to feel like a bone caught between two dogs.

"Evening, lass. I believe you still owe me a dance."

This was completely and utterly unfair. Dirty pool at its dirtiest. She wanted to beat him senseless. Instead, all she could do was smile like a damned fool. "Never let it be said I don't pay my debts."

She recovered her aplomb almost immediately, finishing the dance in stone-cold silence, hoping her frozen glare was enough to rid him of any misconceptions.

All she accomplished was a throaty chuckle and a flash of that damned infuriating dimple. "You can frown all you like, lass, but I know the truth."

"And what's that?" she said as they broke apart.

He caught hold of her hand before she could escape, his fingers encircling her wrist. The scar on his knuckle stood out white against the tan of his skin. "You're pleased to see me."

A flutter in her belly, she tore free. "Aren't you an arrogant sod. I was startled, that's all."

He grinned. She fumed.

The story of their relationship.

Despite her very obvious cold shoulder, he trailed Lucy back to Oliver's table, where she reluctantly explained through a clenched jaw that Michael was an old friend up from Somerset.

While Pamela and Lizzie tipsily batted their lashes, Oliver

smiled indulgently. "Has anyone ever told you how closely you resemble a young Tyrone Power? I think it's the line of the jaw and
perhaps the way you part your hair."

"It's not the full-waiters?" Michael said with a laughing glance
down at his dinner jacket. "Haven't worn this penguin suit since
before the war. Surprised it still fits."

"It fits divinely," Lizzie hiccupped into her champagne flute.

Lucy grudgingly admitted she had a point. On anyone else, the
rumpled knees, crooked tie, and scuffed shoes of his evening dress
would have given off an air of the dress-up box. On Michael, they
hung with old-money-hits-hard-times elegance. Perhaps a result of
years as a scholarship boy. He knew how to smooth a path without
ruffling a feather. Even the hotel staff took him for some down-on-
his-luck earl's son and bowed and scraped accordingly.

Oliver chuckled fondly. "You two should go have a drink. Pamela
and Lizzie will keep me company. Won't you, girls?"

"Of course, Ollie, love," they cooed.

"Actually, I really don't think that's necessary—" Lucy objected.

Oliver paid her no heed, shooing them toward an empty table.
"Go on now. He's come all this way to see you."

Pamela smiled drunkenly. "How awfully roman"—she
belched—"tic."

Lucy would have argued that opinion, but Michael was already
leading her away. Grabbing hold of Oliver, screaming bloody murder, and refusing to let go didn't really mesh with her evening's air
of exotic mystery.

A waiter took their order. She already felt a little tipsy but this
evening demanded to be washed down with copious amounts of
alcohol.

Alone, Lucy leaned across the table, staring Michael down with
what she hoped was a shriveling glare. "What are you doing here?

You're ruining everything. I left you safely back at the bus stop on your way to deliver jam. Next thing I know, you're cutting in and spoiling what was going to be my big moment."

"You mean he hasn't invited you to star in his next picture?"

"He was working up to it," she said with a completely straight face despite the fact that during the whole of their evening, not a single mention of Oliver's original offer had ever come up. He'd either forgotten, changed his mind, or handed out his business card to every female between eighteen and fifty. But Michael didn't have to know that. Let him think she had Oliver eating out of the palm of her hand. "You didn't answer my question."

"I was too busy basking in the warmth of your welcome. I wish you'd come to your senses and give up this ridiculous notion of yours."

"Ridiculous?" How could Michael manage to make her giddy with happiness one minute and a hairsbreadth from murder the next? "Are you saying I couldn't get a job in one of his movies? That I'm not talented or clever enough? That he would only hire me because he wanted to sleep with me? I may look like an empty-headed bimbo, Michael McKeegan, but I do possess some intelligence."

"Of course you do. So stop relying on your pretty face and your slinky maneuvers and use it."

His agreeing with her rather stunted her argument. She took her frustration out on her drink and ordered a second . . . or was it a third? Their waiter was extremely attentive. "You think I'm pretty?"

"Don't be daft. You know you're beautiful."

"But I asked whether *you* thought I was pretty."

His brows drew down into a frown, his mouth thinning almost to an angry line. "How many drinks have you had tonight anyway?"

If that didn't answer her question like a kick in the teeth. Embarrassing heat crawled up her neck and burned in her cheeks. "I'm sorry you had to make the long trip to London just to see me. You could have saved your fare and your breath."

"I didn't come to see you." He took a sip of his pint, his jaw jumping.

"Oh." And no, that was most definitely not disappointment aching her chest. It was simply too many gimlets on an empty stomach. "Oh, well . . . that's good, then, because I'm going to America with Oliver and that's that."

"Fine."

"Good."

"That's settled, then."

"It is."

"Then there's nothing more to say."

"No, there isn't."

They fumed in silence. Michael lit a cigarette. Lucy tried not to glance over at Oliver's table with obvious longing.

"Did you ever find Bill's mother?" Michael finally asked.

"I'm working on it," she mumbled, bracing for his scalding I-told-you-so. If only she'd been able to tell him Bill was safely and happily back in the arms of Mrs. Smedley, he'd have had to concede her accomplishment. Then maybe she'd see more than either tolerant amusement or frustrated disapproval in his eyes.

But there was no self-righteous comeuppance. Not one grumbling remark about her casual inattention. Instead, Michael turned his pint round and round, staring into the glass with a strange tightness to his features, seeming only half-aware of their conversation.

It suddenly occurred to Lucy that she and Michael had much in common—a lifetime of being on the outside looking in, wedged like square pegs into round holes. Michael had shaped himself to fit by learning to be one of the in-crowd, more gentlemanly than any Etonian heir. She had fought tooth and claw against the whole damned lot with their rules and their hypocritical decorum, too furious and full of spite to bend even a little, though it might save her from greater pain.

The only difference was that Michael had chucked it all in to return to the one place where he didn't have to be anyone but himself.

Lucy had no such refuge.

"I suppose if you're not here because of me, you must be here to see Arabella."

He continued staring into his pint as if reading his future within the foam. "I got to thinking about what you said. About taking a chance or always having questions. I knew Arabella and I were a long shot. But for those few short months, it didn't matter. I've wondered over and over if we could have made it work if we'd only tried a little harder. Now I've the chance to find out, how can I just walk away?"

"You must love her very much."

He didn't answer at first. He traced a watermark on the tablecloth, his gaze turned inward, his shoulders hunched. Silently, Lucy watched the past play out behind his stony features.

"I got as far as buying the ring." His hand tightened around his glass; his breath caught, then settled. He gave a sad laugh and a shake of his head. "It was my last night in London before I was due to ship out. It seemed like the perfect moment to propose. I'd be leaving, but I'd have a piece of home that I could dream about while I was gone."

"Arabella had other ideas?"

"She wanted her father to pull strings and have me transferred to a training company or some posting that would keep me in England. We had a huge row about it, and I left for overseas, the ring still in my pocket. Not exactly the grand romantic gesture I'd been aiming for."

"So here's your chance." Her chest was as tight as her smile. "Go in there and sweep her off her feet all over again."

"I don't know what I'd say to her. What we'd say to each other."

"Corporal McKeegan at a loss for words? That I'd pay folding money to see."

"I knew I could count on you for a sympathetic ear," he said with the first hint of a smile.

"You don't need sympathy. You need a kick in the pants." She stood up from the table, swaying only slightly, and grabbed him by the arm.

"What are you doing? Where are you taking me?"

"To Arabella, of course."

"But what about Mr. Oliver? Your big chance?"

"You mean my ridiculous notion?" She glanced over to see Pamela tilting precariously while Lizzie flirted with a busboy. Oliver chatted with a gentleman at the next table. "He's not going anywhere. I'll help you secure your happy ending, then I'll come back and secure mine."

"Just when I think I have you pegged, Lucy Stanhope, you surprise me."

She smiled. "So who's riding to whose recue now, eh?"

The wood-paneled reception room glowed golden warm in the soft light from the wall sconces, while an enormous chandelier gilded the pomaded hair of the dinner-jacketed men and set the precious stones around the necks of silk-clad women sparkling. A groaning buffet stood along a far wall heaped with delicacies most Londoners hadn't seen since Chamberlain's government fell. Waiters glided through the crowds dispensing drinks and savories while a small trio of musicians warred with the clamorous babble of conversation.

Lucy snatched two champagne flutes from a passing tray, handing one to Michael. "Yum. Veuve Clicquot. Nothing but the best."

He downed it in one go. Plucked another while it was still within arm's reach.

"Easy, champ. I don't have time to peel you off the carpet. I've a man to catch."

"Don't remind me," he grumbled.

She shot him a look, but he was staring unflinchingly past a gray-haired man in uniform bearing a colonel's worth of pips and chest medals, over a rather dumpy young woman in an MTC tunic and skirt, and through a hawk-nosed matron of statuesque proportions with a tittering laugh to focus with gun-sight precision on a young woman in a chic off-the-shoulder evening gown in a smoky shade of pink. "There she is."

Lucy didn't need to be told. She recognized her from the photo hidden away in Michael's drawer. Just watching her, she could tell that Arabella was everything Lucy wasn't. She carried herself with that unconscious grace that only comes from being the apple of the world's eye—and knowing it.

As if sensing their gaze, the woman turned and her smile stiffened, her expression frozen in a bewildered mix of pleasure and apprehension.

"She didn't think you'd come," Lucy offered.

"I wouldn't have if it weren't for you."

Something in his tone made Lucy cock him another sideways glance, but his gaze remained focused on Arabella, now gliding through the crowd as if tugged by an invisible cord, her moment of shocked surprise smoothed into polite pleasure.

"What do I say?" he hissed through a frozen smile.

Lucy leaned close, whispering, "'Hello' is always a good place to start."

Arabella pulled to a nervous stop, her eyes darting between the two of them. "Michael . . ." She smiled as if she walked on eggshells. "I can't believe it. Is it really you?"

"It's good to see you again, Bella. Been a long time."

"Two years and three months, but who's counting?"

He cleared his throat as he shifted from one foot to the other.

Good golly, what happened to her gregarious social butterfly? A block of wood had more personality than Michael. Lucy stepped in before this reunion died on the vine. "How do you do? I'm Lucy Stanhope."

"Arabella Nash." The young woman dragged her reluctant gaze from Michael to smile politely. "It's very nice to meet you, Miss Stanhope."

"This is quite a party. What's the occasion?"

Arabella's forehead wrinkled, her rosebud lips pursing as if she was ashamed of the ostentatious display. "My father's birthday. He's been absolutely living at the office recently so Mother decided a party would be just the thing to divert him. It's mostly his stodgy old friends in attendance, but there are a few of us under the age of fifty milling about."

Lucy barely took in the dashing men in uniform and the pretty women in evening gowns until . . . wait a minute . . . she focused on one particular miss whose face looked frighteningly familiar. She'd exchanged her sturdy ARP wool for ethereal Champcommunal silk, but there was no mistaking the no-nonsense sturdiness of Irene Turnbull. So where was Lady Turnbull? Not by the piano. Not by the drinks bar. Not by the—oh dear. There she was. Draped on a very harried-looking ensign.

Neither of them had spotted her yet. There was still a chance to slip away unnoticed.

"Father . . . Sir Reginald . . . your father is Sir Reginald." Lucy's string of cocktails swam uneasy in her stomach. "Sir Reginald is your father."

"That's right. Do you know him?" Arabella looked at her curiously. Michael looked at her as if she'd lost her mind.

"Only by complete coincidence." She tried casually edging behind Michael, praying Lady Turnbull would remain locked in discussion and not look over.

"Daddy's work at Whitehall has simply knocked the stuffing out of him. Barely sleeps. Barely eats. Mother hoped a party at the Dorchester would remind him of better times, but I can't help thinking that nothing will ever be normal again. We won't be normal ever again." As she said this, Arabella tore her eyes away from Lucy's odd crablike lurking to glance hopefully up at Michael.

"If you mean, can we go back to the way things were before the war, then no, I don't think we can," he said somberly. Frankly, he hadn't been anything but somber since they arrived. If he didn't snap out of it soon, he was going to blow his big chance. "But maybe we can build something new."

Bull's-eye! Pink stretched high across Arabella's cheekbones. "Could we?" She girlishly bit her bottom lip. "I'd like that." Placing a manicured hand on his forearm, perfect pink polished nails against the black of his tuxedo, she looked up at him through long dark lashes. "Are you thinking about moving to London? Will you look for a job?"

Lucy didn't wait to hear his answer. She'd done her part. It was up to Michael now.

Oozing her way free of the couple, she headed for the door. If she was subtle and quick, she might be gone before anyone was the wiser. Just before she made her getaway, she glanced back to check on the lovebirds' progress. Arabella had relaxed into conversation and Michael laughed at something she said, their heads bent close, bodies almost touching.

For the briefest of moments, envy knifed Lucy's heart and she caught herself imagining a different happy-ever-after.

An obliging champagne-laden waiter passed.

Then so did the moment.

Chapter 21

So much for not going anywhere.

Pamela and Lizzie were still at the table, a bit glassy eyed and definitely feeling no pain, but Mr. Oliver had been replaced by a pair of accommodating naval officers. After checking in the hotel's restaurant as well as the bar and the ballroom, and skulking near the lifts until the hotel detective started cocking her a suspicious eye, Lucy gave up and asked at the desk.

"I'm sorry, Miss Stanhope. Mr. Oliver has gone out for the evening."

Bloody perfect. She'd been close enough she could taste the damn daiquiris. That would teach her to play village matchmaker.

"Would you care to leave him a message?" the helpful clerk asked.

"Yes, please." She managed to scribble a quick note that included her current address and a burning desire to continue their reminiscences of old times and good friends. And if she happened to spill a splash of perfume on the envelope as she did so, that was no one's business but her own. "If he does return, let him know I'm in the bar."

"Very good, miss."

It took two more drinks and a Sobranie before she could think about the situation without either weeping or cursing. A good beginning. A drunken binge later, she might even get over the fact that she had let a once-in-a-lifetime opportunity slip through her fingers—and for what?

To help Michael rekindle an old flame with a sweet dewy girl who doubtless made it her life's work to be kind to babies and old people, never drank anything stronger than sherry, and knitted scarves for the deserving poor when she wasn't rescuing puppies.

She and Michael would be very happy together, the stupid sod.

A lump formed uncomfortably in Lucy's throat. Best to wash it down with another gimlet.

"Be careful, Miss Stanhope." A tap on the shoulder brought her up out of a tall cocktail glass of self-pity. "That gin you're slurping might very well have started life in an upstairs bathtub."

Could this evening get any worse?

"Good evening, Lady Turnbull." She glanced past to check for oncoming policemen but saw only a hotel porter and two women on their way to the loo for a touch-up.

"I told Irene I'd seen you but she didn't believe me. Said I was mistaken. I am never mistaken." Without asking, she settled into a chair, her flowing orange-and-gold gown drifting about her ankles like a pumpkin-colored cloud.

"Won't you join me?" Lucy asked facetiously.

"Love to. Sir Reginald's party is just what I thought it would be— all hot air and small minds. He's always been a bit of a dull boots, which age has done nothing to remedy." She flagged down a waiter and was brought a glass of barley water and two antacid tablets. "I escaped just before Mrs. Ness-Pryce began describing her latest health crisis. She's probably still in there droning on over her puffy ankles. The woman is a slave to Harley Street." She guzzled the barley water with a satisfied smack of her lips. "Ah. Better than the hair of the dog for preventing a case of the morning-after blue devils."

Was the woman ever going to come to the point, or did she derive enjoyment from playing with her prey like a cat with a rather tired and wilted mouse? Lucy tried to remain aloof, her face fixed in an expression of unconcern while her insides rattled.

"You look as if you could use one yourself." She flagged down the same waiter and a second barley water with antacid tablet chaser appeared. "Who was that young man I saw you with earlier?"

"Just someone I bumped into in the lobby."

"Frightfully handsome. Nice eyes. A bit on the thin side, but pleasing nonetheless."

"He and Arabella Nash are an item."

"Are they? Tip-top girl. Takes after her mother, thank heavens." She settled more comfortably in her chair. "You're probably wondering why I sought you out."

"It had crossed my mind."

"You didn't think I'd put two and two together, did you, Miss Stanhope? But Lady Boxley's cousin was my late husband's sister-in-law, and I remember Lady Amelia Trenowyth's wedding to that brash American financier. It was the talk of London that spring. As was your very premature birth five months later." Her diamond-hard gaze softened. "I spoke to your aunt this afternoon, as a matter of fact. I'm very sorry to hear about your mother."

Lucy's hands tightened round her glass. "You wait. Just when everyone's written her off, Amelia will make a grand entrance. That's what she does. Keeps you guessing. Keeps you hoping."

"Perhaps." She paused. "Lady Boxley is most vexed, you know. So is your cousin. Something about a missing automobile."

"I can explain that . . . and the scratch too."

"No doubt, but neither the whereabouts nor the state of Lord Melcombe's roadster are my concern."

"They aren't?"

"Of course not. It's you I'm worried about—as is your aunt. She's been fretting for days."

"I doubt that. She barely noticed I was there to begin with. I doubt it mattered that I left."

"It mattered very much." Lucy's face must have betrayed her skepticism. "Oh, I know Lady Boxley can come off a bit pompous, but deep down she's an old softie."

"Fathoms apparently."

"When she heard the news about your mother, she worried you might do something foolish while overcome by grief."

"One has to care to grieve." Lucy stared into her drink. "One has to have had a family to feel its loss when it's taken away."

"Perhaps you care far too much." Lady Turnbull stood up to leave but not before placing a thick ivory calling card on the table. "If you ever have need of me."

"I don't understand."

"As I said, your aunt's cousin is my late husband's sister-in-law."

"What does that make you?"

"Your family."

An hour later, Lucy remained at her table, fingering Lady Turnbull's calling card as if it were one of Bill's marked aces and sipping on a pink gin, compliments of a rather snozzled gentleman at a nearby table. Hope for Mr. Oliver's return dwindled, but she was not yet ready to admit defeat and drag herself back to the Connaught with her tail between her legs. Hopefully, Michael's night had gone better than hers. One of them should be able to call their trip to London a success.

A waiter approached and expectation instantly replaced intoxication. "Is Mr. Oliver back?"

"No, miss. There's a young boy at the front desk. Says he won't leave without you and is threatening fisticuffs unless we produce you immediately. I believe he is under the impression you're in some sort of trouble. Guests are beginning to stare and Mr. Blacker, the desk manager, is growing quite agitated. I fear he may call a constable if something's not done."

"This young boy wouldn't happen to have brown hair, freckles, and a mouth like an East India dockworker?"

"That does fit the description, miss."

"Of course it does. Because my night hasn't been a complete disaster."

She followed the clerk into the lobby, where a small knot of people stood huddled off to one side out of the way of the evening's clientele. By the irritated frowns, jabbing hand gestures, and official tone of voice, events seemed to be quickly spiraling out of control.

"Bill Smedley, what the devil are you doing here?" she demanded, pushing her way through to reach the center of the storm.

Startled by her tone, the entire group paused in their worried protestations. A gentleman with his back to Lucy turned around, hands in his pockets, tie unknotted and loose around his neck. "He says he's come looking for you."

See a penny, pick it up. All the day you'll have good luck.

Wasn't that the saying?

Michael McKeegan was beginning to resemble a very bad penny.

Lucy, am I glad to see you." Bill threw his arms around her waist, his face buried in her sequins.

It was hard to maintain one's temper at a greeting like that. Despite her best efforts, she felt herself melting, her own arms coming round to hug him close. His breathing was sharp, as if he'd been running; his body was warm in the chill of the lobby and smelled cleanly of powder and bath soap.

"You're shaking."

He pulled away, straightening with a guilty flush, shoulders squared and hips cocked in a swagger. The little boy giving way to the sullen teen in a split second. "Just relieved to see you're safe is all."

"I'm perfectly safe. But I told you not to leave the hotel room. Oh dear, nothing's happened, has it? I mean, they don't suspect"—she cocked a glance around—"that we're squatters, do they?"

"Naw, we've got 'em bamboozled but good."

She sensed Michael explaining away the disruption with his usual charm until the sharp features eased and the raised voices softened. She had to admit, he was certainly handy to have around, though why was he here and not locked in an embrace with Arabella? And why was she just a little bit relieved?

"I didn't mean to bother you while you was having fun with that bloke Oliver," Bill explained. "But when you didn't come home, I started worrying, and then I heard the guns and the searchlights were blazing."

She'd been barely aware of the antiaircraft guns pounding away close by in Hyde Park. Between the sound-deadening strength of the Dorchester and the orchestra's amazing ability to play along with the rhythm of flying ack-ack, it was easy to forget there was a war going on outside the walls. In fact, everything about this place seemed engineered toward one purpose: to insulate the influential from any discomfort. But step out onto the pavement and the truth could very well explode in one's face.

"I'm sorry you were scared."

"I weren't scared," he replied defensively. "I thought maybe you were. And when you didn't turn up, I started worrying maybe you'd got lost. You're not used to being on your own in London. You don't know it like I do. Anything might happen."

"Too bad nothing did," she muttered.

"Michael said as how I was to look after you, but you said as how I wasn't supposed to leave the hotel room. I didn't know who I should listen to."

"Since you're here, I assume Michael won the day."

"In the end, but while I was going back and forth over whether to come look for you, there was a knock on the door. I hid in the bathroom and, after a bit of banging, whoever it was pushed a note under the door and went away again."

"What did it say?"

"Michael?"

All three of them turned at the sound of Arabella's approach. "Are you coming back inside? We're just about to sing 'For He's a Jolly Good Fellow' and cut the birthday cake. I know Daddy would be disappointed if you missed it."

She stood there in her pink-and-white gown with her pink-and-white china doll complexion and a look on her face Lucy had last seen on that young mother in Yeovil—shy and hopeful and completely smitten.

"I'd love to, but I really ought to see them back to their hotel first." Michael straightened, shoving his rumpled tie in his pocket.

Arabella looked as if she wanted to argue, but her oh-so-proper upbringing stood in the way. Of course, that had never stopped Lucy, but then she'd already acknowledged Arabella was perfection personified while she was . . . well, not.

"You're quite right. Miss Stanhope is new to London, and it

seems she's got herself quite a handful to contend with." Her gaze drifted pointedly toward Bill. "I'm sure she'd appreciate your help. Daddy and I will be here when you get back. Just don't be too long. I've asked the band to play our favorite song." She leaned up on tiptoe and kissed him on his cheek. Had she planted her flag in him, she couldn't have been more obvious about her intentions.

As she trailed back into the party, throwing one last friendly wave over her shoulder, Lucy fought the urge to hurl something heavy at her. And how did she know Lucy was new to London? Or about Bill? Had Michael spilled all her secrets?

"Is that the girl you was talking about on the bus, Michael?" Bill asked. "She's smashing. Like a picture from a book, she is."

Et tu, Bill Smedley?

"But I bet she don't know 'The Four Old Whores from Baltimore' like Lucy does. That's a whale of a song. *The first old whore from Baltimore said, 'Mine's as big as the air.'*"

"Weren't you telling us about a note, Bill?" Lucy hastily interrupted before Bill hit his stride on the rousing chorus.

"Oh, right. It was from Ace. He said we're to meet him tomorrow."

"Who's Ace?" Michael asked, lips still twitching at Lucy's discomfiture.

"How do you suppose he knew we were staying at the Connaught?" she asked, shooting him a hostile glare right back.

Bill was oblivious to it all. "I told you Ace has ears and eyes everywhere. If anybody knows where my mam is, it'll be him."

"I said, who's Ace?" Michael repeated.

"If this is any indication, I expect you're right. Let's just hope he's willing to share what he knows."

"Who the blazes is Ace?" Michael's voice rose.

Lucy glowered. "If you must know, he's an old friend of Bill's."

"Ace and me was best mates before I were sent away. He'll help. I know it."

"I hope so, but don't get your hopes too high," Lucy said. "He's not seen you in years. People change."

"Not Ace."

"Everyone can change, Bill." Michael's words were directed at Bill, but his gaze was locked on Lucy. "Even the people you least expect."

Lucy shut the door to the hotel suite's bedroom. "To see him asleep, you'd never know what a little criminal he really is." She crossed to the sideboard and poured herself a drink. "Gin?"

"No, and neither should you." Michael stood awkwardly in the vestibule, worrying the brim of his hat through his hands. "It's late. I should go."

Ignoring his advice, she poured two glasses and snapped on the radio on her way to the couch. "You can't leave until you tell me about your evening." She pushed the drink into his hand and gently steered him toward an armchair. "So, sit down and start talking."

Despite his protestations, he didn't fight her high-handedness, instead dropping into his seat with a slump-shouldered thud as if the air had gone out of him. "Not much to say. She's the same Arabella I remember. Clever, funny, kind, accomplished."

Maybe Michael was right. She did suddenly feel a bit nauseous. She put the glass down on the table beside her.

"She was very interested in hearing about you."

"I'll bet she was."

"I told her that you were the one who persuaded me to come to London. That it was your determination to go after what you want that convinced me to do the same."

"But you think what I want is complete rubbish."

"I never said that." When she stared him down, he shamefacedly ducked his head. "Okay, I did say that, but even if I think flying off to Hollywood with some California gasbag is mad, it doesn't mean I don't admire you for having the guts to do it."

Stop the presses. Michael admired her? He thought she had guts? Would wonders never cease?

Words hovered on the tip of Lucy's tongue, but before she could respond, Michael looked away, features drawn as he ran a hand absently over the left side of his chest. "It was just like you said it would be. Arabella missed me and wants to start over. We're meeting back at the hotel and going on to a late supper."

Her words were left unspoken, which was probably just as well. Michael was easy. He was straightforward. He saw her as she was and didn't run screaming. These qualities were worth their weight in gold.

Love was the complete last thing she wanted.

Hiding her chagrin, Lucy kicked off her heels and tucked herself onto the couch. "See? Auntie Lucy always knows best."

He gave a soft bark of laughter, dispelling any lingering tension. "Are you sure about that? How many gins have you had tonight?"

"I lost count, but there's still only one of you, so it couldn't have been that many."

The romantic crooning of Frank Sinatra came on the radio. A sudden ache blossomed in Lucy's chest before climbing into her throat, where it threatened to strangle her. She blinked away the betraying shine in her eyes and, snatching up her drink, polished it off in one gulp before meeting Michael's gaze.

He put down his glass. She noticed he'd emptied his in one swallow as well. "Right. Well, I guess I'll be going, then."

"How about another one for the road? Fortify yourself before your lovers' rendezvous?"

"I don't think it would be wise."

She crossed the room to the drinks cabinet once more, feeling his eyes following her. "If you're worried about ruining my reputation, you're at least five years too late. And if you're worried about me ruining yours, well . . . maybe that halo could use a little tarnish."

"I'm not a saint, Lucy. Not even close."

He stood to leave. His dinner jacket was sadly rumpled, his collar button open, and the end of his discarded tie stuck out of his trouser pocket. Lines bit into the corner of his mouth and he carried himself stiffly.

"Michael? Is something wrong?" She put down the glass and placed a palm against his forehead. "You feel warm and your face is all splotchy. It's not the malaria, is it? Or your heart?"

Their eyes locked. "It's not the malaria." He paused for the space of a breath. "Or my heart."

Butterflies banged against her rib cage with the force of cannonballs.

Michael didn't possess the glamorous mystery of Yoon Hai, not even close, but she found she preferred it that way. She had labeled him a sheepdog, but maybe being loyal, brave, and true wasn't such a bad thing to say of someone.

"I don't want to hurt you, Lucy."

His mouth was so close and he smelled of the pungent scent of Yardley's and cigarettes. Heat bloomed in her chest and a shiver of anticipation shimmied up her spine. She had kissed him at the bus depot, a sisterly peck on the cheek. She didn't want to be sisterly tonight.

"That's usually my line," she whispered against his skin. It was all she had time to whisper.

His kiss was just as she'd imagined—and nothing like it. Not gentle and gentlemanly but raw, devouring, demanding. She knew he was drunk. Hell, she was drunk too. But there was more than alcohol fueling their passion. There was loneliness, regret, and disillusionment. An always-potent aphrodisiac.

She didn't have long to enjoy it, though.

"I'm sorry." He shoved her away, his face flushed, eyes bright. "Coming here was a bad idea."

She tried to recapture her earlier cynical distance but it was hard when her lips tingled and her body ached with frustrated desire. "I think it was the best idea you've had in a while."

"Arabella probably thinks I've forgotten about her."

"We wouldn't want her to get the wrong end of the stick." She smiled despite a pressing grinding weight centered in her gut like lead. "After all, if it weren't for Auntie Lucy, you'd still be pining away in Charbury."

She tried to keep the footing light and the banter crisp, if only to protect herself. Michael was a friend. Her only one when it came right down to it. She wouldn't jeopardize that even for a leaping heart.

"I appreciate your restraint," he said with a wry answering smile as he shoved his arms into his coat. Took up his hat.

"Don't forget to send me an invitation to the wedding."

His smile faded and now he merely looked tired and almost puzzled. "You'll be having too much fun in California to be giving us a thought."

"Maybe I'll send up a toast from my lounge by the pool."

"Good night, Lucy, and good luck."

The door closed behind him.

"Damn it." She snapped off the radio. Poured herself another drink. "Damn it to hell." She hurled her glass against the wall, where it shattered.

This time there were no convenient waiters, and an ocean of alcohol wouldn't fix what ailed her.

Chapter 22

Twelve hours and a weak spring sun did nothing to improve Lucy's mood—or this bit of a battered London. The air seemed to carry a patina of grit that itched at her throat and coated her skin until she felt as dingy as her surroundings. Old newspapers blew into the corners of bomb-damaged buildings while today's headlines screamed from a stand in front of the newsagent's shop. A queue of old-age pensioners formed in front of a mobile laundry.

Lucy felt a bit like Cinderella after the ball. Aunt Cynthia's evening gown put aside. Her Hollywood happy-ever-after abandoned. Even the kiss at midnight had been a complete disaster. And to put the cherry on her horrid morning, she had a splitting headache that started at her temples and ended near her ankles. Corpses possessed more joie de vivre than she did.

A truck backfired, crashing through her brain like a machine gun.

"You all right, Lucy?"

"Couldn't be better. Let's just get this over with so I can be quietly miserable somewhere."

This morning, Bill had cocked a wary eye upon finding her sprawled asleep on the couch, and he'd continued to watch her cautiously through his breakfast of porridge and a soft-boiled egg and her breakfast of dry toast and black coffee. But he'd never once come out and said anything about her condition. In fact, he'd been rather reticent—which might have worried her had she any energy to be worried about anything more than putting one foot in front of the other.

Bill led her off the main road and down a narrow shadowed side street. "Ace keeps a room behind his brother-in-law's funeral parlor."

"How convenient. The better to dispose of the bodies, I guess."

"He's not like that," Bill countered.

Lucy cast a wary glance around her. "I certainly hope for our sakes that you're right."

Uneven cobbles threatened her ankles, and mildew climbed the poorly pointed brickwork of the buildings to either side while dirty water gushed out of a broken drain. Overhead, washing flapped in a stiff morning breeze. A baby's plaintive cry echoed from an upstairs window, a man's shouting from another, and two rough-looking boys loitered outside a door. They straightened as Bill and Lucy approached, their eyes hard, mouths pulled into bullish frowns. Bill responded by squaring his shoulders and lengthening his gait to an arrogant swagger. But it was his expression that went through the greatest transformation. A cold emptiness entered his gaze, his features flattening to a sneering hostility. "We're here to see Ace."

"Ace ain't seeing people right now. He's busy."

"Not too busy to see me."

"And who the feck are you?"

"I'm the boy what helped your sniveling self home to your nana when you broke your wrist climbing the fence behind the coal works, Moynihan."

"Smedley?"

"Aye, who'd ya think it was, the Führer?"

They circled him like dogs sniffing for a weakness. "You look different; sound different too. You been gone a long time. Ace is an important bloke now. Don't see just anybody. Got to make an appointment. Got to get by us."

"Oh, for pity's sake." Lucy marched past. "Are we in a damned Jimmy Cagney movie? We have an appointment so step aside."

"Miss!" Bill shouted as she barged through the door.

A young man started up from behind a battered desk, greasy newspaper spread out with a paper disk of fish and chips. He wasn't particularly tall or particularly muscular, and his face bore the scars of an unfortunate skin condition, but there was no mistaking the slyness in his gaze or the menace in his stance.

"Are you Ace?" she demanded.

He buried his surprise almost immediately in a twist of his thin lips and a toss of his head as he studied her slowly and lasciviously. "Depends who's asking."

"Don't get cute. Are you or aren't you? I'm in no mood for games."

"All right. Aye, that's me."

Lucy had been admired by plenty of men, but this was different. She had a feeling it would take a good scrub to erase the feel of those hard eyes crawling all over her. She shoved her distaste aside. "Are you finished, or should I turn around and give you a view of the back side?"

Bill choked, but Ace's mouth turned up in an admiring smile. "The cat has claws."

"Sharp as knives, so don't even think about doing anything

more than looking. You sent us a note about Bill Smedley's mother."

For the first time, he looked past Lucy to Bill. "Did I?"

"Remember me, Ace? Smedley from round on Mansford Terrace?"

He folded his arms across his chest and sat back down. Now that she had a moment to breathe, Lucy noticed packing crates stacked on the floor behind him, some stamped with the name of a company. Others ominously empty of insignia. The pistol in an open drawer of the desk she worked hard *not* to notice.

He plucked at his lip. "Might do. Wasn't you one of them what was always hanging about the back of the pub cadging smokes and swiping empty bottles? Where you been? I ain't seen you about."

"They sent all us boys from St. Ladbroke's School off to live in the country in case of bombings and such."

"That's right. I remember seeing you lads parading down to the station like conquering heroes, mums and dads sniffling, tykes wailing, teachers barking orders like bleeding drill sergeants. And here you are, back again. Countryside spit you back out, did it?"

"Weren't nothing like that. Just didn't get on, so I come back to take care of me mam."

"Seems to me Tilda Smedley has always known how to take care of herself. It was looking after *you* what tripped her up. Maybe she won't be so keen to have you back. Ever think of that?"

Bill reddened all the way to the tips of his ears, but it was his wobbly chin that sparked Lucy's temper.

A nasty right hook would serve the weedy little spiv right, but she didn't want trouble. If Ace was her only path to Bill's mother she'd suck up her own disgust and play the game as he expected it to be played.

Fighting both her distaste and a bad case of nausea, she leaned a hip against the desk and lit a cigarette, tossing the matches aside and leaning back to draw a plume of smoke. "Look, Ace or Valentine or whatever your name is, I've barely slept, I have a hangover from hell, I'm homeless, jobless, and this close to picking up something heavy and smashing it over your rock head—"

"Steady on, ducks. No need for hysterics." He rolled back in his chair. "But I like your spunk. Not a lot of posh dolls like you would stick it to Ace in his own place."

"I like to think I'm unique that way, but did you or did you not send us this note? It's a simple yes-or-no question."

"Aye. I did a little checking around and thought we could do some business."

"What do you mean 'business'? You either know where Mrs. Smedley is or you don't."

He leaned back, putting his feet on his desk, arrogance oozing from every clogged pore. "Oh, I know where she is and what she's been up to. And I could tell you out of the kindness of my heart or for old times' sake, but what's that get me? A medal? Naw, old Ace has expenses. I've got a business to run, so I've got a proposition that could benefit both of us in a big way."

"Do you know how many times I've been propositioned? And by men who would eat you for breakfast and spit out the bones? No thank you. We'll find her ourselves."

He sat up, suddenly all businesslike. "London's a big place, Miss Stanhope. I'm not asking much. My information for a little"—he looked once more at Bill—"assistance with a job. You can't ask for a squarer deal than that."

"I don't think we'd be interested in your kind of job."

"Don't know what it is yet."

She took one more long look at the Aladdin's cave of black-market goods. "I can surmise."

"It's the boy's mam we're talking about." He pushed the folded paper toward her. "Why not let him decide? Or are you afraid he'll choose his old mates over some West End do-gooder?"

"Do-gooder? That's the first time anyone's ever accused me of that."

"Lucy?" Bill said, coming up alongside her; his face had lost its pinkness. He was once again hard, his eyes wary. "It mightn't be so bad to hear Ace out. And if it's only a little job . . ."

"He's conning you, Bill. He's playing you for a sucker. That's what his kind does. It's what he tried teaching you to do."

"Ace?" Bill's gaze moved, unsure, between them. "You wouldn't do nothing that would get us in any trouble, would you?"

"Of course not. What do you take me for?"

"A petty criminal with delusions of grandeur," Lucy snapped.

Ace spread his hands in a gesture of sly surrender. "Sorry, mate. Looks like your minder here won't play the game. You're a sharp bird, Miss Stanhope, but you just might find we do things a bit different from what you're used to. Good to see you, Smedley. Let me know if you change your mind."

"Come on, Bill." Lucy pulled him out the door, slamming it behind her.

Back in the alley, Bill shoved his hands in his pockets, his face gray and tight, but no longer possessing that menacing emptiness she'd glimpsed earlier. "Now what, Lucy?"

Emerging from the shadowy alley into the sunshine was like taking a knife to the brain. She staggered with a hand to her eyes as her stomach rolled ominously at the sour scent of exhaust fumes and frying kidneys. She leaned against a wall, taking slow deep breaths. "Give me a minute. I'm thinking."

Bill kicked sullenly at a can in the gutter. "I'd wager Michael would know what we should do." He slanted her a look from under the shaggy fringe of his hair.

"And take immense pleasure in telling us in patronizing detail."

"He was fun."

"More laughs than Abbott and Costello."

"Clever too."

"He could read and write and even do sums," she said, echoing Michael's mocking answer to her earlier condescension, a hollow pit in her stomach. "A veritable savant."

Bill knocked the can into the street, where it was immediately flattened by a tram. "He wasn't a rotter, was he, Lucy?"

"No," she answered softly, "he wasn't."

An hour later, they had made their way back to Irene Turnbull's flat. Lucy wore a cold compress on her forehead as she watched two antacid tablets dissolving in a glass of barley water. Bill thumbed through a first aid manual left lying open on the coffee table.

"I don't understand," Irene said, pulling on her shoes. She was dressed for work in her ARP tunic and skirt and had the anxious tension of someone running late. "You want me to find Bill's mother?"

"Not at all," Lucy explained. "We want you to help us find Bill's mother. A completely different kettle of fish."

"Smells either way" was Irene's muttered comment.

Bill leaned over, his finger pointing at a word in the manual. "What's that say, Lucy?"

"'Permanganate of potash.'"

Disappearing into the kitchen, Irene hollered from the other room, "If the authorities realize Bill's run away, they'll be on the two of you like a shot."

"What about that?" Bill gestured to another sentence.

"'Perforating wound.'" Downing her tonic in one stomach-soothing gulp, Lucy groaned to her feet and followed after her hostess. The flat's kitchen was enormous and efficient, and looked as if it ought to have a cook bustling about making a royal dinner for twenty. Instead, Irene hunched over a loaf of bread and a cutting board.

"They won't find out because we aren't going to tell them and once he's back with his mother, it will all sort itself out," Lucy explained.

Irene slapped cheese and mustard on her sandwich before packing a bag with her lunch and a thermos. "You have obviously never dealt with the authorities." Racing back into the drawing room, she snatched her hat off a chair and pulled on her coat.

Lucy shadowed her. "Look, according to Bill, his mother works as a maid for a gentleman in the West End."

"That should narrow it down," Irene replied caustically.

"Would it help if I told you he thinks the man's last name begins with a B?"

"Um . . . no."

"It's asking a lot, but I don't know who else to turn to, and you did say you were a dab hand at all sorts of odd jobs."

"Not tracking down missing persons. Besides, I don't work anywhere close to Mansford Terrace."

"But you know people who do. Or you know people who know people . . . well, you get the idea."

"I suppose . . ." Irene hedged.

Bill pointed at a very detailed and very grisly drawing of a head.

"I understand—'carotid artery'—if you can't help. It's asking a lot, and I'm sure you're busy with much more important things." Taking a page from the Bill Smedley book of acting, Lucy affected a rather distinct limp and the always-formidable lip wobble as she trailed Irene into the foyer. "We'll muddle through on our own somehow, it's just my knees are a bit sore this morning after that smash-up with your bicycle . . ."

"You would bring that up, wouldn't you? All right." Irene sighed in defeat. "I'll ask around. Maybe make some calls. Come along with me, and I'll see what I can do."

"Splendid," Lucy chirped, miraculously healed. "I was certain I could count on you."

They emerged onto the street and proceeded to follow Irene, who, even pushing her bicycle rather than riding it, kept up a spanking pace.

"This may sound rude, but why don't you just hand him over to the WVS?" Irene asked as they waited to cross Piccadilly into Green Park. "They'd find him somewhere safe to stay until his mother could be found."

Bill shoved his way between them, his face screwed up in a belligerent jut. "Lucy wouldn't do that. She promised she'd find me mam and she will. You wait and see."

Irene blushed. "I'm sure she will," she said, though she looked anything but as they hurried along the tree-lined footpath toward Buckingham Palace.

Twenty minutes later and out of breath, they turned off Denbigh Street to arrive at a creeper-covered redbrick building bolstered by sandbags. Irene bypassed the ornate pillared portico for a flight of area steps leading to the basement. The room they entered smelled of burned coffee, bad drains, and a nauseating blend of every type of tobacco known to man. An older uniformed gentleman with a walrus mustache stared at an enormous map while two young women spoke quickly into phones. A runner stood hopping from foot to foot in agitation. One of the women slammed down her receiver and barked over her shoulder to the warden, "Explosion, Tufmore Street. Calling for police, fire, and ambulance services."

"There's been no word on an attack from report and control," the man barked.

"Station BR 7 thinks the bomb might have lain there since last week's raid. Workers digging nearby set it off."

"Damn. What a bloody mess. Call in whomever you can reach. Tell them to get all available men and equipment over there."

"Yes, sir."

He spotted Irene, his mustache quivering with agitation. "Turnbull, it's about time. You were due ten minutes ago."

"I'm sorry, sir. I needed to speak with you about—"

"Not now. Grab your helmet and respirator. We'll have personnel from at least half a dozen stations converging. I need you to coordinate. You've got the right accent and the right credentials. People listen to you."

"But, sir—"

"Yesterday, Turnbull."

"Right, sir." She equipped herself before hustling out of the basement wardens' post.

Lucy caught her at the top of the steps as she was taking her bicycle from the rack. "What about Mrs. Smedley?"

"No time now. Where are you staying? I'll phone or send a note round if I find anything out."

"The Connaught under Mr. Fortescue's name."

Irene chewed her lip as she played with the strap of her respirator bag. "Grand-mère told me who you really are. Who your family is."

"I didn't think she'd be able to keep such juicy gossip to herself for long."

"It wasn't gossip. She only said that she knew your mother as a girl and you were very much like her."

Once that comparison might have lifted Lucy's spirits. Now her stomach churned and a cold sweat broke out across her back. So much for the cure-all of barley water and antacid tablets.

"Is that all she said?"

Irene looked unsettled.

"Go on. You can tell me. I have the hide of a rhinoceros."

Irene seemed to consider, then her features smoothed as if she'd made her decision. "She said you were very much like Lady Amelia, but she had high hopes it wasn't in any way that mattered."

"What's that supposed to mean?"

"I thought you might know."

She rode off, leaving Bill and Lucy to keep up as best they could.

"You all right?" Bill asked. "Not gonna shoot the cat, are you?"

"Where *do* you come up with these sayings?" When he continued to eye her with concern, Lucy smiled. "I'm fine. Just a bit winded."

Like Lady Amelia? She had only to glance at her Bethnal Green bodyguard to know that was a laugh. Her mother possessed an entourage of wealthy, powerful men. Lucy had one ragtag boy of twelve.

They continued to follow the clang of bells and the whine of sirens toward a plume of smoke that curled black bellied and shot red with cinders above nearby rooftops. Gawking onlookers gathered behind a line of constables to watch flames devour the remains of a building. Firemen with blistered, soot-smudged faces sprayed the flames while others assisted the wounded from the rubble. A man staggered past, blood soaking his clothes. Another wept against the shoulder of a young woman in a nurse's uniform. A blanket lay draped ominously over a humped shape at the curb just beyond the policemen's rope.

Leaving Bill and Lucy safely behind, Irene conferred with a fire-

man, two policemen, and a man in military khaki before moving on
to a ragtag crowd of survivors being seen to by a pair of ambulance
bearers. She hugged a woman whose shoulders shook with weeping
and spoke to a man in an ARP uniform. Directed an arriving ambulance and organized the setting up of a field telephone.

There was a firmness to her expression and a determination to
her soft features. She neither flinched nor faltered as she worked.
Instead, she took command as if she'd been born to bark orders.
Her father was an admiral. Perhaps leadership ran in the blood.

You were very much like Lady Amelia.

So what ran in Lucy's blood?

Lucy and Bill returned to the hotel just in time for afternoon
tea. She had her heart set on a cream bun and a hot cup of
Darjeeling. Not her usual five o'clock refreshment, to be sure, but
after the day she'd had, it sounded positively divine.

"Miss Stanhope? A letter came for you this afternoon." The
man at the Connaught's front desk handed her an envelope.

"Is it from Miss Irene?" Bill asked, anxiety and excitement in his
voice. "Has she found my mam?"

Lucy hurried him toward the lift and the privacy of their suite,
feeling the curious stare of the clerk drilling its way between her
shoulder blades. Safe from prying eyes, she sawed the letter open
with a finger. A single page fell out onto the carpet. Bill dove for it
as if it were a ten-pound note wrapped round a candy bar.

Almost immediately, his face fell. "It's for you."

She snatched the letter away from him, scanning the swift
slanted writing, her own face showing definite signs of gravity. "It's
not from Michael."

"I never said it was," Bill grumbled.

Come to think on it, he'd been a bit grumpy most of the afternoon. She chalked it up to two packs of gum, a bag of licorice allsorts, and a chocolate bar gathered during their travels around town. The boy seemed to acquire sweets like an art collector acquired oils.

"It's from Mr. Oliver," Lucy said.

"What's he want?"

"He's invited me to dine with him tonight. A car will pick me up at nine."

"Again? How many times you got to see this bloke? I thought we were going to look for my mam today and all we did was muck about."

"I wouldn't call knocking on every door from Regent's Park to Battersea Bridge mucking about."

"I thought you said men was all rotters. I thought you said me and Michael was the only blokes what wasn't. Now you're dolling yourself up to go see this Oliver gent again instead of helping me. That's not fair."

"Give Miss Turnbull time."

"She'll never find Mam. She don't know where to look. She's a toff from the country. What does she know of the city? I say we go see Ace again. Tell him we've changed our minds."

"If you think I'm going to hand over my last few shillings to some penny-ante gangster for information I could get for free, you've another think coming. The man's a black marketeer and probably worse. I wouldn't trust him or any of those boys from the Lion any farther than I could toss them."

"You take that back."

"I won't." She breathed deeply. "If you don't want to wait for Miss Turnbull, we can always go to the police."

"What about your aunt? Or the Sayres? They'll find us out and we'll have come all this way for nothin'."

"I don't like it any more than you do, but maybe it's a risk we have to take."

"No," Bill said, his brown eyes hard with not just anger but fear. "No coppers."

"Then Miss Turnbull is our only option."

"But Ace said he knew where my mam was living."

"Of course he did. He wants you to come begging, but we'll not pay his price."

"Then I'll go on my own. You don't have to come."

"You can't go running about the city by yourself."

"I'm not some mama's boy what don't know his way about. Ace could tell you that if you'd talk to him. He said I was bang up to all the rigs."

"I don't want you hanging about with Ace or his friends. They're all up to their armpits in nasty doings. And they'd drag you in if they could."

"Now you're telling me who I can see and what I can do? You're not my mam. I don't have to listen to anything you say."

"If it weren't for me, you'd still be on the road—or worse, already caught and dragged back to the Sayres."

"I wouldn't. I'd have been fine all by myself."

This time, she hardened herself against his wobbling lip. He was not going to connive her out of her last opportunity for . . .

She shook her head, unsure at this precise moment what opportunity might actually exist, but this was neither the time nor the place to ponder her future. Surely, Mr. Oliver wouldn't lead her on only to knock her down just when she could taste success. "Please, Bill. If you'd just be a little more patient. I'm sure word will come soon."

"I don't want soon. I want my mam now. She needs me. You

heard Mr. Leonard. She's walkin' out with a docker. It's only 'cause she don't have me around to take care of her."

"I understand . . ."

"No, you don't. You're just like all the rest. You say it but you don't mean it. It's just words."

"Bill, please . . ."

"You said you'd help. You promised!" He stormed out the door. Rufus let out a sad little warble.

"Don't you scold too."

Rufus fluttered and was still.

Lucy bathed. "He'll fume and kick about and then he'll come back when he's good and ready."

She dressed. "He's probably out there cadging more sweets off some poor unsuspecting soldier."

She brushed and pinned her hair. "I didn't lie. I really will find his mother."

Perfectly perfumed, attired, and arranged, she closed and locked the door to the hotel suite. Her evening was about to begin, her final chance to persuade Oliver to take her with him when he returned to the United States.

Uneasy, she paused, her hand on the latch, and checked her watch one last time. Nine o'clock and no sign of Bill. Should she? Shouldn't she?

The lift opened.

Taking a deep breath, she stepped inside.

Chapter 23

This time, all her plans fell into place as if they'd been scripted by Metro-Goldwyn-Mayer. The influential man, the sleek car, the grand entrance. Even the night seemed as if it had been created on a Hollywood back lot. The air was soft and brought with it the perfumed warmth of honeysuckle and lilac rather than smoke and mildew. An enormous moon hung high against a sweep of thin clouds and a million stars pricked a velvet sky. Lucy took it as an omen of good things to come and a little bubble of happiness filled her chest.

Finally, after all she'd been through, her moment had come. It was thrilling and, to be perfectly honest, suddenly a bit daunting. Her bubble burst, but she replaced it with a lift of her chin and a stiffening of her back. Butterflies, that was all. They'd pass.

Mason Oliver guided her through to the hotel's promenade, where a table and a bucket of chilled champagne were waiting. Once again, she was offered a feast harkening back to better times and unrationed ingredients. She ignored a repeat of that strange pebble-in-the-shoe sensation. Who was she to quibble over a few steaks and a couple of bottles of bubbly? There would always be haves and have-nots in the world. War didn't change that. It merely made it bad form.

"I apologize for running off last night," Oliver said as he held a seat for her. He wore a sober charcoal suit and a gray silk tie, but Lucy smiled to see a lime-green handkerchief peeking from his breast pocket. "A group of us decided to check out a musical revue at the Vaudeville." He filled two flutes to near overflowing. "We needn't have bothered. Just coming past Piccadilly Circus, the sirens went off." He shuddered. "The noise alone was enough to freeze my blood but then those guns started barking and it was like my brains were about to leak out my ears. Frankly, I don't know how these Brits bear it night after night. I'd have gone bonkers long ago."

"What did you do?"

"What any right-thinking person would do. Fled to the nearest tube station. It was horrible. I had to sit on the platform in the filth. Ruined the seat of my trousers, an old man with bad teeth and horrible taste in waistcoats fell asleep on me, and three fights broke out." He shuddered. "After all that, the Germans didn't even bother to show up. We were all finally let loose like cattle from a pen. It took an hour in the bath and three martinis before I could even think about the evening without growing ill. I can't wait to get back home. My nerves are shot."

And what of those people who called England home? Who couldn't jump on a plane and escape the war? Who endured hardship and tragedy but continued to do what was needed without complaint? Michael and Irene. Patsy and Mrs. McKeegan. Lady Boxley and—much as it pained her to admit it—Sister Murphy.

Lucy's discomfort grew from a pebble in the shoe to a boulder on her chest.

Oliver looked up from his menu. "Are you feeling okay, Miss Stanhope? You look a little . . . off."

"I'm sorry. I suppose I feel almost criminal eating in one meal enough ration points to serve a family of four for a month."

Oliver laughed gently. If he could have chucked her chin in a kindly-uncle manner he would have. "Your conscience does you credit, but see that man in the corner? A member of Churchill's Baker Street Irregulars. The couple coming in? Duncan Sandys and Mrs. Margaret Sweeny. Lord Halifax stays here. So does your minister of war. If it's good enough for the locals, it's good enough for us."

"Of course. If politicians are doing it, it must be all right," she said in her best deadpan.

He didn't seem to get the joke. "Here, forget your troubles in one of these." He popped a canapé in her mouth. It was warm and savory and absolutely mouthwatering. She'd not tasted anything like it since her last dinner at Singapore's Adelphi Hotel, when war had been a few columns in the newspaper or a nightly report on the radio. Something to be tutted over and then dismissed for more amusing entertainments. "Now, tell me they aren't sinfully delicious," he said.

She chewed and swallowed, the boulder barely making room. She tried washing it down with a sip of champagne. "You know, just this afternoon, I was watching them pull bodies out of a collapsed building. Now, hours later, I'm in a world of caviar and cocktails."

"Is that so bad? You like caviar and cocktails, don't you?"

She nearly choked as her champagne turned to poison in her mouth.

"Lucy? Are you all right?"

"Yes, of course. Down the wrong tube." She forced Michael's face from her mind, but his conscience continued to cricket at her.

"Did I tell you about the couple I met on the bus as I was coming to London? Mr. and Mrs. Britt. They've lost four sons in the war."

Oliver tsked with a sorrowful shake of his head.

"And Bill. He's only twelve. He was evacuated at the start of the war. Sent from his home and his mother and the only life he'd known to people who cared less than nothing about him."

"Surely it was for his own good. To keep him safe."

"What of Enzo? He . . . he wants only to marry Sophia Maria and work in his cotton mill in Campione del Garda."

Oliver reached over and patted her hand. "Your compassion does you credit, Lucy, but worrying over it will only put gray hairs on your head and wrinkles on your face. All your good intentions won't change the world." His eyes traveled past her to the approaching waiter. "Now, here comes the soup course."

By now, the weight in her stomach made the thought of food repugnant. She tried shaking off her growing misgivings. "Are you leaving for the States soon?" she asked, hoping he didn't notice she'd not once lifted her spoon.

"London's my final stop. Tomorrow I leave for Bristol to catch a plane home."

"So, this is your last night on the town."

"It is, and I couldn't think of a nicer person to spend it with. Seeing you last evening brought all those wonderful memories of my time in Singapore back. Have you ever heard from that lovely man you had tagging along after you the afternoon we met?"

The boulder blossomed into an ache that spread like cement through her veins. "Yoon Hai?"

"Was that his name? So mellifluous. Like a song or a line of poetry. He was divine, my dear. The bone structure . . . the accent . . . I could have made him a star."

"The last I heard he and his family had fled to China. I'm sure he must be married by now and has forgotten all about me."

"Maybe married, but I doubt he could forget you as quick as that."

Forcing a smile, she focused on choking down a piece of bread.

"Have I ever told you how much you remind me of Lady Amelia?"

First Lady Turnbull and now Mr. Oliver—Lucy wasn't sure she wanted to hear the comparison.

"Oh, not in looks or anything like that. You've a different sort of glamour, but you're both strong and independent. Fierce, if you know what I mean. Willing to fight for what you want."

Now even the bread was too much. Her throat closed on a knot big as a fist. "I've been told that's not exactly one of my more sterling qualities."

"Depends on what you want, I guess."

Lucy's fingers clenched the stem of the glass, her knuckles white. "Amelia wanted power, money, position. She'd do anything to achieve those things."

"Not love?"

"She didn't know the meaning of the word."

"Maybe. Or did she simply look in all the wrong places?"

Lucy had to admit that not all of Amelia's conquests had been industrialists and cattle barons. There was that exiled musician from St. Petersburg and the writer she lived with for six months in Corfu, a waiter she ran off with for a long weekend that turned into three weeks and some chap she met in a queue for the cinema in Melbourne. Anyone who caught her fancy might turn up at the next family day at school as her mother's special friend. But they never stayed long. Amelia would grow bored and move on.

"If love was what she wanted, she could have had it any time these last twenty-one years," Lucy answered harshly. "Instead, I was an inconvenience."

"Yes, that was her tragedy, wasn't it? Chasing some elusive dream while never seeing the real thing right in front of her." Oliver's bright puckish expression faded as he pulled a folded newspaper from his inside breast pocket and laid it on the table between them. A gleam of tears washed his eyes. He made no move to wipe them away. "She left it too late."

Dutch Liner Torpedoed. Daughter of the 6th Earl of Melcombe Among Those Feared Dead.

"Don't you do the same, eh?"

Lucy stared until the newsprint blurred into gibberish. "Excuse me, Mr. Oliver. I hate to dash, but there's somewhere I have to be."

He blew his nose and cleared his throat, and whatever deeper emotion he might have felt at Amelia's passing was tamped back down beneath his primped and perfect exterior. "We haven't had dessert yet. I hear the kitchens do a marvelous chocolate mille-feuille."

"Another time perhaps."

"Of course." He handed her his card. "I'm leaving for Bristol tomorrow afternoon at four. I'll save you a seat."

She paused in the midst of grabbing up her handbag and calling for her wrap. "Do you really think I have what it takes?"

"I wouldn't offer if I didn't think you could be glorious, though I wonder if you're really suited for a life in the movies."

"Are you kidding? Do you know the hell I went through to get to London to see you? Endless days of trains and buses and hitching rides with strangers. A night spent in a rat-infested shed, bomb shelters, bicycle crashes, and creepy gangsters. Why would I go to so much trouble if I didn't want to go with you to Hollywood?"

He stared at her for a long assessing moment and his usual sunny features seemed particularly solemn. "As I said before, Miss Stanhope, you're fierce like your mother and willing to fight for what you want, so maybe you can tell me."

B ill?" Lucy threw open the door to their suite and flipped on the light. "I'm back."

The rooms were just as she'd left them, clothes scattered, the remains of room service on a tray by the door. Rufus's basket by the radiator, where it was warm. But Bill's knapsack was missing. He'd left it beside the couch. Now it was gone.

"Bill, I'm sorry I didn't listen," she called. "We can go look for your mother straightaway if that's what you want." She searched for the bag under the sofa, in drawers, behind the bed. No sign of it. She moved from the living area to the small bedroom to the bath, growing more frantic with each passing moment.

The silent room seemed to echo with the panicked rush of her breathing.

The silent room . . .

No chirping. No fluttering. No scratching against the sides of the basket.

Oh no.

Lucy knelt beside Rufus's basket, lifting the lid to peer inside. A few bread crumbs and a small saucer of water sat untouched. The siskin lay on its side, its legs tucked tight to its belly, its beak agape, eyes staring. Tears burned at the corners of her eyes. Her throat closed around a jagged lump.

Be careful what you promise.

Had Bill come back and found Rufus? Or would she have to tell him and add to the sorrows he already carried?

She shut the basket, her fingers cold and trembling as they fumbled with the latch. Blood rushed in her ears with a sound like the sea and the room tipped and swayed.

Amelia promised to see me off.

She promised us it would be all right. She promised.

Lucy wasn't like Amelia. She never would be no matter how

she tried. Amelia's method of seeking love, if that's what it was, had been selfish and self-satisfying. Love taken with none offered in return. It didn't work like that. Real love ran in an unbroken current. It meant giving without strings. Wanting someone else's happiness even at the expense of one's own.

Keeping promises.

Grabbing up an overcoat, she slammed out into the corridor and punched the lift. The doors opened on a man slouching in the corner, hands stuffed in his pockets, face bleached as bone.

She stared as if she were seeing a ghost. "Michael?"

His gaze narrowed, his body tensing at her distress. "What's wrong?"

"Bill's gone, and it's all my fault."

"Tell me everything." He guided her into the lift with a hand on her elbow.

"I promised him. Don't you see?" Her words spilled out of her in a torrent of recrimination and blame. "I told Bill it would be all right. I told him he would be fine. Nothing is fine. Nothing is all right."

She knew by now that Michael didn't offer sympathetic platitudes. That wasn't his way. A good thing. She would have decked him had he tried. She didn't want to be soothed or reassured. She didn't want to have her emotions minimized or her thoughts belittled. She'd spent a lifetime fighting those who would diminish her. Who would misjudge her. Who would make her invisible.

And in doing so, she had lost herself. She had become someone she no longer recognized.

A stranger within her own tight hot skin.

He guided her like a sleepwalker through the lobby. His touch steadied her. His silent reassurance pulled her free of the dizzying spin of her panicked thoughts.

"Miss Stanhope?" the clerk called out. "There's an issue with Mr. Fortescue's account. We need to speak with you right away."

Michael speared the man with a look that had him hastily backing up, and together, they brushed past and out into the night.

As if mirroring the downward spiral of her evening, the spring warmth had given way to mounting clouds and a misting damp crept up from the pavement to swirl in eddies around their ankles. The bus was nearly full to start, though with each stop farther north and east, the seats opened up, the crowd thinned. By the time they reached Whitechapel, there were only three women in union suits and an older man with a fire watcher's helmet and binoculars left.

She sensed Michael beside her. The warmth from his body flushed her chilled skin. His steady, even breaths slowed the rapid flutter of her heart. His presence kept her from flying apart with impatience at every tug of the cord that delayed their trip. She'd not questioned what circumstances had brought him to her when she needed him most. What she didn't know couldn't hurt her. But tendrils of something very much like happiness pushed against a heart achy and throbbing with grief.

Still, her thoughts slid like Alice down the rabbit hole, splintering and fracturing, notions colliding and overlapping. Bill's final angry reproach superimposed upon her own childish, twisted, and tear-streaked features. Her vows, as hollow as Amelia's had always been.

She closed her eyes, opened her mind, and listened. The engine rumbled and bus tires plopped against the uneven macadam. Tired factory workers snored and a chippie made change. But she heard nothing like a mother's song. Did Amelia even sing? Lucy had certainly never heard her do so. Instead, seeping like fog off the sea came the honeyed tones and false laughter that accompanied Amelia's most scathing criticisms.

You're looking very solid these days, my dear.

A shame you took after the Stanhope side of the family in looks, darling.

Are you sure that outfit's quite the thing, sweetheart?

Dear. Darling. Sweetheart.

She didn't even call Lucy by name, as if they were barely acquaintances. Or as if Amelia couldn't be bothered to remember.

Lucy's eyes snapped open to find Michael watching her carefully, his face sliced by shadow, his pale eyes a pinpoint gleam in the dark.

"Amelia is dead," she said quietly.

Michael shifted beside her. Not so much a movement but an inhalation, a focusing of his attention. His gaze seemed to pierce every wall she erected, every barrier she built. That clear, unfaltering stare peeled away every pretense she used to keep the world at bay, leaving her as exposed as a clam pulled free of its protective shell. In her experience that kind of power over her always ended in grief and pain. But Michael had never once offered her anything but friendship. That was the sign of either a true hero . . . or a complete nutcase.

"Amelia . . ." She choked, tasting the bitterness at the back of her throat, the poison of a lifetime's rejection. "My mother," she repeated, "is dead, and I'm not sorry." Lucy's voice came louder, stronger. A few people glanced over. She didn't care. "I suppose that makes me a bad person, but what else is new?"

Michael kept silent. Perhaps he knew that any interruption, no matter how inconsequential, would dam the flow of words that had to be spoken if she was ever to be free of this toxic resentment. And she knew now that she *had to* be free of it. For all poisons sooner or later destroyed one from the inside out.

"Do you suppose it's my fault?" she asked.

"That your mother is dead?"

"That she never loved me." Lucy tried drawing a breath around the knifing ache in her gut. "Do you think if I'd been a better daughter Amelia would have been a better mother? I tried being what she wanted, but it was never good enough. I was never good enough."

Years of swallowed anger and disappointment became a raw boiling rage at the injustice. Not at her mother's death. That was one small personal tragedy amid a global horror. But that she had been cheated out of her opportunity to finally step free of her mother's shadow and make peace with herself.

"I showed her, though, didn't I?" She gave a harsh laugh. "I got Mason Oliver—Hollywood's own version of King Midas—to take me with him to California."

"Did you? Congratulations," Michael replied. "It's what you wanted."

She sensed his reproach and ignored it. "You're damn right it is."

"Your mother would have been proud."

"She'd have been green. And that would have made it all the sweeter. She'd have finally had to admit I was her daughter. Hell, she'd have made sure people knew she'd given birth to me—the successful movie star."

She continued to feel Michael's every flinch and sway as if she were connected to him by a tensile wire, the smallest vibrations passing between them. It made speaking easier. It made everything easier.

"A proper daughter would weep." Her scratchy eyes burned and her chest throbbed, but no tears threatened. "Not that Amelia was ever a proper mother. Hell, she wouldn't even let me call her Mother, as if it was something to be ashamed of." She fumbled for a cigarette, but her hands shook too badly. Her words, when they came, were soft and broken. "It's a horrible thing to realize your own mother would rather you didn't exist."

They got off the bus at Stepney Green, the streets dark and quiet.

"There's more to being a mother than giving birth," Michael offered, his face now completely lost to shadow, but his lean muscled body a bolstering presence when both her past and her future were crumbling to pieces.

"Someone should have told Amelia that."

Michael's fingers laced with hers, his wide callused palm enveloping hers as he offered a reassuring squeeze. "And then there are those who can love a child even if he doesn't belong to them."

Bill. Out there somewhere. She'd not claim he was either lost or afraid, he'd far too much savvy for that, but he was definitely swimming beyond his depth. "I don't know how it happened. One moment the little fiend was driving me completely mad and now I feel as if I'd die if anything happened to the brat."

Michael smiled faintly. "I know just how you feel."

Chapter 24

Lucy and Michael pushed through the Lion's grungy door and into the smoky interior. A gramophone played a scratchy rendition of "Wish Me Luck as You Wave Me Good-Bye." The same barman stood pulling pints. The same barflies warmed the same stools at the counter. Tables were full; a couple clung to each other on the small dance floor. A group of rowdy boys in uniform were in the private parlor, laughing and shouting and toasting each other's good fortunes.

Lucy shoved her way to the bar. "I'm looking for Bill Smedley. Have you seen him?"

The barman's indifferent gaze passed right through her.

"You have to tell me. It's vital I find him."

"Is it?" He pushed a pint across to a faded narrow-shouldered clerk in a threadbare coat and tie. "Seems to me you've done enough."

"So he *has* been here."

He remained stone faced, turning instead to Michael, who had taken a stool at the bar. "You all right, mate? How about a drink?"

"Ta." He took a long foamy swallow from the pint he was handed.

"I know I mucked things up," Lucy barged in, "but I want to make it right."

"You talkin' about our Billy boy?" the clerk asked.

"That's right."

He broke into a thready and slightly drunken tenor. "*Where have you been all the day, my boy Willie? Where have you been all the day, Willie, won't you tell me now?*"

"You'll get nothing of sense from him," the barman said. "He's been here since noon. The rest aren't much better."

She turned to the men on either side. "I'm looking for Bill Smedley. Maybe you've seen him?"

Neither spoke. She beseeched the men at the tables behind her. Finally, a white-whiskered, rheumy-eyed chap looked up from his backgammon board. "A young lad was in here a few hours ago. Met with the lads what hang about in the back bar. They all went out again a short time after. Haven't seen him since."

"Did they say where they were going?"

"It's best not to know what that lot are up to, then you don't have to lie when the cops come sniffing round after."

"*I have been all the day, courtin' of a lady gay.*"

"Thanks for your help." She had almost reached the door when she noticed Michael wasn't with her. "Are you coming?"

He passed across ten pence for the pint. "Thanks again."

"Anytime, mate." The barman scooped up the coins. Rolling them around in his hand, he seemed to be warring with himself. Finally, he heaved a sigh as he dropped the pennies into the till. "Look, I can't say for certain, but if I were you two, I'd try my luck down by Globe and Portman. There's a warehouse on the corner. Follow the alley to the end and you'll come to a loading bay."

"Why would Bill be there?" Lucy asked, afraid she already knew the answer.

He said no more, merely turned to pull more pints.

She left, hearing the tuneless squall. *"But she is too young to be taken from her mother."*

The mist had thickened, swirling up to press wet and hot against Lucy's face and coat her throat with the taste of rotten eggs and rubber. Overhead, the moon that had shone so bright on her evening with Oliver had been swallowed by low green-rimmed clouds. Michael nearly collided with a sandwich board advertising kosher beef at eight pence per pound. She turned her ankle stepping off a curb. A torch would have been helpful, but neither of them had thought to bring one.

Feeling their way along, they rounded a corner, Lucy coming nose-to-chest with another unfortunate soul caught blind in the blackout. The collision knocked the breath from her lungs and sent her reeling into what felt upon impact like the unyielding edge of a Royal Mail postbox.

"Steady on, miss," said a disembodied voice smelling of cloves, leather, and sardines. "Not a good night to be out. A real pea-souper. You're the second person I've run into tonight. Tripped over a lad and nearly landed on my backside."

"A boy? What did he look like?"

"Couldn't say. He begged a fag off me and away he went."

"Bill—it has to be."

"Hold on, Lucy," Michael chimed in. "It could be anybody. There's no way to know if it was Bill."

"I know it was him." She grabbed the man's coat sleeve before he escaped. "Where did you bump into him?"

"A few streets back just by the Cambridge Heath stop for the 653 bus." He pointed over his shoulder.

"I thought Cambridge Heath Road was that way," Michael said.

"Naw. You've turned yourself all sorts of around, mate. You need to head back down the lane by the old telegraph office, turn left at the second street—not the one by the school, but the other one what runs off toward the church. Turn at the York Hall baths and you'll be on Cambridge Heath."

Thanking him, they followed these somewhat vague directions only to end up right back where they started. What followed felt like a vaudeville act. Did that make her Laurel or Hardy?

"Pack of hoodlums whooping it up by the mission hospital. Told 'em to shove off or I'd call a constable."

"Hanging about smoking fags and rolling dice near that old block of council flats next to St. Lawrence School."

"Young boy, you say? Aye. I bumped into a lad over by the carrier's yard. Begged a pack of gum off a chap in the ambulance service."

"Go back along Bonner Road until you come to the fork and head right until you reach the school."

"Take the shortcut past the Paragon."

"Take the very next left after the church . . . or is that a right just before the church?"

Winded and blistered, Lucy leaned against the postbox. By now, she and it had become very close acquaintances. "We're going to need a Sherpa with an Ordnance Survey map to find Bill in this rabbit warren."

Michael leaned against a building, his head tipped back to rest against the bricks, arms folded over his chest. "This is pointless. We'll never find him in this mess. Maybe if we head back to that café on the corner, we can gain our bearings and start fresh."

"There's no time if Ace already has Bill in his clutches." Her insides quivered with all sorts of dire imaginings.

"You make him sound like a mustache-twirling Jack the Ripper."

"You didn't meet the chap. He gave me the shivers, and I don't shiver easily. He's up to no good and he's going to drag Bill right into the middle of it."

"Wandering in endless circles isn't working. We need to fall back and regroup."

"Then you go find that café and have yourself a nice long sit-down. Maybe even grab yourself a cup of tea while you're at it. I'm going to keep looking until I find him."

"You're not being reasonable, Lucy."

No. She wasn't. She knew she wasn't. She knew Michael was doing his best. More than his best. He had gone above and beyond from the moment she'd rung him up out of the blue and asked for a lift as far as the nearest train station. And now here he was in the middle of London's East End at midnight chasing a boy he barely knew with a woman he barely knew who—oh, by the way—drove him crazy.

Had she left any part of this insanity out?

Was it any wonder he chose caution over calamity?

But logic and Lucy had long ago parted company. And any de-lay, no matter how rational, churned her insides with something very close to panic. She continued to argue, though now she was struck by a strange sense of déjà vu. "I'm being perfectly reasonable. If you don't want to help, fine. I can do it myself."

"That's not what I said," Michael replied, as always the voice of affable reason, damn him.

"But it's what you meant."

"Steady on, Lucy. You're getting yourself worked up over noth-ing. I'm not the enemy. You can stand down." She could barely see her hand in front of her face, but she didn't need a streetlight to know he was laughing at her.

"I'm just a big joke to you, aren't I? A ridiculous tart who's stupid enough to chase halfway across the country after a chance at . . ."

"At what, Lucy?"

"I don't know. A life. A home. A place where I belong. Where I can follow my dreams. Where I can be myself—not my mother's mistake or my aunt's responsibility or 'that girl' that no one quite knows what to do with." She couldn't breathe. She couldn't speak. The fog condensed on her cheeks like tears.

"I don't think you're a joke. Or a tart. Or stupid for chasing your dreams. If I did would I have come to your hotel tonight?"

"I don't know. Maybe Arabella was busy saving puppies or reading to sick pensioners and you were bored."

"I came to apologize for last night."

This just ratcheted her unfounded irritation up a few more notches. "Please. It was a kiss. I was feeling sorry for myself and I never could handle my champagne. Consider your apology accepted and the episode forgotten. You're off the hook. *C'est fini* and all that."

"If you could stop throwing punches long enough to listen . . ."

He grabbed her arm, but she wrenched away. "To what? You telling me what a disappointment I am? I'm well aware, so if you'll excuse me."

"Now you're just being childish."

"Childish? Ridiculous? I don't know why you continue to hang around if I'm so completely distasteful."

"Neither do I," he muttered.

"Why don't you run back to Arabella? Maybe the two of you can play a rousing game of Parcheesi." She stomped off.

"What the hell is that even supposed to mean?" he shouted after her.

But by then, she'd left Michael behind. She'd only gone half a street over before she realized why that conversation felt so familiar. Was this the same panicked desperation Bill had felt? Had he found her patient logic as irritating as she found Michael's?

Oh God, Michael. She'd been horrible. She hadn't meant it.

Any of it.

She turned back, but now the familiar postbox was nowhere to be found. She tried a cobbled side street. Then another. No sign of the blasted postbox—or Michael. She called out, but the green soupy fog warped sound so that voices reverberated strangely and footfalls scraped and tapped like insects. It deadened the spearing lights from antiaircraft batteries and the rising wail of an air raid siren.

Her insides quivered. She hugged herself as a chill swept through her and the cloying claustrophobic damp of the fog finally gathered the strength to become a steady downpour. "Michael?" she called once more. "I'm sorry."

A muffled shout came from somewhere to her left, barely audible over the rain.

Not Michael. A wet cat? A lost child? She called again, and this time the shout was louder, more distinct. And very familiar.

She followed the cries for help, but now something told her to keep silent, afraid of who else might be searching, who else might be out in the dark looking for Bill.

Her hair dripped into her face. Her shoes squished through mucky puddles. Water weighed down her thin coat and plastered her skirt to her legs.

Just past an empty lot, roped off and rubble strewn, stood a large brick building. A wide cement ramp ran up to great hinged doors. The shouts came from an alley running alongside.

"Bill?" she called as loudly as she dared.

"Lucy?" His voice came from a grilled window ten or twelve feet up. "I'm locked in a broom closet."

"How on earth did you . . . never mind. Hold on. I'll be there in a tick."

Feeling her way along the bricks, she returned to the bay doors, which stood ajar, a long thick chain dragging on the ground, a padlock hanging loose in its latch. She stepped inside out of the rain. A cool musty breeze gave the sense of a cavernous space; a snap of a light switch confirmed it. Pulleys hung from rafters. An industrial trolley sat propped by an open equipment lift. A fork-lift was parked beside a lorry with its hood up. A cage enclosed what looked like a foreman's office with file cabinets and desk. Another narrow window was set high in one wall, but this one had no grille. The casing was splintered. Smashed glass littered the grease-stained cement and the piles of folders and correspondence on the cluttered desk.

The warehouse bay itself held floor-to-ceiling stacks of crates, half-emptied of liquor, chocolate, nylon stockings, and French perfume. Tire tracks led down the ramp to be lost in the storm.

The shouts came louder now. Lucy broke off her investigation of this treasure trove of ill-gotten goods to follow the verbal bread crumbs past a series of offices to a locked door at the branch of a passage.

"Bill?" she said, her mouth pressed to the keyhole.

"Lucy?" came a sniffling wobbly voice from within. "Ace locked me in."

"I'll have you out in a trice." She backtracked in search of something she could use to jimmy the door loose. By now, rain drummed against the roof with the force of bullets and a jagged slash of lightning crackled like a spent flashbulb in the dark gap left by the open bay doors. This was followed immediately by a wall-rattling boom of thunder.

Hopefully, the ferocity of the storm would dissuade Ace and his gang of thieves from coming back for the rest of the crates while also keeping the police snug in their station rather than out on the beat, where they might notice a broken window and come snooping.

Another rolling boom vibrated the ground underneath her feet and set the pulleys to swinging, dust caught in the wild sway of the overhead lights. A string of smaller explosions followed. What she had taken for thunder was now recognizable as a German attack.

"Lucy!" Bill's wail possessed a more desperate impatience. "Hurry!"

She counted under her breath as she rummaged in a rolling tool chest by the lorry. One . . . two . . . three . . . four . . .

The explosions seemed to be growing in intensity and proximity, though interspersed with the storm, it was impossible to tell for certain.

Either way, her nerves jumped like live wires under her skin. She drew a deep breath as she snatched up a heavy spanner.

One . . . two . . . three . . .

"Lucy! I'm afraid!"

"I'm coming, Bill."

She ran back down the passage to the closet door. The lights flickered and went out, plunging her into darkness. She stumbled and fell to her knees. Picked herself up and felt her way along the corridor. A near miss rocked the building, bursting against her eardrums and pummeling her chest like a fist.

One . . . two . . .

"Step back, Bill." She slammed the spanner down against the latch. The wood groaned and splintered. Down again. The latch bent and twisted. A third time, the weight pulling on her shoulders and aching her hands. The latch broke away with a crack, and the door swung open. "Bill?"

He fell into her arms, snot running down his chin, eyes red and swimming, his thin body shaking uncontrollably. "Lucy, I'm sorry I scarpered. I didn't mean what I said. None of it."

"No time for tears." She yanked him down the corridor toward the loading bay and the doors beyond. She stepped out onto the ramp, Bill dragging behind.

One . . .

A crack of thunder split the sky. A flash of light burst against her face. She threw up her hands to fight off the sudden blindness of a policeman's torch.

"Oi! What the hell do you think you're doing?"

She wouldn't call Aunt Cynthia. Telephoning Aunt Cynthia was not an option. Aunt Cynthia was a refuge of last—and very final—resort. Yet she was cold, tired, sore, and very close to chucking in the towel. She knew it was bad when she began fantasizing about being back in her bedroom at Nanreath Hall, just she and the taxidermist's menagerie.

The hard wooden bench outside DS Mason's office on which they'd been instructed to sit until further notice bore the graffiti of at least a century's worth of criminals. Bill was currently adding his initials to the who's who of Bethnal Green lawbreakers with the stubby end of a pencil he'd conjured from some overlooked pocket.

At least surly resignation had replaced his overt belligerence in the two hours they'd spent kicking their heels. He no longer referred to DS Mason as "that bleedin' fat stinking copper" nor threatened to bust his way out of "the nick," which Lucy took as a hopeful sign.

She pulled Constable Lewis's borrowed coat closer over her shoulders. It didn't help the slimy cold seeping into every pore, but its comforting scent of pipe tobacco and spearmint gum reminded her heart-achingly of Michael. She immediately chastised herself for being a sentimental heartsick fool. She'd told him to go, and he'd gone. No doubt, he was tucked up in a snug somewhere sipping the foam from his pint and thinking himself well rid of her. He wouldn't be the first.

No doubt he wouldn't be the last.

Raised voices could be heard coming from behind closed doors.

"Don't know what they're so cheesed off about." Bill continued to carve with his pencil. "It weren't a big thing or nothing."

"You broke into a warehouse. That's not nothing."

"I just shimmied through the window and found the key. Ace and the boys nicked the goods. Besides, they'd already been nicked once. Ace was just nicking 'em again."

"That's hardly a point in your favor."

"I only helped 'cause Ace promised to tell me where my mam was."

"Did he keep his promise?"

"No," Bill answered grudgingly.

"Of course he didn't. It was just a way to trick you into doing what he wanted. He dragged you into his crimes and then he left you to take the fall." Bill chewed his sulky lip, his pencil slowing to a standstill. Were her words sinking in? Or was it too late? The answer lay behind that ominous closed door. "The marked deck of cards was amusing; lifting a few coins from that boor on the train in Par was justified—almost. But this is serious, Bill. This is stand-in-the-dock-and-be-sent-away-for-years real."

"Think it'll be the Scrubs for me?"

"I don't know. I hope not."

"What if I told 'em I wouldn't do it no more? What if I said I was sorry?"

"An apology with a heaping side of wobbly lips and sad puppy-dog eyes doesn't magically set things right. You have to mean it. You have to turn your back on Ace and his boys once and for all. Can you do that?"

Bill kicked idly against the leg of the bench, his hair falling into his face, the blanket he'd been given sliding off one shoulder. The clock on the wall inched toward half two. Lucy was in a limbo between exhaustion and panic. She rummaged in her handbag for a cigarette to calm her nerves. Her fingers touched, then closed on Lady Turnbull's now-soggy calling card.

Aunt Cynthia was definitely out of the question, but maybe . . . just maybe . . .

"I won't never do it again, Lucy. Cross my heart and spit." Bill proceeded to do both.

"I believe you. Let's just hope they do."

The raised voices fell ominously quiet.

"What ya think they're doing in there so long, Lucy?"

"With our luck, debating the noose or the chair."

"That's not funny."

"Maybe not, but if I don't laugh, I'll weep."

"You're not in trouble, Lucy, are you? You didn't do nothing wrong."

She leaned back, closing her eyes on her starry-eyed Technicolor dreams. "I did everything wrong, Bill."

Chapter 25

With a rattle of flung gravel, Lady Turnbull jumped the curb in front of her Kensington town house and cut the engine.

"All ashore who's going ashore," she announced, a few hennaed curls escaping her jaunty beret to becomingly frame a face glowing with wide-eyed delight.

Lucy had a feeling hers more closely resembled horrified terror. There were at least three instances when she'd seen her life flash before her eyes and wished she were back in a nice quiet cell in Bethnal Green Station Six.

"That was a lovely invigorating drive," Lady Turnbull said with relish. "I should do it more often."

"I'm not sure that man with the umbrella would agree." Lucy released her death grip on the dash, her legs like rubber, her stomach rolling.

"Pish posh. He was clearly in the wrong stepping off the curb like that. And so I told him with a good mash of my horn."

"I never saw nobody scurry like that, ma'am," Bill chirped. "Almost climbed that lamppost, he did."

"Obviously he possesses an unstable and nervous disposition.

He was never in any danger." She beckoned them after her up the wide marble steps. "I'm an impeccable driver."

Lucy hung back with a hand on Lady Turnbull's sleeve. "I want to thank you, my lady. I know it's late, but I didn't know who else to call."

"Didn't you?" Even in the darkness, Lucy sensed the raised eyebrow, the searching look.

"Crikey!" Bill stared around him at the square of elegant town houses fronting the tidy landscaped park. "This is a spiffing place."

"Isn't it? I was never so happy as when I could hand off the keys to the family's country estate to my son's wife and be shot of the whole dismal place. It was like living in a museum. My little house here in town is much more comfortable, convenient, and just enough for Pidge and myself to manage on our own."

If only Aunt Cynthia held such modern views, but Lucy was almost positive the only way they'd get the old girl to leave Nanreath Hall was in a pine box.

"Come along. Pidge will be wondering what's happened to us."

She'd not even touched the knob before it was opened by a middle-aged gentleman in a robe and slippers. "Welcome home, milady."

Despite his dignified demeanor, relief suffused his thin ferrety features. Lucy would have bet he'd been pacing the floor and twitching back the front curtain for the past half hour.

Lady Turnbull shrugged her coat off onto the manservant. "Of course I'm home, Pidge. Did you think I'd drive into the Thames or fall into a bomb crater?"

"The thought had crossed my mind, milady." He bowed them through to the drawing room, where he had a drinks tray and a platter of sandwiches waiting.

Lucy wasn't sure which she wanted to dive into first.

She grabbed a sandwich.

"Bloater paste, Pidge?" Lady Turnbull inspected the plate with relish. "You do know the secret ways into a woman's heart." She finished her sandwich in two bites and took another.

Lucy returned hers uneaten to the tray. Perhaps a drink instead.

Pidge seemed to read her mind. He stood at her elbow, gin and juice in hand.

"I could kiss you square on the mouth," Lucy gushed.

By only the mere flicker of an eyelash did he acknowledge her enthusiasm. "I'm pleased to be of service, Miss Stanhope" was his ambiguous response.

"Ah, sweet nectar of the gods." She gulped it down, then waited for the usual warm buzzy feeling that haloed the world in a happy glow.

And waited.

Nothing. Tonight, she merely felt nauseated and scraped raw, nerves skittering, thoughts tumbling and turning like rats on a wheel. For probably the first time ever, she waved off a refill and settled for a glass of water.

"Pidge has prepared you both rooms. Should Jerry make another appearance tonight, there's an Anderson shelter in the back garden. I've been using it as a wine cellar since the Blitz ended, but in a pinch . . . eh?"

Had Michael found a shelter during the raid? No doubt he had, and spent the entire time thanking his good fortune at finally being rid of her. She'd been horrid to him since she'd first laid eyes on him all those long months ago. She'd used him, insulted him, bullied him, and taken him for granted. No wonder he'd finally grown disgusted and left her to fend for herself. That's what he'd done. That's what he must have done. She refused to let her mind wander to any other scenarios.

Instead, she focused on Bill, yawning and rubbing at his eyes as he washed down bloater paste sandwiches with a mug of cocoa. Dust caked his grubby clothes and turned his hair a grimy gray. There was a scratch on his cheek and another on his shin. He'd lost a shoe somewhere along the way and his left sock was soaking wet. He was an absolute mess.

Her throat closed around a sob; her stomach swirled alarmingly. Blinking away tears, she crushed him in the biggest, tightest bear hug.

"'Ere now, Lucy. What are you on about? You're squishing me."

"I'm doing what I should have done when I first found you in that horrid closet." She pulled away just long enough to meet his eyes, which were a bit alarmed but otherwise alive with happiness. "And if you ever do such a thing again, William Smedley, I shall take a switch to you myself. Do you hear?"

"Aye, Lucy. I hear."

It was her turn to be squished.

When it rained, it poured. And tonight's storm was relentless. No sooner had Bill been settled in bed and Lady Turnbull retired to her boudoir than the doorbell sounded like a crash of cymbals, followed swiftly by Aunt Cynthia, rather the worse for wear and blinking owlishly.

Lucy recognized that air of weary, rumpled confusion. It was the look of someone who'd wrestled with the vagaries of British public transport and lost. Her aunt's usual stern hairstyle bore evidence of lost hairpins and long hours on windy platforms. Her Dior suit, while still complete with pearls, hat, and matching bag, showed signs of stray train cinders and perhaps a brush with some-one's hairy dog. And her cosmetics-counter sheen had long since worn away to reveal a splotchy exhaustion.

Taking a page from Bill's vocabulary, Lucy breathed a defeated, "Crikey."

Pidge, obviously sensing the coming fireworks, stayed only long enough to suggest that he divest Lady Boxley of her coat (she accepted) and offer her a cup of tea (she declined) before abandoning Lucy completely.

Coward.

In what Lucy could only assume novelists meant when they spoke of "high dudgeon," Aunt Cynthia huffed and puffed like a braking locomotive. Her whole body trembled with a barely sup-pressed inner turmoil until Lucy was afraid the top of her head might explode. "Lucille Miranda Stanhope, what have you to say for yourself?"

No "darling," "dear," or "sweetheart." Not an endearment in sight.

Lucy stood to attention, a strange twisting in her chest and a betraying lump in her throat. "It's wonderful to see you?" She flung her arms around her aunt, feeling the sharp bones of her frame as she inhaled the mingled scents of lilacs and peppermints.

Extricating herself from this surprising reaction, her aunt gawked as if she'd swallowed her tongue.

Frankly, Lucy did too. She'd no idea until her arms had locked round her aunt's middle that she'd been about to throw herself at her. Clearly, she'd taken a harder knock on the head than she'd real-ized at the time.

They both stepped back amid a clearing of throats and an awk-ward glance at their shoes as if the reason for this emotional out-burst might be written there.

Aunt Cynthia recovered first. "I am at my wits' end, young lady. You have stolen, lied, trespassed, and committed fraud. Worse, you've dragged an innocent child into your escapades."

"I wouldn't say Bill was entirely innocent."

"Don't interrupt. I was worried sick with no idea where you'd gone. Do you know the amount of trouble you've caused with your childish foolishness? I've spent countless days chasing you from pillar to post. I've called in every favor and squandered valuable time and resources in keeping your heedless, thoughtless actions from becoming common fodder for the masses"—she paused, suddenly aware of Lucy's rather unconventional ensemble—"is that my dress you're wearing?"

"It might be. Do you like it?" Damp, dusty, and sporting a few torn seams, her refashioned ensemble had survived the night almost intact.

"You stole clothes from my wardrobe and turned them into a . . . into a . . ." Lady Boxley studied her with magnifying-glass precision. "I suppose that collar is quite striking."

Lucy, who had been bracing herself for a crushing blow, was momentarily flummoxed. "Thank you, I think."

Lady Boxley glared, and Lucy resumed her pose of abject contrition. "Where was I? Oh yes. You betrayed my trust, trampled my goodwill, and . . . and . . ."—her hard gaze became assessing once more—"the way the skirt hangs just along the hip there reminds me a bit of Copeland."

Lucy didn't understand the direction this conversation was headed but she decided it was in her best interest not to argue. "Jo Copeland?"

"You know of her? Well, I suppose you are Amelia's daughter. She had an eye for fashion, though I believe she limited herself to purchasing it rather than designing it. You, on the other hand, seem

to have more than fluff for brains. Must come from your father."
She continued to eye Lucy's outfit as if in the audience at a Parisian
fashion parade.

"Are you going to sign me up?" Lucy asked.

"Sign you up?"

"With the WVS or the MTC or the WLA. I'm sure there are
any number of acronyms that would take me."

"No," her aunt replied thoughtfully. "I think I have a better out-
let for your rather unique talents. Madame Evrard lives near Truro.
She's retired now, but in her day she was quite sought after among
the *très chic* Parisian women. I might be able to induce her into
taking on an apprentice . . . if that apprentice was serious about
pursuing such a career."

Lucy hadn't time to digest this remarkable pronouncement before Aunt Cynthia cocked her head, still with a rather fearsome
glare, and added, "If I were you, I'd have chosen a rather more autumn shade to bring out the green in your eyes."

Her aunt knew what color Lucy's eyes were? Would this nonstop series of shocks never end?

"I have a lovely Vionnet. It never worked well with my coloring, but it would suit you perfectly. It just needs a bit of updating
to return it to the first stare of fashion. Actually, I believe there's a
whole trunk of old clothes in the attic. I've never had the heart to
hand them over to the WI for their clothing drives, but you might
find them inspirational."

By now, Lucy felt as if she'd taken one too many blows to the
head—or drunk one too many of Pidge's gins. Surely this conversation wasn't happening. "I thought you were angry."

Lady Boxley's considering frown deepened to one of white-
lipped displeasure. "I am beyond angry. I'm positively furious."

"Then . . ."

"Then what?"

"Then why are you being kind to me?"

Her aunt's expression went rigid as marble. "I'm not being 'kind,' as you so eloquently put it. I am simply mentioning the existence of a trunk in the attic. If you take that as an endorsement of your antics, you are much mistaken."

"But Madame Evrard?"

"Don't fawn at my feet quite yet. When you meet her, you may find that I could not have contrived a more suitable punishment. Compared to Madame, Sister Murphy is meek as a newborn lamb."

That gave Lucy a moment's pause, but only a moment. "Still, I'm surprised you went to all the bother of traveling up here. My mother would have simply sent her solicitor to deal with the situation."

"My solicitor is suffering from a horrid case of influenza and was unable to make the journey." Lady Boxley stiffened in noble umbrage. "And I do not slough off my responsibilities on others."

Lucy's feeling of optimism burst. "Oh, of course."

"Nor, it would seem, if Lady Turnbull's rather incomprehensible explanations are accurate, do you." Aunt Cynthia didn't smile, but there was a softer glow to her usual burning orbs, a smoothing of her furrowed brow, perhaps even a touch of relaxation in those firm downturned lips. "Perhaps you and I are more alike than I thought."

At one time not so long ago that comparison would have sent a shiver up Lucy's spine.

Not tonight.

Before the warmth in her chest could expand, Lady Boxley added in a quelling tone, "A horrifying thought for both of us, I imagine."

Lucy sat at an upper attic window, staring out on the square. No lights burned in the room behind her, so she felt no fear of a warden's reprimand. Beyond the watery glass, the storm had moved to the east, leaving a veil of cloud that hung low along rooftops and curled around chimney pots like smoke. A setting moon left the square across the street a tidy patchwork of shadow upon shifting shadow.

Lucy knew she should be asleep. It would be dawn very soon according to the alarm clock on her side table—already she could hear birds calling from the park's trimmed boxwoods—but as soon as her head hit the pillow, her mind spun in a blur of questions, her eyes locked on the ceiling as if answers might be written among the cracks in the plaster above her bed. The park was no more helpful at sorting out her confusion, but at least the view was more interesting.

She could focus on the scratch of trees against the sky instead of those she'd lost or driven away—Yoon Hai. Lady Amelia. Mason Oliver. Michael.

She could concentrate on the slippery movement of the shadows instead of those she'd found—Bill. Mrs. McKeegan. Lady Turnbull. Aunt Cynthia.

She could listen to the sounds of the city waking up rather than the voice in her head that told her she'd made a complete hash of her entire life since the morning she'd awakened in her airy bedroom on Orchard Road to her mother's scandalized harangue.

Before her on the window seat lay two calling cards. She found herself shuffling them with the same dexterity Bill had once shown with a marked deck.

Mason Oliver's, gilded and embossed, carrying the scent of aftershave and cigar smoke within the heavy-edged stock.

Lady Turnbull's simple script and plain stock, at odds with her elevated position and exclusive address.

Back and forth she shuffled them, one over the other, round and round, shadows lengthening as the dawn approached. Counting pluses and minuses as Bill might have noted aces and queens. Knowing a choice must be made but afraid to make the wrong one.

And thus making no choice.

Back and forth.

Over and under.

America. England.

Leave. Stay.

What dream would she follow?

Which risk would be greater?

A soft knock on the door broke her from the whirl of her thoughts. "Can I come in, Lucy?"

It was Bill, enveloped in a striped linen nightshirt that trailed to his bare toes, the sleeves draping loose over his gawky wrists.

"Of course." She made room for him. "You can't sleep either?"

He climbed up beside her in the embrasure, folding himself in the curve of her body, her chin resting on the top of his head. He smelled of soap and faintly of lavender-scented sheets. Neither spoke, each of them lost in their own thoughts as they stared out on the silence of the park. The shadows lengthened like fingers, then disappeared as the moon sank below the far side of the square.

"I miss Rufus, Lucy."

"Of course you do, but he's flying with all the other birds in heaven."

"Do you suppose he's looking down on us right now?"

"I expect he's too busy eating a feast of worms and seeds until he's fit to burst and singing his lungs out in some big chestnut tree. A heavenly chorus of siskins."

Bill gave a soft sigh. "That sounds nice." He seemed to draw closer to her, his breathing slow and even, until she thought he must have fallen asleep. Perfect. Now she was trapped, her right foot was falling asleep, and she had an itch she couldn't reach without waking him up.

She tried tipping her head back against the window and closing her eyes.

Just as she thought she might finally drop off, Bill's voice pulled her back.

"Do you love Michael?"

A slide of cold infected her, any thoughts of sleep erased. "What do you know about that?"

"Well, do you?"

"I don't think it's any of your business."

"He's keen on you. And he's not a rotter. You said it yourself."

"Yes, of course . . ."

"So why don't you marry him?"

"It doesn't work like that."

"I don't see why not."

"Usually because both people have to be in love—or at least think they're in love—to be married. It's not like picking out a dress in a shop."

The excitement. The infatuation. Then one brought it home, tried it on, and hated it. All right, perhaps it was like picking out a dress in a shop.

"But I saw you kiss him. You thought I was asleep, but I wasn't."

"Then you also saw that he most definitely didn't kiss me back."

"That's not the way it looked to me."

"Yes, well, it was a mistake."

"Maybe, but I still think Michael and you are nice together. He makes me laugh and he's jolly fun. And he knows how to fix an engine and make a paper airplane that really flies and even how to fish with a bit of cheese."

"All fine qualities in a husband." She paused, adding under her breath, "I'm sure he and Arabella Nash will be very happy."

She put Michael McKeegan firmly out of her mind. He was a swell guy who'd helped her out of a jam, but he was nothing like her usual sort of man at all. Neither suavely urbane nor flush with ready cash, and definitely not always up for a good time.

And maybe . . . just maybe . . . that was the point.

Over and under.

Back and forth.

The cards moved in and out like the shrinking shadows in the park.

Chapter 26

If someone had told Lucy only a week ago that she would find herself having breakfast between Lady Boxley—chatelaine of a great estate, caretaker of an earldom, and arbiter of all things proper—and con man, card sharp, and spiv-in-the-making Bill Smedley, she'd have laughed in their face.

Had they also told her that Aunt Cynthia would be taking lessons in sleight of hand from the little swindler, she'd have assumed the world as she knew it had been turned on its head.

"See? It's all making folks look where you want them to 'stead of where you don't."

"Ha! There's the queen."

"Right again, mum."

"What a nifty trick."

The two sat, heads together, the great social divide naught but a plate of kippered herring and a pot of tea wide.

Lady Turnbull sat at the head of the table in a lace-trimmed gold silk robe, rings winking as she nibbled the edge of a piece of toast. "I can't believe no one reported Bill missing for all those days."

Aunt Cynthia glanced up from her dealing. "I've spoken to Loretta Stanley. According to her, those horrid Sayres people kept his disappearance quiet so as not to lose the weekly stipend they were receiving for his care."

"That's ghastly."

"It wouldn't have happened had I been on the committee overseeing evacuations, and so I informed Mrs. Stanley in no uncertain terms. A shoddy lack of leadership, if you ask me. As I've always said, if you want something done right, you must do it yourself."

Lucy caught Pidge's stern eye over her cup of Darjeeling. No robe and slippers this morning. His servant's dignity was ironclad, from the top of his sleek pomaded hair to the tips of his shiny patent-leather loafers, and then he ruined it all with a sly wink of amusement. Lucy winked back.

Last night's misery of indecision remained, but sunshine, hot coffee, and clean clothes always made everything better. She had risen to find her bag retrieved from the hotel and her wardrobe washed, pressed, and put away. Oh, to possess an army of such buttling efficiency.

Now kitted out in something that didn't look like a ragpicker's bargain, she could almost pretend last night never happened.

What if you found you could count on someone else?

Almost.

"I hope the people at the Connaught weren't too beastly, Pidge," she apologized as he offered her another cup of coffee.

"Not at all, Miss Stanhope."

"Really, Lucy. The Connaught?" Aunt Cynthia chided. "It's always been Claridge's for our family and always will be."

"Cooee! Anybody up and decent?" The shout erupted from the entry hall. "Grand-mère? Pidge?"

Bill's head came up like a hound catching a scent. "It's Miss Irene. She's found my mam."

He shot from his chair, tricks forgotten, stampeding into the foyer to meet her and drag her half-resisting into the dining room. She was dressed for work, her felt hat covering a businesslike bun, her gas mask hanging at her shoulder. She pulled up short at seeing the crowd circling her grandmother's table. "I'd not realized you had company, Grand-mère. How do you do, Lady Boxley?"

"I do much better after a good night's sleep, Irene dear." Aunt Cynthia still played with the cards at her plate.

"Pidge, fetch Irene a plate," Lady Turnbull instructed. "You'll join us for breakfast, my dear? Have a proper meal for once instead of living off beans on toast and leftover sandwiches?"

As Irene took a seat, she slid a curious sideways stare toward Lucy.

"Before you ask," Lucy headed her off, "it's a very long and muddled story, but your grandmother has been a peach about everything."

Irene relaxed into a relieved smile. "The more muddled the better if Grand-mère has any say in the matter. She thrives on confusion."

Bill joggled from foot to foot. "You're here about my mam, ain't you, Miss Irene? You found her like you said you would. I knew you was a real corker."

Pidge placed a plate in front of her. She fiddled with her fork. Rearranged her napkin.

A lump crowded out the eggs and sausage Lucy had eaten for breakfast.

"I did ask around, Bill," Irene hedged. "And I put in more than a few calls."

Bill nearly danced with eagerness. "Will I see her today? I can't wait to tell her about Lucy and the spanner and the bombing and the constable what I bruised. And Rufus. And sleeping in a shed. And the sheep."

Irene continued playing with her food. "I'm afraid I haven't heard back yet, Bill. Everyone is doing all they can, but London is a big place and these are busy people."

His dancing stopped. Aunt Cynthia looked up from her cards, her face grim.

"But you promised." His lip wobbled.

"No, Bill," Lucy interceded. "Miss Turnbull didn't promise. I did. She's done what she can. Now it's up to me."

"But you're leaving. You're going to America with Mr. Oliver."

Aunt Cynthia's brows drew low, her lips compressing to a tight white line.

"The arrangements aren't settled, Bill," Lucy explained, casting a wary eye down the table. This wasn't exactly how she'd meant to broach the subject of her decision. She braced herself for the storm she knew was coming.

"Nor will they be," Aunt Cynthia declared right on cue. "You are not going anywhere with some rackety American panderer to be filmed for anyone and his brother to see."

"You sound like a Victorian spinster."

"I sound like your aunt and your guardian while your mother is abroad."

"My mother is dead."

The room went silent. Pidge paused in the middle of pouring a cup of tea. Irene inspected her eggs. Bill drew and held a gasped breath. Only Lady Turnbull remained unfazed.

"You can say it. You don't have to pretend for my sake. Mother is dead."

Aunt Cynthia toyed with her rope of pearls, her fingers running up and down the strand in agitation. "We don't know that for certain."

"I know that for certain." Lucy shoved her chair back and stood in a rattle of dishes. Her heart thundered. Her flesh was cold and clammy. She couldn't catch her breath as she escaped the closing walls of the dining room and all those damned pitying stares.

She fled to the drawing room, where she stood, coiled and aching, her breath coming in snatching gasps. Staring at nothing. Seeing only the wave of a languid hand. The trailing end of a scarf. The car disappearing down the lane to be swallowed by the dusk. This time it would not be coming back.

Loneliness bit deep into Lucy's bones. Tears burned but did not fall.

"You've spent your whole life trying to measure up to your mother. But be careful you don't fall into the same trap as she did, Lucy." She was so lost in her own thoughts, she hadn't heard the click of Aunt Cynthia's heels as she followed her, but now there she stood in her sensible tweed suit, the comfortable scent of her perfume mingling with the far fainter aromas of wind-salty air and musty old house in what Lucy could only think of as eau de Nanreath Hall. "Don't turn your back on what you have in hopes of finding something better round the bend. Sometimes all you'll find is just another bend."

"But what is there for me here?"

"What is it you want?"

Michael had asked her the same question. Lucy thought she'd known. It had been so clear. Her purpose unswerving. Now everything was muddled. Over and under. Back and forth. Stay or leave.

"I want to go home."

"We can leave for Cornwall this morning."

"That's not my home."

"Singapore is lost, Lucy. There is no going back."

"That wasn't my home either. Not really." She crushed her hands into her skirt, feeling the fabric wrinkle and bunch. Her knuckles were white, the veins blue. "It was just a place. Like everywhere I've lived. Just a stop along the way. Never a destination."

"Then where is it you want to go?"

She thought of the little cottage by the millpond, the overgrown garden, the cowshed out the back. It made no sense, this dreaming. A ridiculous folly. A nonsensical lark of an impossibility. A cowshed, for heaven's sake. Who dreams of a cowshed? Still it clung like a burr and could not be shaken. She imagined Parcheesi games and hot cocoa and knitted cardigans and—a happy family.

"I thought I'd know it when I saw it, but I didn't—and now it's gone."

Lucy leaned her head against the glass of her bedroom window. In the washed-out glare of a pale morning sun, the park across the road revealed itself to be far less enchanting. The shrubs were a bit ragged and the weeds a bit encroaching. The most well-tended section was a corner beneath a spreading elm where someone had prepared the ground for a garden.

She drew a deep breath. And then a second. Enough to forestall any humiliating tears and gather her scattered thoughts. Her mother might have been completely wrong about everything else, but she was right about the uselessness of weeping. Tears never solved a problem.

And Lucy's mounted by the hour. She withdrew the calling cards from her handbag, shuffling them between trembling fingers.

Home—she'd spoken the word aloud to Aunt Cynthia, but what did Lucy know of home? Aunt Cynthia had that great ancestral pile on the Cornish coast with roots that pushed deep into the past. Bill had the streets and alleys of Bethnal Green, where whole families lived in a few cluttered rooms and one could spend one's whole life within a few congested city miles. Michael had a close-knit village where neighbors looked out for one another and life moved to the slow turn of the seasons.

What did Lucy have?

She turned from the window to pace the room, chewing a thumbnail in agitation.

What did she want?

Lady Turnbull, no matter how kind she'd been. Aunt Cynthia, no matter how forgiving she'd been. And Pidge . . . well . . . he was a positive dreamboat. Still, Lucy thought she might go bonkers if she spent one more minute quarantined inside the town house turning her life over with the same endless spin of those calling cards.

She slammed out of the bedroom and clattered down the stairs into the drawing room, where Lady Turnbull and Aunt Cynthia sat over a pot of coffee.

". . . a telephone call to Lady Reading."

"Or a formal inquiry with the Ministry of Health."

"I've already sent a note round to the JWO. Lord Bournville sits on a committee there and is a close friend of my late husband's."

"Like the candy bar?" Bill looked up from his deck of cards. Solitaire, she was relieved to see.

"What's that, child?"

"Funny. That name reminds me of something." He scratched his head. "Darned if I can remember what, though." He shrugged and returned to his cards.

"As I was saying," Lady Turnbull resumed, "we should hear anytime. Good old Borny said he'd leave no stone unturned in the hunt."

"Are you talking about Bill's mother?" Lucy interrupted.

Aunt Cynthia added cream to her cup. "She needs to be found."

"And I said I would do it."

The women exchanged a swift glance. The tick of the clock seemed to meet and match Lucy's heart. "We're going out."

"We are?"

"You are?" Both Lady Turnbull and Aunt Cynthia stiffened in their seats. Pidge paused in his dusting. His gaze followed her speculatively as she took up her handbag and Bill snatched an apple from the front hall table.

Bypassing the tepid joys to be found in the park, they left behind the quiet leafy square for the busy thoroughfare of Kensington High Street, passing the great domed façade of Royal Albert Hall, windows boarded up for the duration and sandbags stacked along the curb, but still advertising Sunday concerts, still imposing. Across the way, a group of American GIs were getting their picture taken in front of the Albert Memorial, the prince consort staring down from his pigeon-crowded perch. "Where we going, Lucy?"

"I don't know. Somewhere. Anywhere. I needed to think, and I can't do that with those three watching me as if I might pop off like an unexploded bomb."

"Your aunt is spiffing. Not anything like I thought she'd be."

"She surprised me too."

"She said I reminded her of her son, Hugh, when he was my age. Imagine me being like a real lord. The boys at the Lion—"

"Bill?" she warned, scowling dangerously.

"They won't never know 'cause I don't hang about with them no more." He grinned.

"No one can say I didn't try," she muttered.

Into Hyde Park. Across the Serpentine, where couples wandered arm in arm and children threw bread to the ducks that clustered along the shore. No destination in mind. No route planned.

Only the need to move, to run, to outpace her thoughts and escape the round and round.

Move. Run. Escape.

Was Aunt Cynthia right? Was she in danger of becoming like Amelia? Was that what ran in her blood? Cowardice?

Good-bye was familiar.

Good-bye was safe.

It meant never having to try too hard, never having to risk, never having to change.

Aunt Cynthia said her mother chased happiness. Mason Oliver said she chased love. Lucy chased belonging. And perhaps—just perhaps, mind you—that could only be found by standing still.

They emerged from the park at Marble Arch. A bus poured smoke from a makeshift coal-fired engine. A fire truck clanged its way past. A knot of gentlemen, American by the cut of their suits and the twang in their voices, argued the state of the war as they strolled Park Lane toward Upper Grosvenor and the embassy.

"What are we doing here?" Bill asked, tugging Lucy from her thoughts.

The Dorchester stood across the way; a doorman rolled back and forth on the balls of his feet. Two officers strolled past. A woman emerged from a taxi in a fashionable pencil skirt and a jacket adorned with a handsome fox stole. A stylish hat framed perfectly arranged auburn hair.

She promised.

Lucy froze, the air crushed from her lungs. It couldn't be . . .

Then the woman turned to pay the driver, and it was no one Lucy recognized. A stranger's face.

Her breath returned with a small sob that scraped her throat raw.

Her mother was truly gone, and with her, any desire for a glamorous life in Hollywood.

"We should be getting back, Lucy."

"Yes," she replied, only half-listening. "Yes, we will."

"Her ladyship might have heard from that bloke what's her husband's friend."

"You mean Lord Bournville?"

"That's it! That's where I know that name from."

Lucy came back to the present with a metaphorical clap of thunder. "What name?"

"Bournville. I knew it sounded like a name what I'd heard before. I just couldn't bring my mind to it, but now I remember. That's the name of the gent Mam worked for before the war."

"Are you certain?"

"Course I'm certain. Mr. Bournville—it's the same name as the candy bar. That's how I can remember it so well. Mam always said it was a shame the gent wasn't sweet like the chocolate. 'Stead he was a miserly old tosser what was always coming along behind her to check she'd done her work properly."

"Do you think your mother would still be working there?"

"I dunno. Maybe."

"Come on." Lucy grabbed him by the hand.

"Where are we going now?"

"To find your mother."

"Really?"

Sometimes doing what was best wasn't doing what was right. And if you wanted it done right, you did it yourself. "I promised, didn't I?"

They arrived back at the house to find Lady Turnbull out delivering honey to Mr. and Mrs. Fleischer, compliments of Lower Stokenoor's bees.

Aunt Cynthia had taken the opportunity of her unanticipated

trip to the city to make a formal complaint with the War Damage Commission over a graffitied fresco in Nanreath Hall's blue saloon.

Pidge was in the kitchen polishing the silver.

No one to witness the teeny-weeniest of deceptions. "Canning Town, you said? Thank you very much for your assistance, Mr. Bournville," Lucy said, mimicking Aunt Cynthia in severity of tone and regality of accent. "Lord Gainsborough's solicitors will be most grateful. Mrs. Smedley has been difficult to locate."

Bill giggled.

Lucy shushed him. "Yes, I understand there's a war on."

There was a rap at the door. A ringing of the doorbell. Another knock, louder and more insistent. She heard Pidge enter the hall.

"I'm sure Lord Gainsborough's bequest won't affect Mrs. Smedley's continued employment with you, sir. Yes, I understand. A good dependable maid is hard to find."

There was a murmur of voices. Footsteps heading this way.

"Got to run"—in her haste she stumbled over her drawled vowels and clipped consonants—"that is"—she recovered with twice the ice in her accent—"thank you again, Mr. Bournville. My place of birth? My age? Why, you sly dog. I'm flattered, but really . . ." Lucy made to hang up the phone. "Yes." She faltered. "Yes, of course." By now, she sounded more picture palace than Buckingham Palace. "Cheerio and pip pip! See ya!" she shouted into the receiver as the drawing room door opened.

"A married woman" were the last tinny words she heard before she slammed the receiver down.

Bill gripped his stomach in a belly laugh as a fit of giggles overtook him. "Lord Gainsborough," he guffawed in a series of gasped snorts. "Cheerio and pip pip. You're a corker, Lucy."

"That's one word for her."

Lucy's heart stopped for a moment as Bill looked up from where he'd ended prostrate on the floor. "Michael!"

"Good to see you in one piece, lad." His eyes shifted to meet hers. "Both of you."

Bill leapt up. "We found my mam! Lucy did anyway. She rang up Mr. Bournville and pretended to be a secretary for Lord Gainsborough's solicitors asking after Mrs. Smedley's whereabouts as she'd been left a hundred pounds in the old duffer's will."

Michael lifted a brow in question. Pidge managed to remain impervious, though his eye did stray to the inspiring landscape painting hanging over the fireplace.

"I didn't think he would be as forthcoming if I told him the truth," Lucy explained sheepishly. "It was the first name that popped into my head."

"You always manage to get what you want, don't you?" Michael said with one of those shrewd stares that always left her feeling off balance and underdressed.

She flushed, tightness banding her chest. "Not everything I want."

His eyes flared, but it wasn't with amusement. That was anger burning in those guileless blue depths. "If you weren't a female, Lucy Stanhope, I'd punch you straight in the mouth for running off like that and scaring the shit out of me. What were you thinking? You could have been killed, you great harebrained nincompoop."

Her aunt had grown a heart and Michael had grown a temper. The world really had turned itself inside out.

"You let me go." Even as she said it, she wondered if she was talking about their fight or their kiss. And why it mattered so much in either case.

"Let you? I couldn't have stopped you if I tried. I spent hours searching up and down every blasted street, lane, alley, road, and avenue. But between that bloody fog and the blackout, I couldn't see a damn thing. Finally ended at the police station and they told me a young woman and her accomplice had been brought in on suspicion of looting and black marketeering."

Bill shoved his way between them. "That was us. Lucy broke into a warehouse and smashed a door, then the coppers came and we was taken in, but I landed the bloke five right on the jaw. That'll teach 'em to sort it with me." He spotted Lucy's frown, and his eagerness drained away, leaving only deflated and slouch-shouldered repentance. "But I'll not do nothing like that ever again. Not never," he added in reverent Sunday-school tones.

"How did you find me?" Lucy asked dumbly, trying to understand why Michael had gone to so much trouble to track her down. Probably just his overdeveloped knight-in-shining-armor complex. Didn't he know by now she didn't need saving? Didn't want saving?

Couldn't be saved?

Besides, he had Arabella Nash, a paragon of modern womanhood. Compared to her, Lucy was a complete mess.

"I went to the Connaught but they said you'd checked out. Luckily, a doorman overheard Lady Boxley when she was settling your account. For the right price, he was able to recall the address she gave the taxi driver."

"Who always gets what he wants?"

Pidge stepped forward. "I'd say Corporal McKeegan has shown a marked persistence in the face of overwhelming odds. Tea, sir? I've just put the kettle on."

"Thank you. I'd like that."

"Come, Master William. You can assist me with the tray." Pidge shooed the boy out ahead of him, leaving Michael alone with Lucy.

"You've explained how you found me, but not why."

And just like that, he was Michael again, laughter dancing in his eyes and a smile playing over his square-jawed, clean-cut features. "Because I didn't want to end up bent and wrinkly with a cane and an ear trumpet and all the while pondering what if."

"Oh."

"I should have known you'd land on your feet, lass. You're like a cat."

"No," she said angrily, brought up short by the comparison. "No, I'm not. I'm not anything like a damned cat. I don't even like cats." She swallowed, suddenly tongue-tied. Not a condition in which she often found herself. "I still don't understand. What about Arabella? You dropped everything and came all this way . . ."

"If you must know, when push came to shove, I couldn't do it," he said flatly.

"Do I need to draw you a diagram?" she replied with a mocking glance and a coy arch of her brows. It was that or continue to gape at him as if she'd lost her mind. Which, come to think of it, might explain an awful lot about her day thus far.

A dry smile played over his face. "You're incorrigible."

"So they tell me—repeatedly."

His smile faded, and now he merely looked tired and almost puzzled. "We hit it off just as if I'd never shipped out. Arabella's as wonderful as ever, and the man who wins her heart will be a lucky man."

"But . . ."

"But it wasn't twenty-four hours before she was trying to set me up with a position in Sir Reginald's office and calling round to estate agents about flats in Chelsea."

"That's brilliant—isn't it?"

"It would be if I wanted to count widgets for the military and live cooped up in London."

"Yes, I suppose there aren't many flats in Chelsea with room for a cowshed."

Michael moved to the front window, looking out on the park much as she had done the night before. This afternoon, a kite-flying wind sent spring blossoms spilling like pink-and-white snow across the paths while a row of plane trees stood like sentinels over a man walking his dog and a child jumping rope, their crowns a vibrant green against the gray sky.

He stood with his hands clasped loosely behind his back. "That cowshed is going to be my studio and office when I'm through."

"I don't understand."

He turned toward her, a serious glint in his eye. "I plan to go into the design and building trade. After the war, people will need places to live, and not just trumped-up Nissen huts with a kitchen and a bath, but something they can take pride in. Something they want to come home to. I aim to be the one to give it to them."

"And the old cottage in Charbury?"

"Will be my base of operations. Can't beat a commute of twenty steps out your back door, can you?"

"I take it Arabella didn't see the possibilities in cowsheds and building firms."

"Our conversation never made it that far. I kept waiting for that bolt of lightning I used to feel when I was around her. But it never happened. Not even a hint of a spark."

"You haven't seen her in two years. How can you take one look at her and know you're not in love?"

His gaze met hers, no amusement hidden in those blue eyes now. "The same way I can take one look and know I'm in love, I expect."

Lucy's skin prickled, a queer slippery excitement curling along her limbs and pooling in her stomach. "Now who's being utterly ridiculous?"

He lifted a hand to trace the outline of her jaw, his fingers cool against her flush of fever heat. "That's probably it."

"Tremendously impulsive and exceedingly reckless."

"That's definitely it." His eyes still burned, but now the fire within them scorched with a new and more tempting emotion. Her loyal sheepdog had gone dangerously feral.

"I don't cook," she stammered, her tongue seeming to thicken even as her mind went horrifyingly blank. "I can't clean. I drink too much, smoke too much—"

"Talk too much."

He kissed her. That's right. *He* kissed *her*. And he was sober—at least she thought he was. He didn't taste like alcohol. Instead, he tasted like licorice and tea and maybe toothpaste, his kiss slow and deep and toe-curlingly thorough. His stubble scraped her cheek. Had she been a match, she'd have gone up in flames. He pulled her close against him, his heart thundering under her palm. Her own keeping pace.

The telltale rattle of an approaching tea tray was Pidge's subtle warning signal.

Michael reluctantly let her go, though there was a look in his eye that, well . . . let's just say she hoped it was one promise he meant to keep very soon.

"Does this mean you've decided to stay with Lady Boxley?" he asked.

"It means I have a choice to make."

"Between running off to America or staying in England?"

She kissed him once, then again—just because she could. "Between holding on to an old dream or reaching for a new one."

Chapter 27

The man at the butcher's said it's just up here past the church," Lucy said, studying this down-and-out section of Newham.

Canning Town turned out to be a clustered warren of streets bordered to the west by the India Docks, the south by the Victoria Docks tidal basin, and the north by Barking Road, home to many of the wharfies, factory workers, and clerks employed by the nearby shipping companies, factories, and warehouses. Like its closest neighbors of Silvertown and Poplar, it had suffered from the intense bombing attacks of the last few years, but there still remained, among the blasted crush of ruined buildings and rubble-strewn streets, blocks of shabby terrace houses, shops, and offices where people continued to work and live as if thumbing their collective noses at Hitler's bombardment.

Bill looked around eagerly, his face bright with tamped excitement, but there was no hurry to his pace. He ran ahead to check round a corner, one thin shoulder leaning against the dusty brick of the wall, a hand trailing along the crumbled mortar, his hair ruffled in the acrid tidal breeze.

"Now that the end is in sight, he seems almost hesitant," Michael said.

"I know how he feels," Lucy replied. "Wanting to arrive and dreading it at the same time."

"It's his mother, not a stranger."

"But he's spent years dreaming of being with her. Building it up in his head. Thinking of how it will be when they're together. Once he finds her, he'll have to face a reality that won't be all dewdrops and snowflakes."

"Is that how it was with you and your mother?"

"I would imagine what would happen when we saw each other again, build it up in my head until it was as real to me as you are standing there. Then she'd explode back into my life and it never lived up to my fantasy—not once. You'd think I'd have learned after a while, but I never did. I don't want Bill to face that."

"Bill's mum isn't your mum, Lucy." Michael regarded her carefully. "She sent him away out of love. She'll want him back for the same reason. Wait and see, it'll be all right once they're together again."

The shade of Mrs. Pratchett surfaced like a ghost from the waves. Lucy shivered despite the spring warmth. "Do you ever look on the bad side?"

A dry smile played over his face. "Would it help?" He pointed across the street. "There's number twelve, just like Mr. Bournville said."

Tape crisscrossed the windows that weren't blown out, glass dust and cement rubble crunched under their feet, and washing hung limp and gray from a line in a nearby vacant lot. But children played a riotous game of football farther up the street and a postman whistled as he made his rounds. Two careworn housewives in curlers and aprons took a break from the housework to chat on a doorstep.

They stood with Bill on the opposite corner, his arm looped round a lamppost as he drew circles with his left foot in the dirt. "Suppose she's home?" he asked.

"Only one way to find out." Lucy nudged him forward, feeling the tension stringing his limbs.

As if diving into cold water, he took a breath and plunged forward, arriving at the stoop out of breath and as pale as chalk. With a final glance back at Lucy and Michael, he rapped on the door.

It was as if time froze. The boys at their game, the women on the steps, the postman at his box; all hovered in anticipation. Lucy held her breath. Her hand found Michael's.

Bill rapped again.

Lucy's heart thudded. She was sweating. *Please be there. Please want him back. Please love him.*

The door opened on a pretty woman in her midthirties with the same light brown hair as Bill's, though hers was tied up in a flowery kerchief. Her body went stiff, a hand flying to her mouth. The other gripped the doorknob as if she might faint.

Bill smiled and said something. Lucy could hear the high babble of his chatter. His mother's tones, softer yet no less animated. They flung themselves at each other in a tearful, joyful reunion. She dragged him inside the house and closed the door.

And just like that, it was over.

Bill was back where he belonged.

Lucy should have been overjoyed, yet something felt both incomplete and all too familiar.

Then she realized—he had never once looked back.

"Come on, Lucy." Michael put his arm around her. "We can go. He's home. He'll be all right now."

"Of course." A boulder crushed her chest, her stomach sick and aching. She allowed Michael to turn her away, though her steps dragged, her shoes gray in the swirling dust of the street. "Guess I'm not an expert at good-byes after all."

She stumbled on a broken bit of sidewalk. The boys up the street resumed their noisy game. Unbidden tears washed her vision.

She never heard Bill approach until hands snaked around her middle, nearly knocking her off her feet. The air was driven from her lungs. Her spine was nearly snapped. "Lucy! Wait! Don't leave."

She hugged him back, feeling the press of his bones in his underfed frame, smelling the faint scent of shampoo and the even fainter aroma of cigarette smoke in his hair. Her chest swelled, her throat closing around a hard knot. "I have to go, Bill. But you're safe now with your mam."

"And my dad."

"Your what?" She looked up to see Bill's mother had been joined on the stoop by a broad-shouldered bear of a man with a grizzled beard sprouting from a weathered face.

"My dad. He's come back. Turns out he was a motorman on a tanker, sailed all over the world, but he's home now for good an' all. Mam says he's made a honest woman out of her."

Of course! That must have been what Mr. Bournville meant with his final cryptic comment about a married woman. No wonder Miss Matilda Smedley had been so difficult to find.

Lucy wiped her eyes with the back of her hand. "What if he turns out to be a rotter like all the rest?"

Bill grinned. "Mam says if you want to win the prize, you have to buy your ticket and take your chance. That sounds about right, don't it?"

"It sounds absolutely right." She cast one last sidelong look at the couple standing arm in arm with the somewhat stunned but dewy look of newlyweds. "I guess this is it, then. We did what we set out to do. We got you home."

Bill glanced up at Michael standing nearby. "We got you home too, didn't we, Lucy?"

She rested her cheek on the top of Bill's head. Old sorrows and fresh grief dissolved in the crushing strength of Bill's embrace. Her mother's face swam before her eyes, not pursed with disappointment or icily indifferent, but as it had been that long-ago day at the fair. Tender. Vibrant. Contented. She smelled her perfume. Heard her laughter.

This was the most perfect day ever.

Lucy wholeheartedly agreed.

The afternoon sun stood high to the west.

Lucy watched outside the gates of Whitchurch Airport as a BOAC passenger plane rose up above the far trees in an ascent that would take it out over the ocean on its way to Lisbon, then across the Atlantic to the Azores and finally America.

The roar of the engines vibrated along her bones and down into the soles of her feet. She squinted into the gray sky, a hand to her eyes as the plane ascended. Her chest seemed to lift with the plane, a lightness that brought a smile to her lips.

"Good-bye!" She waved madly as the plane tipped its wings, already high and distant. "Give my regards to Hollywood!"

She stood in the field watching until the plane became a smudge, then a speck, then disappeared altogether. Birds sang in the high hedge bordering the airfield. A petrol truck drove past toward a far hangar. Another plane coughed to life.

"Lucy?" Michael leaned against the door of the estate wagon, obscuring the faded stencil advertising McKeegan's Garage. His shirtsleeves were rolled up, and there was a smear of grease on his cheek. "You coming, lass?"

She stepped to meet him, hand to hand, side by side. "I'm coming."

Acknowledgments

From a hasty one-paragraph proposal, an entire book was born. As always, the process was fraught with false starts, dead ends, and a roller coaster of creative highs and lows. But I was never alone as I battled my way toward "The End," and for that I have to acknowledge everyone who stood with me along the way.

Thank you to my amazing and talented agent, Kevan Lyon, who never lets me rest on my accomplishments but challenges me to reach further, dream bigger, and never underestimate myself. My editor, Tessa Woodward, who answers every question, discusses any problem, and is always there to reassure me when my confidence falters. With help from her able assistants, Nicole Fischer and Elle Keck, she keeps me on track and on time and manages to do it all with kindness, good humor, and infinite patience.

My appreciation goes out to Camille Collins, who looks for every opportunity to shout my success to the world even when I'm too shy to do it myself, and everyone in the HarperCollins family who has taken the time to make me feel at home.

I would still be lost in the virtual weeds without my partners in crime, Do Leonard and Maggie Scheck, who help turn my plot bunnies into words on the page with laughter, munchies, and two big red pens. A shout-out goes to everyone in my tribe at Washington Romance Writers, whose friendship and support has been a constant since the very first day I arrived nervous and frightened in their midst with a crazy idea that I wanted to tell stories for a living.

And last, my love and gratitude to my husband, John. I could never have made this wild journey without him by my side. He is and always will be my definition of brave, loyal, and true. And bear hugs to Georgia, Thomas, and Matthew, who no longer question why Mom and her computer seem to be welded together at times. If I've taught them anything, I hope it's that hard work pays off, love conquers all, and a happily ever after is always worth striving for.

Glossary

ARP—Air Raid Precautions organization. A civil defense organization set up in 1937 whose main duties included serving as wardens, ambulance drivers, fire guards, and communications personnel, and as first aid, decontamination, and rescue workers. In 1941, it changed its name to the Civil Defense Service.

ATS—Auxiliary Territorial Service. The women's branch of the British Army during World War II, the ATS started out serving mainly as cooks and clerks, but by the war's end, it had taken over such essential duties as radar operations, antiaircraft gunnery, and military policing. Princess Elizabeth served in the ATS as a second subaltern during the war.

ENSA—Entertainments National Service Association. A branch of the NAAFI in charge of organizing concerts, parties, movies, and other entertainment for servicemen at home and abroad. It was sometimes referred to sarcastically as "Every Night Something Awful."

FANY—First Aid Nursing Yeomanry. Begun in 1907, this organization trained personnel comparable to today's army medics to assist at field hospitals and as ambulance drivers. It changed its name in 1936 to the Women's Transport Service (WTS) and in 1938 was rolled into the Auxiliary Territorial Service (ATS). A small portion of FANY trained and served in espionage roles as part of the Special Operations Executive.

JWO—Joint War Organization. In 1939, the British Red Cross and St. John Ambulance Corps combined their efforts. JWO worked in hospitals, convalescent homes, and rest stations; provided refugee relief and delivered packages to prisoners of war; and created the wounded, missing, and relatives department to assist in information gathering on servicemen reported missing overseas. The organization was also instrumental in supplying much-needed aid to the German-occupied Channel Islands.

LDV—Local Defense Volunteers. After 1940, this force was known as the Home Guard and unofficially as "Dad's Army." Those otherwise ineligible for military service due to age or other considerations were enlisted to serve as a volunteer auxiliary defense force in case of German invasion.

MTC—Mechanized Transport Corps. This organization provided drivers for military and government departments at home in Britain and abroad. It also took over much of the driving duties for foreign dignitaries unfamiliar with British rules of the road.

NAAFI—Navy, Army, and Air Force Institute. Formed in 1921 to run recreation centers and canteens for the armed services, NAAFI also sold goods and services to the military and their families at home and abroad. By 1944, it managed over 7,000 canteens and employed around 96,000 personnel.

QA—Queen Alexandra's Imperial Military Nursing Service. Created in 1902, this group was the nursing branch of the British Army. Women employed as QA nurses had to be at least twenty-five years old, single or newly widowed, and of good social standing, and have completed a three-year nursing course.

RASC—Royal Army Service Corps. With the exception of weaponry and ammunition, the RASC provided transport, logistics, and supply services as part of the British armed forces.

VAD—Voluntary Aid Detachment. Created in 1919 under the direction of the British Red Cross to offer nursing assistance, VAD volunteers were trained in first aid, hygiene, and sanitation in order to free up male orderlies for other military duties. By World War II, their roles expanded to include work as nurses, pharmacists, radiographers, and lab technicians.

WAAF—Women's Auxiliary Air Force. The women's branch of the Royal Air Force, WAAF worked at such jobs as mechanic, photographic interpreter, and radar plotter.

WI—Women's Institute. Founded in Wales in 1915, WI was a community-based organization for rural women. During World War II, its pacifist philosophy did not allow contributions directly to the war effort. Instead, it focused on food production and caring for evacuees.

WLA—Women's Land Army. Re-formed in 1939, this organization, at its height, put nearly 87,000 women to work on England's farms. No job was too difficult, and "Land Girls" often found themselves doing such things as plowing, lambing, and threshing.

WRNS (Wrens)—Women's Royal Naval Service. The women's branch of the Royal Navy, WRNS mostly covered shore-based duties, working as radar, telegraph, and telephone operators; meteorologists; and intelligence gatherers, and a small number served on motor torpedo boat patrols. By 1944, 8.5 percent of the Royal Navy was female.

WVS—Women's Voluntary Service. Formed in 1938 to help civilians after air raids, this group started out assisting evacuees. But their responsibilities quickly expanded to include organizing lectures on important wartime topics, running mobile canteens, and arranging temporary housing for victims of bombings.

About the author

About the book

Read On . . .

Insights,
Interviews
& More . . .

Meet Alix Rickloff

ALIX RICKLOFF is a critically acclaimed author of historical and paranormal romance. Her previous novels include *Secrets of Nanreath Hall* (HarperCollins, 2016), the Bligh Family series (Kensington, 2009), the Heirs of Kilronan trilogy (Pocket, 2011), and, as Alexa Egan, the Imnada Brotherhood series (Pocket, 2014). She lives in Maryland with her husband and children. ∾

Reading Group Discussion Questions

1. What did you think of Lucy at the outset of the story? Did you find her an unlikable character? A sympathetic character? Why?

2. Mrs. Pratchett and her daughters leave Singapore while Lady Amelia and Fortescue choose to stay. If threatened by war, could you leave everything you own and flee, or would you remain behind and hope for the best? Do you know anyone who's made this decision?

3. Bill and Lucy come from very different backgrounds, but they share many similarities. What are they? What in their lives might have contributed to this resemblance in temperament?

4. Bill is one of thousands of children who left their homes and families during the evacuation of London at the outbreak of World War II. If you were a parent during that time, would you have kept your children with you or sent them away? Explain your choice.

5. All three main characters travel to London in search of something. Do all three find what they are looking for? ▶

6. In the end, Lucy has to make a choice that will affect the rest of her life. What are some difficult choices you've had to make? Looking back, do you feel you made the right decisions?

7. Lucy encounters many different mothers throughout her journey. Which mother did you most identify with? Which mother do you feel played the most pivotal role in the story? Explain.

8. Lucy identifies with Mrs. Britt's desire to ignore reality and live in a dream. Why do you suppose that is? What realities does Lucy ignore? What makes her finally face the truth?

9. Both Michael and Lucy form poor first impressions of each other and slowly revise their opinions over the course of the long trip to London. Have your instincts ever been wrong when it came to someone?

10. Lucy constantly compares herself to her mother, Lady Amelia, throughout the book, and by the end is afraid she is becoming just like her. Are there any ways in which you see similarities between yourself and your mother? Give examples. ∽

Have You Read? More from Alix Rickloff

SECRETS OF NANREATH HALL

Cornwall, 1940. Back in England after the harrowing evacuation at Dunkirk, World War II Red Cross nurse Anna Trenowyth finds herself unexpectedly assigned to Nanreath Hall—her dead mother's childhood home. All Anna has left of her mother, Lady Katherine Trenowyth, are vague memories that tease her with clues she can't unravel. Anna knows this could be the chance for her to finally become acquainted with the family she's never known— and to learn the truth about her past.

Cornwall, 1913. In the luxury of pre–World War I England, Lady Katherine Trenowyth is expected to do nothing more than make a smart marriage. When bohemian painter Simon Halliday enters her world, Katherine begins to question the future that was so carefully laid out for her. Her choices soon lead her away from the stability of her home and family toward a wild existence of life, art, and love.

As Anna is drawn into her newfound family's lives and their tangled loyalties, she must decide if the secrets of the past are too dangerous to unearth . . . and if the family she's discovered is one she can keep. ❧

Sources

While drawing on countless sources to write *The Way to London,* I found these books and websites particularly instructive and inspirational.

Growing Up in British Malaya and Singapore: A Time of Fireflies and Wild Guavas by Maurice Baker
The British Army 1939–45 (3): The Far East by Martin J. Brayley
The British Home Front 1939–45 by Martin J. Brayley
A Bethnal Green Memoir by Derek Houghton
Journey by Candlelight: A Memoir by Anne Kennaway
Luke's Log by K. D. Luke
The West End Front: The Wartime Secrets of London's Grand Hotels by Matthew Sweet
No Time to Wave Goodbye by Ben Wicks

British Red Cross, Caring on the Home Front: Volunteer Memories from World War Two / www.caringonthehomefront.org.uk
Imperial War Museums / www.iwm.org.uk
Remember Singapore / www.remembersingapore.org
WW2 People's War: An Archive of World War Two Memories / http://www.bbc.co.uk

Discover great authors, exclusive offers, and more at hc.com.